A KILLER'S TOUCH

When she looked at him again, he was standing to the side of the bed.

"Just go," she moaned. "Just go, please. You got what you wanted. Please."

But he stood there. Then he moved slowly away, and she thought she had survived it, that he was leaving. She felt the stinging pain, but the thought of him leaving transcended the pain, filled her with hope. She would survive, she felt sure of that.

Then he turned and she could hear the breathing start again, loud and irregular, as he came at her . . . but not the same way this time. He held something in his hand, something shiny and curved, and it was less than a second before her mind registered what it was that he had, and she knew she was going to die.

The edge of the blade felt surprisingly cool. A strange place to use such a thing, she thought . . . unnatural . . .

Gratefully, with one last final scream, Leslie plunged into unconsciousness.

TRANSFORMATION

MARC
BERRENSON

ZEBRA BOOKS
KENSINGTON PUBLISHING CORP.

For Kare,
my best friend

ACKNOWLEDGMENTS

Jon Zonderman's *Beyond the Crime Lab* was of invaluable assistance.

Also, *Miscarriages of Justice in Potentially Capital Cases,* by Hugo Adam Bedau and Michael L. Radelet.

Also, *Cleft Palate Speech,* by Betty Jane McWilliams.

Prologue

There was only the sound of bougainvillea rustling dry leaves against an aluminum screen, the thump and squeak of the bed moaning its labored song, and the soft hum of his breathing becoming louder as he paced himself.

Almost there.

And the darkness . . . always the darkness. He insisted on that. The doors and windows were closed, blocking the light from the outside, his eyes pressed shut as he tried to do the same with his mind.

There were just two luminous hands, yellow-green arrows in the night, and the numbers reminding her that this was no dream, that there was a beginning and an end to their coupling, and it was not one blurred continuum stretching through time . . . that in the darkness they were not alone.

And that even under the brightest light, she could still not see him.

In her mind, with the heat of his body over her, his weight moving slowly back and forth, she told herself to go along with him one more time. Play the game like she always did. His game. It was what he liked, what he needed. It was, she knew, little to ask of her.

But it was also the one thing that was most important.

On this night, as with the others, doubt, like a spider, scaled its invisible web to her brain.

Would it ever end?

Was there anything between them worth saving?

"Call me the name," he whispered, more urgently now. His pace quickened. She could feel him thrusting deeper and faster. Punishing her with it. Reaching inside, trying to get to her center, her being.

She waited, saying nothing. The doubt made her do that . . . something inside fighting back, testing. She realized it was cruel, but she hoped all the same.

"The name," he said, louder this time.

His eyes were closed and his back arched so that when she looked up she saw his chin first, his head thrown back like a wild animal baying at the moon.

"Bear," she whispered. "I love you, Bear."

He moved faster, spurred on by her words, his arms working like pistons at her side, in rhythm with his body. He was at once so far within her he could go no further, yet alone, insulated. In a separate world. *His* world.

"Again," he said.

"I love you, Bear."

For a split second he stopped, his eyes closed, face straining toward the ceiling. His head tossed back, contorted in a spasm of pain. Of pleasure. His breathing ceased, and for a moment she worried that she'd lost him. Then he grunted, and screamed, low and guttural, something from deep inside, primal. His hips pinned her against the bed, his body pumping again and again, driving himself through her.

When he was done he lay motionless, his weight pressing the air from her chest. He kissed her cheek, her ear, then rolled off to the side.

She turned, and within moments felt him behind her, molding his body to hers, his soft breathing tickling the back of her neck.

She couldn't sleep. Questions swirled in her head, demanding answers that she didn't have.

Couldn't have.

She stared at the luminescent clock hands, counting the numbers, the minutes, until the spider slowly descended and she could feel it dangling uncomfortably above the acid pit of her stomach.

In the darkness her tears were invisible, a love message written in sand, washed clean by the tides of time . . . the words existing only as memories in the writer's mind.

Part One

1

Max Becker jogged the stretch of sidewalk by himself, pumping like mad for the first block just in case Deets and Velasquez were still looking. He couldn't have them thinking he was in worse shape than they were. After the first block, though, he snuck a glance over his right shoulder and, seeing neither of his two running buddies, slowed to a walk, grabbing his chest, trying to catch his breath.

He cursed himself (the third time that week, and it was only Wednesday) for not exercising enough restraint at the dinner table. Strapping on the feedbag was something he was very good at. It was a habit that over his fifty-two years he'd been unable to break. He loved food, was just a sucker for a well-prepared meal. To say nothing of the martinis before and the wine during.

It's a lost cause, he told himself, trying to get the arms pumping one more time, feeling his legs cramp and an overwhelming sense of fatigue fall over him like a wet woolen blanket.

The shopkeepers on Fifth Avenue in the Hillcrest area were busy getting ready for another day, unlocking doors, sweeping the sidewalks. A homeless man, wiry, with skin the color of charcoal, gathered his cardboard condominium and placed it inside a shopping cart.

The doors to the chicken pie restaurant were already opened, though when Max peered inside, there were no customers, just a crew of Mexicans busily scrubbing floors and windows. Across the street, a mixed group of commuters, businesspeople and students, waited for the bus that would take them downtown.

Max checked the traffic, then crossed Fifth against the light. He bought a copy of the *Union* at the corner and shoved it under his arm, deciding to run the last two blocks just so Cardozo wouldn't think he'd been dogging it.

The black Labrador greeted him, standing on his hind legs, his front paws balanced against the patio's wrought-iron gate.

"What are *you* staring at?" said Max, feeling that the dog suspected he hadn't run the entire way. He gently cuffed the Lab's massive neck, then opened the gate. Cardozo licked the salty sweat from the back of his knees while Max stripped off his tank top and hung it over the patio wall to dry.

"Great run this morning," he said, entering the living room through the sliding glass door. He headed for the kitchen, Cardozo following close behind.

"I really had Deets and the Honorable Velasquez sucking for air."

Max removed a quart of OJ from the refrigerator and drank straight from the container. He cast an inquisitive eye at the dog, who had taken up his standard position sprawled on the kitchen tile, trying to stay cool, totally oblivious to what his master was saying.

Max didn't like the look he was getting from the dog. Sometimes he thought they'd been together so long that the animal actually understood what he was saying—and didn't much care.

"Don't give me that look," said Max. "I didn't see you out there busting your butt. Jesus. Fucking retriever, my ass! That's a real joke. Here, go fetch." Max raised his arm like he was throwing a ball. The dog didn't move, just flicked an eye up, then back, unimpressed.

"I know, I know," said Max, grabbing the newspaper and heading for the patio. "You're a hunting machine, not about to waste your time jogging around Balboa Park with a group of yuppie housewives and over-the-hill old men."

He plopped into one of the canvas chairs, lifted his feet onto another and tossed his head back, allowing the heat and the intense morning sunlight to penetrate his skin, giving only token consideration to the articles on skin cancer he'd recently read. They'd caused him to limit his sunbathing for a while, until he came to the conclusion that it wasn't in the cards for someone like himself to kick the bucket from skin cancer. Maybe insanity, or cirrhosis, or the dreaded but oh-so-dramatic inoperable brain tumor. But not something like skin cancer. Not him.

The sun felt good, the heat relaxing him, easing the joints. He had no morning court appearances, no clients banging down his door, no problems, legal or otherwise, that needed his immediate attention. It was just the sort of day he liked. He'd spend the morning getting a little color, maybe work in the greenhouse for a while.

He checked off the things he needed to do: feed and fertilize the acid-loving camelias and azaleas; fix that overhead spray that was clogged; transplant the day lily seedlings from flats into plastic pony-packs. Then maybe he'd have time to take a look at the new Jackson & Perkins catalog, something he always enjoyed doing,

15

even though he rarely ordered from it, the prices were so outrageous.

He took the front section of the *Union* and spread it on his stomach, licking his fingertips and quickly flipping through the pages. The bottom page, soaked in sweat, anchored the paper to his skin.

A member of the mayor's task force on waste in government had been accused of taking a plane flight to Miami and charging it to the city, when in fact the woman had spent two nights in a luxury hotel visiting her daughter, who had recently delivered her first child. The member, according to the *Union*, was unavailable for comment. The mayor was, as usual, "looking into the matter."

The Padres had lost their seventh in a row. According to the front-page blurb, all the depressing details could be found in the Sports section.

Yet another medical building had been dedicated, this one for ophthalmological research and treatment, in the name of Jerry Kravitz, the patron saint of bronze dedication plaques, private school building funds, and hospital wings to cure what ailed mankind.

An article on page three caught his attention. Just two short columns. A young woman by the name of Bernadette Slotkin had been raped inside her apartment in the downtown area. She was a waitress who'd been living in San Diego for less than a year. The rape was "particularly brutal," according to the article. There were few specific details, and the police had no clues.

The sun had almost cleared the patio, but its warmth remained. Max felt the sweat running down his spine, dripping into his shorts. He didn't mind the feeling. It loosened him up, kept the bones and joints lubed and oiled.

He put the newspaper back on the table and finished

his juice, smacking his lips at the sticky, pulpy remains at the bottom. He was feeling proud of himself. He'd spotted the article right off, as always. He couldn't control that. It was like being on automatic pilot, zeroing in on what made him feel the worst—another habit he'd picked up that he couldn't get rid of.

Still, he hadn't dwelled on the damn thing. He hadn't allowed himself his usual swan dive into depression over this latest act of common cruelty. And it was common, that was for certain. Most people casually passed such reports by, or read them and thought to themselves, "How terrible," then turned to the funny pages for a laugh before going off to work.

In the back of his mind, where he'd banished the painful memories of Rosalie and Ryan—not being able to rid himself of them entirely, and not really wanting to—he logged this latest incident of brutality. Bernadette Slotkin . . . the name really didn't matter. "Particularly gruesome . . ." Now, *that* was definitely something to consider, something that was sure to qualify for the Maxwell Becker Cruelty Hall of Fame. Max visualized the bronze plaque with his name hanging over the front doors. Jerry Kravitz had nothing on him when it came to chronicling the truly barbarous.

Just stick it back where it belongs, Max told himself—out of the way. And if it raises its ugly head, push it back down. Step on it. It's over and done with. Just like Rosalie and Ryan. Just like those sleazeballs the Carbon brothers. Nothing you can do about it now, even if you wanted to. Just forget it.

Forget it, I said!

Max headed for the shower. He pulled off his running shorts and hung them on the back of the bathroom door. The dog followed, laboriously slinking along, pink tongue lolling from one side of his mouth, slobber in one large gooey globule hanging from the other. He stuck his nose between Max's legs, sniffing.

"Get outta here," said Max, gently shoving the dog's muzzle with the back of his hand. "You horny bastard."

Max sat atop the toilet, waiting for the water to get hot.

"I guess you got a right to be horny," he said, running his palm over the dog's head. Cardozo liked that, or at least, he hadn't said anything to Max to the contrary. But Max could tell all the same, the tongue darting out to lick his wrist, tail wagging. It even seemed as if a smile spread across his wrinkled black face.

"Yeah," said Max, thinking about the previous night. "I guess we all got a right to feel a little horny once in a while—no matter how fucking old we are."

Cardozo barked, confirming Max's suspicion that he'd understood his every word.

2

It was like it used to be during the good times. Early morning. Quiet and crisp, and everyone asleep except him. Nobody after him, yelling at him, telling him what to do. Like back in the Burris Home, before the old folks rolled out of bed. Peaceful.

The image of Old Man Burris and his wife lying next to each other started him remembering, bringing up thoughts he'd kept secreted away beneath layers of other bad memories: a photo album of his childhood burned into a hole in his mind, like a volcano thought to be dormant, unexpectedly spilling forth the molten lava of painful remembrance. There were those who had already been burned by such memories. Scarred for life, as he'd been, by the force of that fiery river of recollection.

And there were those who would be.

He maneuvered the van west on University Avenue toward 163. He'd take the freeway, getting off at Hotel Circle and swinging through Mission Valley, then head north toward Friars Road. The back of the van was filled with newspapers, most of which would be dropped in stacks bundled with bailing wire at the homes of the paperboys who were on his route.

In the darkness the van seemed to operate itself, making the turns as if from memory. It was during this hour of the day that he did a lot of his thinking, his planning. Today was no different.

He considered the stops he needed to make later on, and one house in particular. The image of the woman had occupied his thoughts for the last week, and the last two nights, she'd crept into his dreams. It was time.

At Hotel Circle he turned left—past the shopping malls and hotels that now filled the narrow valley, vying with each other for the tourist dollar—into the residential neighborhoods just north of the commercial complex.

Night was beginning to transform itself into twilight, and a few more cars appeared on the road: early-morning commuters with ties hanging unknotted around their necks, and cups of coffee balanced precariously on car dashboards.

Justin was there, sitting on the opened rear door of his parents' station wagon, rubbing his eyes, yawning and waiting. The boy jumped off the back of the wagon as he pulled to the curb in front of the house.

"Late night, huh?"

Justin didn't answer, but just smiled, yawned again, and began helping unload his share of newspapers.

"Any trouble on the route?" He liked to keep track of his delivery boys, make sure both they and their customers remained satisfied.

"Nope. Couple complaints about wet papers because of the automatic sprinklers. But I took care of that." Justin reached inside the van for another bale. "People coming out early to get the paper. Wanna see whether the cops have caught that guy."

He looked at the boy, confused for a moment, then realized what he was getting at.

"You mean the one who . . ." He wasn't sure whether

20

to use the word with the boy.

"Raped that woman," said Justin, as if he was talking about trading baseball cards.

"Yeah," he muttered. He felt embarrassed at the way Justin had answered. Embarrassed that he already knew of such things.

"Let's hope they do," he said. He was eager to end the conversation. Inside the house he spotted Justin's mother gazing out at them from the kitchen. She was sipping a cup of coffee, barely moving.

"Your folks help you toss the papers?"

"My mom. She drives, usually. I sit in the back of the wagon and do the throwing."

"And she doesn't mind waking up so early?"

"Guess not," said Justin. "She and my dad think it's good experience. Character building, that's what my dad says. And I get to spend the money on whatever I want."

"Yeah," he said.

A distant smile crossed his face, a facade covering his deeper thoughts. Thoughts of his own childhood, when he had delivered papers. Except, there was no mother in his childhood scene. Nobody but a young boy, nervous and unsure, hustling newspapers from a bicycle, when he could get it, but from a wagon on foot most of the time.

And the money, *his* money, that Old Man Burris collected from him each week. And the time out by the smokehouse when he'd kept some of the money for himself, and Old Man Burris had caught him.

"You wanna meet my mom? She's right inside. I'll get her." Justin started toward the house.

"Gotta run," he said, jumping behind the wheel of the van. "Maybe next time."

He waved, gunned the engine, and pulled away. In the mirror he saw that Justin's mother had joined him in the driveway. She was standing next to her son, wearing slippers and a robe, still holding her mug of coffee.

Yeah, right, he laughed, stomping on the gas. The picture of mother and son in the rearview mirror diminished until it was completely gone. He thought: character building, that was it. *Real* character building.

He pulled the van into the carport and headed for his apartment. Some of the local gangbangers had been tagging the side of his building the night before. He always had trouble reading that stuff. Initials mostly. And nicknames: *Flaco, Lt'l Spider, Midget, Big Man, Lonely* . . . Then some names that had been crossed out by rival gangs, then crossed out again. Most of it was old, and despite his efforts to have the manager clean it up, it remained as a permanent reminder of the neighborhood's decay. The graffiti now took up most of the side of the building, and it was difficult to see what the original color of the stucco had been.

Still, he kept track of the names. He could tell how long something had been up there, and what was recently added. He'd even watched some gangbangers tagging the wall one early morning—young kids whose lifetime claim to fame was having their gang monikers spray-painted on the walls of a rundown apartment in a neighborhood that was going to seed.

He thought about what he would like to do to the little punks, if he didn't have other, more important things to think about. Kicking the shit out of some gangsters would be fun, but it might bring attention to himself. He couldn't afford that, not right now, anyway.

Carla was still in bed, snoring. The sheets and blankets were mostly on the floor, except for a corner of the blanket which Carla had pulled over her head. From under the blanket it sounded like a couple of pigs in slop.

He tried to ignore the noise. He was late because he'd stopped to talk with Justin. He pulled on his jumpsuit with the company logo and headed for the bathroom. Hung over the shower curtain were a half-dozen pairs of old nylons like withered snakes hung out to dry. The amber vial of Carla's pills, the ones she used to get to sleep, stood open on the sink, just to the side of a slimy smear of what looked to be soap and makeup from the previous night. He looked away only to see that Carla had used the toilet sometime in the early morning and forgotten to flush.

"Filthy bitch!" he muttered to himself.

He opened the medicine chest, swinging the mirrored door closer. With his special scissors he carefully manicured his moustache. He stood back for a moment, turning his head from side to side, making sure that the moustache covered what it was supposed to. Then, satisfied with his work, he closed the medicine cabinet and headed for the kitchen.

"Leslie Greer," he whispered to himself, checking the list of repair sites for the day. He smiled, thinking about what Justin had said; thinking about what he'd dreamed the night before while he was on top of Carla, changing her face in his mind.

Real character building, he thought, as he left the apartment and headed for the van. It made him laugh out loud.

Leslie Greer hurried her seven-year-old son Randall through the door and watched, as she always did, with a feeling of hope and heartbreak, as the young boy climbed onto the school bus. She remained at the window, watching for a few more moments, even after the bus pulled away leaving nothing but the last cloudy remnants of diesel smoke.

"Frank should be here any minute. No time for breakfast. I'll grab something at the airport." Ted Greer, Leslie's husband, gave her a peck on the forehead. Then, when she grabbed him in a bear hug, he dropped his briefcase and kissed her passionately.

"That's more like it," she said, pulling away for a moment, but remaining in his arms.

"I'm going to miss you," he said.

"Me, too. But it's only a few days, and you have to admit, the traveling has been a little better lately."

He let her go and reached for his briefcase. From the front of the house, a car horn honked.

"That's Frank," he said. He paused for a moment to focus on her face, lifting her chin gently with his fingertips. "Ya know, if I get this promotion, I won't be gone as much. Just the good trips. And some of them we'll be able to take together."

"And?"

He chuckled. "And maybe we'll start working on a little sister for Randy." The horn sounded again impatiently from the front of the house. "Gotta go," he muttered, moving toward the door. "Don't forget the guy's coming to fix the TV."

He sprinted out the front door. Leslie watched, just as she had with her son, as the other man in her life was forced to leave her.

A long, relaxing shower usually worked on these days when the loneliness saddened her. Good and hot, maybe wash her hair. That would take time. Pretty soon it would be lunch, then not that much longer until Randy came home. They'd have dinner together, and talk about Daddy, counting the days until he returned, wondering what special gifts he'd bring back with him.

The sound of the doorbell interrupted her. She was naked, about to step into the shower. Quickly she threw on her robe, pulling the front closed as she approached the door.

"Yes?"

She always asked before opening. Ted had told her to do that.

"All-Valley Cable," said the voice.

The voice sounded funny to her, not quite right. Still, she was expecting them. She clutched the front of her robe more firmly and cracked open the door. The man who stood before her on the front porch was dressed in a gray jumpsuit with the company logo just over the front pocket. He wasn't tall, at least not as tall as Ted, but he was thin and wiry, wearing a baseball cap that she guessed covered a slightly receding hairline. He had a bushy mustache and spoke slowly, with a lisp.

"You called about a problem, ma'am? We've been working in the area. Lots of calls lately."

She hesitated a moment, looking at the man's upper lip, concentrating on the sound of his speech.

"I was here before, ma'am. Needed to get authorization and a part for service." He smiled, then held up a narrow aluminum cylinder. "This is the culprit," he said, keeping the smile. "I need to go up on the pole to install it, but first I have to check the connections inside."

She was about to tell him something about the shower, feeling selfconscious about standing there in her bathrobe.

"Come in," she said, backing away from the door. "You know where the set is." He nodded and headed for the TV in the living room.

"You got another set in the bedroom, don't you?"

Leslie could hear his voice coming from the living room. She was getting used to the hissing sound now. She admired the man for not being overtly self-conscious about it.

25

"Yes, that's right," she said. "Please, do what you need to do. I'll be in the bathroom." She was beginning to relax. She now remembered seeing the serviceman before, along with some others who were working in the area. But Ted had been home then, and the men had done most of the talking.

She heard the back door open, then close. He's outside, she thought. She locked the bathroom door and stepped into the shower, letting the jets of steaming water pound against her neck and back, relaxing her.

He stood in the hallway of her house, listening to the hiss of the shower from the other side of the closed bathroom door. It made him smile, and he felt himself begin to harden.

Still, he had work to do.

He changed the connection on the TVs in the living room and in the bedroom. On his way out, he left the invoice on the kitchen counter, but not before he took a long, hard look at the calendar that the woman had thumbtacked to a bulletin board near the sink. He checked the date he'd seen before, just to make sure. The notation was still there.

He packed up his tools and walked back toward the hall. The hissing from the shower had ceased.

"I'm leaving now, ma'am." He yelled. "No need for you to come out. I left the invoice on the counter. There's no charge."

"Thank you," he heard her yell from behind closed doors.

Thank you, indeed, he thought, imagining what the woman would look like stepping from the shower, all pink and glistening, droplets of water falling from her face, her breasts.

He was still hard, throbbing, as he pulled himself out the front door.

*   *   *

Leslie Greer curled up on the couch, watching TV, sipping a cup of tea. Randy had been read his bedtime story and was now fast asleep. Ted had called from Chicago around dinnertime, saying that he missed them both, but the trip was going well.

She had a paperback mystery she'd been promising herself to start for the last few days. It still lay where it had most of the week, on the coffee table in front of the television.

She was browsing through *TV Guide,* figuring what she'd watch, when she heard the first sound—like a crack, or glass breaking but not shattering. She remained seated, but kept her ears peeled. Probably the neighbors, she thought, or someone out in the street in front of the house. Sounds tended to carry in this neighborhood, especially at night.

Then the next unmistakable sound: a thud. She thought she could feel the house shake.

It was no longer coming from outside.

She slowly got off the couch, still holding her cup of tea, but unaware of it in her hand. Slowly she made her way toward the source of the sound, down the hallway to where Randy slept.

Still listening, but there was no further noise.

She stopped outside her bedroom door. It was partially closed, though she could see inside. She turned and peeked into Randy's room. Her young son was sleeping soundly, just as she'd left him. The windows were closed. Everything looked fine. She began to breathe a little easier. She realized that she was still holding her tea, laughed nervously, and placed the mug on the bathroom counter. Everything was okay, she told herself. It was probably just a cat on the roof; nothing to get worked up over. Though she was breathing more regularly now, she still felt on edge. There was one more room that she hadn't checked.

Leslie quietly slid into her bedroom, almost unwilling to act like she was scared for fear of acknowledging what might be there.

But there was nothing.

The first step, the first blink of an eye revealed only familiar objects: dresser, bed, lamp . . .

Suddenly she sensed she wasn't alone. From the corner of her eye she saw him, a dark, masked blur coming toward her from the side. Then a hand over her mouth and another over her chest, pressing her breasts, hurting her . . .

She didn't know whether to scream. Her first thought was not to wake Randy by crying out. She was so accustomed to remaining quiet while her son slept that her usual practice kicked in automatically, despite the intruder's presence.

He held her, his hand firmly clamped over her mouth. Had she wanted to call out, now she couldn't have. He turned her, still pressing the palm of his gloved hand over her lips, and she saw him fully for the first time. A man taller than herself. Slender, from the looks of him, though he was wearing a lined jacket that gave an indecipherable fullness to his upper body. He wore Levis and tennis shoes.

And he had no face.

The nylon stocking was pulled tightly over his head. She could make out only general features, and then only because she expected to see them. Eyes were mere indentations without size or color. Forehead and head blurred into one murky brown nylon haze. There was a slight protrusion where the nose would be. And the mouth just below, there only because she could hear him breathing heavily from that spot.

He didn't say anything. For a split-second Leslie

28

thought this was a dream, something from TV that she'd carried into sleep with her. Then she was sure it was not. He pushed her onto the bed and came toward her. She hesitated, then screamed.

The slap seemed to come from nowhere. His gloved hand, she thought it was his right, crashed against her cheek and nose, cutting off the scream prematurely. Then another with the same hand, and she heard a crunching sound and felt something wet and warm flowing from her nose.

"Okay, okay!" she cried, hoping to get the words out before he hit her again. Her voice sounded weak to her.

The man held up a finger as if to admonish her, and then nodded his head, agreeing with what she'd said. He reached into his pants pocket and removed a small foil package. She watched with shaking, terrified eyes. The sounds she had taken for granted, the modulated ticking of the clock on the nightstand, the soft whir of the heat blowing into the room from the ceiling vent, the muted squeaking of the bed as she lay on it, all became exaggerated in those precious seconds.

Now what's he doing?

She knew what she was seeing, had known what would happen to her when he threw her on the bed. Still, she didn't want to admit it. Now she was sure, though. There was no turning away. She watched, feeling her body shake, numb to any sensation below her waist, but knowing that her legs were shaking uncontrollably.

The man opened the foil packet, removed its contents, then carefully placed the foil back into his pocket. Then he unbuttoned the front of his jeans and placed the condom on his already hard penis. She thought it seemed a funny thing for him to do. Not as she'd envisioned it in her most horrendous nightmares.

Leslie began to feel faint. She hoped she would pass

29

out, be spared having to see this happen. She thought about fighting back, about screaming and clawing her attacker into submission. Then she thought about being hit again, and about Randy, and that maybe her assailant would leave when he'd finished. Maybe Randy would be spared.

Don't fight, she told herself.

She whimpered and cried out softly as she felt his first painful thrusts inside her. She could practically taste his breath now, fast and wild, as he worked between her legs, a lump of clothes with a hideous deformed face. It was like all those cops-and-robbers shows she'd seen on TV. She'd thought people no longer used nylon stockings as masks. Now she knew better.

For a few moments Leslie lost track of what he was doing. Gazing up at the ceiling, thinking of Ted and Randy, trying to remove herself from the thought that she, Leslie Greer, mother of a small child, a married woman who had never done anything without caution in her entire life, was now having *this* done to her. She was being raped!

When she looked at him again, he was standing to the side of the bed. His pants were buttoned, and both hands were thrust into his pockets.

"Just go," she moaned, pleaded. "Just go, please. You got what you wanted. *Please.*"

But he stood there, then he moved slowly away, and she thought she had survived it, that he was leaving. She'd be all right. More important, so would Randy. She felt a stinging pain between her legs, but the thought of him leaving transcended the pain, filled her with hope. She would survive, she felt sure of that.

Then he turned and she could hear the breathing start again, loud and irregular, as he came at her. But not the same way this time. He held something in his hand. Something shiny and curved, and it was less than

30

a second before her mind registered what it was that he had, and she knew she was going to die.

The edge of the blade felt surprisingly cool down there. A strange place to use such a thing, she thought. Unnatural.

Gratefully, with one last final scream, Leslie plunged into unconsciousness.

3

He could hear the gurgle, then a gasp come from the antiquated Mr. Coffee. Steam rose from the heating plate where he had accidentally spilled water. He could do this with his eyes closed, and often did, his mind wandering off to other, more weighty subjects.

Assistant District Attorney David Gentry took a look at the brownish-green crud at the bottom of his coffee mug, looked around for a styrofoam cup, and seeing none, held the mug under the stream of hot water, occasionally stirring at the bottom with two fingers. Once finished, he dried the mug with a paper towel from the wall dispenser in the small kitchen area that serviced the offices of the San Diego County District Attorney.

I look every year of fifty-five, he thought, checking his distorted reflection in the polished metal of the towel dispenser. Strands of mousy brown hair taken over by gray, combed straight back, receded in two symmetrical paths on either side of his head. A small brush of moustache, slightly darker than what was left on his head, topped a smile that he'd always thought would have looked better on an old man. Perhaps now, he mused, he'd finally grown into his smile.

He removed his wire and black plastic glasses, and caught a blur of his owl-like appearance. He could see almost nothing without his glasses. He held the frames in front of his face, trying to see what he looked like with them off. Presently there were two of him: the larger, less certain, obscured face that he saw outside the outer rim of his frames, then the smaller, detailed, more finite David Gentry within the lenses.

Gentry carefully replaced his glasses, then turned to watch the black liquid slowly rising inside the glass coffeepot.

Outside, through the picture window, Broadway was beginning to clog with early morning commuters, public employees jockeying for a parking place. From where he stood atop the county office building, the people and cars appeared in miniature, like game pieces on some smog-faded, soot-encrusted game-board.

With coffee in hand, Gentry made his way down the hallway toward his corner office. Inside was a wall with the plaques and awards he'd received during his years of public service, along with the memorabilia of big cases he'd handled during his thirty years as a prosecutor. Spying the stack of files on the corner of the desk, Gentry also knew that inside this office were the decisions that he had increasingly come to dread.

In the distance, he heard the susurrous murmuring of faraway conversations, footsteps drawing near, and the jangle of keys. Gentry checked his watch, registering the faces of those attorneys, secretaries, and support staff whom he knew customarily arrived early. He leaned back in his chair, hoisting his feet onto the desk, gently swiveling back and forth.

The magazine was still there where he'd left it the night before, the one with his picture on the cover. It was staring back at him now.

33

Do I really look that old?

He had a lawyer friend, younger than he, who used to say that you know you're old when you find out that the kid that used to babysit for your kids is getting a divorce. Gentry could no longer remember the faces of any of Susan's babysitters, let alone their names.

He was drawn to the face on the magazine, his face. The appearance of seriousness with that partial profile, no smile. Filled with self-righteous arrogance, he now thought.

He had suggested a slight smile to the photographer, but had been overruled. The piece was about the best prosecutors in California, the reporter admonished. "Prosecutors," said the reporter, "are serious lawyers battling against the spread of crime." As if David Gentry needed to be reminded.

At the time, he'd merely nodded and let the photographer and his assistant move and poke and twist him until they got what they wanted: the perfect prosecutor. The true believer crusading for justice (whatever that was). And finally, "The DA of Death." Those were the words printed under his photograph. His epitaph. It still made him shudder.

A voice pulled him from his reverie.

"Oh, you're okay with coffee?"

Gentry nodded, said good morning to his secretary, and watched as she plopped a large canvas bag on her desk and headed for the coffee room, cup in hand.

The magazine article had been complimentary, saying that Gentry was well respected by both his fellow prosecutors and opposing defense counsel. That he'd been the sole person in the San Diego County District Attorney's office saddled with the responsibility of making life-and-death decisions for nearly twenty-five years. That he was to retire from the DA's office very shortly, and was planning on going into private practice, to the reporter's surprise, doing criminal defense work, of all things.

Gentry gingerly sipped from his mug, slurping the brown liquid. His eyes focused on the two-picture metal frame that he kept on his desk. One photo was of his daughter Susan, her most recent from high school. The other was of Jackie, his wife, wearing a sundress, dangling a hat and her sandals from one hand. She was sitting atop a rock. The picture had been taken on one of their beach vacations.

Still, the stack of death penalty cases cried out to him, life-and-death decisions that needed to be made, the cradling of a man's life in your palm, holding it out for inspection, poking and probing, running tests, like a doctor keeping a patient in suspense. Then the decision that was solely David Gentry's: whether this man would face the possibility of execution, or whether his life would be spared.

Gentry opened the first file. He read the defendant's name, and briefly glanced at the statement of facts, along with the defendant's criminal history summary. Clipped to the top of the file was the memo from the supervising deputy. Below that was the trial deputy's memo. Somewhere in the file, Gentry knew, there would be a short memorandum from the department head.

Each memo stated the facts for and against the death penalty. Each attorney, from the lawyer who would actually try the case on up the supervisory ladder, would formally go on record as to his or her opinion: should this defendant face the death penalty?

But it was David Gentry who made the final decision. It was Gentry who would try and make sense from the various memoranda, the defendant's criminal history, the often numerous and conflicting studies dealing with the defendant's background, the facts of the specific case, and any one of a dozen other less tangible factors. It was Gentry who prepared the final memo, the now infamous Gentry Letter.

"Your daughter on one."

Gentry looked up from the file, registered the face of his secretary at the door, punched at his phone, and lifted the receiver.

"Hi, Doll."

"Hi, Daddy. I don't want to bother you, but I wanted to remind you that I won't be home for dinner tonight."

"I remembered. Your dad might be getting old, but I've still got a few years before senility sets in."

Gentry liked to make her laugh. He remembered that Susan was going to some sort of meeting at her school tonight, a woman's group she'd belonged to for the last year.

"Should I call and remind Uncle Max about the meeting?"

"That might not be a bad idea," said Gentry, thinking of his friend Max Becker, and recalling that Susan had mentioned something about Max addressing her woman's group.

"I won't be waiting up or anything," said Gentry, "but do you have any idea when you might be home?"

He heard himself stepping all over his words in an attempt not to seem as worried and concerned for his eighteen-year-old daughter as he actually was.

"Not late," she said. "The meeting starts around sevenish. I'll grab a burger or something beforehand. I should be home by nine, nine-thirty."

"This is that rape thing?"

"That's right. Uncle Max, along with two or three other speakers, will be on the panel. There should be a pretty big turnout, considering what's been going on lately."

Gentry thought of the article he'd read in the

morning paper about the most recent rape attack. It didn't make him rest any easier in his perpetual concern over his daughter's safety.

"Call me when you're ready to leave," he said, giving in to his fatherly instincts. Susan promised she would, and said goodbye. Gentry remained motionless for a moment, his hand still on the receiver, thinking about his daughter. She was all he had now, if you didn't count the job, and that, as the magazine article had correctly announced, would soon be ending.

He'd been unsure whether this was the best time to quit. Susan would be off to college soon, after summer school at Santa Barbara to get a head start on her freshman year. That would leave him in the house by himself.

Thirty years was a long time, doing the same thing, sitting on the same side of the counsel table. He'd fallen deeply into the groove of prosecuting cases, perhaps too deeply to crawl out. He could go it by rote now, having worked his way through the ranks, from handling traffic tickets and preliminary hearings as a fledgling deputy, to his present position, second-in-command in an office of over five hundred lawyers. *The DA of Death.*

Gentry wrote a reminder to himself to give Max Becker a call. They'd been very close at one time, close enough that Susan had grown up thinking Max was actually her uncle. She knew better now, but felt comfortable continuing to call him Uncle Max.

They'd first come to know one another during the Hector and Gonzalo Carbon trial. The Carbon Brothers controlled the Colombian cocaine connection in San Diego. Max Becker had represented Jaime Esquivel, one of the Carbons' mules. Esquivel and some low-level dealers had been arrested and charged with sales. They were all looking at doing substantial

37

prison time.

Esquivel was married, and his first son had just been born. He found it hard to just bite the bullet, take the rap for his bosses. The DA had decided to offer Esquivel a deal: testify against the Carbons and get probation, no prison. Gentry remembered the discussion. Nobody had expected Esquivel to take it. It meant an almost certain death sentence on the street.

The week before the trial, Max Becker had come to him, saying that Esquivel would testify. The trial was postponed, and the Carbon Brothers were arrested on the strength of the information provided by Jaime Esquivel.

Esquivel's wife and baby were sent out of state, and Esquivel was kept in protective custody until the trial. During the months leading up to it, Gentry worked closely with Becker, fine-tuning the testimony of the prosecution's star witness. The two men got to know and like each other, finding that they had more in common than their mutual interest in Jaime Esquivel, not the least of which was children of the same age. The families even got together socially—Sunday barbecues, a Padres game, an overnighter to Disneyland.

It pained Gentry to think of those times, of what he and his friend Max Becker had lost over the years. They'd both had so much that they'd taken for granted.

The Carbon Brothers went to trial and were convicted. Jaime Esquivel testified without incident. Gentry remembered how happy he'd been when the jury had returned with its verdict. He and Max had celebrated with a private little drink at the Westgate Hotel bar. One drink led to two, then more, and before either man realized it, all the defenses came down.

Max, as Gentry remembered it, was the first to bring up the idea of them going into private practice together. With their combined experience, and Gentry's contacts in the DA's office, they couldn't miss, or so Max Becker had said, the liquor lubricating his tongue.

Gentry promised that he'd think about it, though the next morning both men realized, even through their hangovers, that it had been just talk. They were both too entrenched in what they were doing to change.

The conviction marked the end of the good memories for David Gentry. Within months he lost Jackie to an auto accident. Her death clouded any pride and satisfaction he might have taken from the trial.

As for Max Becker, Jaime Esquivel's decision to turn state's evidence signified the beginning of the end. Esquivel was found three weeks later, floating face-down in Mission Bay. Within two months of that, Becker's wife and child would be kidnapped, only to be discovered later clutching each other in an orange grove in Fallbrook, both mother and child dead from bullets fired at close range to the backs of their heads.

Gentry turned back to the opened folder. He put his gruesome recollections behind him for the moment. He took a yellow pad from his desk drawer and drew a line down the center. On the left he wrote the words "Factors For Death," on the right, "Factors against Death."

He had started reviewing this file over a week ago. He'd come back to it, off and on, during the week, as he would the other death penalty cases. He wouldn't prepare the final draft of his Gentry Letter announcing his decision to the defendant and his attorney until he was sure, or as sure as he could be, that his determination was right.

As he wrote, images of himself as he'd gone through the same process in previous cases flashed through his mind. It always happened this way. The images had annoyed him at first, distracting him from the task of choosing life or death, making him doubt himself. But not to the extent that he couldn't work through it. At least, not until recently.

Gentry now sensed himself drifting, not concentrating and worst of all, he felt helpless to do anything about it. First there had been the dream: the ghouls in the cells, hollowed faces asking their questions. Just the one time, but it had thrown him off, surprised him in its suddenness.

Months then passed without the dream reappearing, and he began to relax again. But then, a few months ago, the dream paid him a return visit. Since then, it had come to him regularly, disturbing his sleep, playing games with his mind, even at the office.

Gentry shook his head, trying to jolt himself back to the present. He was right, it was time to retire. Perhaps he'd been doing this job for too long. Perhaps the dream would disappear once he started something new.

He looked down at the paper, questioning just how many more times he'd have to do this. He was tempted to put it aside, leave it for his successor, whoever the poor slob was who inherited his responsibilities. He'd made more than his share of decisions. Who would begrudge him these last few days of peace and solitude?

Slowly and carefully he numbered the entries on each side of the list, wondering if some future society would someday unearth these records of man playing God, and how they would judge David Gentry, the DA of Death.

Max entered the classroom, said hello to a woman who smiled at him, and began slowly to make his way through the groups of females standing busily talking with one another. In the distance he recognized Dawn Daniels, the head of the DA's Sexual Assault Program, speaking with Esther Morse, wife of James Morse, the newly elected district attorney for San Diego County. Susan Gentry gave him a wave from the corner of the room where she was holding forth to a group of high school girls. Max stood his ground, and in a few moments Susan tore herself away from her friends and approached him.

"I thought you might have forgotten, Uncle Max."

Susan reached up and gave Max a hug and a kiss on the cheek. A few of the women nearby turned their heads to watch for a moment, then went back to their conversations.

"I'm beginning to think," said Max, looking about the room, "that this wasn't such a good idea. Am I the only man here?"

"Don't worry," said Susan, smiling. "We're all very civil. Believe me, nobody here is going to attack you."

She moved away quickly, clapping her hands and telling everyone to take a seat.

In the front of the room was a long metal table covered in blond wood-grained formica. Max took one of the three seats behind the table, facing the classroom. The place was filled, all the desks occupied, and some women stood leaning against the blackboard in the back.

To Max's right sat Dawn Daniels. To his left was the president of the local chapter of NOW, a woman Max recognized from her numerous appearances on the local news.

Max wondered if it was just his initial feeling of discomfort, or whether every eye in the room was in fact trained on him. He looked around for possible allies and saw none. He tried to tell himself that these were all civilized women, as Susan had promised him,

41

and that he had nothing to fear. Still, he had to fight an increasingly strong desire to cross his legs and cover his crotch.

"Ladies . . . and, uh, gentleman . . ." Susan addressed the group, flashing a mischievous smile his way. There was a slight titter from the audience, but not enough to make Max feel less uncomfortable.

"Instead of having each of the speakers address you," said Susan, "since most of you are familiar with the issues, and I'm sure have questions, I thought, unless there are objections, that we'd throw the floor open to questions immediately." Susan paused for a moment, switching gears, then picked one woman from the sea of outstretched hands.

"I'd like to know," said a woman wearing a pastel jogging suit and white Reeboks, "what the district attorney's office is doing about prosecuting the person responsible for these hideous rapes we've all been hearing about." The woman's question was followed by a nodding of heads, and it set off a few impromptu discussions among various members of the audience.

"I suppose that question is directed at me," said Dawn Daniels as she folded her perfectly manicured hands on the table.

The Ice Bitch, thought Max. Daniels had an excellent legal mind, but she came across as slightly colder than dry ice. She'd crunched more than her share of careers, groping her way up the DA's promotional ladder.

"Our office," said Daniels, "has an ongoing coordinated effort with the police regarding the person the papers have, in their typical irresponsible fashion, termed 'The Ripper.' We have a number of leads that are currently being investigated. Of course, I am not at liberty, for obvious reasons, to disclose the specifics in public. But rest assured, ladies, we are drawing very near to making an arrest in this case."

Max gave Daniels a look, then quickly turned back toward the audience. He hadn't heard anything about an imminent arrest, and he figured Daniels was just blowing smoke, taking the easy way out. The Ripper, as the *Union*, and now the TV media had begun referring to the suspect, was, as far as Max knew, still at liberty in the community, well outside the watchful eye of law enforcement.

"When?" yelled a couple of voices in unison from the back of the room.

Max watched Dawn Daniels squirm slightly in her seat, the ice beginning to crack. She looked to Susan for help. Then, seeing that none was forthcoming, she cleared her throat. It was only after she had gotten halfway through her answer that Max realized what was happening.

"Soon, very soon," said Daniels. "Believe me, no one is more appalled at the gruesome cruelty of these assaults than I am. Mr. Morse has made the resolution of this case a top priority. It is one of the first things on his agenda as district attorney." Daniels paused, welcoming the smile and acknowledging nods coming from Esther Morse.

"That's not to say that when we catch this . . . *animal* . . . we won't have to jump through all the usual legal hoops that some tricky defense attorney will put in our way to delay and postpone bringing this monster to trial."

Max caught a quick glance from Daniels, as if body language were necessary for her to make the point that he was the only defense attorney in the room. He felt himself sweating, tiny drops of moisture at his back, slowly working their way downward. He thought about uncrossing his legs, but didn't want to appear as if he were losing his cool, which, in fact, he was.

"Believe me, ladies," Daniels continued, "We'll catch this guy, and do our damndest to see that he spends as much of his life as possible behind bars, where he belongs." She smiled, visibly relieved at the applause her comments had engendered. Max felt like punching her, but realized that that would be a cheap shot, and Dawn Daniels had already taken enough of those.

"I have a question for Mr. Becker," said a woman in the front row. She looked familiar, but Max couldn't quite place her. Tall and muscular under a black knit turtleneck, the woman had a mound of bleached blond hair haphazardly pulled up in a bun at the back of her head. Tanned, with etched wrinkles around the eyes and mouth, her face showed signs of a lifetime in the sun. She wore a pair of khaki mountain-climbing shorts with double sets of pockets and flaps front and back. Her long, muscular brown legs tapered into a pair of brown canvas shoes with thick cleated rubber soles that looked like a cross between leather outdoor gear and tennis shoes.

"Mr. Becker, many of us here are aware that you work the other side of the fence, so to speak." She paused, then, not hearing any response from Max, continued. "That is, we know that you spent some time prosecuting cases for the DA before going into private practice."

"That was many moons ago," said Max, cutting into her train of thought, sensing that at the end of this woman's question was a rather sharp pointed object aimed at his heart, or perhaps lower. "I have a general practice now. Criminal, and some civil."

"Ah, yes," murmured the woman. "But mainly criminal defense. Please correct me if I misstate the facts."

The woman was definitely after him. That last bit fairly dripped with venom. Max was still trying to place the face, wondering what he had ever done to this woman to deserve the resentment he heard in her voice.

"How does it feel, Mr. Becker, I mean from a defense attorney's point of view, to be the vehicle by which all the scum and trash of our society skirt the constraints of justice? How does it feel to be used by animals like the Ripper? Don't you ever have second thoughts about representing monsters like the one that left Leslie Greer scarred for life?"

The room turned deathly quiet. In the corner, Max spotted Susan Gentry fidgeting with her hands, alternating her glance from his face to her hands, then back again. She wanted to do something, he sensed, but couldn't. It was obvious that the majority of the women present in the room did not feel that the question was unfair, and were anxious to hear his response.

In the back of the room Max saw a group of women wearing NOW T-shirts, standing just inside the door. He hadn't seen them enter, and figured they must have slipped in while the Outdoorswoman From Hell was busy setting him up.

Max felt the embarrassment within him quickly turn to anger. He had nothing to be ashamed of. He'd suffered more than his share of guilt and remorse related to his profession. And who was this woman to single him out for attack, without even the most rudimentary understanding of how the criminal justice system worked?

"First," he said, staring the woman down, "the way our system works, a suspect is presumed innocent until he is proven guilty beyond a reasonable doubt in a court of law. People accused of committing crimes are entitled to be represented by lawyers. After all, the citizens of this county are represented by the district attorney. Why shouldn't those accused of crimes enter the courtroom on an equal footing?"

He sensed he was losing them. They'd heard all this before, and had stopped buying it years ago. Almost every one of them had been the victim of some sort of crime at least once in their lifetime, and probably more often.

He continued, "It would be nice if the district attorney never made mistakes." Max flashed a scowl at Dawn Daniels, which she returned with a self-satisfied sneer. "But that is not the case. The DA *does* make mistakes. After all, they are human. They are not supermen or women, despite the opinions to the contrary personally held by some of the deputies." A laugh sounded from the back, and Max thought he was starting to turn the corner.

"I'm sure that we all believe in the Constitution. That document gives anyone charged with a crime certain rights. All defense lawyers do is make sure that the government doesn't decide arbitrarily to omit affording those rights to its citizens, regardless of how heinous their *alleged* crimes may be."

"But what about . . ." Again the outdoorswoman, leaping up, raising her hand in the profusion of outstretched hands. She was mercifully cut off in mid-sentence.

"I think it's about time we took a break," said Susan, coming to the front of the classroom. She shot Max a quick glance, like a referree in a prize fight counting out the fallen fighter.

"If any of the panel members wish to stay on and answer questions, they may. There are refreshments set up in back, please help yourselves."

Max was grateful for the rescue, and more than a little impressed by the composure of the young girl. Saved by the bell, he thought—*and* the smarts of Susan Gentry.

"Uncle Max is eternally in your debt," he whispered, as the group of women got up from their seats, somewhat disgruntled at the sudden intermission, but still busily talking and moving toward the food in the back of the classroom. Max looked around for his verbal assailant, wondering if it would look too cowardly if he just quietly slipped out of the room.

"Sorry," said Susan.

"Was it something I said?" he asked, forcing a smile.

Susan smiled. "These women," she said, "are no different than most. There's a feeling of helplessness and fear that starts to spread everytime you have one of these crazy guys who goes around attacking females. Nobody wants to be the next victim, especially not with this guy."

"Who was that woman?" asked Max.

Susan shook her head, saying. "I don't know. It's a public meeting. Anyone can come. I don't know the names of all of the people who are here tonight."

"Mr. Becker?"

Max turned to see Esther Morse standing at his side. A woman in her late fifties, James Morse's wife had the reserved cool, the classiness, that a lifetime of playing second fiddle to the man in the spotlight oftentimes brings.

"I know it's not my place to offer apologies," she said, "but I wanted to say something. Jim and I have stood for law and order our entire lives. We want to see criminals behind bars as much if not more than the next person. Still, it's unfair to take potshots at defense attorneys like that woman did with you tonight. I just want you to know where I stand on that."

Max had met Jim Morse a few times when Morse had been sheriff. He'd seen Esther Morse standing alongside her husband over the years at various public functions. Recently he'd seen her at her husband's side as he was sworn in as the new district attorney for San Diego County. Still, he didn't know the woman . . . not until now, that is.

"I appreciate that," said Max, then shook Esther Morse's outstretched hand with both of his to show that he really meant it.

Max and Susan talked for a while, before Susan asked if she could speak with him privately. Outside the classroom, in the hallway, Max leaned against the wall of lockers, crossing his arms over his chest.

"Something wrong?" he asked.

The young girl he had known since childhood uncharacteristically groped for words.

"No, no," she said. "Nothing like that. It's just . . . well, you know, this summer I'll be going away to college."

"I know," said Max. "It's the only thing your father ever talks about."

"Yeah," she said, embarrassed. "He's pretty proud. When Mom died, he used to tell me that no matter what happened, he'd see that I had food to eat and a roof over my head. And someone to talk to whenever I wanted. College is something he's planned on for a long time." She paused, somewhat unsure of whether to continue.

"So?" Max's voice was gentle.

"You know Dad's retiring. I guess I'm a little worried about so much change in his life so suddenly. New job, me away at school . . . It'll be the first time he'll be by himself in the house. I guess that's what worries me."

Max reached out and placed his hand on the back of Susan's neck. The little girl who used to play games with Ryan, chasing him around the house trying to plant a kiss, had grown up. Womanhood had flattered Susan Gentry with a calm, mature bearing, a keen, inquisitive mind, and a gentleness with others that was remarkable. In her eyes, Max saw the compassion of her father, and in her beauty, the reflection of her mother. He gently brought her head to rest on his chest.

"Don't worry," he said. "You just go up there and do the best job you can. Make your dad and your Uncle Max proud." He saw her smile. "I know you will."

"Thanks, Uncle Max."

"And don't worry about that old man of yours. I'll keep an eye on him. Hell, who knows? We might even go into practice together. Wouldn't that be something?"

Max watched as Susan returned to the classroom, glad that he'd been able to lift her spirits. He thought about the first time he'd met Susan and her mother; the family get-togethers; David Gentry's generosity over the years in putting aside his own grief to help console a friend. Max thought about Jackie Gentry, and how hard David had taken her death. How it had almost killed him.

Then his thoughts drifted to the night Jacqueline Gentry was killed. It was a memory that had lurked beneath his skin, invisible to the untrained eyes, for the past ten years. Like a floating chip of bone, occasionally causing Max severe pain, while at other times dormant, almost forgotten.

Max had kept his suffering to himself, sharing his own grievous images of Jackie's death with no one. Especially not his friend, David Gentry.

He heard scuffing noises from somewhere in the back, and figured it was one of the priests, or perhaps someone cleaning. There was nobody else there. It was a good time to clean. A good time for David Gentry to be alone.

Gentry lit the candle, placing it on the table with the

rest, then knelt, crossed himself, and prayed. The same words at first, the phrases burned into his memory since childhood. Like an introduction and ice-breaker, cutting the awkward, and, he sometimes thought, hypocritical feelings that he brought with him to this place from which he had absented himself for so many years.

His eyes glassed over, and the candles grew into a wall of flame, the light refracted by his tears. He pawed at his eyes with the back of one hand, then wiped the moisture on his shirt. He lifted his head, blinking to clear his vision, then reached for another candle. Dipping the wick to the flame of the first, Gentry lit the second candle, and held it solemnly before him for a moment, gazing down at the flickering solitary light.

The first is for you, my dearest, Jackie.
I'm sorry I failed you. I'm . . .

Gentry pushed the painful memory of his own failure aside. He concentrated on her image, the collage of remembered scenes from a too-short life together, an image that had fixed itself in his mind shortly after her death, when the others had already stopped their mourning. It had angered him that he could not remember everything about her, that the remaining photographs he had of her began to circumscribe his entire perception. He had felt cheated.

Then, miraculously, one day he looked at Susan, and saw *her*. In the beauty of his only daughter, his wife still lived. From that moment on, the photographs no longer defined his memory. The pain took its rightful place inside him, a well from which he could dip his cupped hand to partake of its bittersweet solace. He could now live his life without the feeling that he would die if he couldn't see his wife one last time.

Another sound. Gentry turned to see that he had been joined by an elderly lady who was slowly making

50

her way down the center aisle, limping, and poking a cane methodically at the ground. Gentry returned his gaze to the candles.

Would anyone understand the second candle?

He wondered. He dared not mention it for fear of appearing weak. And the others would think just that. Weakness wouldn't do for the DA of Death—not at all.

He lifted himself off the ground and turned away from the altar, nodding to the old lady as she approached. He paused midway down the aisle to look back. The woman was still there, on her knees, as he had been, holding a lit candle and mumbling to herself.

Gentry thought, *She is a true believer in God. Not one who frequents His company out of fear, or because it happens to be convenient.*

He whispered to himself, *Say a prayer for me, old lady.* Then he turned and walked out the door.

4

"You're an awfully pretty boy, but then, I guess you know that, don't you?"

Billy just stood there, letting the fat man run an oily fingertip down the center of his tank top, gently hooking him between the legs. Billy could smell the man's sour cigarette breath, and was anxious to get it over with. But he didn't show the man that. It was part of the game, to make the man think this was something they were both enjoying.

"I'm going to take a shower," said the man. He made one last grab, squeezing Billy's genitals firmly, cupping them in his hand like two ripe plums.

"I'll be here," said Billy, slowly moving away.

He sat down near the open window and crossed his legs. He knew the man was looking up his shorts. The fat man stood motionless for a moment, smiled, then turned and disappeared inside the bathroom.

Billy thought about ordering room service. He was hungry, and his stomach was starting to rumble. He thought of the piece of cold, greasy pizza he had wolfed down with chocolate milk for breakfast. He could go for a nice steak, maybe a salad with those little shrimp they put on top. The man had promised him a meal.

Billy decided he'd better wait for the man to take care of that. Miguelito had said to let the man do all the talking. *Be quiet, almost like you're not there.* That's what Miguelito had said. Also, that the man was important, and that this could be a sweet deal for them both.

William "Billy Boy" Darling gazed out the window of the seventh floor suite of the U. S. Grant Hotel. His eyes wandered across Broadway to the Horton Plaza, and the strip of green parkway and benches in front. He focused on the familiar faces of the homeless men and women camped out on the benches and sprawled across the grass, some moving up and down the street with an upturned palm in the hopes of a handout from passersby.

They all looked so much smaller from up here, like small insects squished on a windshield, or flecks of grime stuck inside the glass of a picture frame. The giant shopping complex, with its multiple levels of pastel-colored geometric shapes, loomed like some giant watercolor whale about to swallow all the miniature Ahabs.

On the sidewalk below, Billy could see the hotel doorman shooing away a man who had taken up temporary residence in the shady doorway of the hotel bar.

When the car horns and sirens and diesel engine roar from the buses abated, for a split-second, he could catch the electronic chirping of birds, two different kinds, one high-pitched, the other slow and deliberate. He liked that. Thought it was funny that the streetlamps had been wired for sound. Small speakers, he'd seen them, attached to the poles. For blind people, or so Miguelito had explained to him.

Billy heard the fizzle from the shower, and the sound of the fat man singing. The man was happy.

He began to check out the room. A suite. The man had demanded a suite. The man must be important, Billy thought.

They had gone up separately, because that's the way the man wanted it. Miguelito had said he'd stay downstairs, maybe relax in the giant lobby with all that cool, dark marble and mahogany and crystal. Maybe go for a walk, buy an ice cream across the street at the Plaza.

The man had left his clothes in the small dressing area just outside the bathroom. Hung over the chair were the man's pants. On the table, the man had placed his cuff links, tie, wallet, and gold money clip. Billy thought the man was stupid, flashing that gold money clip with all those bills folded over. Almost like he was too important to get rolled.

The man was still singing, looking forward to his good time.

Billy lifted the money clip in his hand, letting it rest in his palm, like his hand was a scale and he was checking the weight. Lots of cash—twenties, folded thick and tight. The clip alone, Billy figured, would be worth a bundle, even on the street.

The hiss from the shower stopped, but the man was still singing. Billy placed the money back on the table. Don't take anything, he told himself, repeating Miguelito's words. The man would be generous, Miguelito had said. This was a sweet deal, and all he had to do was go with the man for the afternoon. Nothing heavy, just the usual.

"I thought you'd be undressed by now."

The man was standing there, wearing the heavy white bathrobe from the hotel, toweling what was left of his hair. The bathrobe was open in the center, and Billy could see the man's hairy roll of fat hanging over what he thought were the puniest dick and balls he'd ever seen.

Billy started to undress.

"That's better," the man said, moving closer. The man kissed him on the lips, and Billy could smell the soap from the shower.

The man said, "You are very young." He started running his fingertips over Billy's shoulders, then down his back and over his thighs. "Very firm, and beautiful." The man looked up, then brushed the hair from Billy's forehead. "Such a pretty boy," he repeated.

Billy saw that the man was getting hard. This was the build-up, he thought. What the man did to get himself going.

Then the man turned away, and Billy figured he was moving to get something. Billy's eyes focused over the man's shoulder, away from his body, so he didn't catch the man's swing.

The first blow rocked him off his feet. Billy staggered backward, hitting his head on the floor lamp, still uncertain what had happened.

When he looked up, the man was coming at him, swinging back and forth with his open hand, making Xs in the air, working on Billy's head and face, each slap bringing a stinging pain.

Billy covered up, surprised and shocked, trying to think, confused.

He found himself curled on the floor near the nightstand, covering his head with his arms to protect himself as the man continued to strike him, first with his hands, then his feet.

"Get up, you filthy bitch!"

Billy could see the man hovering over him. The man's face had filled with blood, spiderlike purple veins streaming from his nose, filling his cheeks. And his chest heaved in labored breathing, causing his flabby breasts to jiggle.

The thoughts were coming too slowly. It was not supposed to happen this way.

Again the man kicked him.

"I said, get up!"

Billy slowly slid up the wall. When he was standing, naked, his buttocks pressed against the hotel wall, the man's mood seemed to change. The man looked at the ground for a moment, then at Billy. A smile crossed his face, peaceful.

"I'm sorry," the man said, slowly reaching out and caressing Billy's bruised and bloodied face with his fingertips. Billy jerked away, then started to relax, thinking the man was weird, but that it was over.

"I am very, very sorry," the man said. "Can you forgive me, Billy?"

Billy nodded slowly. He could feel blood oozing from the corner of his mouth. There was a throbbing pain under his right eye, and he ached all over.

"Thank you," said the man. The man's eyes shifted away for a moment. He moved slowly. Billy wondered if he should leave, if the man expected him to just take off. Perhaps he was disappointed? Maybe Miguelito had been wrong and the man was in no mood for the game.

Then, without notice, the man swiftly brought his knee up between Billy's legs. Then did it again.

Billy barely felt the second knee. The first blow sent an electrical jolt of searing pain throughout his body; his head went numb. He felt like folding himself into the ground and not moving. A burning, painful throb, as if he'd been hit between the legs with a bowling ball, radiated sharp pain down his legs, making them tingle like thousands of razor blades cutting the skin. Death seemed preferable to enduring the pain. He was afraid to look at his genitals, afraid of the colors he might see.

Mercifully, he blacked out.

When he awoke, he was on the floor again. The man was at the bar, still naked, pouring himself a drink. Billy wasn't sure how much time had passed.

Billy got to his knees. The smears of his own blood on the carpet shocked him. He started to crawl to where he had left his clothes, his testicles swinging back and forth felt like they had weights attached. He moved slowly, trying to limit the sway.

There was something not working in his head, causing his arms and legs to shake, and making everything look like it was in shadow.

He started to put his pants on, wincing when the shorts came in contact with his genitals. His balls felt the size of grapefruits. He was still afraid to look.

"Where do you think you're going?"

The man was across the room, holding his drink. Relaxed and smiling, like nothing had happened. Billy was surprised how fast the man had moved.

"You're fucking crazy, man." Billy grabbed his shoes and shirt and slowly started limping toward the door. "You're nuts, man. A fucking loony." All he wanted to do was get out of there. Fuck the money. Fuck Miguelito's sweet deal.

"But the fun's just starting," said the man, stepping in Billy's path.

Billy veered to the side this time, not waiting for the first blow. When the man came at him again, Billy sidestepped, letting the man stumble by, his swinging fist just grazing Billy's ear.

Billy reached for the door, violently ratcheting the handle, but it wouldn't open. When he turned, Billy saw the man coming at him, his leather belt doubled and held in a fist over his shoulder. The man hatcheted the belt swiftly downward, just missing Billy's face but stinging his shoulder. Billy dodged away, and the man followed.

The man was laughing now. He was massaging his genitals as he swung the strap, like a lion tamer in a cage, smiling all the time.

Billy found himself in a corner. The man came at him with the belt, but Billy stood his ground. He tried to push the man away, push him down long enough to get out the door.

The man was short, but heavy, and much stronger than Billy thought. When he began to wind up, about to swing with all his force, Billy grabbed what was closest, a heavy glass ashtray, and thrust it in the man's face. A fountain of blood spurted from the man's nose. He let out a groan and fell backward, grabbing at his face, still on his feet.

The anger had taken Billy over, filling his chest with its violence, bubbling its demand for vengeance. Cornered and scared, Billy grasped the heavy ashtray in his right hand and brought it down on the man's face with all the power he had left.

Another spurt of blood streaming into the air, then another.

The man crumpled to the floor, motionless. Billy stood over him for a minute, thinking that he was still acting, that maybe the man wasn't hurt, but was just playing possum.

But he *was* hurt. The man wasn't moving, and Billy didn't see him breathing, either. Billy gingerly rolled him over with his foot, feeling his toes disappear into the fleshly folds of the man's belly.

On the side of the man's head, just above and to the right of his eye, was a bloody patch of skin that hung down, barely attached to the rest of his face. Above the patch of skin, a mushy purple indentation, a small crater, pushed the bony socket inward, as if the man's eyes were slanted, like an Oriental. The eyeball rested in the corner, pink and white, unmoving. The pupil

58

rolled up somewhere inside the man's forehead.

Billy hovered over the fallen man, wondering what to do. He couldn't think. The eyeball, like a milky olive, a white grape oozing its juices, told him that the man was dead.

Billy could feel his breath running away from him. He was surprised and ashamed when the tears began to pour forth.

What would Miguelito say?

This was his *fault. Miguelito had set the damn thing up.*

Billy looked around the room, trying to find the rest of his clothes. He wondered whether he should take the ashtray with him, then got so confused and scared that he grabbed his shoes and shirt and ran from the room.

When he got to the elevator, he slammed the button with the heel of his hand. He was taking quick, shallow breaths now, his lungs filled with a fire that was out of control.

He caught a glance of himself in the hall mirror. There was blood on his face and hands, on his chest. He quickly put his shirt on and used his socks to wipe the blood from his face. Still, he looked like a prizefighter after a losing effort. He'd just have to hope that nobody saw him on the way out.

When the elevator opened, he thought, for the second time that afternoon, that he was in luck: it was empty. His mind reeled back to Miguelito.

Miguelito's "sweet deal" . . .

Anger welled up in him toward his friend, but only for a moment. Miguelito barely knew the man; how was he to know that the man was crazy? It wasn't supposed to happen this way.

Billy pushed the lobby button, trying to compose himself, trying to remember everything that happened.

Miguelito would want to know everything, that was for sure.

He couldn't put together how it had started. Out of nowhere the man had kicked him. Not playful, like some did, going through the motions like actors, getting off on playacting the tough guy, a light slap here, a pinch there.

No, this one was no playactor.

His mind raced ahead toward consequences, toward what Miguelito would say.

It wasn't supposed to happen this way.

He needed help, advice.

Miguelito would know what to do.

He liked the table in the corner so that he could keep an eye on the whole room. Not that anyone ever bothered him. They'd gotten used to him, coming in once a week to pore over the volumes of past issues.

Interested in history, he'd told the woman at the counter. He'd shown her his employee identification from the newspaper, to convince her that he was okay, one of them.

Still, she seemed suspicious. Fat, with a face like a pitbull and an expression like she'd just bitten into a lemon. As if he would really want to steal some old newspapers!

He pored over the large tome containing past issues of the *San Diego Union*. He didn't enjoy having to act nice to the old bag at the desk, who gave him looks like there was something wrong with him. Looking at his mouth and not saying anything.

But he knew. He watched her stare at his lip, trying to figure it out.

But it was worth it. Once he got settled in his regular place in Archives, he could go over his notes, making entries in his notebook, copying articles from past issues.

Today, he'd found the one he'd been looking for. He had carefully reviewed the article, then made a copy. Now he was reading it over again.

February 18, 1982, Duarte, Ca

The district attorney's office dropped all charges today against Gordon Robert Castillo Hall in a ten-minute hearing in court, thus ending a three-year ordeal for the young man originally convicted in 1978 of first-degree murder.

Hall, serving a life sentence for the shooting death of Jesse Ortiz, had his conviction vacated by the California Supreme Court in 1981. A new trial was ordered based on newly discovered evidence of Hall's innocence. The court cited erroneous eyewitness identification and inadequate representation by counsel at Hall's first trial.

There was strong evidence that another man had done the killing, and several witnesses confirmed Hall's alibi.

The high court also cited the improper actions of the prosecutor in entering into a plea bargain with a percipient witness, Alfred Reyes, a condition of which was that Reyes could not make any statements regarding his observations of the murder without first notifying the prosecutor, giving a written statement to the police, and taking a polygraph examination. The court indicated that such prosecutorial conduct amounted to witness intimidation and deprived Hall of a fair trial.

Hall, who was spared the death penalty only because he was a minor at the time the crime was committed, announced that he had no specific plans for the future, and that he thanked God for his release.

The district attorney was unavailable for comment.

He carefully taped the copy of the article onto a clean page of lined notebook paper. Above the article, he wrote the name of the wrongly accused, and the date. He then flipped through the pages of his notebook, stopping randomly at various clippings he'd collected over the years.

The thin cutouts of newspaper were already starting to yellow, and the tape was cracked in spots. He knew each of the articles by heart, but still stopped to read a few of them each time he opened his notebook.

He flipped to the back section. The pages were newer, unwrinkled. He carefully placed today's clipping there.

He'd spotted another article in the morning edition, but hadn't had time to cut it out. He'd do that tonight, he thought. It was something he would allow himself to look forward to all day.

He started to think of the last woman. The look she had given him just before he showed her the knife. Like it was all over. Like he was going to leave, after all.

The thought of her face made him smile. It made him think of the woman's little scream just before she'd passed out.

It made him think of the part of the woman that he'd taken with him.

The Ripper, that's what they were calling him. He kind of liked the name. It was like that guy in London. He was becoming famous. Maybe he'd start wearing a cape, or something like that. The women would like that, the mystery of it all.

And once he had given it to them, shown them his power like nobody else could, they'd be fulfilled. Just like the woman in the newspaper had been fulfilled.

He'd had to take part of them with him, for his collection. That special part. They'd no longer need that part anyway. He had transformed them. After him, all other men would be second best. He had spoiled them for anyone else.

Yeah, that was it.

He closed his notebook, leaned back in his chair, and watched as the woman at the counter checked the location of an article for another customer.

Yes, he thought. One time with him, and they were all spoiled.

He had made sure of that.

5

They were looking at him, the woman at the cash register and the other one with the little sign that said *Denny's* over the pocket of her uniform. Like they both thought he didn't have the money to pay.

And they weren't far from the truth, he thought. Except, when he reached into his pockets this morning, he'd found a ten that he hadn't remembered putting there.

So now he made a big deal over the ten, looking at it, folding and unfolding it, while he waited for the lawyer to arrive.

Miguelito Gervas was still numb from the night before. He'd gotten into some guy's car off Washington near First, something that he'd been trying to cut down on, and the guy had pulled into the lot behind the bookstore, expecting Miguelito to go down on him right there in the parking lot under the neon sign that blinked on and off, saying, *Adult—Triple X-Rated*.

Miguelito figured that the ten must have come from that. He remembered spending the rest to pay off his outfit, the black leather pants that he now wore, the ones with the fringes up the sides, and the knee-high boots with silver buckles, just like Michael Jackson wore in his *MTV* videos.

He thought of the lawyer, and how long it had been since the last time. Miguelito had been very careful. It had been a while since he'd needed the lawyer. And even this time, it wasn't for him.

That damn Billy . . .

He'd warned him to watch out for the fat one, that the fat one would get full of himself if Billy let him.

Miguelito fingered one of the dozen or so buckles that adorned his black leather boots.

He closed his mind, letting the fatigue and the vague sense of intoxication from the previous night take him away. He could almost see the Central Men's Jail, not the building, but inside, the chipped concrete floor and metal wire beds. The stained bowl sitting against the wall, emitting its 24-hour-a-day dose of shit-smell, like sleeping inside the toilet at the beach.

It would take a while, but Billy would get used to it. After all, *he* had.

Actually, no. He was never used to it. He always knew it was there, a constant reminder that he was less than human. A piece of waste. Shit, himself.

He hated the place, even from the outside, looking through the large iron gates. The one-room buildings with bars over the windows, all with large signs sporting the names of the bail bondsmen in big letters, sometimes a picture, like a cartoon of the bondsman's vulture face, or the Get-out-of-Jail-Free Monopoly card. Like being in jail was some big joke to them.

He could see the lawyer now, getting out of his car and heading for the door. Miguelito ran a hand through his hair and stood up, wiping the grease off on the front of his shirt. The woman from the cash register was already grabbing a menu and moving his way.

Miguelito wondered how the lawyer would take it, whether he could play the lawyer into giving Billy a chance.

Whether the lawyer would need to bring *him* into it.

"Hey, Mr. Becker, you lookin' good." Miguelito put out his hand, flashing his confident smile.

"Mickie."

"How you been doin', Mr. Becker? I been meanin' to call you, you know. Got some good shit goin'." Miguelito held up his palms as if surrendering. A familiar pose.

"Totally legit, don't get me wrong."

"Let's sit down," said Max, motioning for Miguelito to follow the woman with the menus.

They found a booth in the back, where they could still watch the families dragging their kids and their plastic beach toys and chairs down to the sand as well as the longhairs aimlessly wandering the sidewalks, panhandling for nickels and dimes, strumming off-tune folk ballads, throwbacks to the sixties one and all.

"Coffee?" The woman waited. Max nodded. Miguelito shook her off.

"I'll have some juice," he said, his eyes racing across the menu. "You got any grapefruit? I mean, juice?"

"One coffee, one juice. Grapefruit." The woman stopped writing, still waiting. "That it?"

Max nodded.

Miguelito was still consumed with the menu. "And give me some of that corned beef stuff, you know, the hash. With some of those eggs." He smiled at Max. "I missed breakfast," he said, by way of explanation.

The waitress countered, "How you want'm?"

Miguelito was still smiling at Max. Max noticed the small tattoo of a dove perched on a tree limb that Miguelito bore on his left shoulder.

"I think she's talking to you," said Max.

"Oh, yeah. How you think I should have'm?"

"Hon, it's up to you." She began tapping her pencil on the pad impatiently.

"Scrambled," Miguelito finally said. "You got any *chorizo?* I feel like some *chorizo.*"

"No *chorizo,*" she said, then repeated the order and left.

"Nice lady," said Miguelito. "I guess she didn't get dicked last night." He laughed, then added, "At least, not by the right guy."

The waitress returned with their coffee and juice.

"You heard 'bout Billy?"

Miguelito spoke with his head down, slurping from his glass without lifting it off the table.

"Yeah," said Max. "Billy's in deep shit."

"Deep shit ain't the half of it."

Miguelito leaned back in the booth, resting one leg on the cushion. Max spotted the boot with the buckles.

"Nice boots," said Max. "Very low-profile, Mickie. You gonna be doing some moonwalking later on?"

Miguelito flashed his smile. "You like my outfit?" He started to smooth the front of his fluorescent tank top. There was a shadowy gray streak where he had wiped his hand. The muscle-builder shirt was made out of a silk-like material that was sheer enough to show the outline of his nipples.

All part of the plan, Max thought. Miguelito swung both ways, or at least he used to, back when Max had first represented him. He and Billy Darling weren't yet a team back then.

It had started out with sailors, kids from the midwest on shore leave, looking for a place to spend their money, horny from spending months on board a ship cruising the coast of some ungrateful third-world country. *Routine naval exercise*—that's what they called it.

Miguelito had poured himself into a red micro latex sheath and sheer dark nylons ending in black spiked heels. A waist-length rabbit jacket, open at the front, showing a white bra, like a bikini top, contrasted against that milk chocolate skin of his. The hottest bod on the block, or so Mickie used to put it.

Even Max had thought he looked pretty damn good that first time.

Until he realized that he was looking at a guy.

The court stuff wasn't the worst of it. A fine, a few days playing queen of the lockup for all the animals in heat. Miguelito claimed he could handle it standing on his head (and had actually tried).

But sometimes he didn't get away so easy. Some of those farmboys were big, and didn't care much for Miguelito's liberal ideas about friendship. They couldn't appreciate his subtlety, the surprise at the bottom of the box.

A number of his clients decided to take out their frustrations physically, not at all pleased when they reached between Miguelito's legs and came up with a handful of stiff cock instead of what they'd expected, what they'd paid their fifty dollars for.

"Talk to me about Billy," said Max, sipping his coffee. It was bitter, like it had been boiled.

Miguelito fingered the inside edge of his glass, inspecting a piece of pulp that remained on his fingertip, then flicking it away.

"Billy's gettin' fucked over, so fuckin' deep I don't know if anyone can get him out."

"This one of your deals?"

Miguelito nodded, still playing with his glass. "I set it up. The guy was hot for Billy." He turned to Max.

68

"You know how it is with these guys, man. Billy's fuckin' beautiful."

He stopped talking and turned away. Max could see that the hustler's cool facade was chipping away around the edges.

Max said, "So now he's got himself mixed up in a murder beef with one of A. Herbert Reed's closest friends and biggest contributors. Big-time shit, my friend."

Max had seen the reports dealing with the discovery of Jerry Kravitz's body by a housekeeper at the hotel, and the subsequent reports noting her identification of Billy as the person she'd seen leaving the hotel room. Between the blood and prints all over the room, the only thing missing was a business card with Billy's name on it and a videotape of the crime.

"I didn't know who the fuck the asshole was." Miguelito raised his voice. The waitress was at the side of the table with his food.

"Sorry," he said, waving her off.

He looked at the plate of food, picked up his fork, then pushed the plate away.

"I'm losing my appetite," he said. He tossed the fork onto the plate.

In the old days, Miguelito Gervas had been strictly a solo act. With his looks he'd had no trouble getting attention. His youth and pretty-boy appearance kept him as busy as he needed to be.

Now, in his early thirties, Miguelito was feeling the strain; he was beginning to slow down. The booze and the drugs and the sex were wearing him out, and it showed. Though he still had a pretty-boy face, Miguelito was no longer young. Innocence had never been there, but in the beginning, at least, he could fake it.

Those days were long gone. No longer the lissome boy, Miguelito now looked like he was wasting away, little by little, day by day. He reminded Max of an anorexic Sammy Davis Jr.: Little Richard with AIDS.

"You gotta help me . . . I mean, Billy."

Miguelito continued to stare at his uneaten plate of food.

"I feel responsible, man. I warned him, but hell . . . Billy's still just a kid. I shoulda seen it comin', I shoulda seen."

Max was at the bottom of his coffee, but held the empty cup in front of his mouth anyway. He wanted to catch Miguelito's response without looking as if he cared.

"Who's paying?"

"I got some money," said Miguelito. "I could maybe borrow some more from some people."

"You mean take up a collection. Hit up all the hookers and hustlers and try and put together what it's going to cost to hire a lawyer on a murder beef?"

"Yeah," said Miguelito, crestfallen. "Pretty stupid, huh?" He shrugged a laugh, as if he'd given up.

Miguelito looked pathetic. Max thought that if Billy Darling, by some miracle, beat the murder rap and found himself back on the streets, in a few years this is exactly what he had to look forward to.

"I'll talk to him," said Max, motioning the waitress for the check. "No promises."

Miguelito lit up. "That's good, that's cool. No promises. Thanks, man. I really owe you on this one."

Max held up a restraining hand just in case Miguelito, in his excitement, decided to lean over and give him a kiss.

"I'll see Billy today. We'll talk. If I take the case, and I'm not saying that I will because I probably won't, but

70

if I take the case, I'm going to need your help. You know the operation at the Grant. You know about this guy that had his head cracked open. None of your typical, I-can't-afford-to-get-involved bullshit. Do we understand each other?"

Miguelito nodded eagerly.

Max knew Miguelito would say and do anything to get what he wanted. That when it came time for Miguelito Gervas to come through, Mickie would start shuffling his feet, or just plain disappear. Getting involved with the cops or the courts was about as high on his Things-To-Do List as catching a dose of the clap.

"No problem," said Miguelito, all smiles. "Whatever you say, Mr. Becker." He reached for his plate and dug in. "I feel my appetite comin' on strong, like a boy with his first hard-on."

Max didn't comment on the metaphor. Though it struck him, knowing Miguelito as well as he did, as completely appropriate.

He tossed a ten on the table, waved goodbye, and headed for his car, replaying their conversation in his mind.

Miguelito had been right. Billy Darling had gone up in the world, or down, depending on your point of view. He'd represented Billy on a solicitation charge in juvenile court close to a year ago. Chickenshit misdemeanor stuff. The court had sent Billy back to his foster home on probation. It was only a matter of days before Billy once again AWOL'ed from placement. Billy always had Miguelito waiting for him.

But this time was different. Jerry Kravitz, the dead guy in the suite at the Grant, was not your average chickenhawk out to paw the merchandise before settling for a quick blow job. Jerry Kravitz had a place in La Jolla overlooking the ocean and was on the boards of a half-dozen private schools and a handful of major corporations. Kravitz's name usually appeared in the newspaper just after the words "community leader."

But more important than any of that, Jerry Kravitz was one of A. Herbert Reed's best friends and political confidants.

And A. Herbert Reed just happened to be mayor.

"Are you representing this punk?"

Max looked up from his newspaper. Standing in the doorway of the glass-enclosed interview cubicle was Detective Scott Dishell.

"Jesus, Scott," said Max, extending his hand. "How long has it been?"

Max asked the question from rote, the automatic response used to greet a friend one hasn't seen for a long while. Max knew exactly how long it had been. After the words came out, he felt awkward, and could see from the expression on Dishell's face that Scott did also. Both men silently pumped hands before Dishell changed subjects.

"Good to see you," he said. "I happened to be down here taping a statement when I saw your request slip come through."

Dishell glanced back at the deputy checking slips, then took a seat opposite Max at the small wooden table.

The attorney conference room at the men's jail was about half-full, mostly probation officers with long lines of custody interviews. Max spotted Dishell's partner, Jake Benson, seated inside the interview cubicle at the end of the room. Benson was chomping on an unlit cigar.

"I thought Jake would've retired by now," said Max.

"Yeah, so did I." Dishell flashed his partner a look, then smiled. "He's a real piece of work, that one. They don't make'm like that anymore. A real man's man."

Both men laughed.

Benson had been partnered with Dishell during the Carbon Brothers investigation and trial, though Dishell had done most of the work. It was Dishell who had sat at the counsel table next to David Gentry, assisting the DA in the presentation of his case.

Max and Scott, though normally finding themselves seated on opposite sides of the counsel table and with opposing interests, had developed a mutual respect for one another during the negotiations for Jaime Esquivel's testimony. The contact led to a friendship of sorts by trial's end.

"You're still working Robbery-Homicide, I gather?"

"Yep. The drive downtown's getting to be a real bitch, but I like the work. Still the same cramped little desk, right alongside Benson."

Max smiled. He knew Dishell wasn't sure whether he should mention what had happened after the trial, despite the fact that Dishell, like everyone else in the court system, in the city for that matter, was well aware of all the details.

It was like this with friends he met for the first time after a long absence—people who had known him when he was representing Esquivel, then heard about Rosalie and Ryan, then mysteriously disappeared from his life. Avoided him, was more like it. As if what he had might be catching.

But Dishell had not just been a bystander, the average Joe who read about the widowed attorney in the newspaper, clucked his tongue, and said, "What a pity."

Scott Dishell had been there. Called by the deputy who'd discovered the two bodies lying in the culvert near the orange grove, Dishell had been the one who'd notified Max, meeting him that early morning between Escondido and Vista, at the base of the freeway off-ramp.

They had gone together in Dishell's car. Past farms and ranches and oak-covered hills that had once lured prospectors seeking their fortunes in gold. Land that was now cut and gouged to make room for shopping malls and wild animal parks.

Duke Snider . . .

The name drifted through Max's mind as Dishell traveled away from the highway, toward the foothills.

Duke lived around here somewhere. And Lawrence Welk. Mr. Bubbles.

Of all the things to think of . . .

Dishell drove past a split-rail fence and through a gate posted No Trespassing, to where the concrete service road ended in a forest of orange trees that looked like an army of giant gnarled monsters in the moonlight.

Dishell was quiet, eyeing him carefully. Guiding him, staying close, over the thirty yards of dirt path into the groves.

Max had insisted on seeing it for himself.

Forensic was already there. Two men scurrying about, setting up lights and taking measurements. Uniforms in the background, almost indistinguishable, dark, ghostlike figures, standing in front of the headlights from the patrol cars.

A cool, wet mist, ground-hugging fog, swirled at their feet.

He almost missed the bodies.

But there they were. A string outline around them.

It was like someone else at first. Grossly distorted strangers. Nobody that *he* knew.

It didn't register.

He didn't recognize the two naked bodies, adult and child, clutching one another, covered in smears of burgundy and bright red, mixed with mud. Orange balls strewn about on the ground.

Like two players lying spent on a tennis court.

"Maybe we shouldn't do this right now?" Dishell said, gently grabbing his elbow and leading him away.

But it was too late.

What Max had feared most—what he had been preparing himself for—had finally happened. In his dreams he'd already seen this scene: bodies at the bottom of a dumpster behind the shopping center; or washed ashore like Jamie Esquivel; or glimpsed through the window of an abandoned car come upon by strangers : . .

He'd seen it all before.

The image repeated over and over in his mind.

He had tried to appear confident on the outside, putting on the stiff-upper-lip, hoping against hope. While all the time in his soul he knew they were gone.

Max stepped to the edge of the string outline. The techs from Forensics glanced at him, then stepped back, looking to Dishell. The flash pops stopped for a moment while he bent over, one knee on the wet ground, silently inspecting the residue of his life.

They looked almost like mannequins. Plastic. He had trouble acknowledging the truth. Unmoving, skin stained with streaks of blood, eyes staring blankly into the distance. They looked unreal.

He couldn't believe it.

Someone had dumped two plastic mannequins in a field.

How strange.

Max remembered Dishell tugging at him from behind. Lifting him to his feet, mouthing worn words of sympathy.

He heard that voice again now.

"How's your practice been? Still out there defending all the low-lifes?"

"Wha? Oh, that—yeah, same old story." Max brought himself back to the moment, the memories lingering as a sour taste on his tongue. "Some things never change," he said. "Crime-and-punishment's a growth industry, you guys see to that."

Dishell wanted to talk about what had happened. Max could see it in his face. But he was too discreet to ask. Like the others Max had come across since the kidnapping, Scott Dishell just smiled, the unasked question manifesting itself in a knowing look, a tilt of the head, the silent space between them.

I know all about you and somehow that defines how I'll look upon you forever.

Dishell said, "You got yourself into a real can of worms on this one."

"Darling?"

"Word is, they're out to crucify this kid. Big-time shit, Max. I don't need to tell you what's been in the papers. They're painting this Kravitz as something just below a saint."

Max nodded. "I know, I know. Except nobody seems to have hit on the question of what a guy like Kravitz was doing in his birthday suit with a street hustler like Billy Darling."

Dishell smiled. Max could tell it wasn't the first time Dishell had considered the possibilities.

"You're gonna have an uphill battle on that one. Kravitz was a respected community leader." He put up

76

a restraining hand as Max started to interrupt. "I know, I know. That doesn't mean the guy wasn't kinky. God knows, in this business, you can never be sure about anybody or any*thing*. Still, Kravitz was a businessman. There's nothing kinky about a businessman taking a room at a hotel, even in his hometown, if he's doing business. His family claims he was entertaining, and it was more convenient to use the suite at the Grant."

"He was entertaining, all right," muttered Max.

"You'll never prove it," said Dishell. "Darling's a street punk. Narcotics busted him just last month for possession of coke." Dishell paused, seeing the look of surprise on Max's face.

"You didn't know about that?"

"Last time I saw the kid was a year ago. Solicitation beef. He was only seventeen then."

"Yeah, well, he's an adult now, and from what the Narcotics guys say, he's still plying his trade out on the street, strung out from one john to the next."

Max moved a step ahead of Dishell.

"That's the way they're setting it up, then? A burglary, with Kravitz discovering the intruder inside his room as he steps from the shower. They struggle, and Darling cracks Kravitz over the head with something, then splits."

Dishell didn't respond. He just sat there, waiting for Max to speak.

"And the hotel maid sees Darling coming from the room, goes inside, and finds Kravitz dead on the floor."

"Not the most complicated case in the world," said Dishell. "Unless some ambitious defense attorney wants to take a real gamble and go to trial painting Kravitz as some sort of sleazy pervert out for a quick score. Even then you gotta fit the self-defense

77

somewhere in there, otherwise you still have a murder, at least a manslaughter."

Max began to recollect the details of the incident from the TV and newspaper accounts. Dishell was right. The only chance Billy Darling had of beating a first-degree murder charge was to claim self-defense.

The possible scenarios began to present themselves in Max's mind, even before he had a chance to hear Darling's side of the story; even before he'd agreed to take the case.

"Visitor for Darling."

Max looked up, and Dishell turned around.

At the front desk, Billy Darling stood looking over the attorney conference room. He wore the standard County Jail jumpsuit. On spotting Max, he slowly made his way toward the interview cubicle.

"I gotta split," said Dishell, shaking Max's hand. "A word to the wise," he said, lowering his voice. "The DA's got the message from above on this one, Max. Quick justice. Show no mercy."

"The old steamroller, huh?"

"Call it what you want," said Dishell. "Just make sure your ass is covered."

Max watched as Dishell turned, gave Billy Darling the quick once-over, then abruptly strode down the aisle of interview cubicles toward where Jake Benson was already interviewing their suspect.

"Who's that?"

"A friend."

"Looks like a cop."

"He is," said Max, motioning for Billy to take a seat. He could see the look of distrust in Billy's eyes. Consorting with the enemy. Like maybe Max and the cop had been discussing his case, planning exactly how Max would eventually cop him out. The old dumptruck routine.

Max said, "Miguelito mentioned you wanted to talk."

Billy squirmed in his seat, still obviously uncomfortable.

"Don't worry," said Max. "It sometimes pays to have friends on both sides. You never know when you may need a favor"

"Yeah," said Billy, unconvinced. "I guess so . . ."

"So talk."

Billy took another glance at Dishell, then started.

"What's there to say, man? You know what they got me charged with." He shook his head, looking down at the table, away from Max.

Max thought Billy hadn't changed all that much in the last year. Silky golden hair, wavy in the front, combed back to shoulder length, now shaggy around the ears. He needed a cut.

"Let's start at the beginning," said Max. "How did you and Kravitz meet?"

Billy was having trouble getting the words out. It was just like before. Except that was juvenile court, where the stakes weren't nearly so high.

The young man jammed a fist at his eyes. Max could see him desperately trying to hold back the tears. After all, he'd graduated to the big time. No more kiddie-court commissioners giving him community service or a few days in juvenile hall. Most of the grown men in the room with him would think very little of beating him senseless if they sensed his weakness.

"Miguelito set it up," Billy said. "He said it would be easy. That the dude was loaded, an easy score."

"And who else was loaded, Billy? And I'm not talking about cash."

Max watched the muscles in the young man's arms

79

tense. The only thing that might save Billy Darling, he thought, was the fact that he looked like he was able to take care of himself in a pinch. In jail, first impressions were lasting. If you looked tough and acted the part, you could usually get by on that, at least for a while. Billy was well built, the kind of size you'd think twice about before challenging. Yet his beauty, the baby face that had been his meal ticket, would work against him on the inside.

"I did a couple lines that day, beforehand. But I wasn't loaded. Jesus, I wish I were . . ." Billy shook his head, then said, "Things just got outta hand. The guy went crazy."

With his thumb and forefinger, Billy massaged his eyes, covering them from view. When he stopped, both eyes were red and swollen. Max saw his reflection in their glassy pools, an old man staring at his umpteenth client across a grimy county-issue desk.

"How crazy?" said Max. He leaned forward, placing his palms down on the table top.

Billy didn't respond. He dropped his eyes to the table, tracing a nail over some initials that had been carved into it.

"Listen, Billy. If you haven't figured it out yet, you're in deep shit on this one. This ain't juvenile court, where I can just waltz you in with some bullshit social study and talk the judge into letting you go back to placement. You're not leaving this place until this thing is resolved. The DA's gonna charge you with first-degree murder. Do you know what that means?"

Max paused only a second. The tears were streaming down Billy's face now, all pretense of toughing-it-out gone.

"This is a fucking felony-murder, Billy. They say you were ripping the guy off. That makes it felony-murder.

That's the death penalty, Billy. The fucking *Pill!*"

Max pulled back, allowing time for what he'd said to sink in. He knew the young man was scared, and that his threats of dying in the gas chamber would only scare him more. But that was exactly what Max wanted. Billy had been on the streets long enough to have developed that hard shell into which all street hustlers crawled when things got tough—*Don't show your emotions: never let 'em see you sweat . . .* Max was amazed at how often he'd seen it. Kids in serious trouble, with no direction in their lives, still putting on the cool, callous, emotionless facade.

And even though the facade seemed to be cracking for William "Billy Boy" Darling, Max wanted to be damned sure that he didn't see it again.

"It was self-defense, man, he was coming at me. I couldn't do anything else. I had to, man. I had to!"

Billy's voice cracked, and their conversation was beginning to attract the attention of the others in the room.

"Okay, okay," said Max, trying to get the young man to calm down.

"I want you to listen, and listen carefully." Max waited, until he saw something close to a nod from Billy.

"Very slowly, and very carefully, I want to hear your side of what happened. No bullshit."

"I ain't bullshitting you, man."

"Just so we understand each other, Billy, I haven't decided to take this case yet." Max thought of Miguelito, and the fact that if he saw a few hundred bucks out of all of this he would be lucky.

"If I think you're bullshitting me, I'm gonna get up and walk right outta here, and you can take your chances with the PD. You got me?"

Billy nodded. "Where do you want me to start?" he asked.

"At the beginning," said Max. He leaned back in his chair, taking occasional notes, listening as Billy told his story. When he had finished, Max looked away for a moment, trying to capsulize the events of that day into a way he thought they might be presented in court.

"If you're telling me the truth," said Max, "It's self-defense. If you honestly were in fear at the time you struck the man, then that's self-defense. Except that there are a whole lot of 'ifs' in your story. You know this guy was Mr. Big Deal?"

"Now I do."

"Yeah, well, you can rest assured that his family will have their lawyers pushing the DA every inch of the way. And as if that weren't bad enough, Kravitz was a good buddy of the mayor's. From what I've heard, the mayor's office is already putting the screws to the DA to get you tried and convicted as fast as they can. They want their pound of flesh on this case, and nobody much cares how they go about getting it."

"But what about the trial? I get a jury trial, don't I?"

Max smiled. "Yeah, you'll get your jury trial. But just stop and think for a minute. Put yourself in their position. Your jury will be mostly government employees, telephone company, water-and-power workers, people who don't mind doing jury duty because their employers are footing the bill. Middle America. People who go through their entire lives never thinking about guys like you.

"The rest of the jury will be retired people who are afraid to walk out their front door for fear that some young gangbanging punk will hit them over the head and grab their purse.

"If you're real lucky, you might get a young

secretary, maybe a college student, who won't take one look at you and automatically think you're guilty."

"So whatdya mean? I got no chance? I should just roll over and let'm do whatever they want?" The tough-guy facade was beginning to return, except at this point, Max thought, it was okay. Billy needed something to hold onto.

"What it means," said Max, "is that you're going to have to be mentally and physically strong during the time it takes to get this case to trial. You're going to have to always tell me the truth, no matter what. And you're going to have to try and look at yourself and everything you say the way a jury and a judge will look at it."

"So you'll take the case?"

Max hadn't yet decided—at least, not formally, though in his heart he knew he was committed. There was something about Kravitz, the mayor's behind-the-scenes right-hand man dripping with self-promoted good works, that turned his stomach. There was something about Jerry Kravitz that seemed almost too good.

Max thought about his other clients, the work that needed to be done on their cases, and his desire to slow down, take fewer cases, and limit the stress. The last thing he needed now was a high-publicity murder trial that would occupy a large chunk of his life.

"I need to talk with Miguelito again," Max said.

He had been wrong about clients before. Nobody was more aware of how easily an attorney could be taken in by a defendant's consummate job of acting. He had been burned by clients in the past, and each time it happened, it made it just that much harder for the next client, even if totally honest, to gain his confidence.

Max was in the position now where he didn't have to

take every case that came to him. He could afford to pick and choose. It was a luxury with a troubling catch. While he no longer had to defend clients he found untruthful, by implication, those cases he did take weighed even more heavily on his emotions.

For a criminal defense lawyer, thinking too long on the guilt or innocence of one's client, and letting that dictate the manner in which the case was handled, could be a very dangerous practice.

Looking at Billy Daniels' sad, hopeful face, Max realized that he was doing exactly that.

6

For Eddie Deets, Supervising Detective of the San Diego Police Department, the morning runs through Balboa Park had become a passion. Not so much the runs themselves, but all the preparation that went into them. The look. The feel. When everything was right, it was like taking charge, showing himself that even though he was pushing fifty, divorced, and going no further in his job, he still had some control over his life. He still had his little victories.

He started slow. The shoes were new, a pair of Asics Tiger GTXPRESS. He'd had trouble deciding between wearing the Tigers or his old standbys, the Avia 2070s. He decided to go with the Tigers, but was taking it slowly, letting his muscles warm to the task before doing any serious climbing.

He strode down Park Boulevard toward the Florida Canyon entrance to the park. The traffic at this early hour on Saturday was still light, and it didn't take him long, running most of the reds, to find himself inhaling the rich perfume from the Rose Garden. He continued through the park, past the cactus garden to El Prado, where he veered right.

The lawns beside the lily pond and in front of the

Botanical Building were empty, the early morning dew making them glisten emerald green. Deets knew that by midmorning the lawn would be filled with tourists, eagerly taking in the performances of the mimes, jugglers, and musicians along El Prado.

He took a short detour along the Hall of Champions, checking his own reflection in the window. He was wearing a pair of Scott Tinley orange Abstract running shorts, the result of a recent excursion to the local sporting-goods store. They looked like something Jackson Pollack would wear if he were a runner. He also wore his T-shirt from the office, the one with the Red Carpet Realty logo and his name and phone number stenciled below. You never could tell when you might pick up a little business. And the way the San Diego real estate market had bottomed out, he could use every bit of business he could get. He still had another seven years to go before he could pull down his Safety retirement, and even then, he'd need something to supplement his income. He'd been working part-time at Red Carpet, trying to build something he could fall back on when he left the cops.

He jogged past Palm Canyon and wound around through the Japanese Gardens behind the House of Hospitality. That brought him back out on El Prado to the Spanish Alcazar Garden across the street from the Museum of Man. In the morning gloom, the Spanish-Moorish buildings along El Prado took on an eerie, almost foreboding appearance, their gray-shaded facades looking like looming monoliths from a time gone by, bearded conquistadores on horseback bringing civilization to an untamed land.

The hundred bell carillon in the California Tower tolled seven. Deets waited on the grass, slowly jogging in place, trying to stay loose.

It was about five minutes before he was joined by

Rich Valenzuela. Valenzuela came huffing and puffing up El Prado, wearing a worn gray Beethoven sweatshirt and a pair of UCSD gym shorts. He was a good six inches shorter than Deets, but at least ten pounds heavier. His thick mane of black wavy hair fell over his forehead as he trudged the last few yards.

"Max running late?"

Valenzuela spat out the words between breaths, his right hand grabbing his chest, his left on his knee, supporting his doubled-over weight.

"A few minutes," said Deets, barely moving, and barely winded. "You sure you're up to this, Richie? You ought to take it easy at the start, build up slowly."

"No, no. I'll be okay."

Rich Valenzuela was bent over, spitting out the words in quick bursts. "Just give me a sec, let me catch my breath. That's mostly uphill on Sixth." He looked up from his crouch, flashing a smile. Both men knew that Valenzuela was terribly out of condition and that Sixth Avenue was a very gradual uphill.

"All the same, Richie, we'll take it slow. You wanna drop back, catch your breath, go ahead. We'll come back for you."

Deets smiled, then added, "You judges spend too much time sitting on your ass. You gotta get out more often. The body turns forty, everything starts to slow down. If you don't stay on top of it, it's like hell trying to catch up all at once."

"Are we talking about running or fucking?" said Valenzuela. "Cause if we're talking about fucking, Eddie, I wouldn't dare contradict the self-proclaimed expert of San Diego law enforcement. You give this same bullshit speech to your future homebuyers?"

Deets laughed. The two men had known each other for over ten years, Deets as a cop working his way through the ranks, and Valenzuela, first as a prosecutor, then a judge. Valenzuela was now the presiding judge of the San Diego Superior Court.

"Here he comes now."

Valenzuela looked up, having finally caught his breath. Max Becker was slowly jogging toward them on El Prado, just a couple blocks away. Both men took off, meeting him halfway.

"What say we go through the canyon?" said Deets, jogging in place with the others. "Nice and slow for His Honor, here." Max smiled. Rich Valenzuela tried to smile, but it came out looking more like a painful grimace.

"Sounds fine to me," said Valenzuela, with more bravado than common sense.

"Nice and slow," Max reminded Deets. "We'll take a loop around the golf course. It should still be pretty empty."

The three men pounded off down El Prado, Deets retracing his steps back toward Park Boulevard. Max and Deets traversed the canyon in a sort of run-walk, some of the inclines being too steep and rocky to handle at a full gait. Rich Valenzuela plodded along behind, having found his pace by walking every hundred or so yards.

When they got to the golf course, Valenzuela stopped and rested under the purple blossoms of a jacaranda tree near the ninth green, while Max and Deets continued on.

After about twenty minutes, the two men returned, slowing to a walk as they approached.

"How you feel?" asked Max, his chest heaving.

"Good," said Valenzuela. He watched as his two friends continued to walk around, letting their bodies cool down slowly.

"I bet you guys didn't know that these jacarandas were not naturally here?"

Max looked up, wondering what Valenzuela was getting at. Deets continued pacing, swinging his arms back and forth, limbering up, not paying much attention.

"Another San Diego history lesson, Richie?"

"You two could stand a few history lessons," said Valenzuela.

"All right," said Deets, lying on the grass and starting to do push-ups. "Lay it on us, Richie."

"All these beautiful trees, the jacarandas, the palms, were planted by the Mother of Balboa Park. I don't suppose either of you physical fitness studs know who that is?"

Max looked to Deets, who was still pumping away, blowing quick breaths in grunts as he powered up from each push-up.

"No," said Deets, the strain evident in his voice. "Why don't you enlighten us, Your Honor?"

"Kate Sessions. She's considered the Mother of Balboa Park. She was responsible for planting most of the trees. Otherwise, the whole place would look like Florida Canyon, dusty arroyo covered with scrub."

"That's real interesting, Richie."

Max lay down next to Rich Valenzuela on the grass. Deets finished his push-ups, shouting out the number 100 to rub it in, then came over and joined them.

"Nice shorts," said Max. "You planning on entering a beauty contest or something? Maybe pick up some babes on your way to becoming the next Iron Man?"

"Never hurts to look the part," said Deets, smoothing his hand over the front of his shorts.

Max said, "Except that T-shirt's gotta go. You need one of those tank top things, you know, show off the muscles."

Valenzuela snickered.

"Go ahead," said Deets. "Mock me. Just because I'm

not over-the-hill like you two old farts. Richie here's got himself a steady woman, so he doesn't have to worry. You, Becker, seem to have found the celibate life to your liking." He flashed a mischievous grin, holding his palms in the air as if to say, "Go figure."

"Like I always say," said Deets. "To each his own."

Valenzuela's head snapped around. "Like you always say, my ass. Eddie, you've got your nose in everybody's fucking business. It's the cop in you. 'To each his own . . .' That's a laugh!"

The three men were silent for a few minutes, eyes focused on a foursome of golfers teeing up in the distance. It was Max who broke the silence.

"What's the word on the Kravitz case?"

The question had been directed at Eddie Deets. He looked at Valenzuela, who raised his eyebrows and tilted his head, holding back what he might know of the case.

"Is that a personal or professional question?"

"Personal," said Max. "For now, at least."

Valenzuela focused on Max, listening to Deets's response.

"And you'll be sure to let me know," said Deets, "when it becomes professional."

"Of course, Eddie. You know me."

"Yeah, that's why I asked."

Each looked like a cat that had recently swallowed the proverbial canary; each knew what the other was up to, but was willing to play the game, jabbing and cutting in good fun, knowing that the other knew where to draw the line between friendship and professionalism.

"We've got this kid, William Darling. Far as I can see, it's pretty straightforward. Darling gets into Kravitz's room looking for something to take. Kravitz spots him, they struggle, and Darling clobbers him with an ashtray. Nothing very complicated. Darling's got a record—coke possession, solicitation. He's gone up in the world on this one, though. DA'll probably ask for death."

Max nodded, gaining the attention of the other two men.

Valenzuela said, "Seems to me, Max, I recall you representing Darling, or somebody like him, a while back."

"I did."

"I thought you were semiretired," said Deets.

"I am."

"Then what's that look I'm seeing on your face? The one that tells me you got more than just a casual interest in Billy Darling's well-being?"

Max shrugged, then laughed. The other two were waiting for his answer. Max figured they both knew the score, but wanted to hear it from him anyway.

"He came to me," said Max. "Well, not exactly. A mutual friend. Actually, Darling's friend, my former client. I talked to the kid. I'm still not sure whether I want the case."

Valenzuela shook his head. "Gentlemen," he said, standing. "I'd better not hear too much more of this conversation. The chances of me, as presiding judge, trying this case are pretty slim. Still, you never can tell."

Deets nodded in agreement. "Richie's right. The three of us have been bullshitting for so long, we lose track of how it looks. I mean, some reporter or someone could see us one day, maybe overhear us talking cases. Next thing you know, it shows up in the paper, I get a hearing in front of the Review Board, you're reported to the State Bar, and Richie here gets scrutinized by the Council on Judicial Ethics. And we all get fucked, for just a little innocent talk between old friends."

Max's smile matched the one he saw on Eddie Deets's face. Deets was playing possum, more concerned with squeezing information out of Max about his case than with any possible Police Review Board. Deets had been around long enough to know how to cover his ass, and he figured so had the others. All was fair in love, war, and criminal cases.

"Okay," said Max. "What say we leave Billy Darling for the courts? What's your department been doing about this Ripper investigation? I almost got crucified the other night by a room filled with rabid feminists, just because I happen to practice law on the defense side of the counsel table. I tellya, those women were angry—angry and scared."

Deets pursed his lips, then nodded. "Tell me about it. And it's just starting. We don't bag this guy pretty soon, some asses are gonna hit the ringer, mine included. Word's come down that the chief wants this guy made top priority. There's an election coming up, my friends. The last thing the chief wants is to be on the stump answering questions about the goddam Ripper."

"You ever wonder how these guys come up with these names?" Rich Valenzuela didn't wait for an answer before continuing. "These newspaper reporters must sit around for hours trying to figure out some catchy tag, one that hasn't been overused. Considering all the psychos they got running around the state, that's no easy task."

"They'll catch the bastard," said Max. "Either that, or he'll stop, maybe move to another county. These guys either want to be caught, or they fall in love with the publicity. Either way, they make a mistake, get careless. Very few are smart enough to get out when the going's good."

"The question," said Deets, "is how many more

women are going to be raped before he screws up. I hate this damn feeling of helplessness. No ID, no forensic evidence worth a shit. The guy uses a fucking rubber, do you believe it?"

"He takes parts with him, doesn't he?"

Deets swiveled back toward Max.

"How the hell did you know that? We kept that from the papers."

"I have my sources, Eddie. What I'm saying is that these cutters, the ones that take souvenirs, usually have a score to settle. Psychologically, I mean. They're either taking a part that has some meaning to something that happened earlier in their lives, or they're recreating the victim in their own image. Either way, the act of rape, of cutting the victim, is usually tied to some childhood trauma."

"You've been talking to too many shrinks."

"Maybe so, but if you look at these guys, the ones they catch, it's almost always there."

"Pretty vague stuff," said Valenzuela. "Shrink testimony is bad enough. This is really crystal-balling it." He looked to Max, who nodded in agreement. "Still, Max's probably right. Now all we have to do is round up every psycho-slasher in the county and do an in-depth psychological and social history to find our man. No sweat, right?"

"Come on," said Deets, jumping to his feet and starting back. "It's fucking Saturday morning. My day off. I got all next week to try and psychoanalyze this dickhead." He started to jog away. Max smiled at Valenzuela, then motioned that they should follow.

A few paces behind Deets, Valenzuela said, "Give some serious thought to taking that Kravitz case, Max."

Max looked over, seeing the concerned expression on Valenzuela's face. It seemed like everybody had received the word, knew what the result was expected to be.

"Always," said Max. "Always."

The choice was either lowering the temperature for the *streptocarpus,* or raising it for the *sinningia.* As it was, set inbetween at sixty-two, neither plant was showing much growth.

He decided to move the *sinningia* closer to the greenhouse window, hoping that the additional sunlight would raise the temperature a few degrees.

The *clivias* had finished blooming and were ready to be moved to a less prominent place in the garden. Lifting the four clay pots packed with roots, he moved them one by one to a lower shelf in the corner. In their place he set out the Mexican pots he'd purchased in Tijuana, along with the bags of redwood bark and potting soil. He would prepare the pots, settling a layer of bark and soil inside, so that when the annuals were ready for transfer, he could build his bowls of color that with a little luck and careful attention might last him through to fall.

For Max it was the best way to spend a Saturday afternoon. He'd never been a big one for TV sporting events. Sure, if it were the World Series or the NCAAs, he'd usually catch the game. But barring that, he preferred to spend the weekend afternoons puttering around in the garden, talking to Cardozo, having lunch on the patio with his plants.

"Whatdya think, boy? Should we go with the *tolmiea menziesii* tonight?" He held the fuzzy greenleafed piggyback plant in the palm of his hand, examining it. Cardozo rested in a shady spot in the corner.

"I think so. It'll fit perfectly in that pot we bought in Mexico."

94

Cardozo remained motionless, panting slowly, keeping one watchful eye on his master, the other closed.

Max placed the plant on the redwood table, on top of a sheet of old newspaper. His eyes were drawn to the headline Authorities Have No Clues in Ripper Investigation.

He thought about Sabrina and Mitchell, all alone. Just the sort of setup the Ripper preferred, if his past conduct was any indication. Just like Leslie Greer, the Ripper's second victim. A woman and child in the house, alone at night.

He told himself he was probably needlessly worried. After all, Sam had said she didn't give it much of a thought. That she'd lived by herself for as long as she could remember, and wasn't about to adjust her lifestyle because of some chickenshit psycho-rapist.

That was just like Sam, though—Samantha Fleming, the original self-reliant woman, a women's libber since the womb.

Max remembered the incident that had brought them together. It was five or six years after Rosalie's death. He'd just returned, rather half-heartedly, to the practice of law, taking court appointments doled out to him by Rich Valenzuela, not really caring or having the incentive to go out and drum up business on his own.

At the time, he'd been satisfied to accept the court appointments, take the money provided by the county for representing indigent defendants, and not have to worry about settling the legal world on fire. There was something about hustling for clients, living every waking hour concerned with making money, that no longer appealed to him. It was a feeling that had stuck with him, even now.

Samantha Fleming had first said hello from the other side of the glass window inside the attorney-conference room of the woman's jail. She was there because San Diego Vice had felt the pinch from their chief of police, a bible-thumping conservative who'd since been forced out of office and had taken a position up north in Orange County.

Normally, the high-priced call girls worked with relative impunity, providing their specialized services to the movers and shakers of the city. Nothing obvious. Nothing that would raise the hackles of the city fathers (and more importantly, their wives).

Working discreetly out of the Omni Hotel downtown, and the Town and Country in Hotel Circle, the girls took care of business, including the usual *quid pro quo* for law enforcement. The cops had an attitude of "Don't bother us and we won't bother you." And that was just fine with the girls.

Samantha found her arrest more of a novelty than a traumatic experience. She was in the process of bailing out when Max met with her. It was a short meeting. After all, time was money—and business, especially Sam's business, couldn't be transacted from behind bars.

When the case was over, Max had called her. His own sex life since Rosalie's death had been for the most part nonexistent. Sam had a way of talking about things, even Max's loss, that made him feel that he was not hanging out there all alone, that his problems were not as insurmountable as they seemed.

Yet they both knew that the relationship was far from exclusive. He wasn't around day and night, far from it. And she had the rent and other expenses to pay. She was a working girl, plain and simple.

That's what Max had told himself. Over and over, as the years progressed, and he felt the need to be with her grow stronger, even if it was only to talk.

Tonight he would see her for dinner. Her place. A rare event, dinner with Sam on a Saturday night.

Usually it was a big business night for her, high volume. But it was her birthday, and she said she needed somebody to celebrate with, and other than her five-year-old son Mitchell, Max was her only real friend.

He decided the piggyback plant would do nicely. He'd been trying to develop an appreciation for gardening in Sam, though so far he had to admit to mostly failure. She'd managed to kill three fuschias, a basket begonia, and even a ficus that Max had guaranteed as indestructible.

He cleaned up around the garden and headed inside. In the hallway that led to the bathroom were the pictures of Rosalie and Ryan. He'd never had the strength to take them down. Bittersweet memories: the three of them on vacation; he and Rosalie the day they were married; Ryan as a baby, and as a toddler—his first school picture.

He stopped in front of the first picture he'd taken of Ryan, in the plastic bassinet at the hospital. He remembered the day, the nurse wheeling Ryan in after the delivery. Rosalie smiling her marvelous smile, as if they'd done something nobody had ever done before. A miracle. Then the worried look, when the awesome responsibility had set in.

Ryan slept peacefully, his thumb stuck securely in his mouth, cocoonlike in white hospital blankets, like a papoose with a tiny fuzz-covered head sticking out. After the first moments of birth, Max had been relieved to see that everything looked normal. The boy had come out all purple and covered with gook and blood. Max hadn't wanted to sound any alarms, thinking about Rosalie's well-being at the time, but he was convinced then and there that his only son had been born defective, that something wrong had happened in the womb, something terrible.

It made him smile now. He thought about it every time he paused in the hallway to look at the picture. It was the way he remembered Ryan, along with the other pictures—as if, by reinforcing his memory with the celluloid images, he could recreate his history with his wife and son.

And, more importantly, drown out the memory death-slides of that night in the orange groves.

Cardozo let out a soft cry. Max looked down, torn from his memories. He hadn't realized the dog had joined him. He crouched down and wrapped his arms around the dog, running a firm hand over the huge black head.

"You miss them, too, don't you, boy?"

Cardozo barked twice, then licked Max's face.

Talking about their work was one thing he and Sam didn't do. Since the beginning, it was a sort of understanding between them.

At dinner, he told her of his morning run with Eddie Deets and Rich Valenzuela, of the way Valenzuela had huffed and puffed his way back to El Prado, and of Deets's threat to call the paramedics if Valenzuela didn't get into better shape.

He spoke to her of his garden, the effort he had taken in preparing her birthday present, which now sat in the center of the table, after receiving a suitable number of oohs and aahs.

She'd spent the afternoon walking along the Embarcardero with Mitchell, watching the tourists and just relaxing. She stopped for the crab salad at Anthony's, then did some shopping at Horton Plaza. A nightgown, she said, smiling. A birthday present to herself, one they could both appreciate.

After dinner, Sam poured coffee and brandy, and

they spent a couple of hours watching a movie she'd rented.

At eleven, Sam turned out the lights, grabbed his hand, and led him into the bedroom. On the way, she poked her head into Mitchell's room, making sure he was sleeping soundly.

Then they both undressed silently, Max carefully folding his slacks and draping them over the chair. He'd grown accustomed to being quiet during his visits with Sam. Mitchell was a light sleeper, and spent most of his evenings under the watchful eye of the elderly woman next door, who babysat while Sam was out. Sam still wasn't sure how she'd handle things when Mitchell grew older and began asking questions. It was something she rarely touched on with Max, keeping that part of her private life private.

She disappeared into the bathroom for a moment only to emerge wearing the infamous birthday present.

"You were right," he said, his eyes transfixed.

"You like?"

"Very much."

She flicked out the bathroom light, then turned down the covers. The bedroom window was open, but the rest of the lights in the house had been turned off. A cool ocean breeze filtered through the screen, rustling the plastic on the lampshade.

Max felt his way to the bed, then climbed in. They found each other in the darkness, first with hands, then with their lips. Max slowly moved downward, covering her with kisses, tasting her sweet, salty smell. She moved with him, softly moaning, barely breathing as he moved between her legs. First with his fingertips, gently caressing, then his tongue. He guided her gently, until with short, swift, cries of pleasure, she was done.

"Happy birthday," he whispered, lying at her side, listening as her breathing gradually slowed.

She draped a leg over him, moving it up and down against him, making him hard, chewing softly on his earlobe, running her tongue inside.

He moaned softly, trying to move closer, gently straining against her arm over his chest. But she kept him still, wanting to tempt and tease him, to drive him crazy with pleasure.

Finally, when he felt as if he would explode, she slipped her hand down between his legs, firmly gripping him with her hand.

He groaned with satisfaction.

He quickly moved on top of her, easily sliding inside. She was still wet from his tongue. He moved quickly at first, then told himself to slow down. It would be over too quickly.

In his effort to prolong the pleasure, he lost it, felt himself starting to go limp.

"What's wrong?"

"Nothing, nothing. Lost my concentration. Don't worry, it'll be okay. Give me a minute."

She thrust up to meet him, to help him, running a finger down his back, between his legs, gently stroking with her fingernail.

He felt himself coming back, and increased his pace, moving steadily back and forth. He could feel himself harden with each stroke.

"That's it," she whispered. "Mmm."

He felt it coming, almost there. He arced through her, thrusting his hips forward, throwing his head back, slicing forward then back, again and again.

He dropped his head, whispering, "Say the name."

He thought he felt her contract herself around him, closing up, but not out of passion, it was something else. In that split-second he felt Sam close herself to him. He registered the moment in his subconscious, unsure of its meaning.

"I love you, Bear," she said in a monotone. "I love you."

He grunted then jerked, mashing his stomach against hers, shooting inside her until there was no more.

She rolled away from him, and when he brought his body behind hers and draped his arm over her breast, she remained motionless.

For the first time, she didn't grab his hand and press it tightly against her.

7

Mustard squirted from the corner of Deets's mouth. Without putting down the sandwich, he dabbed at his face with a paper napkin, then tossed the napkin onto his desk and took another bite from the oversized kaiser roll. The force of his jaw chomping on the roll sent droppings of yellow liquid plopping down from his hand into his lap.

"Shit!" Deets half-stood in his chair, wiping at his pants. "Goddamn, you'd think a grown man could manage to eat a fucking corned beef sandwich without getting the damn thing all over him!"

"You're making it worse," said Max, calmly munching on two thick pieces of rye bread sandwiching three inches of corned beef. Max placed his sandwich on the waxed paper in which it had come from the deli. He sat on the other side of Deets's desk, smiling as his friend fussed and fumed over his mustard-stained pants.

When Deets pushed aside a stack of folders in his effort to do a little cleaning up, a medical examiner's pack of photos slipped from one of the files. Max picked it up and recognized the name on the outside of the envelope.

"What's this?"

Deets took the envelope from Max, checked the name, then tossed it back into the appropriate folder.

"Ripper's last victim," said Deets, still fussing with his pants. He finally settled back in his chair, leaned closer to the desk so that his chin was about three inches from the top, and stuffed into his mouth in quick fashion the remainder of his sandwich.

"Do you mind?" Max's hand was poised in midair over the folder. Deets shook his head, his mouth filled with food.

Max sifted through the photographs.

"Real nice, huh?"

"Jesus, Eddie . . . these women were butchered." He opened the file and found the medical examiner's report.

"Seems our boy's a frustrated gynecologist," said Deets. "Likes to take something with him after he's done his dirty work." He started sucking on his teeth, working on them with the red plastic toothpick, shaped like a miniature sword, that had come with the sandwich.

Deets said, "They've both had the labia removed. Cut off. Forensic's working on the tool, but it's obviously very sharp, as you can see from the neat incision along the outer edge of the vulva."

"Vulva?"

Deets smiled. "That's the medical term, Max. Let's just say that those women have been circumcised, for want of a more medically accurate description."

Deets belched, wadded up his waxed paper, and tossed it beneath the desk.

"You gonna eat the rest of that?" he asked, pointing at Max's halfeaten sandwich.

Max looked up from the photos at what remained of his food. He'd suddenly lost his appetite.

"Go ahead," he said. He watched Deets eagerly devour the rest of the sandwich in two bites.

"Thought you were on a diet," said Max, still comparing the pictures to the descriptions in the ME's report.

"I was," said Deets, his mouth full. "With the emphasis on the past tense."

"Who you got working this?"

"Leventhal and Levine, for now."

"The Jewish Mafia? Well, they're the sensitive types. At least you won't piss off any of the victims."

"Yeah, and we probably won't find this guy, either. Leventhal's coming off a stress disability, and Levine's got four kids at home, which is about three more than she can handle. Her husband's badgering her to quit, and I have a sneaking suspicion that she's about to pull the plug."

"What happened to the lips?" said Max, spreading the photos like a poker hand on the desk.

"The labia, Max. They don't call'm lips. At least, the docs don't." Deets leaned back in his chair, clasping his hands behind his head. He swiveled back and forth as he spoke.

"To answer your question, I haven't the slightest idea, except the obvious explanation, which is that this perverted jerkoff took them with him."

Max looked up and saw in Deets's expression, the resigned and beleaguered look of the atrocity-weary veteran cop.

"Enough of the goddamn Ripper for now," said Deets. "I got women calling down here almost every minute, wanting to know whether we've caught the sonofabitch, and if not, what the hell we're doing about protecting the community. It's the old I-pay-your-salary routine, you know."

Max nodded. He was thinking about the women's

meeting with Susan Gentry.

"It's just like the goddam Nightstalker," said Deets. "People are afraid to walk the streets. Jesus, we even had a report of a woman who took a baseball bat to some guy selling mops and cleaner door-to-door for the Salvation Army. People are getting real edgy, Max. It's just a matter of time before something totally stupid happens because everyone's so paranoid about this guy."

"You'd be paranoid, too," Max said, "if you were a woman living alone."

"Yeah, guess so." Deets ran his tongue over his teeth, then sucked a few times. "So what's new with Billy Darling? You finally get your head on straight and decide to let some other poor slob represent the guy?"

Max thought of his meeting with Mickie Gervas and Billy Darling. The Kravitz murder was getting daily coverage in the media. Deets, Max figured, probably thought the case was a lock, a slam-dunk for the prosecution. Not worth worrying about.

"I got retained," said Max.

Deets looked at him with a mixture of disbelief and mild disappointment.

"You gotta be kidding, Max. Where's a guy like Darling come up with the retainer on a murder?"

Max didn't answer, and when he didn't, Deets shook his head, laughing softly to himself.

"You're doing this thing for free, aren't you?"

Again Max didn't answer.

Deets sighed, then removed a pack of throat lozenges from his desk, shook one into his palm, then tossed it into his mouth.

"I guess my telling you that you're stupid would do no good?" Deets said, sucking on the lozenge.

"I guess not," said Max.

"Max, listen." Deets rested both elbows on the desk.

In his left hand he held a pen like a cigarette, and with the right he gestured to bring home his point.

"This kid's a loser. Kravitz was one very well-connected man in this town. I don't have to tell you that he and the mayor were like this." Deets crossed the fingers of his right hand like he was making a wish.

"If you get involved in this thing, especially for free, you're gonna come out smelling like shit, just like Darling."

"What if he didn't do it, Eddie?"

"Didn't do it, my ass! You know he clobbered the guy. Come on, Max. The fucking maid saw him. He ain't even denying it."

"Self-defense, Eddie. The kid said he acted in self-defense."

"Whatdya expect the poor bastard to say? That he went in to rip the guy off, got found out, and clobbered the fat rich dude in order to get away?"

Deets paused, sucking on the lozenge, then crunching it with his teeth.

"I ain't telling you how to try your case, Max. Hell, the two of us probably shouldn't even be talking about it. But we go back a lotta years, and I know you'll take what I have to say the right way. At least think about it, Max. There are a lot of powerful people in this town who won't take very kindly to you representing this kid."

Max considered Deets's words. Good advice, as usual. Mayor A. Herbert Reed and his political machine would make representing Billy Darling very difficult. They'd already put pressure on the prosecutor's office to quickly bring the case to trial. What Max couldn't quite understand was why everyone was so willing to overlook the possibility that Kravitz and Darling had something going, and that that was the reason Billy Darling found himself inside the suite at the Grant that afternoon.

"Jim Morse is a nice guy and all," said Deets. "But he's going to come down hard on this kid. They're going to ask for the death penalty. He has to. He's gotta show the voters that they got the tough-on-crime DA they elected." Deets caught himself in mid-breath, about to say something else, but thought better of it.

"What?" Max knew there was more.

Eddie Deets recrossed his legs, then swallowed his lozenge, reaching for another.

"What is it, Eddie? You know something about this case that I should know?"

"Shouldn't tell you," muttered Deets.

"Come on, Eddie. We never played by those rules."

"Okay, okay. It's no biggie. It's just that I heard the DA's going to assign Zellner to the case. It's just a rumor now. Maybe I'm wrong. The way I heard it, now that Gentry's retired, Morse has got the division heads making death penalty decisions on a case-by-case basis. I heard that Zellner wasn't willing to take the Darling case unless Morse personally guaranteed him that he could ask the jury to give the kid the Pill. I guess Zellner didn't figure it was worth his effort unless he could get a scalp to show for it."

Max let the name register for a moment. Nathan Zellner, Nate the Great, Zellner the Zealous. Golden Boy of the San Diego County District Attorney's Office. Long-time friend of James Morse. Zellner was all the things that made for a glamor-boy prosecutor: attractive, arrogant, intelligent, vindictive, and ambitious. Zellner didn't need the money; he prosecuted cases strictly for the fun of seeing people squirm under his thumb.

Max remembered reading a recent spread on Zellner in *San Diego Magazine;* **The Best Lawyers in Town.** In the magazine, Nathan Zellner was pictured in front of his La Jolla bungalow, standing in the driveway with his actress-wife and his black Porsche Carrera, Zellner had his arm around the Carrera.

"That'll just make it more fun," said Max, feeling the false bravado in his voice.

Nate Zellner was arrogant, pompous, and self-centered, but he was also damn effective in getting convictions. He took each loss personally, and there were very few of those. Max knew that Zellner would fight like a cornered animal, use every legal maneuver in the book (and some illegal ones) to get Billy Darling convicted. Nathan Zellner didn't prosecute just any case. Assigning Zellner to the Darling case meant the DA was out for blood, serious about getting this one put to bed early without any surprises along the way.

"Just be careful, Max," Deets warned. Deets wasn't given to melodramatics, and the look on his face told Max that he was absolutely serious.

"Zellner's going to want to make this trial a three-ring circus," said Deets, "no matter what Morse tells him about getting it over with quickly. It's not Zellner's style. You just make sure you don't come out looking like the clown in Nate Zellner's dog-and-pony show."

8

From the window on the second floor, he could see the rolling brown hillside and rocky cliffs forming the eastern tip of the canyon. Houses dotted the edge, overlooking the hundred-yard drop to the base below. Two hikers, college students, from the looks of them, traversed the floor of the canyon, moving steadily west toward the park.

In the distance, he could barely make out the small bridge that spanned Highway 163 and connected the heavily wooded ravine area adjacent to Florida Canyon to the forested edge of Balboa Park. Just an indistinct dark smear, wavering in the heat like a mirage. Almost moving, fluid, like the soft liquid center of a hard candy.

He sat where Millie Burris used to sit with her knitting, looking out on the grounds of the home, rocking back and forth in the old wooden chair that would creak down at them from the open window as they worked in the yard. Sitting in that chair, his feet on the windowsill, gently rocking the chair forward and back, he was aware that the smokehouse was still there, off to the side, in a corner of the yard. Brick and wood, with heavy black iron doors. Almost like a large doll house, or child's playhouse.

Child's playhouse?

The thought made him shudder. He stared at the partially destroyed building as if he could see through the walls, see the inside where the pork and sides of beef, and sometimes whole salmon, were hung and racked to cure.

And the small place where he had found space on the floor to sit, his bruised and bleeding child's knees pulled up against his chest, his back wedged against the corner where the two walls met.

In his mind, the odors still remained, and always would, of food and ashes and smoke . . .

And of his own waste.

He saw himself walking down into the yard, approaching the smokehouse, reaching for the latch on the door, and with great effort, loosening the iron rod and tossing it aside. With one hand, he would heave open the door, only to be confronted with absolute darkness.

A black, bottomless hole into which he dared not step.

But was this a dream?

He continued to rock, halfway between dream and reality, not so far into unconsciousness that he didn't realize he was playing mind games with himself.

He saw himself stepping into the black hole, just as he had before. But this time he had not been pushed. Old man Burris was not standing with a leather strap behind him, showing him the way, bareing his cigarette-stained teeth and laughing.

This time he entered the darkness on his own terms.

He was now invincible.

He had shown them all, made them pay for their transgressions.

The darkness didn't seem so bad now.

At least, not in the dream.

He was pulled from his dream by the sound of crows cawing at the sky, and tapping across what was left of the old wood-shingled roof.

Always the crows . . .

He remembered their harsh caws during those times he'd spent alone in the darkness. It was as if the birds had known he was inside, and that he needed someone or something to proclaim his existence, to herald to anyone who might listen to the fact that he still clung to life within the darkness.

It's just a dream. Just a dream . . .

He moved his eyes away from the window, focusing on the old double bed, the handmade spread with the crocheted yellow and orange flowers arranged neatly on top. His notebooks were there, resting at the foot of the bed. He removed one and brought it back to the rocking chair. The crows still played their noisy song, but it was one he'd grown comfortable with, even after so long an absence.

He began haphazardly sifting through the pages of the notebook. He stopped at an entry he had made a few years before, a case he'd come across while rummaging through back issues of the newspaper. He'd found a book in the library that had mentioned the case, along with many others that he already had in his collection. He began reading what he'd written.

1974. San Diego, Calfornia. Sergeant Jackson.

Convicted of first-degree murder and first-degree robbery, Jackson had been arrested without a warrant. Later, another man came forward and implicated himself in the crimes, and he was tried and found guilty. Jackson was set free after spending ten months in prison. The judgment of conviction against him was vacated. The appellate court described Jackson as an "innocent man, convicted and imprisoned for crimes he did not commit."

He let the notebook rest on his lap. The facts of the article filled his thoughts. He felt himself falling back into the dream again, except that this time, it was the victim in the article, and not him, who sat scrunched up in the darkness with only the sound of the crows and the pain of his own tears for company.

He pulled himself away from the smokehouse, away from the yard and the long gravel drive that led up from the main road. He focused on the humpbacked hillside in the distance, and the occasional car snaking its way through the canyon below.

This was the perfect place, he thought—not just because it was high on a hill and would give him warning of intruders, though that was definitely something to consider.

He felt at one with this place, as if he'd come full circle, and had, by some cosmic quirk of fate, been dropped back to where it had all begun, in order to complete the tale.

This is where it has to happen.

If he'd been the type to believe in God, he thought, he'd have deemed it to be divine intervention that had caused him to end up at this house once again, at this particular time. It made him feel good, thinking about the luck of the whole thing.

He put the notebook back on the bed and removed a brown envelope from inside one of the other notebooks. He carefully unclasped the flap of the envelope, then gently shook the contents onto his lap, not looking directly at what he was doing.

That was his custom. The first look was always the

worst. He'd found that if he looked away, catching only a quick glance of photos and not concentrating on each detail, it was less painful.

Monster Boy . . .

Slowly he began to move his eyes to the pictures, then away, each time spending a second more on the face.

Turn away.

It isn't so bad, is it?

Sneak another look.

That's right. Not that bad.

Running a fingertip over the photo.

Familiar.

An old friend.

He wasn't sure who'd taken the photographs, or how old he'd been. That he'd been at least a few years younger was obvious from the pictures. Anything more was just guesswork.

And he couldn't have asked, the pictures were not his.

He'd come across them one day while cleaning the office. He remembered that clearly. He'd just turned ten, and his years at the Burris foster home were just beginning. It had been too tempting to see his name neatly typed on the manila folder inside the ugly green metal cabinet without giving it another look. When no one was watching, he slipped the folder from the cabinet and rifled through it.

Now, with the pictures resting on his lap, he almost wished he never had.

Monster Boy . . .

He hadn't needed the file with his name on it to know that the pictures were of him.

After all, he was the only one, wasn't he?

Day after day, hour after painful hour, the others, the children and adults, would remind him. It was not

113

just the teasing and taunting, but their painful silent looks. Expressions that were both sympathetic and at the same time horrified. The flattening of the nose, the flaring at the edge of the cleft, rendering the misshapen nostril stretched and contorted into some freak-show rendition of reality.

The mark of the devil, that's what he'd heard old man Burris whisper to his wife shortly after he'd arrived at the home. Art Burris had always been a big one for the Bible. The eye-for-an-eye, hellfire-and-damnation type. And it had been the young boy, the Monster Boy marked since birth, who'd quickly become the focus of the old man's perceptions of evil on earth.

He put the photographs aside, turning them over so there wasn't a chance that his eyes would be drawn back to them. Bile in his stomach slowly worked its way to his throat, making him aware of each sour breath. The anger bubbled into his chest, filling his head with intense heat. He imagined his eyes were powerful lasers focused on his enemies, past and present, incinerating each of them into oblivion with just a look.

The newspaper article about his latest victim came to mind. It calmed him, made him think back to when it happened. The woman had been good, just lying there, letting him show her his power. Even the kid hadn't made a peep, inside his own bedroom, safe within his nice warm bed.

What did he know about people?
What did he know about darkness?

The woman barely screamed when he took his part of her, as if she really didn't mind. As if once he'd had her, she understood that she would no longer have any use for that part.

It made the Monster Boy, the Ripper, smile, thinking about that. He was beginning to relax now,

114

the anger reduced to the small, fiery ball that always burned in his chest just beneath the skin.

His mind filled with thoughts of the woman and her little boy as he flipped through the pages of his notebook. His eyes came to rest on the diagram, the one he'd designed himself. There were still some kinks in the system, things he'd have to work out before he was ready. The chemicals might be a problem. The ones the prisons actually used might not be available, at least, not to him. Still, there were substitutes that would be just as effective, maybe even better.

He tried not to get carried away with the thrill of what it would be like, what that singular moment would mean to him, and ultimately, to the one person on whom all this, his very life's breath, had been focused.

The crows had stopped cawing. The sun had cast a gray blanket over the far side of the canyon. It was time to leave. He moved toward the door, turning to face the room one last time, making sure everything was in order. He glanced at his clipboard which rested on the nightstand just inside the bedroom door. His eyes immediately focused on one name on the list. He'd already driven by several times, even gone inside once. He planned on stretching this one out a little. Maybe make one more visit to be sure everything was just right.

The cops were starting to increase the heat. He'd need to be even more careful now. He figured that waiting, letting the situation cool off a little, would be the wise thing to do.

But the feeling was coming over him, stronger than ever, honing his senses to a razor's edge. He might not be able to wait much longer. He felt the blood pulsing through his body, making his head throb, just as it had with the woman. She'd been so easy, and this one looked the same. Just a quick in and out. The woman would be alone.

Grabbing the clipboard, he took the stairs two at a time until he reached the bottom with a thud. His eyes drifted up through the ceiling to the second floor, and he visualized where he had been and what he'd done. He thought about the darkness inside the smokehouse, and about finding the photographs from so many years ago.

He needed to get moving, he told himself, if he expected to be at the woman's house on time. He closed the front door, then bounded down the porch steps and trotted toward the van.

A voice inside his head was telling him to take it easy, to let time pass. But it was barely audible. The feeling was coming on too strong now, drowning his patience and caution in an angry sea of emotion.

One more time, he told himself, heading down the hill toward the main road.

Just this one more time.

She stood at the door, her hand on the knob, waiting. Through the window in the door she could see the black Lincoln parked in the driveway. The driver had already honked once.

"I thought you were going to drive yourself to the office," she said, giving her husband a peck on the cheek. She could taste his spicy aftershave.

"My predecessor always used a driver," said James Morse. He was fingering the knot of his tie. "How do I look?"

"Like the new DA of San Diego County," she said, grabbing his arm and holding him at the door a few seconds longer.

"I'd have to find the driver a new job," he said, "and besides, it's damn convenient having him around when

I need to see the troops. Like today. We'll be traveling from one end of the county to the other. It'll be after seven before I even get back to the office. At least with the driver, I can do some of the paperwork in the car."

Esther Morse smiled. "I'll keep dinner warm," she said. She knew and respected her husband well enough to believe that the driver's services would not be wasted on anything other than business. He'd had the use of a driver when he'd been sheriff, so it wasn't an altogether novel experience for him to be chauffeured back and forth to work.

She watched the Lincoln back out of the driveway and pull away, then returned to her morning paper and coffee.

The newspapers still featured stories about the Ripper. The stories contained what Esther Morse recognized as wild speculation, catering to the paranoid blood-lust of the community. It sometimes seemed as if the entire female population of the city was in hiding, reluctant to go about its daily business for fear of becoming the next victim of this demon. Not a day went by without someone claiming to have seen the Ripper based on the rather general composite drawing police artists had created. The Ripper had allegedly been spotted at a half-dozen of the local shopping malls, standing in line at a supermarket checkout, and one observer had him seated in his car, stopped at an intersection, waiting for the light to change. It was worse than Elvis.

It pained Esther Morse to think of her husband throwing himself into the center of this storm. There was great pressure on law enforcement to find the killer quickly. The golden aura of election night still hung over their heads, but only barely. The honeymoon between James Morse and the voters would soon be over and Esther Morse hoped, it would not end in political divorce.

She heard a knock at the front door. As she moved toward the door, she quickly ran through which of her neighbors it might be at this early hour.

Through the window she saw the hat first, then the uniform. Her mind quickly clicked to the telephone call she had made the previous day. She opened the door.

"Cable company, ma'am."

Esther Morse recognized the young man who had removed his hat and now stood on her front porch smiling. It was impossible to forget that smile.

"Come inside," she said, opening the door and standing back. "You know where to go. Can I get you a cup of coffee, or something?"

9

The U. S. Grant Hotel on Broadway was the center of elegance and refinement in the San Diego of the early twentieth century. Built in 1910, it had by the late seventies fallen on hard times, as was typical of the entire downtown area. Once the meetingplace of the monied elite, society's darlings, the Grant was forced to close after a stretch of years that had it looking more like a flophouse than the crown jewel it had once been.

With the redevelopment of the entire downtown area and the renovation of historical San Diego, the Gaslamp Quarter, and the Horton Plaza complex of shops, restaurants, and hotels, the Grant saw its rebirth.

In 1985, the grand dowager of San Diego hotels was completely renovated. The elegant and formal atmosphere of the early twentieth century returned. Cut-crystal chandeliers discreetly illuminated mahogany-paneled sitting rooms. Luxurious oriental rugs over rich marble floors padded the footsteps of guests. Liveried doormen were posted at the entrances, graciously opening the enormous brass portals, assisting guests with packages purchased during shopping sprees across the street at Horton Plaza.

Max had always liked the Grant. The staff was solicitous without being haughty. The place was generally quiet, except for the hubbub of traffic and downtown noise rising off Broadway.

The Edwardian lobby of the Grant lived up to the hotel's former glory. No atriums or glass-enclosed elevators here. Everything reeked of old-world elegance. From the small wood-paneled elevators to the abundance of polished brass to the enormous sitting-room lobby with its ornately carved walls, Palladian pillars, and elegant antique furniture, the Grant was destined to be reborn into the twenty-first century in style.

It was definitely the sort of place a person of Jerry Kravitz's stature would choose to spend the evening.

But not a home-away-from-home for the likes of Billy Darling.

And not the sort of place you'd expect to find someone murdered.

Max checked his watch, figuring he had time to wander upstairs and get a look at the suite before his breakfast meeting with David Gentry. He'd all but decided to take on Billy Darling as a client, despite Eddie Deets's advice to the contrary. To Deets, Darling was just another sleazy street hustler whose fate wasn't worth a passing thought, let alone the time and trouble of defending him in court against a murder charge. Max was still not altogether certain that Deets was wrong.

He waited for the elevator, inspecting his reflection in the polished brass doors, wondering how the hotel managed to remain in business with so few customers. There was nobody in the lounge except the bartender, a young man standing inside the rectangular bar, sporting a white shirt with a black clip-on bow tie. He was busy watching a portable color TV, while

120

vigorously polishing a glass. Occasionally a house-keeper or waiter would stroll by, whisking at invisible dirt, or moving an errant glass or napkin.

Max took the elevator to the eighth floor. Once the doors closed behind him, he found himself standing in total silence, except for the hydraulic hum of the elevator as it moved upward.

The lobby on each floor was large and spacious, in the old style. A huge Palladian window filtered sunlight into the eighth floor lobby from the Broadway side of the building. In the center, on a polished wood table, an enormous floral arrangement gave a splash of daring color to the otherwise staid interior.

Max followed the numbers on the doors until he found the room he was looking for. He expected that the door would be locked, and it was. The cops would already have finished with the room by this time, but whether the hotel would still keep it closed off was questionable. Since there didn't seem to be any great demand for rooms, Max wondered if the hotel management might have agreed to an informal request by authorities not to use the room until the murder investigation had progressed further.

From around the corner, he heard the sound of elevator doors opening, then the squeak of wheels and the bump of a cart as it was shoved over the crack between the elevator and the hallway. Max could tell that the cart was moving his way. He turned and headed toward the noise, meeting up with the hotel house-keeper as they both rounded the corner.

"Not very busy this time of year, huh?"

The housekeeper gave him a look of incomprehension, then smiled and nodded. She had stopped rolling her cart, but still had both hands resting on the handle. She was young, with short black hair. Her uniform fit snugly around a bony body that didn't have a pound to

121

spare. She eyed Max with silent suspicion. Max wondered if she spoke English.

"Terrible what happened here," he said, gesturing toward the room. The housekeeper followed his hand, staring down the hallway for a moment. Max had the feeling that she understood him, but was hesitant to get involved.

"I don't suppose they're using that room, at least for the time being."

"It's locked," the housekeeper finally offered in clear and precise English, albeit with a slightly Southern drawl. She dug into the front pocket of her apron and pulled out an electronic pass-card. "I've got the keys," she said, flipping the card over in her hand. "To clean the rooms."

Max had positioned himself in front of the cart. He wanted to take a look at the room without alerting hotel security. He could have taken the accepted route of advising the management of his representation of Billy Darling, and his desire to inspect the scene of the crime. The hotel would have undoubtedly had their security people contact the police, who in turn would have notified the DA's office. He'd eventually get his chance to see the inside of the room, but only in the company of hotel and law enforcement observers.

By slipping inside surreptitiously, Max hoped to find something that might have been missed by the cops, and to also have some time to himself there. Over the years, he'd learned that people often unknowingly disclosed secrets. A quick smile, a faraway look, perhaps an answer too eagerly offered. Rooms and places were sometimes the same. You could get a feeling for the exact moment of the crime, and what the occupants of the room might have been thinking, by standing inside alone, projecting yourself back in time and place.

"I suppose," said Max, "that all the rooms on this floor are pretty much the same."

The housekeeper began fiddling with a box on her cart, sorting the soaps and miniature bottles of shampoo and lotion as she spoke. She seemed to no longer regard Max as a threat. Just another guest, though an inquisitive one.

"Except in the middle," she said. "The room where the man was found is right here—803." She pointed. "I'm supposed to clean it today." She tapped her finger on a clipboard containing a sheet of paper with numbers listed in columns. "Been closed because of the police, but it's on the list this morning."

"You mind if I take a look?" said Max. "I won't disturb anything. I'm doing an article for a magazine about the murder, and I thought, well, if I could just take a quick peek at the place where the body was found . . ."

She seemed to hesitate for a moment.

"We'll be interviewing all the employees," he added. "Taking pictures of the hotel for the magazine."

"Pictures?"

Max pulled a notepad from his jacket. "I could take your name and background information now," he said. "And send the photographer by later to get a shot of you in your uniform."

The housekeeper smiled bashfully, then quickly ran her hands down the front of her apron, smoothing the wrinkles. She tossed her head back and whisked a few errant hairs from her forehead.

"Well," she said, pursing her lips in thought. The card-key rested in a tray at the back of her cart.

"I don't suppose it would do any harm," she said. She started to shove the cart down the hall. Max followed at her side.

"Just a quick look," she said. "I shouldn't, but I don't

123

see as anyone would mind your giving the place a quick once-over. It's going to be cleaned today anyway."

They stepped in front of the door. The housekeeper pulled out the card and inserted it into the lock, then shoved open the door.

"Go ahead," she gestured, waiting for Max to enter the room first. After they were both inside, she closed the door behind them.

The bed was still unmade, and Max figured it hadn't been touched since the police investigation. There were still spots of blood on the carpet and the wall near the door. Max stood in the center of the room, slowly taking it in. The housekeeper stood behind her cart, just inside the door, clucking her tongue in disbelief.

"I know I saw it on the list," she said, incredulous, checking the clipboard once more. "There," she pointed, stabbing at the paper with her finger. "Right there—803. For today." She tossed the clipboard onto the cart. "I swear, they must've made a mistake. This place ain't ready to be cleaned. Least, not by me." She gazed down at the bloodstained carpet. "That ain't gonna come up, no way. They're gonna have to put a new carpet and new paint in this place." She clucked again and started toward the telephone.

"Wait just a second," said Max.

"Gotta call," she said, without conviction. She seemed satisfied to let Max remain inside for a few more moments, more interested in what a magazine reporter might want to do at the scene of a murder than in cleaning another hotel room.

Max replayed his interview with Billy Darling in his mind, slowing it down so that he could mentally walk through the crime step by step, matching Billy's words to the images inside the room. Of course, the heavy glass ashtray had already been taken as evidence by the police. Kravitz's personal property, his clothes, the robe he'd worn, had also been logged into evidence, marked and numbered for future reference.

What remained inside room 803 was a stifling, almost choking airlessness, as if the breath of Kravitz and Billy had been sealed inside, tainting the space with their intense passion and fear.

Max could sense that fear, standing inside the room where Billy had stood. He pictured Jerry Kravitz coming from the shower, cornering Billy that first time, taking him totally by surprise.

The police report had indicated that among Jerry Kravitz's personal property was a gold money clip containing a little over twenty dollars in currency. That fact had struck Max as odd. The cops hadn't overlooked it either. A guy like Kravitz would carry around a wad, not just twenty dollars.

Sure, he could have been running a little low, except that's not what Billy had said. Billy had seen the roll of money while Kravitz was in the shower. If Billy was telling the truth about not taking it himself, then there was some other explanation for what had happened to the cash. Max looked at the housekeeper.

"You weren't the one who found the man, were you?"

She shook her head, then averted her eyes. Max thought she was hiding something. He came closer. He was trying to remember the name of the housekeeper listed in the crime report, the one who had discovered Kravitz's body and notified the front desk.

"It's for the magazine," he said.

She didn't answer. The magazine trick was no longer working. He had said or done something to frighten the young woman. Max decided to take a stab at it, knowing that if he waited until the time of trial, the emotional trail would have turned cold.

"It's the money, isn't it?"

He saw her eyes lift momentarily, flutter, then close.

"You saw the man's money. The bills he had in the money clip."

"I didn't take nothing," she mumbled. Her eyes were watery. She had set her jaw in a display of emotional defiance, but her eyes betrayed her.

"I didn't say that you did," said Max.

The woman had lied to him about not being the one who'd found the body. Max was sure that she was now also lying about the money. He tried to picture how it might have happened. The young woman entering the room, the initial shock of seeing Kravitz's naked body on the floor, the crushed and bleeding skull, the blood on the carpet and walls.

Then, moving slowly into the room, spotting the large wad of bills on the table in the dressing area . . . thinking about how many months of cleaning rooms that money represented . . . thinking about her family, putting food on the table, buying a nice warm coat to wear during the cold morning bus rides to the hotel . . .

After all, who would notice? The man had so much money; he was rich. She could tell that by the way he dressed. And by the gold money clip containing all those crisp twenty-dollar bills.

"You have to go," she said, reaching for the door. She opened it, then quickly jerked her cart outside. Max followed her out. She hurriedly locked the door, then briskly pushed the cart toward the service elevator.

Max watched as she waited for the elevator doors to open. She kept her eyes riveted on the doors, as if she was afraid to look back at him. When they opened, she followed the cart inside and disappeared.

Max still had the frightened face of the housekeeper

on his mind as he took his seat downstairs in the Grant Grill. David Gentry was already at the table, poring over the front page of the *San Diego Union*.

Max said, "Anyone else in this city been murdered that I should know about?" He smiled, then reached across the table to shake Gentry's hand.

"Just the usual," said Gentry. "Some guy from San Francisco, bends spoons with his eyes, wants to help find the Ripper. Says he needs to be in the rooms where the victims were attacked. He gets visions."

Max reflected about his own thoughts inside room 803.

"These guys seem to come out of the woodwork," said Gentry, "everytime we get one of these serial psychos. I've never known one of 'em to be any real help on a case."

Gentry reached across the table, dipping his hand into a small woven basket and removing a croissant. As he spoke, he spread raspberry jam on half of it.

"They'll catch this guy, but it won't be because some psychic got a mental image of the killer from stroking the victim's clothing. The cops will beat their brains out doing all the legwork, dotting the i's and crossing each t. Keeping lists, and cross-referencing everything. They'll get everybody's statement in writing, nice and neat. Work up a few artist renditions of this guy, the whole nine yards.

"But you know how they'll finally break it? Somebody will give them a tip, maybe unknowingly. Somebody will say something to somebody else, and that person will get busted, or anxious for the publicity, and mention it to the cops."

"What about Ramirez?" said Max, referring to the LA Nightstalker murders.

"Ramirez was a fluke. How many times, Max, you know of where the killer is ID'd by some kids playing in

127

the street and the whole neighborhood chases the guy down and beats the shit out of him? It just doesn't happen. Those people were lucky they weren't killed trying to catch the guy."

Max remembered the outdoorswoman at Susan Gentry's meeting, thinking she would give any assailant a run for his money, even the dreaded Nightstalker. It would be poetic justice, Max mused, if the Ripper picked her as his next victim.

The waitress came and took their order. Max sat opposite Gentry, in one of the red leather tuck-and-roll booths, beneath a framed oil painting of an English hunting scene. A few yards away, Mexican chefs in tall white hats worked furiously over open grills, preparing breakfasts and jabbering to each other in Spanish.

Max asked, "How's your practice?"

"Slow, Max. Very, very slow."

"That's how it always is when you start out. I remember spending the first few months sitting behind my desk reading novels."

Max thought Gentry looked okay, nothing to worry about. Part of the reason for the meeting had been Susan's concern that her father seemed a little shaky. Gentry was not the sort to wear his emotions like clothes, but Max felt he knew him well enough to tell if there was a major problem.

"I got on the juvenile panel," said Gentry. He sipped on his coffee, then winced when it burned his tongue.

"Good steady work," said Max.

"Yeah. The other day I had a kid charged with stealing another kid's bike." Gentry laughed. "One day I'm sitting in my office in the court building deciding whether some guy should get the death penalty or not, the next I'm representing Dennis the Menace." He shook his head.

"Hey," said Max, "it's work, right? It pays the bills."

"Yeah, I guess you're right. " Gentry paused, then laughed to himself.

"I'm sitting in court with this kid while the trial's going on. The kid's wearing a jacket, with a T-shirt underneath. It comes time for the kid to testify, he takes the stand, unzips the jacket so you can see the front of the T-shirt. You know what the damn thing says? It's one of those Bart Simpson deals. You know, Bart Simpson's face with a cartoon caption above it. This one says. *'I didn't do it. You didn't see me do it. You can't prove anything.'*"

Both men chuckled.

Gentry continued, "And the kid's wearing this thing while he's testifying! Can you believe it?"

"Who was the judge?"

"McDermott. That was the only good thing about it. He's so senile, he probably didn't notice." They both laughed again as the waitress arrived with their breakfast.

"What happened to the kid?" said Max.

"Whatdya think? When was the last time you won a case in Juvenile?"

Max paused a moment to think, then said, "Last year. The DA lost their eyewitness midway through the trial."

"That's about what it takes," said Gentry. He flicked at two oily fried eggs with his fork, staring as the bright yellow centers formed a small pool at the edge of the plate.

Max said, "I don't remember you complaining much when you were on the other side of the counsel table."

Gentry smiled. "You're right. You have to try both sides to appreciate the difference. Now it's my turn to be treated like shit by some snot-nosed young prosecutor who thinks he knows it all."

Max motioned to the waitress for more coffee. He

watched as she poured, first for him, then for Gentry. He'd decided that Susan Gentry's concern over her father might be more the result of her own guilt than of any emotional problems her father was experiencing. As Susan had said, her going off to college marked the first time the two of them would be apart. Max figured she probably was used to playing mother hen to her dad, and that the upcoming separation would be as traumatic for her as for him.

Besides, Gentry was a rock. He'd proven that much after Rosalie and Ryan were kidnapped. At the time, it hadn't been very long since he'd lost his wife, Jackie. Yet it was David Gentry who was always there with a supporting hand, an open ear, an expression that said, *go ahead, lay it all on me, there's nothing so big that we can't handle it together.*

While the two friends had grown apart in recent years, the shared experiences of ten years ago served to bind them forever. Max wondered if he appeared in Gentry's thoughts as often as Gentry appeared in his.

Gentry waited until the waitress was finished pouring the coffee before saying, "Word has it you're representing Billy Darling." He leaned back, dabbing at the corner of his mouth with a napkin, waiting for Max to respond.

"And who did you hear *that* from?"

"I still have my spies," said Gentry. "Besides, what's the secret?"

"I haven't formally taken the case yet."

"But you're going to?"

Max considered the question. He'd determined to represent Billy Darling, and he wondered now why his initial response to Gentry's inquiry had been tentative. He'd been cautious automatically, without thinking.

"Looks that way," said Max. He reached for his coffee. Gentry was shaking his head in disbelief.

130

"That's going to be a tough one, Max. Zellner's got it, and you know what that means."

"Yeah," said Max. "Daily press conferences, and having to see the Great Nate's smiling face on the six o'clock news every evening."

"And," Gentry added, "the death penalty for Darling."

"If they can prove it," snapped Max. "Zellner may think all he has to do is show up for this one, but believe me, he's in for a surprise or two."

Max saw the inquisitive look on Gentry's face. He really had no surprises in store for Nathan Zellner. Not yet, anyway. Just the defense attorney's eternal hope that something would develop in the case prior to trial that might help his client.

Max realized he was getting worked up over nothing. David Gentry was on his side, he knew that. Getting all fired up this early in the game served no purpose. Still, there was something about Gentry, about Zellner and Deets and all the others, that irritated him. Something about the fact that everyone considered Billy Darling's conviction a forgone conclusion. And about the fact that nobody seemed even remotely interested in looking into Jerry Kravitz's reasons for being with Billy at the hotel in the first place.

Sensing Max's discomfort, Gentry steered the conversation away from Billy Darling.

"I bet you Zellner wishes they'd assign him the Ripper case. It'll be front page news for weeks."

Max hadn't been listening. He looked up, realizing he'd missed most of Gentry's comment. He smiled, then nodded.

His mind was not on David Gentry, nor the Ripper. He was back inside room 803, standing in the center, thinking through what Billy Darling had told him, and staring at the young housekeeper who had thought it so important not to tell him the truth.

Max was entrenched in a dream where he and Samantha were making love. At least, he thought it was Sam when he was finally awakened by Cardozo. All he knew was that he was erect. All he could remember was making love to a body with Sam's face. Yet during the dream, the body hadn't moved. No smile, no moans of pleasure. A plastic doll.

He liked to think he had some insight into the meaning of dreams—at least *his* dreams. He tried to piece it together, thinking about the way Sam had seemed more distant the last time they'd made love.

Sam was still on his mind as he shuffled into the kitchen to make coffee.

Cardozo was there, holding the newspaper in his muzzle, waiting for Max to pour his breakfast into the bowl.

"I'll trade you," said Max, grabbing the paper. The dog wouldn't let go. It was their daily morning ritual. Not until Cardozo's bowl was filled with kibble would he let the paper drop to the floor.

"There," said Max, pouring the food into the bowl. "Now will you give me the damn newspaper?"

Before Max finished, Cardozo had let the paper fall and was busy burying his nose deep inside the bowl.

Max took the newspaper and went out to the patio with his coffee. He quickly surveyed the garden, thinking to himself what chores needed doing that day, then plopped down in the chair and opened the paper.

The headline on the front page caused him to choke on his coffee: *DA's Wife—Ripper's Latest Victim.*

He was halfway through the article when the phone

rang. Max took the paper back inside and lifted the receiver, still concentrating on the article.

"Max, this is Richie. I suppose you've heard?"

"Wha? Oh, yeah. Got it right here. Haven't even read it yet."

"Well, don't bother," said Valenzuela. He sounded agiated, in a hurry.

"It's Esther Morse. Yesterday, early evening. I found out about it late last night. They wanted to keep it under wraps until they figured how to handle it."

"And they're sure it's the same guy?"

The words from the paper were popping into his mind at the same time Rich Valenzuela was speaking.

"Looks that way. Brutal, Max. I'm telling you, this guy is a real sicko. Cut her the same way. It's hard to believe someone would go to the bother, leave the woman alive afterward. Jesus!"

"How is she?"

"In intensive care. She'll pull through. Morse's scheduled a press conference this afternoon. The man's pretty shook up. Deets says there's no way the DA can handle this thing now. They're talking to the attorney general, but they've got problems too. The AG and Morse are close buddies. Looks like they'll recuse themselves."

Max was trying to keep up with Valenzuela's commentary. The image of Esther Morse at Susan Gentry's women's meeting, the classy lady, kept spinning through his mind.

"That's one of the reasons I'm calling. We need to talk, Max. And I'd rather not do it over the phone."

"How's the park, near the bell tower, in about half an hour?"

Valenzuela said that was perfect and hung up. Max got dressed and grabbed the long leather leash that he kept by the back door.

133

"Come on, boy," he said, "we're going for a walk." He snapped his fingers and stepped out of the way as Cardozo practically crashed through the door in his excitement.

He almost spilled his beer when he heard it. He hadn't been paying much attention to the TV. It was on in the living room, and he was in the kitchen, making a sandwich and sipping on the end of an ice-cold bottle of Coors. Breakfast of Champions.

By the time he got to the set, the reporter was already halfway through her story. He stood motionless, within a foot of the screen, glued to the broadcast. Within a few seconds, the reporter had completed the report on the Ripper's most recent victim.

He took a deep slug from the bottle, trying to fight down the heat that was rising in his chest. Something had gone wrong—or at least, that was his first impression on hearing the news.

He hadn't known.

How could he?

Still, now that it had happened, what did it mean?

He brought the beer to the sofa, sat down, and rested the bottle on the cushioned arm. He thought back to the woman: how it had happened, what she'd looked like, and what she'd said while he was doing it. He could feel things beginning to calm down inside him, like everything wasn't so bad after all. He liked that feeling. He'd had it before, when he was a kid, only then, most of the time things stayed as bad as he thought—or got worse.

He balanced the cold bottle on his chest, resting the neck on his lower lip. He replayed in his mind the part of the news broadcast he'd heard, making up what he thought he'd missed. It was fun, making up a story about himself, what he'd done. He started to make up additional news stories, like what he expected to hear this evening, and the next day, and all the days that they searched but couldn't find the famous Ripper.

In the reflection of the bottle, he could see his smile. As always, his mind jumped to the photographs he'd taken from the Burris Home, and then, in turn, to his dream.

In the dream, he was standing in a courtroom. There was a glass wall between where he stood and where everybody else was. He couldn't get to the others, couldn't make them hear what he had to say.

The one who had done it was there, in the dream. He had seen pictures of him in the newspapers and in magazines, and sometimes even on television. The one who had done it was always in the dream, standing in the courtroom on the other side of the glass wall, pointing in his direction and laughing. The others, the judge and lawyers, the jury, would join in the laughter. The only one not laughing was the defendant, who always appeared in the dream seated on the witness stand, averting his glance as if he was ashamed.

And now, without even knowing it, he realized that he'd exacted a certain revenge.

The Monster Boy as the Ripper. Come full circle. So perfect.

The DA's wife . . .

It made his mind race with excitement to think about what he'd done. He felt fear and exultation at the same time. A point of no return had been passed. He'd reached a higher level from which the fall would now certainly be deadly, but from which the view was magnificent.

They would come after him now, use all their power to dig him out.

He wouldn't let that happen, though.

He thought of the women he'd raped, and those he'd slept with. He thought of the Burris Home, his notebooks and articles—and the secret place out in back.

A plan crept into his mind and took up a place behind his eyes, out of his view, but directing his observations, his actions. The plan would be the culmination of everything he had lived for. It would be his final act, a testimony to his being. A rejection of the dream.

It would be his fate.

10

Miguelito Gervas stepped over the old man sitting in his own urine on the soggy tile of the bathroom floor. The old man was mumbling to himself, though his eyes were closed. Miguelito thought the old man was sleeping, maybe having a dream where he was doing a lot of talking.

The place reeked of piss. Miguelito thought that in a few more minutes the scummy brass floor drains would be totally clogged and the water would start to rise. It would spill out the door into the entrance corridor before one of the maintenance people decided to do anything about it. Miguelito had seen it before. He was just glad to get inside and comb his hair before the water got too deep.

It was still early. Heading for the cafeteria, Miguelito could see only a small group of people waiting in front of the elevator doors—guys in suits with briefcases and newspapers under their arms, and ladies dressed like business people, except for the tennis shoes on their feet and the high heels they carried for changing into later.

Miguelito shoved his hips through the turnstile, grabbed a pink plastic tray, then put it back. He headed straight for the grill in the back, passing the rows of desserts and salads. Quickly surveying the overhead menu, he pressed his chest against the glass divider to get a better look.

"Breakfast burrito," he said to the little overweight Mexican chef who stood in front of the grill. The chef was tapping a long stainless steel spatula on the edge of the cooking surface, while singing along with mariachi music that was coming from somewhere in the kitchen.

"Eggs and chorizo," said Miguelito. "Potatoes," he added, pointing to a large mound of shredded hash browns steaming in butter on the grill.

He helped himself to some coffee. As the liquid streamed into the cup, he gave the room a once-over, making sure there wasn't anyone there who he couldn't afford to have see him. He had some warrants out, some chickenshit misdemeanor bullshit. There were some cops who would know that, and who would know him. They might try and hassle him about it, even down here, this early in the morning.

When he returned to the grill, the plate with his burrito was sitting on the counter. The cook looked at him and smiled, still poking the spatula at the sizzling food, and singing along with the music.

Miguelito paid the cashier and found a table in the corner where he could keep an eye on people as they came in.

He was finishing his burrito, thinking about getting another and wondering if he had enough money, when he noticed the lawyer standing just inside the eating area, holding a cup of coffee and looking around. When Miguelito met his eyes, he held up a hand and the lawyer headed toward the table.

Miguelito put the remainder of his oozing burrito back on the plate, and wiped at his mouth with his paper napkin as the lawyer pulled up a chair and sat down.

"You got something on your face," said Max, handing Miguelito another napkin.

"Thanks." Miguelito gave a couple of brisk strokes to his face, then neatly folded the napkin and slipped it under the edge of his plate. He felt like eating the rest of his burrito, but thought he might be embarrassed in front of the lawyer if it fell apart when he picked it up. Instead, he removed a pack of cigarettes from his jacket pocket and lit one up.

"You seen Billy lately?"

Miguelito hurriedly blew a plume of smoke over the lawyer's head before answering. "Yesterday," he said, tapping the ash into a neat little pile on the corner of his plate. He still wanted that burrito, and hoped to finish it once the lawyer left.

"He looked okay," Miguelito shrugged, then brought the cigarette to his lips, but quickly put it down. "I *guess*. Who knows, man? That place . . ." He paused, thinking about Billy and what they would be doing to him inside.

"You gonna get him out today?" Miguelito was trying not to sound as worried about Billy as he was.

Max smiled, then sipped his coffee. "Today's just the arraignment," he said. "The DA won't put on any of his evidence. They don't have to prove that Billy committed the murder at this stage. After today, Billy's case will be set for a preliminary hearing. Even then, they don't have to prove him guilty beyond a reasonable doubt, only that there's strong suspicion he did it. Then he'll be arraigned again, but this time in Superior Court. The DA will have to bring him to trial within sixty days of that date."

Miguelito smiled, then repeated, "So you gonna get

him out today?"

The lawyer was talking lawyer talk, which, as Miguelito had learned from experience, was usually just so much bullshit. What was the bottom line? That's what he wanted to hear. The lawyer could save all his courtroom talk to impress the judge. When would Billy get cut loose? That's what Miguelito wanted to know.

"It's a no-bail case," said Max. He had a feeling that Miguelito knew that already. That going through all this was old news.

"I'll ask the judge to set a bail, but even if he does, it's going to be high. Higher than Billy will ever be able to make."

"How high?"

"Half a million," said Max, matter-of-factly. "Maybe a quarter. Depends." He slurped down the rest of his coffee. "Either way, it doesn't really matter, does it? There's no way you or Billy are going to come up with that sort of cash, right?"

Miguelito shook his head. "Shit, man, that don't seem fair. Don't they gotta prove Billy did it first? I could see them setting some sorta bail, you know, not too high, just to keep him around. But shit, this is like locking him up and throwing away the fucking key! They know Billy don't have that sorta cash laying around. The fuckers know they can keep him in the can for as long as they fucking want. Shit, that really sucks, man."

"They have sixty days to bring Billy to trial after his arraignment in Superior Court," said Max, aware that the cafeteria had filled up since his arrival, and that Miguelito's raised voice had drawn the attention of people at nearby tables. He tried to speak calmly, hoping Miguelito would follow his lead.

"If they can't put this thing together within that time,

then the judge will have to dismiss the case." Max paused, looking at Miguelito, knowing that he wasn't telling Miguelito anything he didn't already know. Miguelito had been around long enough to know his rights, all the motions he could run in court, which private defense lawyers and PD's were dump trucks, and which would fight for their clients.

And what you had to do with your head in order to do time without going crazy.

There was nothing else to say. Every case was the same when it came to this point. Max wouldn't know just how strong the prosecution's case was until the preliminary hearing, maybe not even then. The DA didn't have to call all their witnesses at the prelim. Most prosecutors held back, not wanting to disclose any more of their strategy than they had to—saving the best, the big artillery, for trial.

Max looked at his watch, then grabbed his briefcase. "It's in Division 4," he said, backing away from the table. "I'll see you there."

Miguelito nodded and waved a lazy hand in Max's direction. "I'll be there, man," he said, as Max turned and headed for the exit.

Miguelito watched him disappear from view, then lit another cigarette. He started thinking about whether he trusted the lawyer. After a minute or so, he decided that no lawyer was worth trusting, even the ones that said they were honest. Sure, some were better than others, but they'd all go through the motions in court, act like they were your asshole buddy. Like it really hurt them to see you go down. Like they were truly sorry that all those promises they'd made when they took your money hadn't worked out.

When it came time to actually do time, the lawyers would walk out one door to their Mercedeses and their car phones, and guys like him and Billy would leave through another, usually in handcuffs, with some brownshirted courtroom bailiff pushing them along.

Miguelito tapped the end of his cigarette. He felt sorry for Billy, and at the same time thought Billy was stupid for letting this happen. He hoped Billy would get smarter in the can. He'd have to. It was either that or get killed.

Miguelito didn't want to see Billy come to any harm. It made him think of when he was young, like Billy, and of all the shit that went on inside the jail when the deputies weren't looking, or didn't care. Billy might not be tough enough to handle that.

Miguelito felt himself getting too involved, like it was him inside the can instead of Billy. It was unhealthy to get too involved about somebody else's bad luck. Even if it was for a friend.

Miguelito tossed his cigarette into the styrofoam cup, listening to it sizzle.

No, he thought, it wasn't good to spend too much time watching out for the other guy. Hell, just sitting here in this room with all these court people and cops was taking a big chance. What if somebody spotted him? He could end up getting popped on warrants.

And why? Just because he was there for a friend? He couldn't say anything to help Billy in court. At least, nothing that wouldn't get him in a shitload of trouble. Sure, he could tell the lawyer that he knew the fat guy, that he'd been with him before. That the fat guy liked to beat on people before he got his rocks off. That what Billy said about the fat guy was true.

But shit . . . who'd believe *him?*

They'd take one look at him and figure he was trying to cut himself a deal. They'd run his rap, and then start asking about the warrants and his priors, and he'd be up there sweating bullets, trying to think of excuses.

Miguelito decided nobody'd believe him. That it was better to keep quiet. He'd done what he could. He'd found the lawyer and gotten him to take Billy's case. That was more than anyone had ever done for him.

Miguelito nodded, as if agreeing with himself. He got up and took a few steps toward the door. However the rumble in his stomach made him return to the table and grab what was left of the burrito, stuffing it in his mouth as he walked from the room.

Max waited patiently inside the court, then got up and approached the counsel table as his case was called. His head swirled with images of Billy Darling and Jerry Kravitz's flabby body—courtesy of the coroner's photos—lying on the floor of the hotel room.

But Kravitz and Darling were in the background. They stood in second position, right behind what Rich Valenzuela had proposed to him the previous morning.

Valenzuela had met him at the park. The two friends had watched Cardozo romp around the grass, sniffing at plants, chasing other dogs. After a few minutes of making small talk, Valenzuela had dropped his bomb.

"I talked to Deets," he said, his eyes on the dog, no inflection to his voice.

"They're going to appoint a special prosecutor to handle the Ripper investigation from here on out. AG and DA have a conflict of interest."

Valenzuela then turned and faced him.

"The job's yours if you want it, Max."

Max was about to question Valenzuela's sanity. But he remained silent, letting the other man speak.

"I know you're going to say that you're no prosecutor, that it's too much work. That your head's

143

not into that sort of thing."

"Perfect," said Max, smiling.

"I also know you well enough to believe that you're the perfect man for the job. You have the time. You were a helluva prosecutor at one time . . ."

"Over fifteen years ago!"

"Still, you don't forget how to do it. It's lawyering, no matter which side of the counsel table you sit on. You're a damn good lawyer, when you put your mind to it."

"But that's it, isn't it, Rich? My mind hasn't really been in it for the last ten years."

Valenzuela didn't have a quick comeback for that one. Max's ghosts, the demons that plagued him over Rosalie's and Ryan's deaths were something outside his control. Only Max could deal with them.

"At least think about it," said Valenzuela. "The presiding judge makes the assignment, and I'm picking you. You've got twenty-four hours to mull it over."

Max had left the park telling himself there was no way in hell he was going to take this on. After all, he was semiretired, and proud of it. To take charge of a major criminal investigation at this point in his life would be madness.

Yet the more thought he gave to the possibility, the more he felt something tugging him into the fray. He still hadn't made up his mind, but he had until the afternoon to tell Valenzuela of his decision.

Max was pulled from his thoughts of Rich Valenzuela and the Ripper by the unpleasantly familiar needling sound of the prosecutor's voice.

"Your Honor, the People would strenuously object to the setting of any bail in this case. As the court is aware, this is a brutal slaying of one of the city's most prominent citizens. And for what reason?"

Nathan Zellner paused in his oratory, allowing the courtroom audience to take in his slender, well-muscled frame, his celebrity profile, and his Giorgio Armani double-breasted suit. Zellner's mother had been a starlet of sorts during the fifties, and it was rumored that little Nate had even done some acting as a child. Max could see the ease with which Zellner the Zealous had made the transition from camera to courtroom.

The Billy Darling case and the performance of Nathan Zellner were a treat for the retirees, the professional courtroom watchers, who daily moved from courtroom to courtroom observing the proceedings. Normally, the three or four old men constituted the only audience to the run-of-the-mill tedium of the criminal courts.

But today was different. Nate the Great was in action, strutting his stuff. The audience section of the courtroom was filled, not just with professional courtroom watchers, but with lawyers and clerks, and staff from other courtrooms, along with the press. Everyone was anxious to see the Great One in action. And the Great One knew it.

Max sat next to Billy Darling on the other side of the counsel table from Nathan Zellner. Zellner was arguing against the setting of any bail, reciting for the judge what he expected the evidence would prove.

The housekeeper, Zellner claimed, reading from a condensed version of the police reports he had paper-clipped to the outside of his case file, would testify to finding Jerry Kravitz's body in room 803, just after seeing Billy Darling run down the hall toward the elevator. She identified Billy's picture from a photo lineup.

The forensics experts would testify to finding Billy's fingerprints all over the hotel room, and more specifically, on the glass ashtray that the deputy coroner determined was the likely murder weapon.

Max remained calm as he listened to Zellner rail against the moral injustice of allowing someone of Billy's ilk even the slightest opportunity to make bail. Max knew it was an exercise in futility to even ask that bail be set. Any bail, on any murder, would be too high for Billy to make. Zellner also knew that, except he was not the type to pass up an opportunity to perform before the local media.

Zellner continued, now pacing back and forth behind the counsel table, gesturing dramatically to the packed courtroom.

"The defendant, Your Honor, has almost no local ties to the community. He lives on the streets, and is a significant risk to the community." Zellner shook his head, giving the judge and the audience a knowing smile. Max wished he would wrap this thing up and sit down.

"No, Your Honor, I know that this court is not foolish enough to take that chance."

Max looked up and noticed that the judge was busy reviewing another file, and apparently hadn't heard or taken offense at Zellner's last comment.

In the audience, seated on opposite sides of the courtroom, were Miguelito Gervas and Eddie Deets. Deets had his arms crossed over his chest and wore an impatient scowl. Miguelito squirmed nervously in his seat, grimacing and pursing his lips everytime Zellner drew near. It looked to Max as if Miguelito was about to spit at the prosecutor.

"The People are recommending that no bail be set in this case," said Zellner. He started to sit down, then rose suddenly. "And, if I may, I would like to remind this honorable court that this *is* a death penalty case.

The defendant, upon his conviction, is looking at either spending the rest of his life in prison, or dying in the gas chamber. I think that in itself, Your Honor, would be motivation enough for Mr. Darling to skip bail." He sat down, a self-satisfied smile flashing across his face.

Max looked at his client. Billy hadn't said a word during the arguments. He'd spent most of the hearing staring down at the dark wood of the counsel table, which is what he was presently doing, except that the legal pad Max had given him was now covered with small gray circles where his tears had dropped.

For a moment, the courtroom was quiet. Both counsel and the audience looked to the judge for direction. The judge had his head in a file and hadn't realized that Zellner had completed his argument. After a few seconds, he looked up, spotted both counsel seated at the table, then grabbed his gavel, pounded it once, and said. "Motion is denied. There will be no bail in this matter."

Within seconds, the judge bounded from the bench into his chambers, and the bailiff was at the back of Billy's chair, pulling it and him away from the counsel table, and leading Billy back into the custody lockup.

Max began to pack his things.

Miguelito raced up to the railing that separated the audience section of the courtroom from where the lawyers operated.

"Mr. Becker?"

Max turned at the sound of his name. Miguelito had his hand raised like a child in a classroom.

"Another one of your little faggot clients, Becker?"

Nathan Zellner had moved to the center of the counsel table. He held the DA's file on Billy Darling under one arm, and gestured toward Miguelito with the other. Max noticed that Zellner had taken the precaution of remaining outside Miguelito's reach when he made the comment.

"Fuck you, asshole," said Miguelito, smiling, and not missing a beat. It was as if he'd been saving the comment during the courtroom proceedings, waiting for just the right moment.

Zellner tried to appear nonplussed, but found himself at a rare loss for words. He maintained his distance from Miguelito, who was now poised at the divider, ready for his next volley. Zellner knew he was probably safe from attack, here inside the courtroom, but while it was rare that prosecutors were assaulted in court, it was not totally unheard of for lawyers to be confronted and sometimes pushed around by witnesses and defendants.

"Ahh," said Max, making a sniffing gesture, as if there were something in the air. "The smell of Zell." He smiled. He knew Zellner didn't like that one. Zellner's dislike for that particular comment and all the various nicknames, was well known among the defense bar.

Zellner didn't respond, though Miguelito started to chuckle, repeating the words over and over, *smell of Zell, smell of Zell,* which only served to anger Zellner even more.

"Caught your article in *San Diego Magazine,*" said Max. He had his briefcase packed and was ready to leave. "'The Ten Best Trial Lawyers in Los Angeles.' Very impressive, Nate. Loved the car. Mommy buy that for you?"

Zellner curled his lip in a sort of half-smile, half-snarl.

"You're in over your head on this one, Becker," he said. "The little faggot is going to get the Pill. Juries don't like faggots bashing the heads of their community leaders."

148

"I'm sure," said Max, "that you've figured out an explanation for why Kravitz was in a hotel room with Mr. Darling in the first place?"

"Easy," said Zellner, flashing a cautious look at Miguelito, who seemed to be enjoying the barbed repartee between lawyers. "Kravitz was there on business. Not so unusual. Your client decided to slip inside and see what he could take. Kravitz was well known as a big spender. Flashed his moneyroll around for everyone to see. Some people are stupid that way." Zellner gave Miguelito an accusing stare.

Zellner continued, "Darling gets inside, sees the money, and takes it. But not before Kravitz finds him. There's a scuffle, and your client clobbers Kravitz over the head with the ashtray." Zellner smiled, holding his palms up at his side. "Simple," he said, keeping the smile on his face.

Max had to admit that Zellner's theory was the easiest to accept. The jury would take one look at Billy, decide that Zellner was right, and close their ears to anything Billy had to say in his own defense.

Billy's biggest problem was the missing money. Had the twenties not been taken from Kravitz's room, Billy's story of self-defense might find some receptive ears. But the way it stood, nobody on the jury would believe that Jerry Kravitz was as kinky as Billy Darling said, or that it even mattered, once they learned of the stolen money.

Max's mind quickly flashed to his conversation with the hotel housekeeper, and to what he thought she was holding back. He made a mental note to try talking to her again.

"Don't be too sure," said Max, unconvincingly. He lifted his briefcase from the counsel table and headed for the door, leaving Nate Zellner and Miguelito

149

Gervas to their *machismo* staring contest.

Eddie Deets was waiting outside. He stood in the corner, leaning against the wall, in casual conversation with a couple of uniformed officers. As Max passed, Deets excused himself and hurried to join him.

"Like I said, Max—this ain't gonna be any cakewalk." The two of them walked briskly toward the elevator.

"Hell, Eddie," said Max. "I didn't expect that it would. You'd think after doing this for as long as I have that a guy like Zellner wouldn't still get on my nerves. I tellya there are times when I feel it would be worth my ticket just to get the satisfaction of strangling that clown."

"He's no clown," said Deets. "He knows exactly what he's doing. He won't make any errors. He'll wait for you to do that. I always felt that he used that attitude of his to get the advantage. He eggs other lawyers into making it a personal thing, which usually leads to them making mistakes. The guy knows exactly what he's doing, Max. Don't let him get to you."

Deets paused for a few moments.

"I suppose," he said, "that you've made up your mind on the Ripper?"

Max smiled, playing a little cat-and-mouse with his friend.

"And?"

"I'm going to do it, Eddie."

Deets slammed him on the back.

"Good move, Max. The two of us working together, finally. It'll be great. I'll fill you in as soon as we get back."

"Hopefully," said Max, "both you and Richie will feel the same way after a few months."

On the way back to the station, Max started to calm

150

down. He mentally took stock of what needed to be done on Billy's case, who needed to be interviewed, what evidence could be gathered for presentation at trial.

He hoped to get Billy's trial completed before the Ripper investigation began to take up too much of his time. Unless it was postponed, Billy's trial would be heard within the next three months. Max figured he'd be able to handle both the Ripper investigation and Billy Darling's case as long as the Ripper wasn't arrested in the near future, which didn't seem likely.

Levine and Levinthal, along with the rest of the support staff, handled the day-to-day investigation chores, and so far they'd come up with nothing. But once they made an arrest, Max knew that everything would heat up, and he'd find himself devoting all his time to prosecuting the Ripper.

"This is what we have so far," said Deets, handing Max a large accordion file. They had returned from court and gone straight to Eddie Deets's office. Within the file were reams of paperwork, some pages loose, others stapled together in notebooks.

Max, feeling the weight of the file and still thinking about preparing for the Billy Darling trial, said, "Make it short, Eddie. Is there anything in here that I need to know right away?"

Deets plopped down in the chair behind his desk. He reached into a desk drawer and removed a bag of caramels, his hand shaking one out. Then he paused for a second, grimaced, and tossed the bag back inside the drawer. "I'm eating too much sugar," he muttered, even as he reached for a crystal jar of hard candy that he kept on his desk. Quickly removing the plastic wrapper from one, he tossed the shiny red cube into his mouth.

"I thought you were on a diet," said Max.

Deets waved him off. "Nutrasweet."

"If you're asking whether we've got a suspect," said Deets, chewing on the candy and poking at his teeth with his finger, "then I think you already know the answer to that one. Shit, if we only had something, *anything . . .*" He shook his head. "I'd love to get the press off my back. Even a suspect who we could question would help. We're getting hundreds of calls, Max. I just tell 'em to say we're zeroing in on an arrest, and that for security reasons, we can't disclose anything more."

"The usual bullshit," said Max. He was looking over the paperwork dealing with the Ripper's most recent victim.

"And now, with Esther Morse as a victim . . ." Deets sighed. He reached toward the jar of candy and pulled out another.

"I don't need to tell you, Max, that Jim Morse wants this guy hammered, and hammered good. Can't say as I blame him."

"And Morse's not alone. The DA, the sheriffs, everyone wants to get this guy. Morse may have rescued the DA's office from prosecuting the case, but I get three or four calls a day from those guys wanting to know what we're doing."

Deets's concern seemed real to Max. Eddie would sometimes put on a performance to bring home a point. But this was no show; the pressure was really on, and it was getting to him.

"Just the fuck what I need," said Deets, "having the goddamn DA breathing down my neck in addition to the mayor's office, the press, and every women's group in the county."

The photographs of Esther Morse looked similiar to

those of Leslie Greer, the Ripper's second victim—except with Esther Morse, Max realized as he sorted through the stack of pictures, he was looking at someone who he'd actually met, someone he knew. Max remembered Mrs. Morse approaching him at the women's meeting. He remembered her encouraging words, and her classy appearance. A friendly fish in a sea of piranha.

Now, looking at the photos of what had been done to her, he experienced the downside of that familiarity. He could not dispassionately toss the pictures aside. There was a face, a person who was connected with the pictures. This atrocious carnage had been committed on the body of someone he knew, a friend, someone with whom he had shared kind words. This was more personal.

Max said, "Richie said she'll be all right?"

Deets made a gesture with his head, tossing off a silent comment. "Depends on what your definition of 'all right' is. She'll live, if that's what you mean. The wounds will heal. The physical wounds, that is." He muttered something unintelligible under his breath. "Sex is pretty much out of the picture," he added.

Max thought about that for a moment. The Ripper had transformed all of his victims physically. The mental conquest, displaying his dominance, had not been enough for this man. For most rapists, the mental game was what it was all about: asserting power over the helpless victim.

But this guy was different. There was an added dimension to his violence. He didn't maim with an eye toward killing. On the contrary, the neat incisions, the surgeon-like precision of his acts, testified to the Ripper's desire to have his victims live on as walking examples of his handiwork. For this monster, there

153

was something about physically transforming these women that was at least as important, if not more so, as the rape itself.

"I've decided to partner you with an experienced officer," said Deets. Max could tell from the smirk on Deets's face that there was more to it than that.

"We'll keep Levine and Levinthal on the case. You'll want to talk with them about what they've managed to run down. At least they're familiar with what we've done so far." Deets readjusted himself in his chair.

"I'm assigning Phyllis Draper to assist you on this thing," said Deets. He waited for Max to respond.

Max ran the name through his head, unable to go beyond the general familiarity of having heard the name somewhere before.

"Phil Draper," said Deets. "She's an experienced rape investigator." He paused, as if uncertain whether to mention what was on the tip of his tongue. Finally he said, "Phil's being transferred from Vice. I expect her to be up and running on this case by next week."

Now in Max's mind the name was matched with a story. Still no face, but he definitely had heard the name before.

"Isn't she the one that sued the department? Some sort of discrimination suit?"

Deets muttered, "Yeah, but that's all over now. She was going through a divorce. Real messy. She was hitched to a lieutenant in Vice. Things didn't work out. When he filed for divorce, she went a little crazy. Both of them working the same unit didn't help matters."

"So you're getting her out of there, and dumping her in my lap to cool off, right?"

Deets raised a restraining hand. "Now, wait a second, Max. It just happened to work out that way." Deets was talking fast, which Max knew from

154

experience was a sure sign he was lying.

"Phil's a good cop. She got shafted in that divorce. The lawsuit was just a way of striking back. She thought she got screwed on the promotion list, and if you ask me, she did. Her ex was the supervisor who wrote her promotability rating. But that's all behind her now. Believe me, Max. she'll do a good job."

Max snapped, "Have you slept with her, Eddie?"

Deets looked shocked, but Max could tell it was put on.

"She's a friend, Max. Just a friend."

"Is that a no?"

Deets didn't answer. He quickly unwrapped another candy and tossed it in his mouth.

"I'll take that as a yes," said Max.

He wasn't that upset with Deets. Eddie had his allegiances, his emotional baggage from nearly thirty years of clawing his way up the ladder. If Phil Draper was half as experienced as Deets claimed, she'd be fine. Max realized he needed all the help he could get on this one. He just hoped that he wouldn't have to spend too much time playing Phil Draper's divorce counselor.

Augustus McDermott made sure they took away the empty glass before putting down a new one. What with the Judicial Council investigation and the courthouse rumor mill going full speed, he couldn't afford to be seen tossing down bourbon with two or three empty glasses on the table.

They wanted him out. Gus McDermott wasn't exactly sure who *they* were, but he knew he was being watched.

It angered him to think of the injustice of it all. After nearly thirty years on the bench, it had all come down

155

to this!

"Get you another, sir?"

Gus looked up from his drink and his worries eyeing the slender young cocktail waitress. There had been a day, he thought, when, with a wink and a smile, he'd have had the young lady in bed.

Gus shook his head. He watched the short skirt, the underpants clearly visible, the rear end swaying back to the bar.

He tried to recollect what his lawyer had told him about the Judicial Council hearing. They were evaluating him—*him* of all people. Some young whippersnappers filled with self-importance were passing judgment on matters they knew nothing about. They hadn't been there; they hadn't had to sit in court listening to witnesses lie and watch lawyers primp and perform for their clients. What did *they* know?

Gus slurped the rest of his bourbon, threw a twenty on the table, and pushed back his chair.

He still had some time. The council always moved slowly, taking testimony for weeks, then postponing a decision sometimes for months. Meanwhile they couldn't touch him.

Let 'em talk behind my back, he thought. Let 'em say I'm too old, senile. What do they know? I'll show 'em, I'll show each and every one of them.

He glanced around the bar before getting up, looking to see who might be watching him. When he thought it was clear, he carefully stood up, keeping both hands on the edge of the table for support.

His head swirled as he got up, but not as much as it sometimes did. He blinked twice, trying to bring the bartender and then the front door into focus. With one hand still on the table, he started to walk toward the door.

Outside, the cool night air made him feel a little better. Facing his car door, Gus reached into his pocket for his keys. He'd done this a thousand times. He found the ring and lifted it, holding the keys in the palm of his hand. *Which key?* he mumbled to himself. *Which key?*

He picked one, then inserted it into the door, twisting his wrist at the same time. Nothing. He tried again, this time putting the key in the other way. Still nothing. Gus removed the key from the door and put the ring of keys back in his palm. With his fingertip, he poked around the ring, looking for the right one. He could hear voices coming from the bar, and for a moment, he lost track of exactly where he was. He looked up, saw the neon sign glowing in the darkness with the name of the bar, then registered that he was in the parking lot. He tried another key, and this one worked.

Getting inside, he dropped the keys. When he bent over to search for them, his head struck the steering wheel. He felt a sharp sting just over his right eye. Okay, okay, he told himself, you're a little worse off than you thought. Just sit a minute and get it together. First the keys. They've got to be on the floorboard somewhere. Reach down slowly and pick them up. Then start the car.

Gus retrieved them and managed to get the right one inserted into the ignition. When he started the car, it revved loudly, and it was a few seconds before he realized that he still had his foot on the gas. He let up on the pedal and shifted the automatic transmission into gear, and the car lurched forward toward the exit.

Everything was going to be all right, he told himself. He stopped at the first red light. His head was beginning to clear now, though there seemed to be a whole circle of red lights, and he was having trouble deciding which one to watch. It didn't matter, though, because when one turned green, they all did. A sort of Christmas-wreath effect, he thought.

He'd only traveled about a mile when he heard the sound of someone's voice crack the night air, and saw the flashing red lights in his rearview mirror. For a second he thought he was looking back at the Christmas wreath. But then he connected the voice with the lights, and then the siren. It was the cops.

"Good evening, Officer," said Gus. He smiled, like he wasn't really drunk on his ass. In the back of his mind, he thought about all the drunk drivers he'd heard testify in court. He could feel himself sinking with every word.

"Have you been drinking, sir?"

Gus thought about that one. The young cop just stood there, leaning over, smelling the inside of the car. Gus thought, shit, you know damn well I've been drinking.

"Just a couple," said Gus.

"May I see your driver's license, sir?"

Now it was getting worse. Gus didn't remember whether he'd even brought his wallet, then thought he might have left it at the bar. He reached into his coat pocket and tried to remove the leather billfold that he knew was usually there. He was so relieved when he felt the wallet that he smiled at the cop. The cop didn't smile back.

"Here we go," said Gus, lifting the wallet from his pocket.

Midway between his pocket and the open driver's window, the contents of the wallet spilled out. When Gus looked down, he saw about a dozen rectangular pieces of plastic, some coins, a few scraps of paper with phone numbers written on them, and a picture of his dog all scattered on his lap.

"Oops."

"Please step out of the car, sir."

"Wha . . ."

"Just step out of the car."

The cop had lifted his flashlight and was shining it in Gus's face. Gus lifted his hand to cut the glare, while at the same time trying to open the door. He stumbled out of the car, using the driver's door for support. He was aware that some of his credit cards and pictures had fallen into the street.

"Never mind those," said the cop, as Gus started to bend over to pick up the spilled contents of his wallet.

The cop said something about field sobriety tests, and that Gus should watch what he was doing. Gus watched as the cop stood on one leg, holding out the other leg, balancing. Gus remembered that one. He'd seen it done a thousand times in court, and had practiced it inside the bar with his drinking buddies, showing them how well he could do the test. They had all agreed that he'd performed the tests perfectly.

Gus smiled, then took up his position on the side of the road. He lifted his right leg, looked at the cop, then felt himself falling over. The cop caught him just before he collided with the side of his car.

"Jesus," said Gus. "That's my bad leg. I can't do it on that leg even when I'm sober."

The cop smiled.

Gus thought about what he'd just said, and decided there was something that hadn't sounded quite right. But he went on.

"Give me another one," he said.

The cop went through three more tests. Gus touched his fingertip to his nose, did the alternating handclap, and recited the alphabet, he thought, to the cop's satisfaction.

When he'd completed the tests, Gus started to get back inside his car. He was glad he'd practiced the tests so many times. He wasn't familiar with the area, and had picked the bar because it was on the way home and he felt nobody would recognize him. He told himself that he'd have to remember this bar the next time, how the cop must have been watching as he'd come out, figuring he'd have an easy arrest.

"You're under arrest, sir."

Wait a minute . . .

Gus felt the cold metal of handcuffs pinch his wrist. The cop had one hand on the cuffs, the other pressed against his back, pushing him toward the patrol car. The cop palmed the top of Gus's head as they neared the door, pushing him into the back seat of the car.

Once inside, Gus could see that there was another cop sitting in the front passenger seat, sipping a cup of coffee. He heard him tell the driver to head straight to the station, that this would cap off their shift.

The station seemed to be just around the corner. Gus was feeling sleepy. He was thinking about the trouble he'd managed to fall into, but the urge to sleep was stronger than anything else. He rested his head against the vinyl back seat of the patrol car for a few minutes. It smelled like someone had recently thrown up on it. The smell didn't keep him awake, though. He was surprised, after what seemed too short a time, to feel someone shaking him.

"Come on, old-timer." The driver-cop was helping Gus from the back seat. "You'll have plenty of time to sleep it off later."

They directed him into the station, and sat him down in a small room next to a table. On the table was a box-shaped machine with lights and dials. Gus wasn't so far gone that he didn't recognize it.

The cop fiddled with the switches on the machine for a minute, then placed a tube in Gus's mouth and told him to blow.

"Harder," said the cop, watching the needle on the machine jump. "You have to blow harder."

Gus did as he was told, now watching the needle himself. It seemed to jump clear across the dial, where it stayed a moment, then dropped down. The machine started clicking, and Gus watched as the cop pulled a small card from the box. Looking at it, a smile crossed the cop's face.

"Jackpot!" said the cop.

Judge Augustus McDermott closed his eyes, realizing that he was dead in the water.

Max tried her apartment door. No answer.

He sat outside at the curb, drumming his fingers on the steering wheel, thinking. After a few minutes, he cranked the engine and eased the car down the street.

He thought he knew where she might be.

He hadn't spoken with Samantha since their last night together, her birthday. He'd left early the next morning, leaving Sam and Mitchell in blissful sleep. He'd had a worried feeling at the time, something unpleasant sticking with him from the night before. He'd felt a coldness between them. He wasn't sure whether it was real, or the vague, nebulous remnants of a dream.

Still, in her sleep, Sam had mumbled something to him, a quick grab around the neck as he bent down to give her a parting kiss. The coldness had disappeared.

Must have been a dream . . .

Max headed toward Harbor Drive and the Embarcadero. The sky was a flat, cloudless powder-blue. A soft breeze had blown the smog and morning fog out to sea. The blue-tiled dome of the Santa Fe Depot glistened in the bright afternoon sunlight.

He slowed, pulling the car to the side as he passed the Maritime Museum. Crowds of tourists huddled around the three ships, the *Star of India,* the *Berkeley,* and the *Medea.*

Not seeing Sam, he pulled the car further south, turning in at the parking lot next to Anthony's. He put some coins in the meter, looked both ways trying to figure where to start, then headed on foot toward Seaport Village.

The walk was packed with sightseers taking advantage of the great weather. At the B Street pier, an animated group of people in Bermuda shorts and casual flowered shirts waited in line in front of the pink-and-blue structure for day-trips to Catalina and Ensenada.

Still no sign of Sam and Mitchell.

Perhaps they were somewhere else?

Coming here had been pure guesswork. She said she'd brought Mitch here before. But that didn't mean they'd made it a regular thing.

Max continued south on the Embarcadero, passing the Navy's eleventh naval district complex. Huge, gray hulks—destroyers and carriers—loomed in the distance like giant granite mountains, floating cities.

The crowds increased as he neared the shops and cafés of the Village. The place was a magnet for tourists, and the city planners, realizing this, had concentrated much of their development efforts in recent years to build up the area, adding high-rise hotels and a convention center.

Across Market Street, Max spotted the complex of hacienda-type buildings that had once housed the

162

Police Department, a vestige of his former years as a prosecutor. The complex was now abandoned and pegged to become part of the Seaport Village expansion.

At the Broadway Flying Horses Carousel he spotted them. Mitchell was seated atop one of the handcarved unicorns, beaming from ear to ear. Sam was standing at his side, supporting him as the carousel slowly revolved.

Sam spotted him before the ride was over. She waved and whispered in Mitchell's ear. He also waved and then quickly brought his hand back to the pole for fear of falling off.

Each time the carousel spun past him, Mitchell would smile and Sam would wave. Max wondered if he should get on.

He thought he could see something in Sam's face, some reticence, and wondered if it was just his imagination. A little of the old Maxwell Becker paranoia.

A little of the dream?

As the carousel twirled, he second-guessed himself for the hundredth time about his relationship with Sam. He'd told her from the beginning that long-term commitment was out of the question. He wasn't ready, might never be.

Yet look what had happened.

Four years had gone by, and she was the only woman he'd managed to have any relationship with that had lasted longer than dinner and a movie.

So what does that tell you, schmuck?

The paranoia buzzed around his head, and he felt like swatting it.

Go ahead, take your best shot. Then the whole world will know just how crazy you are. Like those bums on

163

Broadway, talking to themselves, fighting battles with imaginary villains.

Imaginary?

The carousel stopped. He watched Sam lift Mitchell off the unicorn. The two of them carefully stepped down from the carousel and walked toward him, hand in hand.

"I'm glad I finally found you," he said, kissing her forehead and lifting Mitchell into his arms. He held the young boy in the crook of his arm while he silently mouthed the words *"Ice cream?"* to Sam.

She nodded.

Max said, "I don't suppose a big boy like you still eats ice cream?"

Sam smiled and Mitchell screamed in delight, "I do, I do."

They bought Mitchell a cone and found a table under an umbrella to sit down.

Sam said, "I would have thought a casual afternoon stroll was out of the question for you now."

"You heard about the Ripper?"

"It was in the paper and on TV. They also mentioned the Kravitz case."

"Yeah."

She locked eyes with him not letting him get away.

"I suppose we'll be seeing less of you, at least until this is over?"

Max watched Mitchell lick the sides of the cone, trying to keep up with the melting ice cream.

"About the other night . . ." he said.

He struggled for the right words.

"I don't know if this is the right place or time . . . I know you were upset. You have a right to be . . . I don't know what to say. I . . ."

She held up a restraining hand.

"You don't have to explain anything," she said. "Believe me, Max, I never bought into that hooker-with-the-heart-of-gold routine. We both knew the score when we started."

She paused, swallowing hard. He noticed that her eyes had become glassy.

"Sorry," she whispered, looking around the table, grabbing a napkin. She blew her nose.

"What's wrong, Mommy?"

A quick turn.

"Nothing, dear. Mommy just got something in her eye."

Max felt like an outsider, trespassing on something he had no right to see.

Sam said, "I'm not going to ask you for a commitment, Max. I said I wouldn't do that in the beginning. It wouldn't be fair for either of us. I know you still love her, the memories . . . It may sound strange, but I love you for that.

"But you have to understand where I'm coming from. I'm not getting any younger, and Mitchell is getting to the point where I have to think of his future. I can't keep doing what I do and expect him to understand."

"I know," said Max. "I've thought about that, too."

"So you'll understand when I say that I have to make a decision. Mitchell deserves better than a part-time mother and no father. Please, I want you to understand that I don't intend this as an ultimatum. I wouldn't want you under those circumstances anyway."

"Do you have any plans?"

He asked, wanting to say something and not knowing what to say. Before the last word passed over his lips, he realized it was wrong, incredibly insensitive.

"What I mean is . . ."

"I know," she said, with a half-smile—a sorry attempt at fighting off the tears. She turned away, using the napkin to clean up Mitchell's face, keeping busy while she tried to compose herself.

"We've got to get back," she said, lifting Mitchell off the seat and setting him on the ground. When she looked up, her eyes met his, but this time she quickly turned away.

"Will I see you again?" he asked.

She grabbed the young boy's hand and started to leave.

"I think," she said, turning to face him, even-toned, without a trace of animosity or anger, "that's up to you, Max."

He watched them walk off, disappearing in the traffic on the other side of Harbor Drive. He walked over to the carousel and ran the palm of his hand over the polished wooden horses and unicorns, mythological creatures. He thought about Sam and Mitchell and what Sam had said.

And about what his beloved Rosalie would have wanted him to do. "Bear," he could hear her say, her words soft in his ear, "follow what's in your heart."

Sweet Rosalie . . .

He jumped off the carousel platform, thinking about that, and wondering if there was anything still left in his heart.

11

Max called and suggested, if she didn't already have plans, that they meet over the weekend and go over strategy for the Ripper investigation. Phyllis Draper said okay, but Max had the feeling that he was intruding, as if once he'd suggested it, she'd felt trapped, uncomfortable about turning him down.

As he drove out to Draper's home, Max thought about things. He figured they were already off to a lukewarm start as partners. Not that that was all that unusual, meeting each other over the telephone for the first time.

He tried to tell himself that a certain amount of awkwardness was to be expected—welcomed, in fact. It showed a mutual respect: two people not taking one another for granted.

Still, he had a funny feeling about teaming up with a total stranger.

He drove west on Highway 8 to Sunset Cliffs, then south toward Cabrillo Point, hugging the west side of the peninsula. The jagged finger of land forming the westernmost edge of San Diego Bay was still partially shrouded in early morning fog. A stack of cars lined the street near Bermuda and Santa Cruz Avenues, surfers and sunbathers taking the stairs down to the beach, getting an early start.

Max followed the road, keeping one eye on the street numbers and the other on the steep cliffs to his right. The address came up on him fast, a wooden sign with rusted metal numbers at the mouth of a gravel drive. He turned off, checked the numbers on the sign with his scribbled notes, then proceeded down the gravel road until it forked. There were three or four houses at the various tines of the fork. Max determined which way the street numbers would run if this was a typical suburban development, then tried the house furthest up the drive.

On a plateau, standing higher than the others, stood a small ranch-style single-story wood frame house. The cedar roof shingles had weathered dark gray and were splintered and patched in spots. White paint peeled from most of the wood surfaces, exposing older, more yellowed paint underneath. Oak barrel planters, the only attempts at landscaping, stood on each side of the dirt walk leading to the front door. A Toyota Corolla was parked in the shade of a towering oak at the end of the gravel drive. Toward the rear of the property, Max spotted an old set of rusted free weights stacked against the side of the house.

The house was cradled in back by a gently rising hillside. The giant oak shaded one end of the house, and the sloping hillside did the same for the other. The mountain brush was dry, though some wildflowers could still be seen poking white and orange heads through the brown underbrush.

Two dogs, mutts, came bounding from nowhere to greet the car as Max pulled within a few feet of the dirt walk. Once the dogs had stopped barking and were bowing their heads under Max's gentle hand, the place became eerily quiet. The only sound was a distant, irregular tinkle coming from a set of wind chimes near the front door.

"Good boys," said Max, petting the dogs, glad they were friendly. He closed the car door, listening to the slam and thinking that in this silence the noise would be sufficient announcement of his arrival. A few minutes passed, and still nobody emerged from the house. Max thought he saw a curtain move at one of the windows.

He could barely see the rooftops of the other homes just down the road. Each seemed to occupy its own little niche, set off against the undulating hillside.

Max stood overlooking the bluff, taking in the view, noticing that in the distance—it seemed like miles away—he could make out a string of tiny gray rectangles, a naval convoy of some sort.

"Once the fog burns off, you can see a lot better."

The voice came from behind him. He thought he recognized it, and as he turned to meet it, a certain feeling of foreboding came over him.

It was her.

Phyllis Draper stood on the front porch, hands on her hips, staring at him. Max returned the stare, still not believing that this had happened to him. He thought he must be mistaken. There was no way that this woman could be the Phil Draper that Eddie Deets had chosen as his partner.

But everything fit—the divorce, the discrimination suit against the department, her living out here, isolated. She was the same one, all right. Phil Draper was the outdoors woman from the meeting at the high school.

"Ain't it a kick?" she said, though she appeared less humored by the situation than her comment indicated.

"You?"

"You expected Starsky and Hutch?"

Max shook his head in disbelief.

"It wasn't my idea of the ideal assignment, either," she snapped. "Now, are you going to just stand there with the dogs all day, or are we going to get down to business?"

Max thought of getting back inside his car and driving away. He would let a few days pass then talk with Deets, tell him it would never work with Draper, and stonewall his friend into getting him a different partner.

"I've got some coffee brewing," she said. She headed toward the house, then turned back. "Come on," she smiled. "I don't bite."

Max followed her inside. The front door opened directly into a living room which was a large space dominated by a river-rock fireplace that occupied the entire back wall. A heavy mantel, really only a thick piece of gnarled oak that had been imbedded in the rock, ran the length of the fireplace. The mantel was covered with various athletic trophies: small golden figures in various poses adorned with wreaths and the like.

A sectional sofa covered in a country print of sturdy fabric occupied the other corner of the room. A colorful homemade quilt was draped over the back of the sofa. A weathered oak barrel like the ones outside served as a cocktail table. It was covered with a disk of clear glass. Some wildflower peonies in an old jelly jar decorated the table.

The window on the other side of the room opened onto the back of the house. Most of the view was the hillside, which had been cleared for about twenty feet before it once again became wild and turned into the sturdy brush that dominated the landscape.

Phil Draper came in holding two mugs of coffee and a bottle of Jack Daniels under her arm.

"I like a little splash," she said, setting it all on the

170

coffee table. "Tends to warm things up a little quicker."

Max was still in shock. This was the woman he could have strangled the other night. He'd had nightmares about this woman. He thought he'd seen the last of her, and now this.

"Don't get yourself so worked up about it," she said, as if she were reading his mind. "You were fair game up there. I didn't like that bitch from the DA's office any more than I liked you." She smiled. "You just happened to be the lucky one that night."

"Lucky, my ass," said Max.

He took the bottle of Jack Daniels and poured a generous amount into his coffee. He was close enough to the mantel to see that the trophies and plaques were a mixture of surfing and bodybuilding awards. He stole a glance at his new partner, confirming, even under her loose-fitting outdoor clothing, the possibility that the bodybuilding awards were hers. He looked around the room, expecting to see the graduation picture of her son, who Max figured was the recipient of the surfing trophies.

"They're all mine," she said, matter-of-factly. She sipped carefully at the edge of her mug, watching him closely. Seeing his look of surprise, she added, "I still surf. Started as a kid with my dad." Her head turned to a small photograph of a man in his fifties, standing in the sand next to a large surfboard. The picture seemed dwarfed by its loneliness on the wall.

"He was a cop, right?"

She nodded, clucked her tongue, then poured some more whiskey into her cup.

"All my men have been cops," she said. From the acid tone in her voice, Max had the feeling there was more to be said.

"Dad was the best of the lot," she continued. "And even he was no bargain. Drove Mom nuts. She finally saw the light and left him, shortly after my first marriage." Draper laughed wryly.

"Now, there was an event," she said, slurping down what Max calculated was whiskey with just a touch of coffee.

"Dad showed up at the wedding plastered. Which was nothing unusual for him, except Jack's side, that's my ex—my *first* ex—were all teetotalers. The wedding pretty much set the tone for our short, and very unsweet, marital relationship."

Max watched her talk and drink, and drink—and drink. Phil Draper seemed a lot softer around the edges this time around. The outdoorswoman who'd plagued his dreams had turned into a sort of nostalgic drunk, like a guy at the bar spilling forth his problems to a sympathetic bartender.

Except that Max felt sure Draper wasn't drunk. She'd put down a good deal of whiskey, but he could tell it wasn't the liquor that was talking. She'd evidently made a decision to tell him about herself. The whiskey just helped things along.

"After my second marriage hit the crapper, I decided to pack it in for a while, give celibacy a chance." She paused, glancing toward the window as if she expected to see somebody looking in.

"You heard about my lawsuit, I'm sure?"

Max nodded.

"Yeah, I'm famous for that one," she chuckled "They don't fuck with me anymore, I can tell you that. I don't know that I'm the most popular cop on the force, but believe me, now they think twice about messing with Phil Draper."

"Deets says you're coming from Vice. Something about not making the promotional cutoff."

She arched her eyebrows, her lips poised at the rim of her cup.

172

"That how he put it?" She took a quick sip, then placed the cup on the table. "He would, wouldn't he? Put it that way, I mean. I got screwed, and Ed Deets knows it."

She stopped, catching herself before blurting out her next thought. This was the part, Max guessed, that had something to do with Deets sleeping with her. The part she was holding back.

"Listen," she said, pushing herself back on the couch and crossing her legs on the table. "I don't know what Deets has told you about me, and I don't know what you might have heard on your own. But you can believe what you want. There's probably nothing I could say now that would affect that anyway.

"As I see it," she said, "we're both starting something different, something new. Now we can form all sorts of opinions about each other right off the bat, build walls, nurture our little secrets behind masks. Or we can decide that catching this psychopathic asshole is more important than the differences that might exist between us.

"Now, I could sit here and tell you that we will never be able to work together. That you're just another sleazy defense lawyer without the balls to go after this guy. I could say that since you're a man, you really are incapable of understanding what catching this guy means to women.

"I could say a lot of things, Becker, that I'm not saying." She grinned, seeing the smile on his face. "I asked around about you, just as I'm sure you did with me. I know a little about where you're coming from. And what I heard makes me think that those things I could have said about you would have been out of line. I'm willing to give you a chance, Becker. That's what this big long speech boils down to."

She waited for his reply, head slightly tilted to one

173

side, flashing a self-satisfied smile, and projecting a calm, knowing expression.

"You make one helluva first impression," Max finally said. He was surprised to find himself thinking that this unlikely partnership just might work. Phyllis Draper, in her faded Levis, leather mountain boots, and wrinkled Pendleton, with both dogs at her feet, might just be what he needed. She wouldn't admit as much, but Max felt Draper was out to prove herself, and would work her ass off on this case, just to be able to shove it in the face of those in the department who had treated her unfairly in the past.

She gently poked at the dogs with her foot, moving them out of the way.

"I want to show you something," she said, motioning for Max to follow. She walked toward the front door, then turned down a short hallway. At the end of it she entered a small bedroom. At least, Max thought, it had originally been intended as a bedroom. Now the room contained no bed or dressers. Nothing except two sand-covered surfboards stacked against the wall in the corner, and a large chrome-and-black metal contraption that stood in the center of the room and reached within a few inches of the ceiling. Max had seen universal gyms of the same sort in some of the health clubs around town.

"This for you?" he asked.

Draper didn't answer. She removed her Pendleton, revealing a spandex bodysuit clinging to solid muscle underneath.

"You caught me during my normal workout time," she said, straddling the small padded bench and pulling on a pair of leather gloves. She lay back on the bench, positioning herself under the rubber-gripped handles. Her breathing became deep and regular, increasing in intensity until, with a loud grunt, she pushed the handles to their full extension over her chest, held the weight, arms outstretched, for several seconds, then brought the handles slowly down. She did ten more repetitions of the bench press before she sat up.

"I'm impressed," said Max. He wasn't joking. The metal pin that fit between the black iron plates and determined the weight of the lift was out of sight somewhere down below the level of the bench. The weight increased as the pin moved downward. Above the pin, the last number that Max could see stenciled in white on the plates was 180.

"If we ever find ourselves in trouble," she said, not even breathing hard, "I want you to think of what you just saw. If there's any rough stuff, I want you to know that you can count on me carrying my weight."

Max was a little embarrassed. He'd harbored no thought of playing machismo games with Phil Draper; she wasn't the type. And even if he had, after her display at the bench press any silly ideas of that sort had been permanently banished from his mind.

Max sat down next to her on the bench. "You know something," he said, grabbing his chest and acting faint. "I was wondering if you could get the case file out of my car. I'd get it myself, but I'm a little winded from just watching you."

She laughed, then pushed him off the end of the bench.

Max felt a little uncomfortable, sitting at his usual table at Mr. A's, nursing a martini and waiting for Esther Morse to arrive. The table overlooked Sixth Avenue and Balboa Park. The rolling green hills of the park were covered in shadow, as were the buildings in the distance. Only the top of the bell tower still shined bright, reflecting the last slivers of sunlight.

He had suggested meeting at his office, or her house, whichever she preferred, whatever would be less of a strain for her.

Esther Morse had surprised him, though, suggesting that they meet for a drink, someplace with people.

"I've got to get out of the house," she said, "before Jim and the half-dozen cops he's got around here drive me crazy. I'm developing a terminal case of cabin fever."

Max suggested the bar at Mr. A's, then offered an early dinner, which to his surprise, she eagerly accepted.

The Ripper investigation was plodding along, nearly six weeks since the last attack, and going nowhere. The guy was careful, very careful. Randomly spacing his victims, making preparation and vigilance all the more difficult.

So far all they had were the victims' statements, all pretty much the same. The assailant, depending on which victim you believed, ranged anywhere from five-ten, to six-four. He was either of medium build, or slight and wiry. None of them saw his face or heard him speak.

They had all agreed on the knife, though. It was sharp and curved, and he carried it in his jacket pocket.

And then there was the use of the condom. Each of the women said the same thing. Right before intercourse, the Ripper had removed a foil package from his pants and slipped the condom over his penis, each time in open view of his victim.

The guy was smart. No visual identification and no telltale pieces of evidence left at the scene.

Max had tried to interview Leslie Greer again, but her husband had asked him to hold off. In the weeks since she'd been attacked, her emotional condition had deteriorated. She was still under the care of psychiatrists, he said.

Max hadn't wanted to push the issue, though he intended to speak to the woman in the near future. He'd asked her husband to let the authorities know once things stabilized sufficiently to have his wife questioned without risking her emotional well-being.

Max looked up from his drink and his thoughts of Leslie Greer to see Raphael, the maître d', escorting Esther Morse to the table.

"Thank you for meeting me on such short notice," he said, standing and helping her with her chair. She was dressed in a linen business suit and appeared calm. Max was surprised at her composure, expecting that she'd exhibit some outward change in her appearance after her experience.

Raphael stood to the side, arms crossed, beaming, like the proud father.

He probably figures, thought Max, that I've finally met someone serious.

In the years that Max had eaten at the restaurant, he'd almost always dined alone. Raphael would joke with him about fixing him up with a nice Italian girl, a relative of his.

"Can I get the lady something from the bar?"

She looked at Max, then turned, saying, "I'll have what he's having.

"I have to admit," she said, adjusting herself in the chair, "that Jim wasn't totally in favor of our meeting. At least, here. He made me bring along one of his bodyguards, or at least, that's what I call them. They're regular cops, but they seem like bodyguards to me." She jerked her head in the direction of the bar. Max noticed a young man seated at a table, sipping an orange drink and staring at them. He looked like a fish out of water, his bulky muscular frame stretching his inexpensive suit.

"But I couldn't stand it in the house any longer. Jim

177

only cares about my safety, I know that, but he can be suffocating sometimes."

Raphael brought two fresh drinks and placed them on the table.

"Cheers," she said, lifting her glass, but not waiting for him to clink. She took a long swallow of the clear liquid, smacked her lips softly, then took another.

"Marvelous."

"They make the best," he said.

"Listen, I didn't mean to hoodwink you into a free dinner invitation. I'm sure you've got better things to do with your time than wine and dine an old bag like me."

"You underestimate yourself," he said, thinking how right first impressions could be. The more he was with this lady, the more he liked her.

"You might have seen that look I got when you walked in. Raphael likes to play mother hen. He feels sorry for me when he sees me come in to eat alone. People are funny that way. Not that I always prefer my own company, but there are plenty of times when I'd rather enjoy a good meal by myself."

"But this isn't one of them?"

Max shook his head, then took a sip of his drink.

"I know you've gone over the events of that night a dozen times already," he said. "I've read all the statements, the crime reports, etc. Your husband has probably told you that we're still banging our heads against the wall on this one. We've got a very general description of this guy, not enough to match him with any of the known violent sex offenders on our lists."

"And you want to know if there might be anything I forgot to mention?"

"I thought I'd try."

"Well, Mr. Becker . . ."

"Max."

"Well, Max. I wish I could help you, but I've told the

178

police everything that I can remember. Believe me, I've gone over that scene in my mind a hundred times. In my dreams." A partial scowl flashed across her face. "It always plays out the same."

Max wondered what this woman was holding inside. The physical scars had healed, were healing, but there was something in her exaggerated bravado that made him think that emotionally, Esther Morse had just set out on the road to recovery.

"Leslie Greer said that she was hit, struck in the face by her assailant. That even while he did that, he didn't say a word, just motioned for her to be quiet."

Max put his finger to his lips, simulating the gesture.

"I could say the same," she said. "Except for the striking. I passed out during the rape, but before that, when he grabbed me and threw me on the bed, he didn't say a word. And, of course, he had that stocking over his head, so I couldn't see his face."

Her body shivered, but she covered it quickly by reaching for her martini and turning away from him toward the window.

"Are you all right?"

She turned back and gave him a hopeful smile. "That's the million-dollar question, isn't it?

Max waited.

"Yes," she said, returning her gaze to the window. The sun had set and the park was shrouded in darkness. The lights of the city twinkled in the distance.

Max tried to place the statements of each of the victims in his mind, like plastic transparencies, one over another, to see where they differed and where they remained the same. The Ripper stuck to the same routine, sneaking in at night when the man of the house was gone, raping his victims, then very carefully, surgically, cutting them up, leaving no trace of himself at the scene.

179

Esther Morse turned from the window and said, "I want you to promise me something, Mr. Becker— Max . . ." She put down her drink and folded her hands in front of her. "I don't want you to feel sorry for me or for my husband. I don't want you to think how tragic or sad it is that this has happened. That won't do either of us much good. I want you to feel what I feel right now, what I've felt ever since that night—anger, Mr. Becker. I want you to be angry, just like I am. I want you to catch this bastard, make sure he's either killed, or locked up forever."

Max saw her composure begin to crack. Despite her efforts to set her jaw and look tough, her lower lip quivered with fear. Or perhaps, Max wondered, it *was* anger.

She quickly recovered and reached for her drink, taking slow deep breaths.

"Sorry," she said, shaking her head. "I told myself I wouldn't do that."

"We don't have to talk about it anymore," said Max.

Esther Morse wiped her eyes, carefully dabbing with her napkin to avoid smearing her eye makeup.

"I hope that doesn't mean that dinner is off?" she said, smiling. "All this crying has made me hungry." She lifted the martini glass to her lips, draining the rest of the liquid.

Max motioned for Raphael, then turned and placed a reassuring hand on hers.

"We'll catch him, Mrs. Morse," he said, trying to bolster her spirits. "You have my word on that." He paused, then added, "You just take care of yourself. It looks to me like you're doing a damn good job of that already. I don't know whether I'd have your strength, I can tell you that right now."

Esther Morse was a brave woman, yet even she was having trouble reconciling what had happened to her.

Max wondered whether the other two victims would ever find the strength to recover.

"It's all a facade," she said, smiling. Raphael was standing at the edge of the table, waiting and listening.

"I'm really a wreck underneath."

Max could tell she was joking, or at least had not intended that her comment be taken seriously. He wondered if the shell of composure cracked when she was at home, alone with her husband.

"You could have fooled me," said Max. "How about another drink while we order dinner?"

It was the part of the morning that Phil Draper liked best. The surf had only been average, two-to-three-foot swells and choppy. But that was okay. She'd gotten everything she could out of the waves, and now she sat on the sand with her arms wrapped around her knees, gazing out at the Pacific.

Though she'd toweled her hair dry, she was still cold. The frigid ocean air stung her ears. She pulled the hood of the old sweatshirt over her head as protection against foggy swirling morning chill.

She felt alive, like a loose wire filled with a powerful electrical current, jerking freely in the air. Wild and dangerous—and pure. This was the part of her life that nobody could take from her.

But this morning her thoughts strayed from the majestic beauty of the ocean. She kept coming back to her meeting with Max Becker and the reports on the Ripper case that she'd been poring over for the last few days.

Even out in the surf, in the murky green bottomless depths—where normally she concentrated solely on the waves, catching the right one, mindful of the inherent danger of playing this game with nature—her mind

181

drifted back to her work.

There was something in those reports that was tugging at her, just beneath her area of recall. She knew if she concentrated too hard on what that something was she'd lose it. It was one of those subconscious impressions that would eventually surface when she least expected it to.

So she remained on the sand, watching the translucent gray clouds become increasingly dark and threatening as they shifted over one another, like a photographic negative of the real thing. The frosty air numbed her fingers and toes. She dug her toes into the sand for warmth, and pulled the sleeves of her sweatshirt over her hands.

It was nearing time to leave. The idea that eluded her was still out there. She could feel it and sensed that the indistinct images now running through her mind would soon sort themselves out. Then she would have it.

It had happened this way before. She liked to think of it along the lines of one of those bingo machines that tossed scores of ping-pong balls inside a clear glass cylinder, then systematically selected the balls, one at a time, organizing them in an orderly line of numbers.

In her case, each ball would bear a letter, and when all the balls had been selected, the clue that she'd been searching for would be there, spelled out for her.

She had already reviewed Max's interview with Esther Morse, and had repeatedly gone over the crime reports. In fact, she had read them so many times she could now envision each page, where certain details appeared on the page, and how the various paragraphs of the reports related to each other.

She had been consumed initially by the cruelty of the violence. The photographs depicted in graphic, bloody detail the malevolence of this monster. It had taken her a few days to get past that cruelty, to put her own hatred aside and concentrate entirely on the facts. Ultimately, she realized that if she had any hope of capturing this demon, she'd have to relive each attack as if she'd been there, which meant not skipping over any detail, no matter how small or trivial.

She'd also have to get into the Ripper's head, think as he would, and her hatred of the man would only get in the way of doing that.

It finally came to her as she slid her surfboard onto the roof of the car. She'd been adjusting the towel under the board when the realization hit her. Just as she knew it would, when she least expected it. And it had come together because of something Esther Morse had told Max, something they'd both considered a mere aside at the time. Something that had not been mentioned in the first crime reports.

Doing the grunt work herself, taking a personal interest, had paid off. That made her feel good.

She hurried to get back home, to make the call. She could feel the adrenaline from the morning still pumping through her body, now helped along by the excitement generated by her discovery.

Maybe it's just a coincidence, she told herself, turning from the highway onto the gravel road. Maybe I'm getting excited over nothing?

As she drew closer to the house, she thought about bouncing the plan off Max first. After all, he was in charge and maybe he'd have his own ideas on how to handle it.

Once inside, though, she went straight to the phone. She couldn't wait any longer. She was barely aware of her still shivering body. The dogs moved anxiously at her feet, sensing her nervousness. She quickly found the telephone number from the inside jacket of the case file and dialed. A woman's voice answered after the second ring.

"Hello?"

"Is this Leslie Greer?"

"Who wants to know?"

She was not surprised at the woman's tone of cautious suspicion. After what this lady has been through, she thought, I don't blame her one bit for being a little paranoid.

"This is Investigator Draper. I've been assigned to your case."

"But I thought Mr. Becker was handling . . ."

"We're working it together," she said. "I have the reports on your case and the others. This will just take a few seconds."

"Well, uh . . ."

"If you like, you could call Mr. Becker and have him verify who I am."

"Uh, I guess that isn't necessary. It's just that I've repeated my story so many times already."

"I can appreciate that. I know that Detectives Levine and Levinthal have questioned you, in addition to Mr. Becker, so I'll try not to go over the same ground."

"Okay."

Her mention of the other two investigators seemed to put Leslie Greer at ease, as Draper had intended it to do.

"I really only have one question," said Draper. "It has to do with something that may mean little to you. In fact, it may turn out to be unimportant, but we're trying to follow all possible leads.

"What I want to know is if you had any cable TV service during the week or so before you were assaulted. I know that sounds a little strange, but . . ."

"I did. But how did you know?"

Phil Draper could hear the fear in the woman's voice. It mingled with the excitement and anticipation she felt churning in her own stomach. She told herself

184

to remain calm, not to sound too excited, not to get this victim's hopes up. But the way she felt, the sudden electric jolt in her chest, made it hard for her to do that. She removed the composite drawing from the file, along with the notes from her interviews with the other victims.

"Ms. Greer," she started out slowly. "Could you please describe the serviceman the cable company sent to your home? Take your time."

12

"Who is this guy?"

"His name is Fredrickson. He's the office manager."

"You talked to him?"

"Briefly. Nothing specific. Just that we needed some information. He was cooperative. Says he used to be a reserve sheriff."

They were in the unmarked detective's car, heading into Mission Valley. Draper had filled Max in on what she'd learned from Leslie Greer. The crime reports on the first victim mentioned that Bernadette Slotkin had also received service to her cable television during the week before she was raped.

As it turned out, all three victims had received cable TV service during the weeks leading up to their attacks. All from the same company, All-Valley Cable.

Draper parked the car in the lot and she and Max entered the building. A receptionist immediately showed them into Dan Fredrickson's office. Draper did the introductions.

"Glad to meet you," said Fredrickson, shaking hands with both of them and motioning for them to sit down.

Fredrickson was a large man, over six-six. He had

sandy blond hair cut close in a military-style buzz, around a pudgy florid face that reddened when he laughed. He wore a short-sleeved white shirt with a clip-on supermarket tie. Holding up his powder-blue Levis was a thick leather belt with a large silver-and-turquoise buckle. A pair of scuffed leather boots completed his wardrobe.

Fredrickson said, "Now, how can I help you?"

"It's come to our attention, Mr. Fredrickson, that your company serviced certain households on certain dates over the last month or so."

"We service a lot of households," he said, letting out a belly laugh. "Biggest licensee in the county, and don't let any of my competitiors tell ya any different. Just what area are you talking about, Mr. Becker?"

Max provided the names, dates, and addresses.

Fredrickson jotted down the information, looked at it for a moment, then reached for the phone.

"Arlene, send me the book on the Vallejo tract."

He put the phone back on the hook, saying, "If it was one of our crews, the book will tell me."

The office door opened, and the woman who had greeted them outside entered carrying a large notebook filled with pages of computer printouts.

"Here we are," said Fredrickson, plopping the notebook on his desk and rifling through the pages. He compared his handwritten notes with the information in the notebook.

"Yep," he said, stabbing a finger at the printouts. "You're right. Our people did all those jobs."

Draper felt her heart jump and start pumping faster. "Mr. Fredrickson," she said, "we need the name of the technician who did the work."

Fredrickson smiled, shaking his head.

"More than one," he said. "We had a whole crew out there working that tract. And this other one's in the

Coronado tract, which is also ours. But still, we're talking a major cable reroute. Lots of trucks and equipment. A whole slew of men working those jobs."

Draper's heart dipped.

"But surely you have the names of the employees who did work at specific houses? Wouldn't you show an invoice, a work order that had to be signed off?"

"Maybe. Depends. Sometimes, if it's a big job, they don't specify a particular address. What I mean is, a man could work a yard, even get into the house, and his name wouldn't necessarily appear on any of the paperwork, except maybe the supervisor's list of who's working which crew. But that doesn't help you find out if a particular man entered a particular house. Which, I'm assuming, is what you're after?"

Max nodded.

"Wish I could be more help, but unless it was a specific return call by the same technician, you're going to have to talk with the job supervisor, see if he remembers anything."

Fredrickson lifted his palms in the air.

"Sorry 'bout that."

Dan Fredrickson's information about the job supervisor proved less complicated than they'd expected. The supervisor provided them with a list of five technicians who'd worked the two tracts which included the residences of Bernadette Slotkin, Leslie Greer, and Esther Morse.

They split up the list, Draper taking the first three names, Max the last two. Both understood that this was a longshot at best, that since the areas involved were receiving a major service from the cable company, the coincidence of all three victims having cable service was not as great as they'd originally thought.

188

Still, it was all they had to go on. Forensics had still not come up with anything, and each of the victims had been interviewed and reinterviewed. Max did not want to put himself in the position of badgering the women any further, making them feel like victims all over again. He was acutely aware of how easily that could happen, and of the strains and intrusions into their privacy that any future court appearances would cause.

He'd obtained photographs of each of the men from Fredrickson, a bit of luck there—company policy. Otherwise he would have had to figure some other way to present each of the servicemen to the various victims for identification.

As it turned out, each of the women identified more than one of the servicemen as either working inside or around the house during the cable installation.

Two of the men weren't identified by any of the victims, and Max was tempted to drop them from the list, but thought better of it after Draper convinced him that any of the five would have had access to the homes, even if they had not been seen by the victims. He compromised, putting the two who had not been picked out at the bottom of the list. He took one and gave one to Draper. That left one on his list and two on Draper's who had actually been seen by at least one of the women.

Danny Jackson had been identified by both Slotkin and Greer. He lived in a trailer complex in Solana Beach, along with his three dogs, two cats, and enough hunting rifles to supply a small army. He drove a banged-up red Toyota four-by-four with a sticker on the back window that said, "No Fat Chicks," and another on the rear bumper that read, "Ban Criminals, Not Handguns."

When Max met him, Jackson was seated on the steps

189

of his trailer, cleaning his rifle.

"Looks like an antique," said Max, pulling out a business card and handing it to the man.

Jackson inspected the card, then placed it in his shirt pocket, apparently unimpressesd.

"My daddy give it to me. T'was his daddy's before."

"Ahh, an heirloom. You're lucky it reached you in such good shape. Guess it hasn't been used much."

Jackson didn't answer. Just kept polishing away at the barrel with a soft, oily cloth. He looked younger than his twenty-seven years, with skin that hardly showed the trace of a blond beard. His curly blond hair was pulled back in a loose ponytail. He wore a Coors beer T-shirt. There was a pack of cigarettes tucked into his rolled-up shirtsleeve. He was within the height and weight descriptions provided by the victims.

Max mentioned the dates that the three women had been raped, asking Jackson if he remembered where he'd been.

"Listen, Mr . . ." Jackson pulled out the card and read the name, "Becker. I know why you're here. You're lookin' for someone to pin that murder rap on. The Ripper. Well, mister, you're barkin' up the wrong tree. I don't know nothin' about those women, 'ceptin' I might have worked on their cable system. That's all. I never killed nothin' human in my entire life. Never had the need.

"And to tell ya the truth, sittin' here, I can't say *what* I was doin' those nights. Probably sittin' right here, doin' what I'm doin' now."

Max felt like he was in the Ozarks somewhere, thrown back in time. Still, the good-old-country-boy routine could be a ruse.

"Then you've got nothing to worry about," said Max. "And you wouldn't mind making a statement, letting me take your fingerprints."

"Go 'head, print all you want, Mister. If I was in those houses, like you said, my fingerprints would be all over the place anyway. Don't see how that proves nothin'."

The country-boy had a point. This whole conversation, Max figured, was probably a waste of time. Despite Jackson's guns and his loner lifestyle, Max had a feeling about him, something that told him the country-boy was too obvious, not the type of psychotically precise assailant they were looking for. By the looks of him, Jackson had neither the patience, the skill, nor the inclination to surgically carve up his victims.

Max asked a few more questions, then told Danny Jackson to call before going on any trips. He made an appointment for him to come down to the station to be printed and give a formal written statement.

When he got back into town, Max stopped at the station to check in with Draper, find out if she'd had any success. He found her in the officer's lounge, feet up on the coffee table, chomping on an apple, carefully perusing a fitness magazine.

"Any luck?"

Through a mouthful of apple, she said, "Dexter said he was with his in-laws on the nights that the Greer and Slotkin women were raped. Watching TV one night, at the movies the other. Called them from the house, dialed the number, and let me ask the questions. They corroborated the whole thing."

"Great, that's two down. Jackson hasn't provided an alibi, but he doesn't seem the knife type. We'll keep an eye on him, but I'm not real optimistic. That leaves us with the two off the list, and what's his name . . ."

"Harris Fourcade," said Draper, tossing the magazine on the coffee table. "Met up with him this afternoon. At a job site. A little hard to understand, speaks with a lisp. Says he was with his girlfriend on the

191

dates in question. That he's always with her. Comes straight home after work. Also offered to call her for me, even bring her down."

"Whadya think? Is he bluffing?"

"Who knows? He fits the description, height and weight. But so do the other two. By the way, I also got the employment paperwork on the two that weren't ID'd. Neither of them fit the description. Taylor is short and fat, and too old. Davis is very large and very black."

"Are Dexter and Fourcade coming down to make a statement?"

"Fourcade said he would. Dexter balked initially, gave me his 'Why me?' routine. But he eventually backed down, said he could come during the next few days. They're both waiting for my call."

Max walked over and poured himself a cup of coffee. It tasted bitter and overheated. He poured in a few tablespoons of powdered creamer to cut the acid taste.

"Why don't you take off," he said. "This cable angle was grasping at straws from the get-go. We'll start fresh tomorrow morning."

"Yeah," she said, stretching, then standing and doing a few quick kneebends. "I'm going downstairs, work-out. You care to join me?" She smiled.

"I wouldn't want to show you up," he said, taking her place on the couch and spreading out the Ripper file folder on the coffee table. "Don't break anything."

Max sipped on his coffee, arranging the case files on the table like a fan, a poker hand, wondering what his next draw would yield. He looked through them again, then decided he'd had enough, the words jumbling on the page as he read, his mind playing dyslexic games.

There was still plenty of light when he got home, so he changed into his running clothes, grabbed Cardozo's leash, and headed for the park.

"And how was your day today?"

He huffed his words to the dog as they jogged down Sixth Avenue, receiving the occasional odd looks from passersby.

"Mine?" he answered. "Nice of you to ask. Well could have been better. Ya see, boy, this Ripper character is one smart asshole. Covers his tracks real good. Got us jerking ourselves off trying to catch a lead. Probably laughing the whole time."

Max headed into the park, jumping onto the grass to cushion his steps. On the lawn near the lily pond, a mime was entertaining the last few tourists, first doing his silent juggling routine, then the one where he was supposedly trapped inside a glass house, pressing his hands on the walls, trying to get out.

Max had seen it dozens of times before, and he guessed, so had most of the tourists. Yet they continued to watch, and laugh when they were supposed to, and many threw coins into a large cardboard box marked "Donations."

Max hated mimes. He never got the point of the whole thing.

He called for Cardozo, who had wondered off to sniff a tree. The dog cantered back, wagging his tail and slobbering all over Max's shoes.

"Come on, boy. Let's head home."

He'd gotten to the very edge of the park, near the entrance, when it struck him. He whirled, his chest heaving, both from the exertion of the run and the knowledge that had just come to him. Like a filmstrip run at full speed, the images of the three Ripper attacks sped through his mind, along with a voice, his own, reciting facts from the various reports and interviews.

He had it.

It was there, just behind his eyes, ready for him to grab.

He wrapped Cardozo's leash around his right hand and took off, running in the opposite direction of his home, downtown, toward the station.

"Where's Draper? Is she still here?"

The desk sergeant looked at Max as if he'd just escaped from mental health court.

"I'll check, Mr. Becker."

The sergeant reached for the phone, still eyeing Max warily. Max stood on the public side of the desk, in the waiting room, holding onto the counter, trying to catch his breath. Cardozo had found a place in the corner near a potted plant to park himself.

It had been the mime. Max hated mimes, but he was in love with this one. The mime had given him the clue, had triggered the connection. At least, he hoped it was a connection.

After a few seconds of whispered conversation, the desk sergeant hung up the phone. "She ain't here," he said. "But she left a message in case you called in." He lifted a piece of paper on which he'd been taking notes, reading slowly:

"There's a reason why Mr. R. never spoke to his victims."

The sergeant looked up, his brow furrowed, confused.

"That make any sense to you?"

"Yeah," said Max, smiling. "All the sense in the world, Sergeant."

She was already awake, staring at him and smiling.

"You had a rough night last night, baby," she said, caressing his forehead with her hand. He hated it when she did that.

"Talking up a storm," she said. "Couldn't make much sense of it. You worried about something, hon?"

He rolled away from the girl, knowing that this would have to end, that the girl would only be trouble.

"Whatsa matter, baby?"

She was back on top of him now, straddling him like she hadn't got enough last night. She had that little schoolgirl pout that she seemed to think he liked. In fact, he thought it made her look stupid.

"Get off me," he said. She looked surprised, even hurt. That was good.

He rolled off the bed and headed for the bathroom. Once inside, he closed the door and sat on the toilet. He'd have to tell the girl that he was going away. Yeah. Maybe that an old girfriend had come back into his life and he was going to live with her. That would work. After all, Carla was with him mainly for the booze and the pills. She'd find someone else to get her loaded, some other guy's place where she could crash and sleep it off.

He'd been worried about the dreams. For years he'd talked in his sleep. Even at the Home, the other kids used to wake him up, laughing at whatever it was he'd been saying.

Maybe Carla had heard too much? He thought about that for a moment, then remembered what she'd said, and considered how stupid she was, and the spaced-out condition she'd been in last night. He decided not to worry about Carla—not yet, anyway.

He planned the day ahead. First he'd dump Carla, hopefully after convincing her to find someone new. Then he'd drive to the Home. He'd climb the stairs to the rocking chair that looked out on the yard. There he'd be with his thoughts and his notebooks. He'd spend the afternoon there, thinking about the way things had changed, and planning what to do next.

There he could have his dreams without having to worry about somebody listening.

He remembered only parts of last night's dream. The courtroom scene was in it, but this time *he* was the one who was on trial. The prosecutor was still the same, though; that never changed. The prosecutor called the woman as a witness, and the woman pointed at him and said that he was the one who did it.

Now, remembering that part of the dream made his stomach churn, but it also made him laugh. Imagine that slut thinking she could get away with pulling that kind of shit on the Monster Boy!

The dream-woman who had pointed him out had looked pathetic in her tattered and burned clothing. Her skin had been charred black, so that only her eyes were white. She was crying and pointing her scorched finger at him, like the ash tip of a cigar.

He wondered how much of that Carla might have heard. The dream was beginning to overlap with reality. It was only a matter of time before he said something that Carla recognized, a name or even a place. Then she'd ask him about it the next morning in her stupid baby-talk way. He wouldn't explain, but that might make her even more curious.

He didn't need that, and he didn't need her.

Especially with the cops climbing all over themselves trying to capture the Ripper. Carla was a loose end that he definitely could do without.

"You gotta split," he said, pulling on a sweatshirt as he emerged from the bathroom.

"But baby, I thought . . ."

"Now," he said. He picked her jeans off the floor and threw them at her. "I got a van full of papers to deliver."

He watched as she pulled on her jeans, all the while pouting and talking under her breath. He wanted to get her to move quicker.

"Here's fifty bucks," he said, tossing the money on the bed. He let her kiss him, then tapped her on the ass and forced himself to say, "Come on, baby. I'm in a hurry."

She grabbed the money and headed to the door, stuffing the bills into her pants pocket, along with her underpants. She giggled, then waved, then slammed the door behind her.

He thought she'd never leave.

He shuffled into the kitchen and spooned some instant coffee into a mug, then turned up the gas under the pot of hot water. The blue-yellow flames licked around the edge of the pot. He listened to the boiling water gurgle inside. He wondered what Carla would think if she knew he was the one, the Monster Boy, the person the papers called the Ripper.

He brought his coffee to the small dinette and sat down. Yesterday's paper still lay where he had left it the night before, on one of the kitchen chairs. There was an article he would cut out today, one for his collection. It was about the lack of progress the police were making, and the new cop they'd assigned to supervise the investigation.

Not that that really mattered; they'd never catch him. He was too cautious, too clever. He knew all about how the cops worked, how they could connect blood-types through semen. He'd taken care of that. As with Carla, he'd leave no trail that they could follow.

But the more he thought about it, reveled in the importance of what he'd done, he found himself almost wishing that they'd discover him, just so he could explain to them how clever he'd been.

He saw himself standing in a room filled with cops, telling them how he'd done it—how he'd deceived them. The cops would be in awe, shaking their heads in disbelief and admiration.

He was still in his reverie, accepting daydream applause, when he was pulled away by a knock on the door.

He wasn't expecting anybody. Who could it be?

He looked through the peephole in the door. The cheap magnifying glass distorted the face.

Standing on the landing outside his apartment was a middle-aged blonde, wearing flats, and dressed in a pair of plain beige slacks and a matching blouse. Even in the flats, Fourcade could tell she was tall.

He cracked open the door, wide enough to make his voice heard, maybe scare her away.

"Yeah?" he mumbled. He thought she was trying to sell him something, like those ecology freaks that go door-to-door for donations.

The woman reached into her pocket and removed a black leather billfold, then flapped it open and thrust it into the crack for him to see. A detective's shield.

"Investigator Draper, Mr. Fourcade. I'd like to ask you a few more questions, if you don't mind."

Part Two

13

"Who's the girl?"

Phil Draper glanced toward the reception area, then turned back to Max. "Fourcade's girlfriend," she said. "She was just leaving the apartment when we took him in."

Max kept his eyes on the young bleached blonde in the reception area as Draper filled him in on the events leading up to her taking Harris Fourcade in for questioning.

"Just like you, it finally hit me," she said. "The one thing that all three women had in common: the guy never opened his mouth. Strange. Sometimes they don't say much, but there's usually something, a grunt, an order barked at them. But this guy didn't say a word."

"I'm surprised we didn't catch it sooner. Why we didn't ask ourselves whether there might be a reason behind the silence."

Max said, "It was easy to miss. Who could have figured?"

Draper pursed her lips, silent for a moment, then went on.

"Anyway, I took Fourcade's picture over to show

Daniel Greer. The kid's pretty damn young. And he didn't get that good a look. But I could tell he locked on something in that photo lineup."

"Did he pick him out?"

Draper hesitated. "Not exactly. He seemed afraid. Not unsure, just scared. I asked him if any of the faces looked familiar, like it was no big deal what he was doing. The kid hesitated, looked at his mommy, then pointed in the general direction of Fourcade's photo."

"Doesn't sound too strong."

"It's not, yet. I got him to say that Fourcade looked the most like the man he saw in his house that night. I'm sure he knows it's him, that he's just plain scared."

"Vibrations from his mother."

"That's for sure. The woman's an emotional basketcase."

"What about Slotkin? She didn't pick out Fourcade initially. Did you show her the picture?"

Draper pulled back, hesitant about answering.

"She seems to have disappeared," she said. "We're still looking. The address we have for her is no longer any good. Landlord says she moved out, left no forwarding address."

"You're kidding?" Max tried to recall the facts of the first Ripper attack. Bernadette Slotkin. She was in her early twenties, the youngest of the three victims. She'd dialed 911 herself, and by the time the first units arrived, the paramedics already had her en route to the hospital. The first time she was interviewed by the police as to what happened was early in the morning on the day following the assault. The initial reports were on the skimpy side, since she was still woozy from the sedatives. Either from shock, or because of the drugs, Bernadette Slotkin had recalled very few specifics about her attacker. Max had been meaning to talk with her further, but hadn't yet had the chance. Now it appeared that they'd have to spend additional time and resources trying to locate the woman.

"I've got Levine following up on it," Draper said. "I spoke to the patrol officers who took the report. Slotkin was single, lived by herself in a rental house. Did some sort of secretarial work part-time. A little flaky, according to the cop who originally interviewed her. Of course, at the time, they had no idea that she was just the first in a series of victims. The cop said he had the feeling that she didn't want to get involved, just wanted the whole thing to disappear."

"And so she disappeared instead."

"You know how that works," said Draper. "For some women the embarrassment and humiliation of going through the court system is worse than the actual rape."

Draper paused, considering what she'd just said. Max had the feeling that no matter how long she thought about it, Phil Draper would never understand the attitude that allowed a victim to give up in the quest for revenge.

"What did Fourcade have to say on the way down?"

"Not much. I told him I wanted to ask him a few questions. He said, 'About what?' I mentioned the Ripper investigation and he clammed up."

"Has he demanded a lawyer?"

"Not yet. I tried to make bringing him down here as low-key as possible. Like he really wasn't a suspect. I asked him if he would mind coming down for a while, answer some questions. That we'd bring him back to his apartment when we were finished."

"And he bought that?"

"He seemed concerned about the girl. Almost like he didn't want her to be involved."

"Protecting her?"

"I'm not sure. Maybe keeping her in the dark would

be more like it."

"Mmm." Max wondered what the bleached blonde's involvement might be. What she knew.

"She was in the parking lot when we brought Fourcade down," said Draper. "She followed us down in Fourcade's van. Do you want her questioned?"

"Not yet," said Max. "Where's he now?"

"Room 3." She gestured with a toss of her head in the direction of the small interview cubicles that lined one side of the hallway adjacent to the detectives' room.

Max said, "What about the press?"

"As far as they're concerned, we're still looking for a suspect."

"So now we have Mr. Harris Fourcade, who has tentatively been identified by two of our victims as having serviced their cable TVs during the week they were attacked. None of the victims can ID him as the assailant, since the Ripper wore a stocking mask during each of the attacks."

"Except Daniel Greer," said Draper. "He said the man who stopped at his doorway was not wearing a mask."

"Yes," said Max, contemplating his next move. "Daniel Greer. For what that's worth."

"And we've got Fourcade's prints," said Draper, "inside the Greer and Morse residences."

"Which," Max interrupted, "Fourcade or his lawyer will claim were placed there by him at the time he was working on the cable."

"One's on the headboard of Esther Morse's bed," said Draper.

"And she has a television in that bedroom?"

"Sure, but it's at the other end of the room from the headboard."

"But he could have been in the bedroom legitimately

to service the television, right?"

Draper didn't answer.

"And he could claim, as I'm sure he will, once he's had time to think it over and talk with a lawyer, that he might have placed his hand on the headboard for some totally innocent reason."

Phil Draper resented Max's questioning, but realized that he was just doing his job, playing the devil's advocate. They needed enough evidence on Harris Fourcade to justify a filing, which meant enough evidence to ultimately convince a jury of his guilt.

What they had so far fell far short. Draper realized that without a stronger identification by Daniel Greer, she was relying on Fourcade making a mistake in order to provide the missing pieces. But all Fourcade had to do was refuse to answer their questions, and they would be forced to release him.

She and Max and everyone else working the Ripper investigation were feeling the public pressure to make some progress on the case. Now, she was having second thoughts about the wisdom of bringing Harris Fourcade in for questioning so soon.

"How are we doing with the warrant?" asked Max. He had drafted a warrant for the search of Fourcade's apartment. He'd sent Levinthal over to get a judge to sign the warrant, but hadn't heard anything back yet.

"Leventhal's on his way to the apartment."

"You realize," said Max, rather uneasily, "that the probable cause for that warrant is almost nonexistent. We're on very weak ground here."

"The judge signed it, didn't he?"

"Sure, we sent it to someone we knew would sign anything. That doesn't mean that some other judge, later on, won't look at the warrant and decide that the signing judge must have had his head up his ass when he authorized the search."

Max got up and grabbed the case file. The process of second-guessing his own legal decisions was just beginning, and he was already tired of it.

"Come on," he said. "Let's see what Mr. Fourcade has to say."

Harris Fourcade was seated behind a square wooden table in the middle of the interview room. Through a small window in the door, Max watched him for a moment. Fourcade appeared calm. He had his hands folded in front of him, and was slightly reclined in the wooden chair, staring at the wall.

"What's with his lip?" Max whispered to Draper.

Draper shrugged. "Looks like a harelip, something like that. The moustache covers most of it."

Max opened the door and strode into the room.

"Good afternoon, Mr. Fourcade," he said. Phil Draper followed behind, saying nothing.

"I'm Investigator Becker. I believe you've already met my partner, Investigator Draper."

Fourcade nodded in Max's direction, then his eyes darted toward Phil Draper, who had taken up a position behind Max with arms folded, leaning against the wall. Max took a seat opposite Fourcade at the table.

Max said, "Now I don't know how much Investigator Draper might have told you about this case, but I'm going to fill you in on why you're here." Max smiled, trying to warm up to the task, trying to put Fourcade at ease. Fourcade's expression remained impassive.

"We're investigating the Ripper case, I'm sure you've heard of it?"

"The one who raped those women."

"That's it." Max heard a slight lisp as Fourcade spoke, a hissing sound, reminiscent of a whisper.

"So why me?"

"Well, I was just about to get to that," said Max. He

started to poke around in his case file, as if he were looking for something. He wanted to give Fourcade time to digest the importance of his being there.

"It's come to our attention," said Max. "That during the week of their attack, your cable company serviced the homes of the three women who were raped."

Max waited for that to sink in, noticing no change in Fourcade's expression. His hands remained calmly folded in front of him, his eyes staring straight ahead, his breathing slow and steady.

"In fact, two of the victims have identified you as the serviceman who was inside their homes."

Fourcade waited a moment, then in the silence that had developed between them, he responded "So?"

"We've also discovered your fingerprints inside the bedroom of one of the victims."

Fourcade looked to Draper, then back at Max. He unclasped his hands and began twisting a ring on his left forefinger.

"Wouldn't my fingerprints," he said, his eyes fixed on the ring, "necessarily be inside the homes if I was working there?"

Max checked the eyes, seeing that they were steady, unafraid. He realized he wasn't going to get anywhere with Harris Fourcade. Not without something more dramatic to use against him, something that would shock him into making a mistake.

"Perhaps," said Max.

There was a knock on the door, followed immediately by the entrance of Carl Levinthal. Levinthal approached Phil Draper and started whispering. After a few seconds, Draper motioned for Max to step outside.

Max excused himself and followed Draper and Levinthal into the hallway just outside the interview room.

"They found a nylon stocking in Fourcade's apartment," said Draper. Max could hear the suppressed excitement in her voice. "It's down at the lab now," she added.

Max turned to the reception area. The blonde was still there. "Fourcade's girlfriend?"

"Maybe," said Levinthal. Levinthal still seemed shaky, and Max wondered if perhaps he had returned from his stress disability layoff a little too early. "She seems to have slept there on and off. It might be hers."

"Anything else?"

Levinthal shook his head. "We found the stocking rolled up in a corner of the closet."

"By itself? I mean, you didn't find the matching one?"

"Nope."

Max glanced at Fourcade through the window. "Phil, get Fourcade a doughnut and some coffee. Tell him we had a minor emergency and that we'll be back to finish our interview shortly. Then take a statement from his girlfriend. Find out whether she lives with him at the apartment. Don't mention the stocking."

Max turned to Levinthal. "Carl, get down to the lab and light a fire under those guys. I want to know if there's anything there. We've got a couple more hours at most with Fourcade before he starts to get antsy. I need to know about that stocking right away."

Max watched as both Draper and Levinthal went their separate ways. He had tipped his hand with Harris Fourcade. If Fourcade was, in fact, the Ripper, then he now knew that they were onto him. If they turned up nothing with the stocking, nothing that incriminated Fourcade, then he would have to be released.

Max was fighting the feeling of regret that was coming over him. Deets was calling daily for reports on their progress. The media was starting to get nasty, criticizing the lack of results. When Fourcade's connection had surfaced, they'd jumped on it. Now, he thought, perhaps he had jumped too quickly.

"They found a hair." It was Levinthal on the phone, calling from the lab.

"In the nylon?"

"Yeah. Dark, probably black or dark brown."

Max thought of the bleached blonde, figuring that her natural color was probably black. Just their luck.

"Male or female?"

"He didn't say," said Levinthal. "I don't think they can. Here, let me put the lab guy on the phone."

Max waited a moment before a different voice came on the line.

A distant, somewhat aloof, "Yes?"

The lab technician even sounded like an egghead.

"This is Max Becker. I'm the one who sent the stocking down to you guys. Levinthal says you found a hair?"

"A single hair," the technician dryly confirmed. "Embedded in the nylon."

"Man or woman?"

"What?"

"Is the hair from a male or female?"

Max heard the technician chuckle.

"There's no way we can tell you that, not with what we've got."

"What about running a blood-type on the hair?"

Again the technician chuckled. It was starting to get on Max's nerves.

"Let me explain to you," the technician said, speaking like teacher to student, "what you might be able to do with this hair. First, you obviously want to connect this hair in some way to a suspect. The only way of doing that specifically is by DNA-typing. We don't do that here, though I am aware that the FBI went on-line with DNA-typing facilities in 1988.

"But that's not your major problem. In order to even have the opportunity to DNA-type this sample, and I'll try to be as simple as possible in my explanation, we'll need to first amplify, then analyze the hair. Every cell in every organism has a chain of molecules called a double helix. No two people are the same in this regard, except for identical twins. You may have heard of 'genetic fingerprinting'?"

Max grunted.

"Well," the technician continued, "that is simply a layman's term for the process of DNA-typing. By analyzing a tissue sample or sample of body fluids, the specific genetic fingerprint, so to speak, can be determined. You match this sample with one from a given suspect, and *voilà*, you've got your man."

"Of course," the technician elaborated, "It's never quite that simple. This is still very experimental stuff. The process is hardly over three years old in this country. From what I understand, some courts are still a little reluctant to recognize it as a reliable means of identification. Also, it is often impossible for labs to give a definitive answer because the specimens either are not large enough or were degraded, usually by bacteria, from having been exposed to the elements."

Max thought about the first two victims and how the paramedics and ER doctors, in their haste to render aid to the suffering victims, had shaved and swabbed their patients, all but eliminating the possibility of finding any of their assailant's pubic hair.

"That's not the case here," he said.

"Probably not. Except, like I said, the FBI is the only government lab I'm aware of that's now doing extensive DNA-typing, though I know that locally there's a movement to collect and store blood samples from convicted sex offenders in the hope of someday DNA-typing the samples for reference."

"So give me the bottom line," said Max. "Is this hair useless, or what?"

"Not useless. I could give you blood type, most likely. If that helps. They're running it now. Of course, blood type doesn't always narrow the list of suspects, especially if the type is common. We could try to DNA-type what we've got, except I don't have very high hopes for that."

"Why's that?" Max figured the technician's job was to dispassionately look at evidence and render objective scientific opinions. Still, he was finding the total lack of encouragement depressing.

"DNA from inside a hair shaft is from the mitochondria and cannot be typed sufficiently to identify a person. On the other hand, the DNA from hair-follicle cells attached to hair that has been pulled out *can* be typed."

"What have we got?"

"A little of both, and not much of either."

Max began to connect what the technician was telling him with Harris Fourcade. They could probably type the hair as to blood, and that might eliminate Fourcade as a suspect, but would not automatically incriminate him. If the hair was subject to DNA-typing, something Max had only briefly read about but had never actually experienced during his legal career, they might be able to find Fourcade's genetic fingerprint in the sample of hair.

But what did that prove? Only that a strand of Harris Fourcade's hair had somehow found its way into the nylon stocking. Perhaps because Fourcade had pulled the stocking over his head prior to raping his victims, or perhaps because the stockings belonged to Fourcade's girlfriend who lived with him and shared his closet. Even with the matching genetic fingerprint, there was room for Fourcade to wiggle out.

The lab tech said, "You wouldn't have come across any semen, would you? Maybe some pubic hair?" There was a note of skepticism in his voice.

Max smiled, thinking that that would be nice. A good sample of body fluid to match up with the suspect.

"No such luck," said Max. "It seems our rapist knows a little something about DNA. Either that or he's inordinately fastidious. No pubic hair. At least, none that we were able to gather as evidence. All the victims say the assailant used a condom."

"A condom? That's incredible!"

Max could hear the lab tech clucking his tongue in disbelief.

The technician continued, "These guys are getting smarter every day. If all you've got is this bit of hair in the stocking, it's going to be a real longshot matching it up with anyone." He paused for a moment. "Hold on," he said.

Max listened to the muted conversation on the other end.

"The blood type is O-positive," the lab tech said, coming back on the line. "Very common. I'm afraid it's not much help, though it might eliminate your man as a suspect."

"See what you can do with the DNA analysis," said Max. "This is top priority. If you need authorization from the Big Boys, just let me know."

He hung up the phone, replaying the conversation in his mind. The only thing he could do now was to get a blood sample from Fourcade. They'd need a warrant for that, unless Harris Fourcade was willing to provide one voluntarily. Max didn't have high hopes for that.

212

He figured as soon as he mentioned anything about blood samples, Fourcade would be on the phone to his lawyer, and that would be the end of that. Any experienced criminal lawyer would tell him to refuse to provide the sample until the entire case could be reviewed. A blood sample could always be provided later, once the lawyer had had an opportunity to read the reports and speak with his client.

Max was about to return to the interview room when he spotted Phil Draper heading his way.

"The girl's name is Carla Janis," she said. "She's known Fourcade for about three months. Says she met him at a bar. Nothing exclusive. Sees him every couple of weeks, or so she claims."

"You think she's lying?"

"I asked her whether she's sleeping with him. She just shrugged and said, 'Sure,' like it was no big deal. I have the feeling that Ms. Janis spreads it around, and that she's probably got items of clothing in a dozen closets all over town."

"Great." Max couldn't help but think of all the legitimate, perfectly lawful ways that Fourcade's hair could have ended up where it had.

Draper said, "She says she can't recall whether she was with him or not on any of the evenings that our victims were assaulted. I think she's hedging her bets. The stocking is probably hers, but she had no idea Fourcade was using it."

"*If* he was," Max added. "I want to get a blood test for him. Get Levinthal to use the form warrant. Fourcade may agree to give it voluntarily, but just in case, I want to have that judge's order ready."

"No need," Draper said. She opened the manila folder in one hand like a paperback book, and removed a California driver's license.

"Carla Janis brought this with her," she said,

handing the license to Max. Max looked at the card with Fourcade's picture on the front, then flipped it over. Fourcade had one of those stickers attached to the back of the card that designated emergency medical information, including blood type.

"O-positive," Max mumbled to himself.

"Is that good?"

Max looked at Phil Draper, then at the face of Harris Fourcade staring up at him from the card.

"Maybe," he said. "Just maybe."

Harris Fourcade was still seated at the table when Max entered. He was licking his fingers. A square of wax paper, slightly crumpled, lay on the table in front of him. Fourcade was removing doughnut crumbs from the waxed paper with his fingertips.

Max said, "Everything okay?"

Max had entered the room, not yet certain whether he was going to go with what he had and file charges against Fourcade. He realized the case was still weak, especially if Daniel Greer's identification didn't hold up in court, which, from the sound of it, was a distinct possibility.

He also was aware of the public pressure to make some progress toward resolving these crimes. He was banking on the lab coming up with something more specific during the DNA testing. Those Forensics boys could do wonders. He'd seen it before in dozens of cases: the miracles of modern science applied to capturing the bad guys. But such sophisticated laboratory analysis would take time, which was a commodity in short supply.

Max still half hoped that, once confronted with the facts, Harris Fourcade might make an admission, or at least say something that could be used against him at trial. Suspects often unknowingly made incriminating statements, thinking that if they refrained from offering outright confessions, they wouldn't get hurt. Perhaps Fourcade would take a chance at offering an alibi that would later fail to pan out. Perhaps he would put himself someplace or with someone only later to be caught in the lie.

"Ya know, Mr. Becker," said Fourcade. He had finished licking his fingers and had taken a long sip from the paper cup of coffee, that Phil Draper had brought him. "I've been thinking about what you said."

Max's ears perked. Perhaps this was what he was hoping for. Perhaps Fourcade was going to say something that he'd live to regret and make their job a whole lot easier.

"It seems to me that I shouldn't have to come down here to answer your questions, unless you think that I had something to do with what happened to those women."

Max sensed the shift in mood. Fourcade was asserting himself now. He seemed to have an objective in mind. If there was still any hope of getting him to talk, Max knew he'd have to prompt Fourcade now. If the suspect were allowed to proceed at his own pace, he might gain confidence along the way, and eventually realize that he had nothing to gain by answering questions.

"Not necessarily so," said Max. "We're just here to gather evidence. Now . . . ."

"I don't think so, Mr. Becker." Fourcade was smiling now, and Max realized that he had been toyed with, manipulated. He'd underestimated Fourcade and Fourcade knew it, and was now throwing it back in his face.

Max strongly suspected that Harris Fourcade was the Ripper. Not because all the evidence unmistakably pointed in that direction. On the contrary, if they didn't come up with something solid linking Fourcade to at least one of the victims, the case would likely be tossed out of court. Yet there was something in the hard edge that Fourcade was now revealing that caused Max to believe that this man could very easily rape and then mutilate his victims; that something was in his expression of callous arrogance.

Fourcade said, "Don't you have to advise me of my rights?" He shot Max a self-satisfied grin.

"Is that what you want?"

There was something in Fourcade's smile, the hint of curled lip under the bushy moustache, that unsettled Max. He focused on the sneer, listening to Fourcade's words. His mind quickly flashed on the fact that in each assault the assailant had not only been masked, but had not spoken a word to his victim. He and Draper had been right: the Ripper had needed more than merely a visual disguise.

Still, was it enough to convict him?

"Never mind," said Fourcade. "That won't be necessary. I know my rights, and I'm not about to say anything to you. In fact, since it seems like you're going to continue holding me here, I want to see my lawyer now, before anything else happens."

Max closed the folder and pushed back his chair. He was at the door, readying to leave, when he said, "You'll get your phone call. Give me the attorney's number, and I'll place the call."

Fourcade's expression took on an intense sparkle, like an idea had exploded in his head and was flashing its bright light through his eyes. He still had that grin, only this time Max had the feeling that Fourcade was not just pleased with himself, but was laughing specifically at him.

"David Gentry," said Fourcade, his face illuminated

with anticipation. "I want to call David Gentry. He's my attorney."

Max thought he heard his heart as it plunked into his stomach.

He didn't need to look up David Gentry's phone number. He knew it by heart.

14

It was strange, he thought, the way things sometimes worked out. Of all the cases he expected not to get, the Ripper trial would have headed the list. Still, here he was, waiting for the jailers to bring down Harris Fourcade, a man whom he didn't know, but who evidently knew him. A man whom Max Becker had said was to be charged with the rapes and mutilations of three women.

David Gentry found himself wondering, since leaving his post at the DA's office, what the sheriff's deputies who manned the attorney conference room of the jail thought of him. He wasn't sure how many of them actually knew who he was, what he had been. Some of the old-timers would have to be aware that he had spent a long and illustrious career prosecuting cases.

He figured that most of the veterans would take his change of allegiance in stride. After all, it wasn't the first time a prosecutor had switched sides. Some of the best criminal defense lawyers in town had received their instruction while working their way through the DA's office.

Gentry wondered if the slightly uncomfortable sensation he was feeling was more the product of his own mind than the ill-will of those in law enforcement whose paths he had crossed since becoming a defense attorney—residue of the nagging doubts about the morality of what he was now doing, and the decisions he had made while on the other side of the counsel table.

It made him think about lighting another candle.

The dream had taken up permanent residence in his mind, and was now playing itself out. Gentry saw himself inside the cell, staring at those few faces that he could still recall. As always, in the dream he was rendering his explanation, justifying his actions to those men with whom he shared the cell. The men were never physically threatening. There had been times when he was jolted awake in a cold sweat, that he would have preferred the physical threat to the emotional pressure, the guilt.

I was just doing my job.

In his mind's eye he could hear himself utter those words.

The system put you here, not me. You must understand that.

He was still trying to get through to the stone faces of his cellmates when he heard his name called.

"Mr. Gentry, are you okay?"

Gentry looked up. Standing opposite him was a slender man Gentry guessed to be in his late twenties, dressed in a San Diego County Jail jumpsuit.

"Uh, yes," said Gentry, clearing his throat, pulling himself back to reality. "Sorry."

He motioned with his hand for the young man to take a seat. It disturbed Gentry that he hadn't been able to put aside his dream even for the short time that it took the sheriffs to bring Harris Fourcade down from his cell.

"That's okay, Mr. Gentry. If there's anyone who can understand being a little groggy from loss of sleep, it's me." Fourcade smiled and kept the smile on his face until he saw Gentry relax.

"I tell ya," said Fourcade, "between the noise, and the smells, and the other inmates hassling you all the time, I figure I'll be lucky to get a couple hours a night in here." He shook his head. "I'm not used to that. I usually get my seven or eight. If I don't, I start to get a little spacy. You know what I mean?"

Gentry smiled, then nodded. It struck him that Fourcade had easily jumped into their conversation without even introducing himself, as if the two of them had known each other for years and were merely going over old times, instead of discussing an upcoming death penalty trial.

He was intrigued by the way Fourcade's upper lip seemed to curl up into his bushy moustache. He had seen people with cleft palates before. However, he wasn't sure if that was Fourcade's condition, since most of the lip was covered with hair. There was a hissing noise at the end of certain syllables when Fourcade spoke. Gentry concluded that the young man had adapted to his physical condition as best as he could, and that the susurrous hiss was something Fourcade had learned to live with. In any event, he didn't seem self-conscious about it, and Gentry admired him for that.

"I have a few things on my mind," said Gentry. "Other cases."

Fourcade just nodded.

Gentry figured he had bought the lie. Both men were silent for a moment.

Fourcade wasn't what David Gentry had expected. Slender, well-groomed, not exceedingly big or overpowering, he had anticipated something more, some sort of demon or monster. A guy you could pick out of the crowd.

"I've read some of the reports," said Gentry, tapping his pen on a legal folder that lay on the desk between them. "There's more, according to the prosecutor. They're putting together a complete package for me. I should have most of what the cops have by tomorrow."

"How does it look?"

Gentry paused before answering. This process of engendering confidence in clients was still new to him. If he was still a DA, he'd just tell Fourcade that they were going to slam his ass, go for the max.

Every time he spoke to a client now, though, he had to fight that prosecutor mentality that automatically came to the fore. He'd seen defense lawyers talking to their clients during his years as a prosecutor, and he knew that an important part of the game was developing a good attorney-client relationship.

Cons almost always lied, even to their lawyers, but if they thought their lawyer was doing all that was possible for them, they were a lot easier to deal with.

Gentry didn't want to build up Fourcade's hopes. But neither did he want to sound so pessimistic that Fourcade would think he was being dumped by a shyster who was just out for the fee.

"They've got your prints inside the houses," said Gentry. "They've got two victims identifying you as servicing their televisions during the week prior to the attacks."

Gentry paused, reaching for a sheet of paper buried underneath the police reports. "And," he said, showing Fourcade the lab report, "they've got this hair that they found in a nylon stocking. The stocking was removed from the inside of your closet."

Fourcade looked carefully at the one-page form

from the lab.

"All in all," said Gentry, "they really don't have much."

He was beginning to get excited about the case. Max had called him from the station, telling him of Fourcade's request. Max had sounded depressed, but had tried to hide it with jokes about the two of them going head-to-head on the Ripper trial. Beneath Max's light-hearted banter, Gentry had sensed his friend's uneasiness with the situation.

"So you can get me outta this place, right?"

Gentry let out a nervous laugh. "Not so fast," he said, holding up a restraining hand. "They're still working on connecting this hair to you and to the victims. They've filed three counts of forcible rape, mayhem, attempted murder, and burglary."

"Burglary?"

"Yes. When you enter a dwelling with the intent to commit a rape or other serious felony, it's burglary. You don't have to steal anything."

Fourcade nodded, silently digesting Gentry's legal explanations.

"Now, some of these crimes overlap. While they could convict you of all counts, they could not sentence you on each and every count." Gentry caught himself and added, "Of course, that's assuming they can make any of this stick against you. The way it looks now, I don't see how they can get past the preliminary hearing."

"When's that?"

"Ten court days after the arraignment," said Gentry. "Unless we agree to a continuance. Waive time, I mean."

"I'm not waiving anything," said Fourcade.

"I agree. Time is on our side right now. If they get to the prelim with little more than what they have now,

222

you stand a good chance of having all the charges dismissed."

Gentry hesitated, knowing that he needed to talk with his client about finances, and that this was as good a time as any. The girl, Fourcade's girlfriend, he assumed, had come to him with a cash retainer. But Gentry needed to get the issue of attorney's fees out of the way with his client before they started to talk trial strategy.

"Your girlfriend," he said, starting out a little wobbly, "has given me five thousand dollars." Gentry stopped, the words stuck in his throat. As a DA he was not used to receiving such large chunks of cash, though he had often heard stories of enormous fees being paid to some of the more high-profile defense attorneys. Quoting fees was difficult. Gentry was unsure how much he should charge Fourcade for his services, or whether he should demand the entire fee up front. If he went to trial without getting paid in full, on the promise that the money would be forthcoming, there was no chance in hell, should he lose at trial, that Fourcade would send him the rest of his fee from the state prison.

Gentry said, "The fee for the preliminary hearing will be ten thousand."

There, he thought, it's out. If Fourcade balks, I'm not going to back down.

It was less than he'd heard a lot of defense attorneys charged. And this was the high-publicity case of the year.

"No problem," said Fourcade. "I'll have Carla get it to you within the next couple of days."

Gentry was gaining confidence. He wanted to get past this money business and on to the discussion of Fourcade's defense.

"That'll take you through the preliminary hearing," Gentry said. "If the case is dismissed at the prelim, then you won't owe me anything more. If we go to trial in Superior Court, though, I'll need an additional thirty thousand before the arraignment."

"No problem," said Fourcade, more eagerly than Gentry had suspected. "I've got the money, Mr. Gentry. I want the best, and you're it. If that's what it takes to hire the best, then so be it. Don't worry. You just let me know when you need the cash, and I'll see that you get it."

That had gone easier than expected, Gentry thought. It was the first time he'd had to quote such a large fee, the first time he'd been retained on a serious case. He was certainly starting out big, having his first big client accused of being the Ripper. He had to wonder, though, looking at the young man seated opposite him, whether Max Becker had moved a bit too soon on this one. Harris Fourcade certainly had the opportunity to attack these three women, but where was the hard evidence putting him at the scene of the crimes? The hair in the stocking could be easily explained. As far as Gentry could determine, Max would need to find some trace of Fourcade that he could link with one of the actual assaults, and not merely to Fourcade's being present in the victims' homes.

"I assume," said Gentry, "that your girlfriend, Carla, will be willing to testify for you, if it comes to that?"

"Uh . . ." For the first time, Gentry saw a slight degree of uncertainty in Fourcade's expression. It disappeared quickly.

"Sure," he said. "Carla lived with me. Those nylons are hers." He gestured with both arms outstretched. "Hell, there's a million ways my hair could have gotten into those stockings." He laughed slyly, as if embarrassed. "I mean, we slept together, Mr. Gentry. I'm a little embarrassed by this, but I used to like to undress her, before we had sex, I mean." Fourcade waited for

224

Gentry to nod, then went on.

"Carla liked when I kissed her, all over, if you know what I mean." He paused, then continued. "I'd run my lips down her leg as I pulled off her stockings. She got a charge out of that, and, I have to admit, so did I."

Gentry smiled, more to make Fourcade feel at ease than anything else. It was the type of explanation that he had expected Fourcade would offer. Though embarrassing, it had the ring of truth. As long as Fourcade's girlfriend backed him up, there'd be no way Max would be able to disprove it.

Unless Max and his army of lab technicians came up with one of Fourcade's hairs in the vaginal specimens taken from the rape victims, Harris Fourcade's little sexual foreplay story would run very nicely in front of a jury.

Gentry was already thinking of other explanations. Fourcade's servicing each victim's TV was easy to explain. The Ripper had narrowed his list of victims down to a well-defined geographical area. All the victims lived in the same two general areas. All-Valley Cable Company just happened to service both areas under their state license. Was Harris Fourcade to be convicted of rape and assault merely because he'd had the misfortune of being assigned to service the accounts within his employer's jurisdiction?

That was a jump that Gentry figured no jury would be willing to make without some further evidence linking Fourcade to the actual attacks.

"I'll talk to Carla," he said. "The police have already taken her statement."

"I know," said Fourcade. "She told me when I called her."

Gentry's prosecutor mentality immediately kicked in. He wondered just what Fourcade and his girlfriend had talked about, besides finding the money to hire a lawyer.

Gentry fought off his suspicions, pushing them aside for the moment. Why should he doubt Fourcade's word? Here was a young man with little or no prior contact with the law. Someone with an obvious physical disability, who had apparently overcome that disability. He was gainfully employed, minding his own business, when out of nowhere he's accused of being the heinous Ripper, based on very scanty evidence at best.

"Can I ask you how you found me?" said Gentry.

Fourcade looked briefly confused, then said, "I saw the article about you in the magazine. You know, 'The DA of Death.' I figured, *there's* a guy who knows his way around the system. If I ever get in trouble, I thought, he's the one I want on my side." Fourcade smiled.

Gentry felt somewhat embarrassed.

"Besides, I kept hearing your name mentioned on the TV everytime there was some serious case. By the time I saw the magazine article, I pretty much knew who you were. You have one hell of a reputation around here, I can tell you that. All I had to do was mention to that guy, Becker, that I wanted you on the case, and he looked like he'd seen a ghost."

Fourcade chuckled.

"And the cops in here all seem to know who you are. It gives me a sort of respect that the other inmates don't get.

"And there's something else," said Fourcade, his tone becoming more somber. "I didn't have a mom or dad around much when I was growing up. I read in the article about your wife, the way she passed away and all. Well, what you said about getting on with your life and taking care of your family kind of stuck in my

226

mind. I hope you don't mind me talking about this, but it was just something I thought about."

Gentry forced a smile, telling Fourcade that it was okay. He was slightly surprised that the magazine article had had such an effect on the young man. There had been only a few sentences dealing with Jackie's death. The writer had insisted on mentioning something about it. Gentry had made a point of answering most of the personal questions as tersely as possible. In the end, they'd agreed to the short reference about Jackie and Susan. He'd seen no harm in it since his fellow employees in the DA's office were already aware of his history, as were most of the other people he worked with.

What surprised Gentry more were the conclusions that Harris Fourcade had drawn after reading the magazine piece. A lot of cons figured: once a prosecutor, always a prosecutor; the DA was the enemy, the bad guy, trying to lock them up. They weren't aware that many ex-DA's were now plying their trade on the defense side, and that for many lawyers involved in the system, the decision of whether to become a prosecutor or defense attorney was often determined by which side had a job opening at a given time. A large number of lawyers coming straight out of law school applied to both offices, and took the job that was offered to them first.

Harris Fourcade, in his own way, seemed to understand this. He seemed smarter than most cons, Gentry thought. Any good criminal lawyer would tell you that in order to be successful in trial, you had to be able to think like the other side, to anticipate the other guy's moves before he made them. Thirty years as a DA had taught Gentry most of the tricks, and given him the ability to spot and take advantage of his opponent's weaknesses. Switching to the defense side, he'd told himself, was just a variation on the academic exercise of practicing law. He kept reminding himself that there was no moral issue involved in representing criminal defendants, that every person accused of a crime was entitled to their constitutional right to counsel.

"Mr. Gentry," Fourcade said slowly, his mood still serious. "I know you've been involved in a lot of serious cases, and that you've probably talked to a bunch of guys in jail like me. I hear the stories from the other inmates about how they tell their lawyers that they're innocent because they think that way the lawyer will work harder for them."

"I'll tell you right now, Mr. Gentry, I'm not lying to you. I wouldn't do that. I have no idea why I'm here, and I had nothing to do with those women. I've saved enough money over the years to pay your fees, Mr. Gentry, but I have to admit that once this is done, it'll be like starting all over again for me. I'll be financially drained.

"Not that I'm begrudging you your money," said Fourcade. "You're the best, and the best don't come cheap. I just want you to know, to believe, that I had nothing to do with those women." He paused; his voice had cracked on the last two words.

Gentry noticed Fourcade's eyes becoming glassy. The image of Harris Fourcade, pawing at his eyes, wiping away his tears, stuck in Gentry's mind. It was an image he'd seen before, not in real life, but in his dream. It was the face, one of the faces, he saw in the cell. That questioning look, the expression that asked: *Why?*

"I'll do my best," said Gentry, meaning every word.

Fourcade was pleased with the way it had gone. It was all he could do not to clap his hands together and yell. All his years of careful collecting, of concentration and focus, were about to pay off. Even he was surprised at how well things were working out.

He followed the red line painted on the floor, careful to hug the wall as he was expected to do. He kept his distance from the other inmates, the blacks offering their jive-talking threats, the Mexicans their menacing scowls. He made his eyes look straight ahead and kept to himself.

If the lawyer knew what he was talking about—and he certainly did, that was the beauty of it—he'd be out of this place and back on the streets in about two weeks. He could do two weeks in here by being careful and watching himself—keeping an eye on the animals.

The bit about the lawyer's wife kept repeating itself in his mind. That had been a stroke of genius, he thought. He hadn't been sure how Gentry would take it, but one look at the lawyer's face told him that he'd hit the jackpot. A dead-center bulls-eye. Gentry had gone all soft and watery over it. The lawyer had really liked him for that.

The rest was all flattery and stroking . . . and money. The thought of losing forty grand upset him for a split-second, until he realized that it wouldn't be forty grand. He'd be out the ten for the prelim, but that was a small price to pay for putting the lawyer in his plan, right where he wanted him.

Who the hell was that?

Fourcade had been thinking about the lawyer, not paying much attention to the other side of the custody corridor. Just a couple of beefy deputies dragging an injured inmate between them. This one looked really fucked-up, like somebody had taken batting practice on his head.

But that face looks familiar . . .

He stopped for a moment, watching the sheriffs pulling the inmate's limp body toward the infirmary.

There was a trail of blood from where they had dragged him down the hallway. It made the red line on the floor look wavy in spots.

Fourcade continued to watch as the deputies jerked the lifeless body down the corridor. He could no longer see the face, though the memory of what he had quickly glimpsed remained in his mind. The face was definitely familiar, but the recollection was buried so deep that unless he saw it again, he knew there was no way he'd remember.

"What the fuck do you think *you're* doing?"

Fourcade turned to see another deputy with his hands on his hips, standing no more than six inches away. The deputy was giving Fourcade his serious look, like he was pissed and about to beat on some prisoner's head, and Fourcade was the closest one around. Fourcade's first thought was that they were serving Mexican food for dinner—he could smell it on the deputy's breath.

He blurted out, "Nothing, sir," then skirted around the deputy and quickly made his way along the painted red line and back to his cell.

Billy Darling's first knowledge that they were there, inside his cell, was when he looked up from his sleep and saw the two sets of eyes staring down at him. He blinked, thinking that he was still dreaming. He still wasn't afraid. His mind had yet to register the significance of the two faces so close to his.

"Ooo-wee, that's one fine piece of ass!"

Billy felt a hand pressed firmly on his crotch. He knew if he moved it would hurt.

A voice said, "You wanna be nice and let me go first? Or do I have to fuck you up?"

Billy could see the one that asked the question had a

large scar over his right eye. He was smiling and talking to the other one. They looked alike to Billy, two huge black faces, gold and white teeth glittering as they smiled at one another, arguing over who was going to be first.

Finally, the one with the scar shoved the other man out of the way, then turned toward Billy.

"Yes siree," he purred, slipping his hands inside Billy's pants and fondling his genitals. "We gonna have fun, now, aren't we, white boy?"

Billy could see the other man smiling and watching, as he leaned against the wall in the corner.

"Come on, sweet meat," said the first one, grabbing a handful of Billy's shirt in his fist and lifting him off the bunk. Billy felt himself suspended in air for a moment, then he fell, thudding to the concrete floor. When he rolled over, he saw that the first one already had his pants down around his knees, and was fondling his penis.

"Don't hurt him too bad," said the one against the wall. "Save some for me."

The first one just laughed.

"You can't do this," Billy said, hearing the weakness in his voice. He looked through the bars of the cell, expecting to see a deputy, but there was none. He yelled for help.

"That's not nice," said the first one, smashing his fist into Billy's mouth. Billy felt a tooth at the back of his tongue, caught in his throat. He tried to cough, but the tooth wouldn't come out. He swallowed hard, and could no longer feel the tooth.

"What you think, sweet meat? You think the Man don't know we in here? You think the Man's gonna come in here and save your little white ass?"

Both black men started laughing. Laughing loud enough for Billy to be convinced that what the first one said was true. Nobody was going to intercede. The deputies knew what was going on and intended to do nothing about it.

It hadn't yet struck him that the deputies were the ones who had set this whole thing up.

The first one thrust himself at Billy, holding his penis in one hand and resting the other hand on the back of Billy's head.

"Just take that big thing in your mouth, white boy. That's it, nice and easy. Ooo-wee, that do feel good!"

Billy did as he was told. The first one worked his hips back and forth. Billy rolled his eyes, catching a glimpse of the fat man's belly. Billy was choking. The force on the back of his throat made him want to vomit. He saw the inmate's head thrown back, breathing heavily. Billy prayed it would soon end. The first inmate placed his hands on either side of Billy's head, directing the action. Then the inmate groaned, and Billy felt his mouth fill with sticky liquid.

Billy fought off the impulse to choke, as he swallowed some of the first one's semen. He didn't have time to think about what to do next, since the other inmate was quickly on top of him.

"Suck me off, white boy."

The second one had replaced the first. He straddled Billy, shoving his erect penis into Billy's mouth. The second one worked back and forth, but before he came, he removed his penis.

"We gonna try something a little different," he said, turning Billy around and pushing him to the ground. Billy felt the inmate's rough hands pulling his pants down. He heard a spitting sound, then felt a wet finger in his anus. Within seconds, Billy knew that the second inmate was inside him. He winced at the sharp, painful jab of the second one's penis, ripping its way in and out, as the hand from behind continued to hold him down.

After a few moments, Billy heard the second one groan, and felt something warm and syrupy running down his leg. Billy assumed that it was over, that the two had got what they had come for.

But he was wrong.

"Now we gonna leave a little message," said the first one.

The first one came closer. Billy was on all fours on the ground. He saw the man's leg swing back, and before he could dodge the blow, he felt the thud of the shoe as it crashed into his nose. Then another blow, but this time from the second inmate, and harder.

Billy felt a sharp jolt, like a bone being driven into his brain. With the first kick, blood sprayed out from his nose. There was blood in his eyes and on the floor and walls of the small cell.

Billy lay on his back, arms outstretched at his sides. He could see both men standing over him. The second one still had his pants down. His penis dripped semen as he massaged himself.

Billy's head felt like a lead weight, too heavy to lift. The inside of the cell was spinning, rendering unclear the ghostlike images of the two men and everything else inside.

Billy closed his eyes, trying to get away. It didn't work. He both heard and felt the first kick to his ribs. There was a crisp cracking sound before the pain. Taking a breath, it seemed like somebody had ripped a hole in his lungs. The hurt was so intense, he tried not to inhale again, which only made the next breath worse.

"You fucked with the wrong guy," the second inmate said. "The Man don't like what you did to the dude."

Billy was trying to make sense of what was being said. He thought he had made the connection—the fat rich guy in the hotel—when he felt the second kick in exactly the same place. An intense fire burned inside his chest. An explosion.

He could feel himself going under and was grateful for it. By the time the third kick was delivered, he was already unconscious.

The next thing Billy recalled seeing was the red line painted on the jail floor and his own legs dragging behind him. He thought that he must be in a dream, since everything seemed hazy, and he was flying— floating down the painted red line without having to take a step.

15

"Will the boy testify?"

"I think I can talk his mother into it. It depends."

"On what?"

"She's worried about his safety. It's only natural."

Max considered Draper's point, then said, "Tell her we'll make sure there are no problems of that sort."

He paused, noting her questioning look.

They were having coffee in the courthouse cafeteria. There was an elevated area in the back, somewhat secluded from the rest of the cafeteria, which was reserved for nonsmokers. It was where Max usually took his coffee when he had a court appearance downtown.

"She mention the Carbon brothers?"

Draper shook her head, then brought the cup of coffee to her lips, blowing on the rim, trying to avoid his eyes.

Max's thoughts wandered to his last big case. He'd been on the other side of the counsel table, at least in the beginning. Once again he told himself that the decision to testify against Hector and Gonzalo Carbon had been left up to his client. It wasn't anybody's fault.

But he couldn't escape the blame for Jaime

Esquivel's death, no matter what mental games he played with himself. He'd advised Esquivel to seriously consider taking the deal, to testify against the Carbons.

Esquivel had had no real choice. Max had known that. He'd also known that Esquivel, once he snitched on the Carbons, would be dead meat on the streets.

What he hadn't known, what he naively hadn't even considered, was the length of the Carbon arm of retribution. It had never crossed Max's mind that they'd go after *him*.

Prosecutors and defense lawyers mixed it up on serious cases with hard-ass defendants on a daily basis, and rarely became the object of attack by those defendants. The sleazoids normally went after each other, "street justice," they called it. Snitch and you were fair game. The rule was, keep your mouth shut, do your time, and get even when you got out.

He didn't blame Leslie Greer for questioning the safety of her son. The Carbons had managed to exact their revenge, even from behind bars. It had cost him dearly. It had cost him everything.

At the time, David Gentry and the others had vowed to get to the bottom of the kidnapping, to punish those responsible. And Max had watched, paralyzed by grief, as the days turned into weeks, then months, without a resolution.

In the end, nobody was brought to trial. They never caught the ones who did it.

Max could remember very clearly that autumn day almost ten years ago when David Gentry took him to Presidio Park, overlooking Old Town. They sat on a bench surveying the rolling grassy hillside scattered with picnickers.

"They're putting the case on the back burner," Gentry had said. The pain of relaying the message had been obvious in his expression.

"We can't tie either of the Carbons to the kidnapping. Nobody's willing to come forward and testify."

Max had felt little animosity toward those who had made the decision. By that time, he'd realized that killing the Carbon Brothers would not bring his family back. The revenge factor had receded into the background; the flames had become burning embers in the recesses of his mind.

"Ya know, Max," Gentry had said, trying to console him. "This could be a fluke. Maybe it was some crazy that was responsible for this, someone totally unrelated to the trial and the Carbons. It happens all the time. Have you ever thought of that?"

Max had thought of it a good deal. He wanted to believe that Rosalie's and Ryan's deaths had nothing to do with him, with his work. With the decision he'd made to have Jaime Esquivel testify. With his lack of foresight, his failure to protect his wife and young son, who had the right to rely upon his protection in such matters.

But it was too much to swallow.

Jackie Gentry's death shortly after the trial was explainable: an auto accident. They'd reconstructed the accident and determined she'd run off the road, plain and simple. No personal blame.

But the bodies in the orange grove were different.

They were *his* fault.

Also plain and simple.

The more he thought about it, the more Max understood Leslie Greer's concern. In the end, there was no way that he could absolutely guarantee Daniel Greer's safety.

At some point the Ripper case would become ancient history. Once Harris Fourcade was in prison, everyone's memory would dim. The newspapers would be filled with the grisly details of more current atrocities perpetrated against the citizens of San Diego.

A jury might not give Fourcade the death sentence. Maybe something less. If he was a good boy in the joint, did what he was supposed to do, and stayed out of trouble, he could look forward to being released after serving only half his sentence. If he wasn't stupid enough to threaten people from behind bars, there was no way to stop him, once he was released, from taking his revenge against those who had put him away.

"It's a longshot anyway," said Draper. "The kid picked out Fourcade's picture, and I think he's pretty sure that Fourcade was the one inside the house the night his mother was attacked. But I have to tell you, he's young. And he's scared."

"Will he qualify in court?"

"Probably. I mean, he knows the difference between right and wrong. He'll answer all the questions the right way. I don't think that's going to be the problem."

"Then what?"

"He's a little kid. You know how that goes."

Max nodded, running a fingertip around the rim of his coffee. He did know how difficult it was to use a young child as a key witness. They were often easily confused as to times and dates. Frequently, unless very well coached, child witnesses would simply agree with whichever side asked them the last question.

While defense lawyers couldn't get away with badgering children, it was easy to lead a child into giving a desired answer simply by convincing them that that was what was expected.

"We'd better get back to the office," he said, checking his watch. "You told them ten sharp, right?"

Draper nodded, slurping the rest of her coffee. They traveled together back to the station.

Leslie Greer and her son were already there, waiting.

Someone had seated them in the anteroom just outside Draper's office.

Leslie Greer looked nervous, sitting ramrod straight in the wooden chair, knees pressed together, mechanically sipping on a cup of coffee. Her son, Daniel, was seated next to her, shoulders slouched, blowing into the top of an empty Pepsi bottle.

Max greeted mother and son and escorted them into Draper's office. He motioned for them to have a seat on the worn vinyl sofa, while he sat on the edge of the desk, trying to look relaxed. Draper sat in her chair behind him.

"First let me assure you, Mrs. Greer, that you and Danny have nothing to worry about. This sort of thing happens every day in our courts. Believe me, you have the power of the entire police community behind you on this."

Leslie Greer nodded, trying to smile. It came out more like a quick twitch, then a shrug. She looked more frightened than her son, and Max thought, with good reason. One victim in the family was one too many.

"Now, Danny," said Max, warming to the task. He couldn't help but think that Ryan had been only a couple of years older when . . .

"I need to ask you some questions, questions that you've probably heard before. I want you to think real hard before you answer them. Do you think you can do that?"

The young boy nodded.

"Good. First, you remember when Ms. Draper showed you those pictures?"

Another nod.

"Well, Ms. Draper said that you thought one of the men in the pictures looked like someone you knew, someone you might have seen before. Is that right?"

A look at his mother, then another nod.

"A man you saw the night your mommy was hurt?"

Nod.

"Danny, I'm going to show you those pictures again. I want you to point that man out to me, the one you saw that night. Now, this is just between us here in this room. A game to see just how smart you are. You play games in school, don't you?"

"Sometimes."

"Good. Well, this is like those games. Just like your teacher asks you questions when she plays games with you in school, I need to ask you questions about this man."

Max reached behind him for the photo sixpack.

"Do you remember this, Danny?"

A nod, as he took the photo lineup card, laying it on his lap.

"That's the same one Ms. Draper showed you. Can you show me the man you picked out for her?"

Daniel Greer pointed directly at the picture of Harris Fourcade, then looked up.

"Excellent," said Max. "I can see you're really good at this game."

The young boy smiled.

Leslie Greer looked even more nervous than when she'd entered as if she saw her son sinking deeper into the system, getting increasingly more involved, and was worried whether it was the right thing to do.

"Now, the next part of this game, Danny, is for you to tell me what you saw this man do. Do you think you're smart enough to do that?"

"Sure I am."

"Good. Okay, you get this part right, and believe me, I think you'll be the smartest boy that I've ever had playing the game."

"I saw him at the door," the boy said. "Just standing

240

there. Like a shadow. A ghost, ya know?"

Max heard Draper clear her throat. He tried not to wince, not to let the boy know how he felt about that last answer.

"Good, Danny. Now, he must have been more than a ghost. I mean, you saw his face, right?"

Nod.

"And you picked his picture out. And this man here, the one in the picture, he doesn't look like a ghost to me."

The boy seemed confused now. Max realized he was losing him.

"I guess what you meant when you said he was a ghost is that he was hard to see, because of the shadow, right?"

Anxious nod of the head.

"And that you saw his face, but not for a long time. Only long enough to know that he was there and to know that this one here, the man in the picture, is the same person?"

"I guess."

Max was beginning to lose hope. Danny Greer was the typical six-year-old, very suggestible, and very frightened of the unknown. No judge, no matter how sympathetic, would tolerate the type of leading questions he was asking now. In court, Danny would be on his own, putty in the hands of an experienced defense lawyer.

"Okay, Danny, you know the difference between right and wrong, don't you?"

Nod.

"And between telling the truth, and telling a lie?"

Nod. His eyes wandered off to the posters on the office wall.

"Now, when you tell a lie, you get in trouble, don't you?"

241

"Yes."

"And your mommy's taught you that it's always better to tell the truth, right?"

"Yes."

"And when you go to court, or when you talk to someone like me, you know that you're supposed to tell the truth, don't you, Danny?"

"Yes."

"Because you would get in trouble if you didn't, right?"

A nod, the look more worried now.

"Now, Danny, this next question is very important. The most important question of the game. Win this one, and you win the whole game. Champion."

A quick smile, eyes back.

"When you picked out this man's picture, the one that was in your house when your mom was hurt . . . you were telling the truth then, weren't you?"

The young boy paused, thinking.

"He's the one I saw," he said. "That one there."

"And you're really sure about that, right?"

Nod.

Max thanked Leslie Greer and her son, and had one of the patrol officers show them to their car. When he returned to the office, Phil Draper had her feet on the desk, her head resting against the back of the chair, and was staring at the ceiling.

"Well, Sherlock, whatdya think?"

Draper didn't answer. She didn't move. After a few seconds, she said, "Gentry will make mincement out of that kid. Hell, a first-year law student could demolish him in less than five minutes on the stand."

The idea of going up against his friend David Gentry had swirled unpleasantly in the back of Max's mind for some time now. Fourcade's choice of counsel had been a shock, though Max had attempted to hide his anxiety. He still continued to wonder how Harris Fourcade had chosen Gentry.

Max knew that friend or no, David Gentry was a professional, and that he'd handle the case like a pro. Which meant that he'd do whatever he had to to defend his client, including cross-examining young Daniel Greer until the boy didn't know his left from his right, up from down. Draper was right, it would be a cakewalk.

He and Gentry had had a few friendly conversations about the case since Fourcade's arrest. But recently Max had gotten the impression that Gentry was actually convinced of his client's innocence. Max wanted to take Gentry aside, remove him from their adversarial courtroom relationship and talk to him friend-to-friend.

Max wanted to convince Gentry that his client was guilty, that despite the weakness of the circumstantial case against him, he was convinced that Fourcade was the Ripper. He wanted to tell Gentry that now, with the evidence of Danny Greer's identification, the case against Harris Fourcade was more than just a few weak links in a chain of circumstantial evidence.

But he didn't.

Max had gone through the motions of complying with discovery, turning over to the defense all the pertinent information about the case. If he had decided to use the identification testimony of Danny Greer at the preliminary hearing, he would have been legally compelled to prepare a report dealing with the young boy's identification, and to have supplied David Gentry with that report, along with a copy of the photo lineup card that was used in the identification. It would probably have necessitated a short continuance of the preliminary hearing in order to allow Gentry to review the newly discovered evidence. The time might possibly have helped the prosecution bolster its case against Fourcade, but in all likelihood, Max concluded, a delay caused by such a disclosure would have done more harm than good. It would have allowed the defense a shot at discrediting the prosecution's eyewitness prior to trial.

"It's very weak without the kid's ID."

"It's weak even with the ID," said Draper. "But it's your call, Max."

"What if we hold the kid back, don't have him testify at the prelim. We get the case in front of a favorable judge, one that's not going to want to dismiss one of the biggest criminal cases of the year. Put on the victims, the cable company evidence, the nylon stocking. Have Forensics testify to the blood-type connection. We work on the kid between now and the trial, have someone out there, someone he learns to trust, coaching the kid. Coach him until he's able to withstand Gentry's cross-examination."

Draper said, "That's a lot of ifs. Another one is what if you're wrong, and the judge finds that there's insufficient evidence at the prelim and boots the case? Or better yet, Gentry gets wind of this whole thing and starts bitching about us witholding evidence under the discovery order?"

Draper was right. They couldn't hold back the information about Danny Greer's ID much longer. Gentry and Fourcade had a right to that information, and withholding it could lead to a dismissal.

Max made his decision.

"I say we go with what we've got, leave the kid out of it for now."

Draper smiled. "So, Coach, who you got in mind to hear the prelim?"

*   *   *

They were able to wrangle the prelim in front of Jeanette Oldfield, an ex-city attorney. Oldfield was due for reelection within the year, and was not likely to go out on any political limbs. Besides, Oldfield had a reputation as a law-and-order judge, a second prosecutor in the courtroom.

As expected, Judge Oldfield held Harris Fourcade to answer on all charges, without the benefit of Danny Greer's testimony.

Max and Draper found themselves, four weeks after the prelim and two weeks after Fourcade's arraignment in Superior Court, waiting for David Gentry to arrive to argue his 995 motion to dismiss the charges.

Max's first surprise of the morning was discovering that the regular judge, Lenore Phillips, had called in sick. The clerk informed him that they were in the process of trying to find a temporary bench officer for the day.

Max and Draper had taken seats in the front row of the courtroom in the audience section. The DA regularly assigned to the court was busy reviewing a stack of case files at the counsel table. Two public defenders were whisking themselves in and out of the custody lockup, interviewing clients. The bailiff sat at a desk just inside the wooden gate that divided the court staff from the audience. He was talking on the phone and using a yellow fluorescent marker to highlight various names on a computer printout of defendants in custody.

When David Gentry entered, he said a formal good morning to Max, conversed briefly with the clerk, then headed for the lockup.

Max's second surprise of the morning came when he saw the flabby red face of Judge Augustus McDermott in the doorway that led from the judge's chambers into the courtroom.

On seeing the judge, the clerk hefted a stack of court files, one of which was the Fourcade case, and handed them to McDermott. The doddering old man then disappeared into chambers.

Draper said, "Is that who I think it is?"

Max nodded.

"Shit!"

"Don't worry," said Max, though he was less than confident himself. "I'm sure McDermott has got more important things on his mind these days. There's no way he's going to want to draw any more attention to himself than he has to. The press and the Judicial Council are watching his every move. The last thing that old codger would want is to throw himself into the spotlight by dismissing the most important case of the year."

Draper considered what Max said, then nodded in agreement.

"Besides," said Max, "I'm sure McDermott wants to make short shrift of this calendar. They probably dragged him from his normal court, and I'll bet he's not overly happy about that. He likes to hit his regular watering holes at lunch, tank up for the afternoon."

Draper looked at her watch. "We're going to have some time," she said, getting up. "I'm going to make a call. You need anything?"

Max said no. He watched as she skirted her way down the aisle. Phyllis Draper was dressed for business today, wearing heels, instead of her usual flat-soled shoes. It made her appear even taller. The Pendleton shirt had been replaced by a conservative white silk blouse worn under a light-colored tweed blazer, and a rather too tight-fitting linen skirt. Max had seen her so often in her outdoorswoman attire that meeting her in court this morning he'd almost not recognized her. It took him a while to get used to the new image.

A few minutes after Draper left, David Gentry emerged from the custody lockup, paused a moment to converse with the clerk, then approached Max.

"I don't know whether I should be pleased or pissed off," said Gentry. He stood on the other side of the railing.

"McDermott's crazy enough to do anything," said Max. "Though I doubt, with what he's got going on, that he'll want to take any chances on this one."

"Chances, my ass," said Gentry. "Hell, Max, we both know that this case should have been kicked at the prelim. You may have something up your sleeve that you're saving for trial, but if McDermott follows the law, this 995 should be granted."

Max gave Gentry a sly smile. He knew his friend was probably right.

"David," he said, "I wouldn't want to deprive you of such a big fee by allowing this case to be dismissed before it even gets started."

"Yeah, right," muttered Gentry, returning Max's smile with one of his own. He had received the second five thousand dollars, just as Fourcade had promised. Fourcade had been upset at the preliminary hearing when the judge had refused to dismiss the case. Gentry was feeling a little self-conscious about that, feeling that he had perhaps built up his client's expectations.

"I gather," said Gentry, "that they're shifting McDermott around, figuring that if they keep him moving, he won't be in any one court long enough to do any real harm."

"He's probably not long for the judicial world," said Max. "The council should be about ready to render their decision. Word is that they're going to remove him from the bench any day now. Everybody pretty much figured that from the beginning. The guy's pissed off too many people. McDermott's probably the only one that's still holding out any hope."

Max had just finished speaking when Augustus McDermott came back inside the courtroom, holding the stack of files. He plopped the files on the clerk's desk and announced that he was ready on all cases. He directed the clerk to get the lawyers organized for calendar call.

Max swallowed hard, wondering if he was right about McDermott. He looked okay this morning, though Max knew that he kept a flask in his jacket pocket, and took nips even while on the bench. Using an obvious subterfuge, McDermott would cough, then bend down, sticking his head beneath the bench, as if looking for a tissue. While out of view, he'd take a few slugs from the flask, then pop back up, his face flushed, smacking his lips.

"I've asked for priority," said Gentry, placing his briefcase on the counsel table. Max got up to join him, still wondering whether he'd made the right decision about Danny Greer. It was too late for second-guessing now, but that didn't stop him from doing it anyway.

He took a seat opposite Gentry at the counsel table, thinking that at least he'd have his answer very soon.

Augustus McDermott closed and locked the door, then returned to the desk. He'd brought the bottle in a brown paper bag and kept the bag inside his briefcase. With the bag upright inside the case, he slipped the bottle out and placed it on top of the desk.

He carefully poured from the bottle into the flask, spilling some on the desk blotter and cursing. When the flask was full, he capped the bottle and returned it to the bag, then locked the briefcase. With his sleeve, he wiped off the few drops of whiskey that had spilled on the desk.

There, he thought. He was set now . . . except for the smell.

Gus McDermott looked around the strange chambers for a minute. If this were my chambers, he thought, I'd spray the hell out of it with air freshener. He got up and headed for the bathroom. Inside, he found a can of Glade, Spring Bouquet. He watched, holding the can in his outstretched hand, as the aromatic mist filled the room, masking any smell of the Wild Turkey that he'd spilled.

That's more like it, he mumbled to himself. He sat down behind the desk, giving it one last sniff test, before lifting the first file from the stack that the court clerk had given him.

He quickly rifled through the file, seeing that the case was on calendar for a 995 motion. He hadn't heard one of those in years, since such motions did not exist in Juvenile Court. He quickly looked over the preliminary hearing transcript, thinking that all he'd have to do was listen to counsel's arguments, then sustain the findings of the municipal court judge. He'd be on safe ground that way.

Gus McDermott was barely paying attention, about to slip the flask from his coat pocket, when he spotted the name on the neatly typed page of testimony. He stopped thinking about the flask. He felt the blood rush to his head and saw his hands start to tremble. He raced through the transcript, trying to catch the gist of the witness's testimony, feeling the anger mounting inside him with every sentence.

"Goddamn asshole," he muttered.

He finished reading the testimony, then read it again. His mind was already focusing on getting even.

He thought back to the first time he'd seen the lab report on his own drunk driving case. The name was there, just like in the prelim transcript. The same guy, a supervisor, signing just below the lab tech who'd actually done the work.

The supervisor. The one who would testify at trial that he, the Honorable Augustus McDermott, had driven his automobile while drunk. The one the Judicial Council had questioned, just before arriving at their decision.

Gus had heard the scuttlebut. It was only a matter of days, perhaps hours, before the council took formal action.

Gus McDermott, the courtroom personnel whispered behind his back, was soon to be history. Another judicial relic put out to pasture.

Well, he'd show them. He'd show them all!

There was still one last judicial act for him to perform, a final blow to be struck. In one swift stroke he'd get his revenge and cut them all down to size.

He reached for his flask and took a good long pull, came up for a breath, then took another. He needed courage for this. He needed to get even, and this was his chance.

He knew he wasn't thinking as clearly as he should, that he was taking a chance to even consider doing this. This was a damn big case—the biggest!

He tried to calm himself. He forced himself to again carefully read the entire transcript.

When he finished, he was surprised at how clear, how obvious, his course of action was. The transcript was incredibly weak, almost totally bereft of hard evidence. The prosecutor, Gus thought, had probably figured that he'd push this case through based on the seriousness of the charges, even though the evidence against the defendant was flimsy.

Gus knew now that he could get his revenge, and still come out on top. All he needed to do was point to the transcript. Any judge or criminal lawyer worth his salt would have to admit that it wasn't even a close call. It was obvious that any reasonable magistrate should have determined that the prosecution had failed to show even a strong suspicion of guilt.

Yes, that was it. He would simply be following the law.

And they couldn't hold *that* against him.

He would act like he was just doing his job. Nothing personal. He had objectively reviewed the transcript and honestly thought that the case should be dismissed. No yelling or smiling as he rendered his decision. And certainly no jokes about the lab report. In fact, he mused, he wouldn't even mention the lab tech's testimony. Nothing about the blood-typing of the hair, or all that DNA mumbo-jumbo.

Gus McDermott then had a vision of himself. In the vision he was seated in court, presiding over the 995 motion. He saw himself as he always did: dignified, respectable, and wise. He was imparting wisdom, making decisions in his own magisterial fashion. He saw himself looking up from the court file, saying the words, "The 995 motion to dismiss is granted," then tossing the file down to the clerk.

It would take all his judicial restraint, he realized, not to gloat in his triumph.

Gus McDermott got up from the desk and put on his robe. He opened his chamber's door, stifling a smile and muttering under his breath, *Vengeance is mine, saith Augustus McDermott.*

Fourcade turned, smiled at Max, then winked. David Gentry saw his client's actions and motioned for him to remain quiet. Gentry's own emotions were on the verge of racing out of control. The impossible had happened: Judge Augustus McDermott had granted his motion. McDermott had dismissed the Ripper case.

Max and Draper sat motionless at the counsel table, stunned.

Gentry had argued his motion, and Max had subsequently responded. McDermott had calmly inquired as to further argument; then, hearing none, he decisively announced that he found the evidence in the transcript insufficient, and granted the motion to dismiss. McDermott then bounded off the bench and disappeared into chambers.

Max noticed Phil Draper staring at him. He could see Fourcade congratulating his lawyer, pumping his hand, both attorney and client all smiles.

Max was aware that there was a next step to take, a decision on the future course of this case that needed to be made. Yet at that moment, everything seemed distant, even the voices of others in the courtroom. For a few seconds he couldn't organize his thoughts. Images floated randomly before his eyes: the faces of Deets and Valenzuela, the photographs of the mutilated women, Esther Morse at the restaurant . . .

He also thought of young Danny Greer, and what his mother would say when she found out that her attacker had been set free by the same judicial system she'd been promised would protect her son.

"We have to refile," whispered Draper. She was haphazardly placing loose papers into a case file. He could see the fire in her eyes, and the way she was concentrating on not looking at Fourcade.

She knows herself, Max thought. He realized that Phil Draper knew that she was on the edge, that if she watched Fourcade with his shit-eating grin, celebrating his victory, that she might do something stupid, something that would not only affect their case, but something she would regret when she'd had time to cool off.

"If we refile," said Max, feeling his own sense of emergency beginning to dissipate, "that'll be our last crack at him. If something happens then and the case gets kicked, we'll be out of court for good."

He thought about the rule that allowed prosecutors to file the same felony charges only twice. They'd taken their first shot at Fourcade and had blown it. They'd get only one more try and they couldn't afford to take any chances with that one.

Max watched as Fourcade practically floated back into the lockup. They would transport him back to county jail, where he would pick up his things prior to being discharged. By dinnertime Harris Fourcade would be back on the streets, a free man.

Max fought against second-guessing his decision not to use Danny Greer at the prelim. It was too late now. They still had one more shot at it, and the next time he'd pull no punches. He'd put the young boy on the witness stand to identify Fourcade. Perhaps by then, the lab would have something more concrete tying Fourcade to at least one of the rape victims.

"I didn't think he had the balls to do it."

Max looked up, drawn from his thoughts of Danny Greer and lost opportunities. David Gentry stood a few feet away. He had packed up his paperwork, said goodbye to his client, and was on his way out.

"You got lucky," said Max, then immediately regretted it. It was a bush-league response, especially with David Gentry.

"Maybe," said Gentry. He allowed Max's jab to pass. He'd been there himself. Prosecutors losing big cases were not all that common. And this one was more than just a big case.

"Listen, Dave," said Max, extending his hand. "I shouldn't have said that. You did a nice job. You were right, the case was close."

"You're going to refile," said Gentry, as if it were a foregone conclusion. "Will you tell me when so that I can walk my client into court?"

"Sure," said Max. He paused, deciding not to get involved in a discussion of when he thought the case might get refiled. He wasn't at all certain himself.

Max added, "Fourcade probably thinks you're the greatest thing since sliced bread."

"He's happy," said Gentry, low-keying his victory. "After all, Max, he's an innocent man. The system worked. We should all be happy."

Max looked at Gentry as if he were a stranger. Gentry, he thought, had bought Fourcade's entire story, swallowed it whole. Max felt like grabbing his friend by the lapels and shaking some sense into him. But he didn't.

"Yeah," Max whispered to himself. "I bet the victims are real happy."

He'd spent two weeks in the jail ward of County General Hospital, recuperating from his injuries. Getting off the bus at the Central Men's Jail, he still limped, but for the most part his head had cleared. His face was still swollen and discolored, and he found it hard to breathe because of the tape around his ribs and the splint the doctors had applied over his broken nose. The last person Billy Darling expected to see as he trailed along in line, handcuffed to the inmates in front and behind him, was Harris Fourcade.

At least he was pretty sure it was Fourcade.

He only got a quick glance as the guards hurried the line back inside the jail. Fourcade was at the far gate, in the company of two deputies. And Fourcade, to Billy's surprise, was dressed in civilian clothes.

The guards halted the line of prisoners for a few

254

seconds, allowing Billy a longer look. It had been close to ten years since he'd last seen Harris Fourcade back at the Burris Home. There had been a substantial difference in their ages, so he had never known him that well. But everyone at the Home, no matter how young, was aware of who Harris Fourcade was. You couldn't easily forget that face.

Yet it was not just the face that Billy was thinking about now. His mind drifted back to when he'd last seen Fourcade. He quickly attempted to compute how old Fourcade would be, ultimately deciding that the inmate he was looking at was just about the right age. He had the same general build, and was about the same height as Fourcade was when he'd left the Home.

The moustache was the thing, though. The Harris Fourcade that Billy remembered never had a moustache. Old Man Burris wouldn't let him grow one.

The line began to move again and Billy stole one more glance at the prisoner being released.

Billy wasn't surprised to learn that Fourcade had ended up in jail, all things considered. Not that *he* had any right to talk.

Still, Fourcade always had a hard, defensive edge to him. He hadn't been the toughest kid in the Home, but Fourcade was always the one involved in the most fights. He had a sort of mental toughness that he continually tested. He made a practice of challenging anyone who commented about his appearance or who even looked at him the wrong way. Fourcade had taken more than his share of lumps from some of the bigger boys, but never without getting in a few good licks of his own.

Billy headed down the line until they reached the main gate. There, the deputy in charge unlocked the heavy steel chain that connected the wrists of the inmates. Billy rubbed his wrists, glad to be rid of the handcuffs.

The two thugs who had sent him to the hospital were nowhere to be seen. The sheriff acted as if nothing had happened.

They herded Billy into a dayroom, where they held him until after dinner. It was nearly eleven before he was placed in a cell.

The main thing on Billy's mind as he dropped into the cot was sleep. He rolled over, feeling his body go numb with slumber almost immediately.

The last thought that flashed through his head was an image of himself standing in line, watching Harris Fourcade being released, and wondering whether Fourcade, like himself, ever had nightmares about the Burris Home, and the old brick smokehouse out back.

16

David Gentry was excited. He'd been concerned that the Harris Fourcade preliminary hearing would spill over, botching up their plans. But it hadn't. In fact, it couldn't have worked out better. Fourcade was behind him, the refiling of charges did not appear imminent, and Max had promised to call him if, in fact, the prosecution was going to give it another try.

So Gentry packed up the station wagon, not worrying about Harris Fourcade.

It was the day he'd been looking forward to, and dreading, for the last year, ever since Susan had received her acceptance from Santa Barbara.

Santa Barbara!

He could recall the afternoon the acceptance letter had arrived in the mail. He'd seen the envelope first. He tried to remember all the stories from over thirty-five years ago. Whether the size of the envelope gave away the contents. Whether a thin envelope meant a rejection, a thick one an acceptance, with all those marvelous forms to fill out.

He remembered standing at the front door when Susan got home from school. He had the envelope in his hand. Susan knew exactly what it was the minute she set eyes on his grinning face.

They'd both been waiting for word, along with thousands of other high school students. He recalled how perfectly calm Susan appeared, while his own heart pounded inside his chest like a pile driver. It was almost as if her total pleasure was in seeing his happiness.

So now the day had finally come. They had wedged most of her things into the car the night before. Now he was trying to find an empty space for those last few items: Susan's stuffed animals, her stereo, the pictures that had been hanging on the walls of her bedroom for as long as he could remember.

Gentry felt a constriction in his throat and tears welling up. He had cried a little the night before, nursing a cup of coffee by himself at the kitchen table after having packed most of Susan's things into the back of the old wagon. She'd gone off for one last night with her friends, and he had been left alone with his memories. He had walked through the house, stopping every few steps, thinking about something that Susan had said or done in that exact spot. The house was filled with memories for him.

It wasn't until last night, sitting alone in the silence, that he fully appreciated that his daughter was actually leaving. Then the memories began to crowd in, pressing the breath from him.

He heard their voices. Jackie and a very young Susan laughing together.

He remembered the arguments between mother and daughter, the braces and contact lenses, and more recently, Susan explaining to him through her tears about a lost love, or pining away in her bedroom, talking nonstop on the phone about the latest hunk.

Her bedroom was the most depressing. All the picture frames had been packed away, and the walls were bare. Susan had always kept pictures of her friends and things she had clipped from magazines thumbtacked to the walls. Now, all that was left were the squares of slightly discolored paint where objects had once been.

The stuffed animals that had competed with her for space on the bed were neatly packed away in boxes, some destined for the car, most for the garage. The closet had been cleared of all her clothes. Only the old coffee urn and a pair of too small shoe skates were left on the overhead shelf.

Gentry removed the skates, remembering the day he had bought them, recalling how excited Susan had been when he'd brought them home and stenciled her name in black marker on the back.

That was when the tears had come.

The intensity of the crying had surprised him.

He tried to tell himself that this wasn't an end, but a beginning; that Susan would be back. That what was most important in his life had not been taken from him forever.

All his talking, though, had not stopped the tears. In the end, he had turned out the light in her room, left a short note to Susan about getting up early, then returned to his bed to cry himself to sleep.

"You'll come up in a week or so, won't you, Dad?"

Gentry heard her voice coming from inside the house. He imagined that despite his Herculean efforts, his sadness was obvious.

Now, he thought, she'll try and cheer me up, make believe that this isn't as big a thing as it seems, that things will always be the same between us. Susan was good at that. It was one of the many reasons why he

259

loved her so much.

"They have a family day a few weeks after orientation," she said, walking down the porch steps carrying one of the boxes of stuffed animals. "By then I should be set up in the dorm. You could stay in one of the motels nearby, and we could make a weekend of it."

He took the box of animals from her. "Do these go or stay?"

She poked her nose inside, then looked at him and smiled. "I don't suppose my roommate would appreciate my filling up the dorm with stuffed teddy bears."

"I suppose not," he said.

He was losing it again. The memories fell on him like a warm afternoon thunder shower. Running for cover would have done no good. He turned and carried the box back to the porch, not bothering to wipe the tears from his face. He put down the box, then sat on the cool cement steps. Susan came over and joined him, crouching opposite him, holding his hand in hers.

"Pretty stupid, huh?"

It was all he could think to say. It wouldn't be fair to her, he thought, telling her why he was crying, why he loved her so much, and how sad it made him feel to think about her going away.

"Oh, Daddy," she said, still rubbing the back of his hand. She flashed that smile of hers, the one he'd seen so many times, the one she'd smiled several years back, when he'd finally broken down and allowed her to go on her first car date.

He'd never been very good at letting go. He felt overcome, then as now, with the bittersweet pain of changing roles. Susan was now the strong one, understanding that doing the right thing was often painful.

He wondered if it would have been any different if Jackie had lived. Perhaps he would have grown more detached from his daughter's everyday life, casting Jackie in the lead role of disciplinarian and confidante.

Yet despite the sweet ache of letting go, he knew he wouldn't have had it any other way.

Once in the car and on the road, the tears disappeared. They would have the next four or five hours together, he thought. Just him and his daughter: the magnificent young lady he had raised in her mother's image.

He was coming to understand that this was not a permanent goodbye. He wasn't losing Susan, just letting her get on with the rest of her life, which to his great happiness, he was coming to understand would always include him.

Father and daughter headed up Interstate 5, hugging the coast, filled with expectation, and already making plans for his next visit.

Max was surprised to see Miguelito seated in the hallway. He was slumped on one of the heavy wooden benches, eyes closed, holding the glowing stub of a cigarette in one hand. It looked as if his fingers were on fire. Next to him on the bench was a large Styrofoam cup with part of the rim chipped off. Little white pieces of white Styrofoam, like petals that had fallen from a flower, littered the ground beneath him.

Max could see that though his eyes were closed, Miguelito was not asleep, just resting. His lips quivered, but not as if he were cold. More like he was talking to himself, repeating something he had thought of, or heard somewhere. The air around Miguelito was filled with the slightly nauseating aroma of body odor covered by sweet cologne.

The glowing orange stub had burned down almost to the skin by the time Miguelito pulled himself from his lethargy and brought his hand to his mouth for one final drag. It was then that he spotted Max, staring at him from a few feet away.

"Mr. Becker," he said, the words coming out slowly, slurred. Everything about Miguelito this morning was coming out slurred. Max wondered if he was on something, or just coming down from the night before.

"You look like shit," said Max.

Miguelito smiled, brushed some errant cigarette ash from his lap, then wiped his nose with the back of his wrist. He snorted a few times then swallowed hard.

"Sorry," he said, tossing the cigarette to the floor and crushing it with one of the same silver-buckled boots he had worn at their first meeting.

"Got a virus or something," he mumbled. He again drew the back of his wrist across his face. "Must be going around."

"Yeah," said Max, thinking that Miguelito was still high, but on the way down. "You got that expensive kind of virus. Seems like a lot of people around here got the same thing."

Miguelito didn't laugh. Instead he asked, "You gonna get Billy out today?"

"Yeah," responded Max impatiently. "I'll just walk in there and tell the judge it's okay to cut Billy loose. I'll tell 'im that I talked with you and that you gave me your word that Billy would make his appearances. Then you could address the court yourself, Mickie. I'm sure you'll make a great impression this morning, all bright-eyed and bushy-tailed."

There was something that kept Miguelito hanging on, some reason why, at a pretrial hearing where nothing very important was going to happen, Miguelito Gervas found it worth his while to be hanging around at 8:30 in the morning in the cold courthouse hallway, under the influence of any one of a number of controlled and restricted chemical substances, and providing the cops with a living example of probable cause for arrest.

He must be feeling guilty over Billy Darling's arrest—perhaps, Max thought, even more guilty than he had initially surmised.

"This is just a pretrial," said Max. "We'll set a trial date, maybe discuss when the pretrial motions are to be heard. It shouldn't take more than a few minutes. If I were you, I'd get into the head and see if I could get my act together. Either that, or make myself scarce. You're likely to get busted for being under the influence if you sit here much longer."

Max peeled off a five-dollar bill and five ones.

"Here," he said, stuffing the bills into Miguelito's pants pocket. "Get yourself some coffee and some breakfast. You've got my number. Call me later and I'll fill you in on what happened."

Max turned away from Miguelito and started down the hallway.

"Hey, thanks, man," said Miguelito, in a loud slur.

Max looked back. Miguelito was bent over, poking at the ground with his hand, as if he were pulling weeds, picking dollar bills off the floor. Max watched Miguelito stuff the money back into his pockets, then slowly pace off the fiteen or twenty steps to the men's room. Miguelito walked as if he were cross-country skiing in slow motion.

It would be a miracle, Max thought, if he didn't get

himself arrested before the morning was over.

Nathan Zellner was already seated in the jury box inside the courtroom when Max entered. Zellner was talking to the calendar deputy from the DA's office. There were three private defense attorneys seated in the jury box, waiting for the judge to take the bench. Both the clerk and bailiff were busy on the phone. As Max entered, Zellner made a determined effort to act as if he weren't there.

This is going to go quicker than I thought, Max said to himself.

He was standing alongside the courtroom clerk, waiting for him to get off the phone, when the bailiff got his attention, motioning him to the small desk near the lockup door.

"For you," he said, holding the telephone receiver in his outstretched hand. "Make it quick, I'm expecting a call."

Max took the phone from the bailiff.

"This is Becker," he said into the receiver. He listened as Phil Draper told him that another woman had been attacked.

"Same as with the first three," she said, without going into detail. Max knew exactly what she meant.

"Except," Draper added, "this time the Ripper has added a new wrinkle to his act. He killed this one."

They had just passed Thousand Oaks, having gotten stuck in bumper-to-bumper traffic in LA, and were again bordering the Pacific and the bleached white-sand beaches of Ventura and Carpinteria. The coastal mountain range rose gently in the distance.

Gentry drove the car north, the road paralleling the

railroad tracks on one side, the Pacific Ocean on the other. In the distance, oil derricks, like giant black insects perched atop the water, rhythmically pumping up and down. It reminded him of those desk toys that bob up and down in a glass of water.

He turned to Susan. "You hungry?"

He wasn't, but wanted to prolong the trip.

"I could eat."

"Good. We'll stop in Ojai. It's a little out of our way, but we have plenty of time."

He gazed out the window for a moment, then said, "You know, there's a place there that's nice. Your mother and I . . ."

He stopped, surprised that a memory from so long ago, one he was sure had disappeared, had crept back into his thinking.

He continued, "Your mom and I stopped there once, back before you were born."

For several seconds Gentry disappeared, alone with his memories, letting his mind fill with the images of that day long ago.

"Maybe not," he muttered. "It's about twenty miles out of the way. We'd have to get off the main highway." He looked to Susan for confirmation.

"If you want to, Dad," she said. "There's no hurry. Whatever you want."

"No. No, it's okay."

He was having second thoughts about conjuring up old memories. He didn't know if the restaurant even existed anymore. Experience had imparted to him the painful realization that those sorts of side trips down memory lane usually didn't result in happy endings. It was just never the same the second time around.

"There's a place in San Luis Obispo," he said, his mind drifting to past trips, "called the Madonna Inn.

Every room is different. They've got one called the Caveman Room, all done in rock. They've got a thing in the men's room where instead of a urinal, you walk up to this wall of rock and a waterfall starts cascading down right in front of you." He laughed, thinking about the first time he'd been there. "It's done with an electric eye. I was almost afraid to go to the bathroom. You can imagine what a shock it is, a bunch of men standing there, pants down, ready to go, when all of a sudden the wall of stone springs forth with water. The county put me up there on one of my trips to Atascadero. We were only there for a night, but I'll never forget that bathroom."

Susan said, "Is that where Harris Fourcade would have ended up? Atascadero, I mean."

"Maybe. Depends. The Department of Corrections moves people around based on bed space. The facility at Atascadero and the one at Patton State Hospital are set up to house mentally ill prisoners. They're supposed to have programs to treat rapists and child molesters. He could have ended up in one of those places, or he could have found himself in the general prison population."

Gentry hadn't given any thought to Harris Fourcade since they'd started their trip. He hadn't seen or heard from Fourcade since the day Judge McDermott had dismissed the case. He had instructed Fourcade that the charges were likely to be refiled and to stay in touch.

"It's kind of funny," said Susan. "You representing Fourcade, and Uncle Max prosecuting him after Uncle Max went through that grilling at the meeting we had. I didn't like to see that happen to him, but I'm glad it wasn't you up there."

Gentry chuckled. "Me, too."

"I suppose that means that Uncle Max will be

starting from scratch again? It seems like they'll never catch that guy."

"They'll get him," said Gentry, then caught himself, realizing that Susan might have meant that they'd never catch Fourcade.

"I mean," said Gentry, "that they'll eventually catch the one who's committing these crimes."

"You're convinced it isn't Fourcade?"

He looked at her, about to answer in the affirmative, when the thought struck him that there was no way he'd ever leave his daughter alone with Harris Fourcade. The inconsistency in his own thinking made him hesitate before answering. It was the sly smile that he'd seen on Fourcade's face that he now saw in his mind's eye.

"He never admitted as much to me," said Gentry. "The evidence against him was weak—so weak that I don't think anyone could have proved that Fourcade was the Ripper."

"Uncle Max seemed to think so."

"Well . . ." Gentry thought about responding, giving some long explanation of why prosecutors think the way they do, but he decided against it.

"That's why we have trials," he finally offered. "That's why judges and juries and not prosecutors, are given the ultimate decision in determining guilt or innocence."

He'd heard himself uttering those same words hundreds of times before. It was what he told himself when he was alone with his thoughts. Those were the words he repeated over and over again in his dream, even as he felt himself going under.

Kneeling in front of the candles, saying his prayers, those same words swirled in his mind.

In his dream, he could see himself standing inside the

cell on death row, mouthing the words to all the stone-faced prisoners. His lips would move, but there was no sound. Those sentenced to death just stared at him. They couldn't hear him; they couldn't understand.

"There's the sign," he said, pointing to an advertisement for the restaurant. He pulled the stationwagon ahead of an old van, then onto the freeway offramp.

"I could eat a horse," he said. "How 'bout you?"

17

"Whatdya got?"

"Single adult female," said Draper. "The name's Jill Fernault. Mid-twenties. According to the neighbors, she's lived in the house a little less than a year. Worked part-time at a preschool. Was going to college to get her teaching credentials. Her folks own the place, at least their name's on the utility bills."

Max and Draper were standing just inside the front door of the small suburban bungalow. The usual crowd of neighbors and interested onlookers had gathered in the street in front of the house. The uniformed units were positioned on the sidewalk holding the crowd at bay.

"Forensics here?"

"In the back," said Draper, leading the way.

He followed her down a short hallway into a back bedroom. The house smelled stuffy, like old clothes or newspapers. The musty decayed smell diminished and became something else as they neared the bedroom. Max recognized the familiar coppery odor that he'd always associated with fresh blood.

Inside the bedroom, the Forensics lab techs were busy hovering over the body, magnifying, inspecting,

269

and gathering samples. Two young men wearing jackets from the coroner's office lounged disinterestedly in the corner, waiting for someone to give them the go-ahead to take the body.

Jill Fernault's nude body lay motionless atop the bed. Her arms were at her sides, her legs slightly separated. A lab tech had positioned himself in the V between her legs. He was inspecting the gaping bloody wound at close range, using a magnifying glass and tweezers.

"Same as the others," said Draper. "The labia have been removed. He must have either taken them with him or disposed of them, because we haven't found them."

The lab tech who was hunched over between the dead woman's legs was removing samples with a swab. The area of the bed under her lower body was stained a dark crimson. Someone had placed a piece of clear plastic on the bedspread underneath the dead woman to prevent the blood from soaking the clothing of the people working the body.

"How long has she been dead?"

"Less than ten hours," said Draper. "Apparently he used the same knife to slit her throat."

Max's eyes were drawn to the purple meat-market gash that stretched from ear to ear. The blood had frothed over the wound and stained the woman's skin, giving her neck the appearance of a pinkish-red napkin that had been tucked in below her chin.

"What about the cable?"

"I checked," said Draper. "She's got an outside aerial. The area is serviced by cable, but the house isn't set up for it. There's one TV in the living room, but like I said, it's hooked up to an outside antenna."

"A copycat?"

"Could be. We'll have to wait for the autopsy, see if

270

they can give us anything on the weapon. It's kind of hard to tell from here."

Max knew what she meant. The woman's body was covered in blood. The area between the dead woman's legs was bathed in red and purple, like someone had dumped a can of paint on her genitals. The coroner would have to clean her up, then take a closer look to determine whether the same cutting instrument had been used, and if so, whether the incision was similar to that of the other victims.

"Where was our boy during the last twelve hours?"

"I sent Levinthal out to his apartment," said Draper. "Haven't heard anything back yet."

"Get on the horn and tell Levinthal to stay there until Fourcade shows up. Tell him to grab his ass as soon as the little prick shows his face."

"What about his lawyer?" said Draper. "The guy's not gonna open his mouth without Gentry knowing about it first."

"Call Gentry and . . ."

Max interrrupted himself, remembering that Gentry was on his way to Santa Barbara with Susan.

"Gentry's out of town," said Max. "We'll worry about that later. Meanwhile, let's find out where Fourcade is."

Max gave some instructions to the lab tech and the coroner's deputies. He and Draper then retraced their steps back down the hallway.

In the small kitchen, Jill Fernault had kept a bulletin board on which she had tacked recipes, photographs of herself and friends, bills that needed to be paid, a half-dozen "While You Were Gone" telephone messages from her preschool, and some handwritten scraps of paper reminding her of things to do. Max glanced at the board, hoping to see the name All-Valley Cable Company, hoping to see something that would link the dead woman in the bedroom to Harris Fourcade.

"I already checked," said Draper, coming up behind him. "There's nothing."

"Take the whole thing anyway," said Max. His eyes darted around the board as he looked for a familiar name, place, or number. He fingered through Jill Fernault's telephone messages. They were tacked together in the lower corner of the board. Just the usual stuff: concerned parents wanting to conference with her about their child; Mrs. Fernault asking if her daughter would be home on Sunday; a doctor returning her call about a sick student. The normal residue of everyday life.

Still, Max wanted the bulletin board. Perhaps something would come to him later. Perhaps the lab would find something, anything, to explain why the Ripper, or whoever it was, had selected Jill Fernault as his latest victim.

Max pulled his hand away from the stack of telephone messages. He was readying himself to go back into the bedroom. He visualized Jill Fernault on the bed. This was the part of handling homicides that he'd never fully gotten used to—probably never would.

As preparation, he filled his senses with the sight and smell of blood, replaying the images of carnage he'd seen in the bedroom. It was what he had to do so that he didn't toss his cookies and embarrass himself.

Max was concentrating so fully on preparing himself to face the gore that he barely had time to completely read one of the telephone messages. All he saw were the words scribbled across a piece of notepaper: *"Newspaper subscription/Will you be home?"*

The words meant nothing to him.

Their importance wouldn't register until it was almost too late.

272

                    *   *   *

He was finally set. In the end, he decided to scrap the
gas chamber idea. Too many problems. And buying
the chemicals would create a trail that the cops could
follow right to him. He didn't need something as
complicated as all that, even though it was what he had
used in the dream.

Instead, he found some rubber tubing in the storage
shed of the Burris Home. He bought a simple plastic
dust mask at the hardware store, along with a tube of
silicone caulking. The dust mask had an elastic band
which held it snugly against the face. He attached one
end of the rubber tubing to the mask, using the silicone
caulking to make the seal airtight. On the other end of
the tubing, he connected the rubber nipple that would
fit snugly around the exhaust pipe of the van. He
hadn't tried it out yet, but he was sure it would do the
trick.

The dream had changed over the last few nights. He
no longer fought the dream. He knew that it was about
to end, that his life was moving into and overlapping
with the dream.

The faces that had washed through his nights were
becoming clearer. They were now looking at him with
expressions of shock, as if seeing him for the first time,
recognizing his importance.

The lawyer, as always, was there in the dream. Only
now, the burning light of fear and recognition flashed
in the lawyer's eyes.

It made him feel good, thinking about that look. It
was the look of suffering he would soon see on the
lawyer's face, the dream becoming reality.

He dropped back behind the station wagon. He let
up on the gas, allowing the other car to pull ahead, then
eased the van off the freeway. He kept his distance,

following the station wagon into the foothills, then into the restaurant parking lot.

He figured they were stopping for lunch. He passed through the lot and parked the van on the street. He watched as the lawyer and the girl walked hand-in-hand into the restaurant.

They still didn't know.

He thought: first he'd make the girl suffer—the father's only child. Just like the lawyer had done to him.

Then the lawyer.

Just like in the dream.

18

Phil Draper awoke feeling wired. In the darkness she slipped into a pair of sweatpants, an old long-sleeved T-shirt, and a heavy sweatshirt.

Padding barefoot down the hallway into the kitchen, she poured food into the bowls for the dogs, turned on the coffeemaker, and glanced out the front window at the swirling fog.

The moon bathed the earth in a mysterious glow, like the uncertain luminescence of a neon sign flashing in a dark alley.

She returned to the bedroom, put on her tennis shoes, leaving them unlaced, and headed for the weights.

On a cushioned vinyl-covered mat in the corner, she started stretching. Lying on her back, she gazed at the ceiling as she went through her warmup, her mind focusing on Harris Fourcade and not on the exercise.

Fourcade was the reason she hadn't been able to sleep. The information she'd sent for weeks ago had finally arrived at Children's Services. Due to the usual bureaucratic bungling, the package had sat in the mailroom downstairs for nearly a week before someone had finally noticed it.

A secretary had called her last night, acting as if it were Draper's fault that the package had been lost. With some begging and pleading—and, finally an out-and-out threat—Draper had managed to convince the secretary to send it by county messenger to her house the next morning.

Straddling the narrow exercise bench, she draped her elbows over the support bar and grasped the weight. She began her first set of curls, watching the weight slowly move up and down, enjoying the sound of the heavy steel plates clanging together. The dogs had finished eating and had taken up their familiar positions curled around one another atop the exercise mat.

Draper hoped that the information from Children's Services would provide the key to understanding Harris Fourcade. They'd had a sketchy background workup on him at the preliminary hearing. It consisted mainly of Fourcade's rap sheet and a supplemental criminal history including a DMV printout.

Except for a few traffic violations, Fourcade's adult criminal record was clean. Draper knew that any juvenile record Fourcade might have was legally confidential, sealed by the court against unauthorized eyes—at least, certain unauthorized eyes.

Draper managed to convince a friend in the clerk's office to run a printout of Fourcade's name on the computer for juvenile arrests, which led to her discovery of a battery charge filed against him in 1974. The case was filed by the DA in juvenile court, but never adjudicated. A twelve-year-old Harris Fourcade had been put on informal probation and the case had been dismissed.

Draper completed her second set of ten curls, then moved to the military press. She adjusted the pin for the proper weight, then positioned herself under the bar, spreading her legs for balance. She concentrated on controlling the weight, heaving it up over her head, then slowly bringing it down. She alternated bringing the bar down, first behind her head, then in front. She focused on the lift, pushing the thoughts of Fourcade aside for the moment.

Once finished with the set, Draper moved around to the bench on the other side. Positioning herself on her stomach, she stretched out, hooking her ankles under the padded weight bar. She began to lift, pulling her feet back toward her waist, then letting them return. Her legs were in good shape from a life of ocean swimming. She could do this one without thinking. Her thoughts returned to Fourcade.

She'd made an unauthorized trip to the archives to retrieve Fourcade's juvenile case. It was amazing what flashing a badge could do. They wouldn't let her take the file with her, but she didn't have to.

Inside Fourcade's juvenile file was a report from the probation department on his suitability for informal probation supervision. It mentioned that Fourcade was a dependent ward of the court, having been placed in a foster home at the age of seven. The battery complaint arose from a fight that Fourcade had had with one of the other wards at the foster home. With this information, Draper had been able to dig up the number of Fourcade's dependency court file, which she hoped would contain information dealing with his initial placement in foster care, along with any other pertinent information that Children's Services possessed on Harris Fourcade. This was the package she was now waiting for.

Draper went through the rest of her workout, finishing with two sets of bench presses. By the time she was done, sunlight streamed into the room from two small back windows, and the house had begun to warm up. She removed her sweatshirt and was toweling the perspiration from her face and neck when both dogs started to bark. She followed the dogs to the front door, telling them to hush, and shooing them away with her foot.

Opening the door, she found a large manila envelope on the welcome mat. The messenger had already returned to his car and was heading back up the gravel driveway to the main road.

The envelope was the size of a small briefcase, with a flap closure at the top fastened with heavy brown string. The words: "SAN DIEGO COUNTY DEPARTMENT OF CHILDREN'S SERVICES," were printed in bold black lettering on the front. Below that was the word, "CONFIDENTIAL." There were lines printed on the face of the envelope, places for the signatures and dates of those people who would have occasion to inspect its contents, however the lines were blank.

Draper dumped the contents of the envelope onto the kitchen table. She went to the counter and poured herself a cup of coffee, then returned.

Most of the documents were reports and social studies from Children's Services. The department was obligated to monitor its wards, preparing written reports on their status under foster care. Children's Services had recently come under fire for failing to adequately supervise its foster care homes. There had been reports of children being removed from foster care homes due to allegations of sexual molestation, only to be placed elsewhere where the same thing occurred.

The manila envelope contained a half-dozen short-form reports dealing with Harris Fourcade. From the records, Draper learned that Fourcade had been bounced around among three or four different placements during his first years in foster care. He eventually ended up where he'd started, at the Burris Home, a privately owned foster care facility located near the Hillcrest area.

Draper put the reports in order by date, then began reading. The paperwork painted a picture that was not all that unusual.

Fourcade had been brought by his mother to the Burris Home at the age of seven. Apparently—the reporting Children's Services worker was unclear about this part—Mrs. Fourcade had left her son on the front porch, then disappeared. By the time the people at the Burris Home realized what had happened, the mother had left town.

Young Harris Fourcade had been able to provide Children's Services with his name, his mother's name, and their last place of residence, which, upon further inspection, proved to be a flophouse downtown.

Fourcade denied knowing who his father was, saying he'd never met the man, and that his mother had used her own name for as long as he could remember.

Children's Services ran a record check on Mrs. Fourcade, discovering that her first name was Dolores, and that she had applied for a California driver's license, claiming she was a single woman. She'd applied for the license under the name Fourcade, which she indicated on the application was her maiden name.

There was additional paperwork in the file dealing with two surgical operations on Harris Fourcade that the county had authorized to repair a cleft palate condition.

Draper's mind jumped back to her first meeting with Fourcade, the hissing noise he'd made when he spoke, and the moustache that covered most of his upper lip.

According to the hospital's follow-up reports, the surgeries resulted in some minor improvement in Fourcade's appearance and speech. The doctors indicated that because of Fourcade's age, further surgical intervention might be cosmetically beneficial, but only on a long-term basis. They recommended a series of operations over the next eight to ten years.

The physicians stated that normally a cleft condition such as Fourcade had could be almost completely eliminated if the surgery was performed at the toddler age, but Fourcade's maturity presented additional obstacles to complete success.

The final letter in Fourcade's medical file was from the head of Children's Services, who in a terse, one-paragraph response to the social worker's request for funds, stated that due to budget constraints, any further cosmetic surgery for Fourcade would have to be put off indefinitely.

According to one of the final reports prepared by Children's Services, Harris Fourcade had found his niche at the Burris Home. The social worker had written that although Fourcade remained a loner and still suffered from periodic violent outbursts of temper, the operators of the Burris Home found enough gradual improvement in his performance to recommend that he remain there. He went to school and stayed out of trouble. While his speech was still impaired, the social worker reported that Fourcade was making progress.

The author of the report stated that she had interviewed Fourcade and found that despite his obvious speech impairment, he was able to communicate with others. She recommended that Fourcade remain at the Burris Home until he attained the age of eighteen, at which time he could stay on at the home if his services were needed, or begin life on his own as an emancipated adult.

Draper went back to the earlier reports. She tried to imagine what sort of crisis would cause a mother to leave her seven-year-old child on the doorstep of a foster home and then disappear. Draper was aware that this sort of thing was not uncommon. She'd dealt with cases of women who had left their unwanted babies in trash cans or on the doorsteps of churches—anything to rid themselves of the responsibility.

But Fourcade had been seven when he'd first arrived at the Burris Home. His mother had taken care of him for the first seven years of his life. Draper wondered what might have happened to Dolores Fourcade to precipitate such a sudden and shocking act.

She also wanted to know where Fourcade's father fit into the picture. Was he just a one-night stand? Was he totally unaware that Dolores Fourcade had borne him a son?

She started to make a list of things to do. The first thing she wanted to include was finding Harris Fourcade. They'd had his apartment under surveillance since the last attack, but hadn't seen a trace of him. His girlfriend was not much help, either. She claimed not to have seen Fourcade since his release from jail. It seemed as if Fourcade, like his mother, had disappeared into thin air.

The first item Draper wrote on the list was to tell Max what she had discovered. The next was to check the marriage records for the late fifties and early sixties to see if Fourcade's father was more than just a one-night stand.

After that she would make a few phone calls to see if the Burris Home still existed and to find out if anyone there remembered young Harris Fourcade.

*   *   *

281

The newspapers usually arrived a day or two late. By the time he got to them, they had been splayed out all over the dayroom. The sports section was always the hardest to find, as it was the favorite of most of the inmates—at least, those who could read.

Billy had just finished lunch and was killing time in the dayroom until the deputies took him back to his cell. He'd eaten quickly in hopes of getting to a telephone and calling Miguelito.

The only one who'd come to visit him in the last month was the lawyer, but that was okay. Billy understood why Miguelito had to make himself scarce. Still, he wanted to talk with his friend, maybe get his advice on what he should be doing.

There were always lines at the phones. The sheriffs told the judges that the phones were always open to inmates, that the courts didn't have to make specific orders allowing inmates a designated number of telephone calls. This was only partially true, though. It was up to the deputies to decide if you were allowed access to the phones. And even if the sheriffs did let you get to a phone, there was always someone standing right behind you pushing you to get off. For Billy Darling, that person was almost always bigger and meaner than he was. It made for limited time at the telephones, and very short conversations.

Today was no different. By the time he'd returned from lunch, all the phones were in use and there were lines of three and four inmates ahead of him.

Billy plopped down on one of the dayroom's ripped vinyl couches and absentmindedly paged through the newspaper. His attention was immediately drawn to a photograph on the front page. He recognized a smiling Harris Fourcade being escorted back into the custody lockup by a courtroom bailiff after having his case dismissed.

Billy scanned the article, learning for the first time that Fourcade had been charged in the Ripper investigation. The article mentioned that the charges against him had been dismissed based on the insufficiency of the evidence. Fourcade's lawyer was quoted as saying he was pleased to see that justice had been done.

When Billy got to the part quoting the prosecutor, he had to read the words twice. He wondered if it was the same guy, if *his* Max Becker was the same as the prosecutor quoted in the newspaper. He decided that it couldn't be, that the similarity in names was just a coincidence, maybe a typo.

Billy lowered the newspaper and saw that the phones were still busy. He would have to ask Miguelito about this. After all, the name was pretty common: Max Becker. He finally decided that the prosecutor of the Ripper was probably just another guy with a similar name.

Yeah, that was it. No big deal.

Billy let his mind drift back to the Burris Home. He'd pieced together most of the story since first spotting Fourcade in jail. Seeing Fourcade being released had brought back bitter memories of the big house out in the middle of nowhere, and of old man Burris and that stupid wife of his collecting their county checks and making sure that none of the kids said anything at inspections that they weren't supposed to.

Billy had quickly learned to follow orders there and to answer only when spoken to. One time alone in the darkness of the smokehouse had done the trick for him. It was like that for the other kids, too.

All except Harris Fourcade.

Billy could see Fourcade standing at the door to the smokehouse. Old Man Burris was behind him, making an example of Fourcade to the other kids. But all

Fourcade would do was snarl, his lip curled back in angry defiance, looking into the darkness, not showing his fear.

Billy remembered the story Fourcade had later told him about what had happened to his father. Billy hadn't believed Fourcade then; nobody else did either. They all thought he was full of shit. They all thought he was making it up to try and seem more important. Lots of kids did that at the Home, trying to look tougher than they were.

But now, with the newspaper containing Fourcade's picture resting on his lap, Billy wondered if perhaps the story had been true. He wondered if what Harris Fourcade had told him about getting even was more than the typical bullshit of a foster kid shuffled between foster homes, trying to sound tough.

The deputies were lining up inmates, readying them for return to their cells. The last of the prisoners were hastily saying their telephone goodbyes. Billy took his place behind the others, still thinking about Harris Fourcade. It was probably all a big coincidence, he told himself, just one of those weird tricks of memory. That's what Billy was thinking as he shuffled along in line.

All the same, by the time he reached his cell, Billy had decided that he'd skip breakfast the following morning and place a telephone call to Max Becker.

"You have two collect calls from Billy Darling," she said. "I didn't know whether you wanted me to accept the charges, so I didn't."

"That's okay," said Max. It was Saturday morning and he was talking to his answering service. "If Billy Darling calls again," he said, "go ahead and accept the charges, and give him my home number."

284

"Your home number?"

"Yeah. Don't worry, it's okay."

Max hung up, wondering about the wisdom of disclosing his number. He usually didn't. In fact, he hardly ever gave clients his personal number. But he figured that Billy hadn't been ringing his office number off the hook like most of his other clients. Billy had been satisfied to wait and get information about his case during their regular jail visits. For Billy to keep calling, Max thought, there must be something important on his mind.

Max was in his running shorts and shoes, wearing a T-shirt that Deets had given him. The front of the T-shirt read: *Old Lawyers Never Die, They Just.Do It In Their Briefs.*

David Gentry had called the night before, asking to get together. Gentry had said that he was feeling a bit lonely since Susan had left for Santa Barbara.

Max wondered if Gentry was being honest, or whether he was using Susan's departure as an excuse to smooth things over between them. They hadn't talked much since the Fourcade case was dismissed.

For Max, the Ripper investigation was stuck, bogged down by its own weight. He wasn't any further along toward refiling the charges against Fourcade. If anything, the inconsistencies in the last attack had thrown them off the scent completely.

Phil Draper had also called with some babble about investigating Fourcade's history. Something about a foster home and Fourcade's mother using her maiden name. Max had the feeling that Draper wouldn't give up until she'd finally pinned something on Fourcade. It had become a holy crusade of sorts for her, and Max worried that her actions were based solely on her hatred of the man.

The legal reality hadn't changed. They still had only

the slightest circumstantial evidence linking Fourcade to the first three victims, although they had finally discovered the whereabouts of the first victim, Bernadette Slotkin. Levine had located her in Oakland, waiting tables in a small seafood restaurant. She promised to keep herself available, though now it didn't seem all that important.

David Gentry had suggested that they take a run together, with the caveat that they not talk cases. Whether Gentry in fact wanted to commiserate about Susan's leaving, or just wanted to keep the bridges open between them, Max was glad he'd agreed to the suggestion. A long, slow run through the park was just what he needed.

The phone rang just as he spotted Gentry pulling his car into the driveway.

"Hello."

"Mr. Becker, this is Billy. They gave me your number, said it was okay to call you here."

Max said, "Yeah, Billy, no problem. What's up?" He heard Gentry knock at the front door and went to open it.

Seeing him on the phone, Gentry entered silently, closed the door, and draped his equipment bag and towel over a kitchen chair.

"Start again," said Max. "I didn't hear the first part." He sat down next to Gentry at the kitchen table.

"I saw this picture in the paper," said Billy. "I thought I recognized the guy before, but I wasn't sure. Now I'm sure."

"Sure of what, Billy?"

"Sure that it was him," said Billy.

"Who?"

"Fourcade. Harris Fourcade."

"What about him?" Max felt a chill at the mention of Fourcade's name.

"I knew the dude," said Billy. "At the Home, back when we were both kids. He was older than me, but I still remember the guy. I didn't know you were prosecuting the dude. I guess you are, huh?"

Max's mind flashed to the information Phil Draper had provided.

"Wait a minute," he said. "You mean that you and Fourcade were at the same foster home?"

"That's right."

"You're sure about this, Billy?"

Max noticed Gentry listening attentively. Gentry grabbed a notepad and pencil and placed it on the table in front of him.

"As sure as I *can* be," said Billy. "It was a while back. About ten years ago. I was around seven or eight. Fourcade was older, almost ready to leave. Except, that wasn't his real name."

Max listened to the silence, expecting Billy to continue. He was aware that Billy might be about to provide the information that Phil Draper had been racking her brains trying to locate. Yet he still wasn't convinced that it had much relevance to the case.

"You still there, Mr. Becker?"

"Yes, yes, Billy. Go on. I'm listening."

"His real name was Harrison. That was his daddy's last name. The full name, his daddy's, I mean, was Jake Harrison, if I remember right. Anyway, when his momma brought him to the home, she made him promise not to mention anything about his daddy, and to use the name Fourcade instead of Harrison.

"He was named John, after his daddy. I guess when he got to the Home, they got the name mixed up. Either that, or he decided to use part of his daddy's name as his first name, and his momma's name as his last. It was a long time ago, Mr. Becker. A lot's happened since then. And I didn't believe some of what he said. You know how kids are."

"He told you all this?"

"Yes, sir. I thought I'd forgotten most of it, but when I saw him being released, I started to remember. Then, when I saw his picture in the newspaper and read about you prosecuting him, most of the rest came back. Fourcade's a hard dude to forget, you know what I mean? We didn't have it so good at the Burris Home, but Fourcade had it worse than anybody. He and Old Man Burris didn't get along at all. Anyway, I've been trying to call you for the last two days. You're one hard dude to get ahold of."

"Yeah," said Max. "Sorry."

He was piecing together Billy's information, trying to quickly determine what bearing it had on the case. Even though Phil Draper would be happy to learn of Fourcade's true name, it didn't appear that this newly discovered information brought them any closer to pinning the Ripper crimes on Harris Fourcade, or on anyone else, for that matter.

"I just thought you should know," said Billy.

"Thanks."

"Sorry about calling you at home."

"That's okay, Billy. Don't worry about calling me if it's something important."

"Well," said Billy, "they're telling me that I have to get off. Mr. Becker, could you do me a favor and maybe mention to Miguelito the next time you see him that I wouldn't mind talking to him? It gets a little lonely in here sometimes."

Max tried not to think of what might be happening to Billy inside. It was part of the insulating attitude that came with being a criminal defense lawyer. You didn't want to get too close to the bad guys. You didn't want to let them work their way under your skin. It only led to trouble.

"I'll do that," said Max. He hung up the phone.

"A break on the Darling case?" said Gentry. He was still seated at the kitchen table.

"I doubt it."

Max was uncertain how much of his discussion with Billy he wanted to disclose to David Gentry. He assumed that Gentry would represent Fourcade if the charges were refiled. And what Billy Darling had disclosed seemed to have no real bearing on the case. Not yet, anyway.

Max wasn't even sure how much of it was true. Billy wasn't the most credible of historians. Like Billy had said, there were a lot of kids in foster homes that made up stories to convince themselves that their lives weren't as desperate as they knew they were. Billy Darling, Max thought, was probably no exception.

Max decided it wouldn't do any harm to fill Gentry in on the conversation.

"Billy Darling says he knows Fourcade. They were in the same foster home together as kids."

Gentry's eyebrows raised, but nothing more.

"He says that Fourcade is not his real name. That his real last name is Harrison, and that he was named after his father."

Gentry's expression remained impassive, calmly taking in what Max was saying.

"Fourcade's real name," said Max, "is John Harrison, after his father, Jake."

Gentry bolted ramrod straight against the back of his chair. His chest heaved with a deep breath, and his eyes opened wide. He held his breath for several seconds, then rolled his eyes toward the ceiling, exhaling in a slow whistle.

"What?" said Max.

Gentry closed his eyes. He moved his head slowly back and forth, as if in a trance, disbelieving.

"What is it?"

Gentry opened his eyes, then gripped the edge of the table. Max noticed his knuckles going white.

"I knew a Jake Harrison," he said, in a monotone.

To Max, it looked as if David Gentry had been visited by the dead. As it turned out, he wasn't far off the mark.

"He died in prison on death row," said Gentry. "Convicted of murder. I was the one who recommended the death sentence."

19

They decided to hell with their pact about not talking cases. Gentry spent another half-hour at Max's place trying to brainstorm with the information Billy Darling had provided. Neither man felt much like running anymore.

"Let's put aside whether Fourcade's the Ripper or not," said Max. "Let's say he isn't, okay? Do you think it's just a coincidence that the first lawyer he calls when he's arrested is the DA who helped put his father on death row?"

"But you said he didn't know his father."

"Darling said that. The kid was seven or eight years old. Do you really think his mom never mentioned anything to him about where he came from?"

"It's possible," said Gentry. "Fourcade's mom and this guy shack up a few times, she gets pregnant, he disappears. It's not exactly Ripley's Believe It or Not."

Max could see that Gentry was playing devil's advocate. Like in law school, when as a student you were assigned to argue one side of an issue regardless of your personal beliefs. It was a skill that grew to be second nature with lawyers. It was the type of thing that could really screw with your mind if you didn't remember that it was all an academic exercise. Gentry hadn't gone that far—yet.

"So you're saying that of the thousands of lawyers in this city, Harris Fourcade just happened to pick you, and it had absolutely nothing to do with your putting his dad on death row? By the way, what happened to him?"

"He died."

"Not in the gas chamber?"

"No. Prison fight. He was killed—knifed, I think. It was a long time ago."

"So your decision about going for death really had no bearing on whether he lived or died?"

"Probably not," said Gentry.

His eyes wandered toward a small framed picture on Max's kitchen counter. It was of Max standing with his arms around Rosalie and Ryan. It triggered something in the back of his mind, something important. The thought lasted for only a split-second, then disappeared.

"I'll relay the information to Phil Draper," said Max. "She can check out Jake Harrison's criminal history, perhaps pull the original investigative reports, if they exist. See what she can find out about this Burris foster home."

Gentry used Max's phone to contact the deputy DA assigned to weekend duty. As a favor, he arranged for Gentry to gain access to the DA's office and their files on a Saturday.

An hour or so after leaving Max's home, David Gentry found himself dressed in his fluorescent nylon running shorts and his Nike's, seated in a room just down the hall from his old office, going through boxes of old death penalty cases that were awaiting placement in storage.

As a prosecutor, Gentry had always managed to

keep the death penalty files with him, claiming that he would be responsible for finding the space to store the records, and that, on occasion, it was helpful to consult certain files in preparation for his interviews with the media.

Up until the last ten years, the number of death penalty filings by the DA's office hadn't been high enough to present a storage problem. Even after California had passed the Death Penalty Initiative, which revived the use of the gas chamber, the first death penalty cases amounted to a mere trickle in the ocean of criminal filings.

In those days, the filing of a death penalty case was a major media event. Only certain deputies, those with proven expertise and experience, were allowed to prosecute such cases. The public defender's office also had a policy of allowing only senior trial deputies to represent defendants facing the gas chamber.

Things had changed drastically in the last ten years, with the increase in drive-by gang shootings, drug murders, and the prevailing attitude on the streets that life was worth only as much as a Rolex watch or a pair of Air Jordans.

In recent years, one could enter any superior court in the county on any day of the year and observe at least one death penalty case, often more, winding its way through the courts.

In his years as the DA of Death, Gentry had compiled a master list of cases that covered every death penalty decision he'd made during his tenure as a prosecutor. The cases for a given year were organized alphabetically by the defendant's name. At the front of each case, he had placed a yellow preprinted form containing the defendant's name, the date the case was filed, the trial deputy's name, and the name of the defense attorney. Attached to the yellow sheet were copies of the various memoranda from the trial and from supervising deputies relating to the death penalty issue, along with a short summary of the facts of the case and the background of the defendant. A copy of the Gentry Letter was also included.

Gentry had referred to his master list countless times in providing statistics and examples to reporters and government officials. He had also found occasion to refer back to prior decisions he'd made in order to maintain the continuity in policy that he'd always considered of paramount importance.

He concluded from the fact that he discovered his master list in a box underneath three other boxes that whoever was currently making death penalty decisions for the DA's office had little or no concern with continuity.

Gentry located the Jake Harrison file and began to review its contents. On its face, the memoranda and attached reports reflected a strong case against Harris Fourcade's father.

Jake Harrison had been charged in a liquor store robbery. The reports alleged that Harrison had shot the store clerk at point-blank range after the clerk had handed over the money from the cash register. According to the sole witness, the clerk had his hands on top of the counter at the time the fatal shot was fired.

This was important, because if the clerk had been reaching for a gun, though it was not legally sufficient to create a self-defense situation, it might have provided sufficient mitigation to dissuade Gentry from recommending the death penalty.

The sole witness in the case was a transient who had been standing outside the store at the time of the robbery. Admittedly drunk, and with bad eyesight, the transient had identified Jake Harrison as the shooter, saying that Harrison had run right past him upon leaving the store. The transient, after repeated questioning by the police, had stuck to his story and his identification.

The memos from both supervising deputies were short, recommending that the death penalty be sought. The trial deputy included what knowledge he had, prior to trial, of the defense he expected Harrison to offer.

Harrison had told the police that he had been by himself at a Padres game the night of the robbery, but hadn't been able to corroborate his alibi. Harrison had said that he stopped off at Bully's on Texas Street for a couple of drinks on the way home after the game. But upon questioning by the police, the bartender couldn't be sure whether he had served Harrison or not.

Harrison had a lengthy record for theft, having done a stint in Chino for a robbery he'd committed in L.A. that had been reduced to grand theft-person. His rap sheet reflected that he'd been in and out of local jails for everything ranging from petty theft to assault to credit card forgery. At the time of the murder, Harrison was on probation for possession of a concealed firearm.

The police never recovered the murder weapon, and Harrison steadfastly adhered to his alibi. The trial deputy mentioned in his memo that the defense was requesting a polygraph examination to prove the veracity of Harrison's story.

Gentry flipped through the file, finding no documentation that the polygraph was ever administered, which was not surprising, considering that even now, over twenty years later, lie-detector evidence was still considered too unreliable to be admissible in court.

Attached to the Gentry letter were two pages of handwritten notes. Gentry recognized the handwriting as his own. The notes were his initial evaluation of the case, along with his impressions of the credibility of the prosecution's star witness based on a personal interview he'd had with the transient.

Reading the notes again, Gentry sensed the uncertainty that he'd felt at the time of the interview. The witness had admittedly been drinking the night of the shooting. He'd told Gentry that he couldn't see the face of the shooter during the robbery, but had been within a couple of feet of the man afterward.

In his notes, Gentry had written not only that the witness appeared defensive, but that he also seemed to enjoy the attention he was receiving from both the cops and the media since he'd become involved in the investigation.

Gentry paused for a moment, looking away from the Harrison file to the stack of boxes that almost filled the small room. The Jake Harrison case had been one of the first he'd decided. Still, there was nothing about this particular decision that had stuck in his memory.

Other cases had bothered him, plaguing him with uncertainty. Had he made the right decision? Was he missing something? Had an innocent man been sentenced to death?

It was the stuff of nightmares, the dreams in which he spoke, without being heard, to the gathering of faces he'd condemned to die. *Why me?* they all said, their lips mouthing the silent question.

Gentry saw a twisted and perverted reflection of himself in the blank, shadowy expressions of those awaiting death.

Why me?

He normally didn't include his notes in the master file. There had to be a special reason for doing so. On the few occasions that he had, it was to explain his decision-making process, to elaborate on some issue that he had not wanted to include in his Gentry letter.

He always kept these notes separate from the formal DA's case file, considering them more his personal property than part of the public record.

But he had attached two pages of notes to the master file on Jake Harrison.

The more he thought about it, the more he felt that there was something about Harrison's case that remained unexplained.

In the end, he'd gone along with the supervising and trial deputies, and authorized the trial deputy to seek the death penalty. Harrison's long criminal history, his lack of a corroborated alibi, the apparent certainty of the prosecution witness, the cold-blooded shooting, all pointed toward death.

And in that sense, Gentry mused, he had been right. The addendum from the trial deputy reflecting a jury verdict of death served, in a way, to vindicate his decision.

Yet in his handwritten notes, Gentry could see what the others could not: he saw himself agonizing over the decision, as he had agonized over many such decisions. Between the lines, he recognized his own uncertainty, the intense guilt he felt over having to play God with the life of a man whose name he had all but forgotten until now.

Only Jake Harrison knew if he was truly guilty. The lawyers and the courts constructed a fiction to which they all swore allegiance. Part of the oath was that you could question the facts and question the law, but you never questioned the system itself. The alleged beauty of the system—what made it work, according to its participants—was that each of its members knew his role and didn't go beyond it.

Jake Harrison had been represented by counsel who had presented his client's alibi as best as his legal skills and personal desire would allow. The People of The

State of California had, within the rule of law, presented the case against Jake Harrison. Twelve members of the community had considered both sides and determined that Harrison had been proved guilty beyond a reasonable doubt and to a moral certainty.

The system, its supporters would later claim, had worked once again. It had justified its existence. Jake Harrison was water under the bridge. It was time to move on to the next case.

What more was there to consider?

Gentry spent the drive home thinking about Jake Harrison, frustrated with himself for not being able to remember every detail.

He could no longer recall what the prosecution witness looked like, nor could he recall his own thoughts upon interviewing the transient, other than what he had scribbled in his notes.

Gentry wondered just how much of his father's history young Harris Fourcade had been privy to. Fourcade had been left at the foster home about the same time that Jake Harrison was sentenced to death. The mystery of Dolores Fourcade's actions had been solved. It didn't take much for Gentry to piece together what must have happened: a young mother alone in the world, the father of her child sentenced to death. No money, no other person to turn to for help. Perhaps she'd never really cared for the boy. Perhaps, for her, Fourcade, like his father, was just a painful living reminder of the mistakes she'd made in life.

Perhaps it was, as he had argued with Max, just a coincidence that their paths had crossed once again some twenty years later.

Gentry's thoughts were still focused on Harris Fourcade when he walked through the door and saw the light on his answering machine blinking. He punched at the button, listening to the tape rewind as he shuffled off to the refrigerator for a beer.

There was only one message, a female voice Gentry didn't recognize. He poured the beer into a glass. He was not paying close attention to the voice, about to flick on the TV, trying to rid himself of the image of Jake Harrison, when something the voice said made him stop dead in his tracks. He heard the glass of beer drop from his hand to the floor. Thoughts of Harris Fourcade and Jake Harrison raced uncontrollably through his mind. He pinched his eyes tightly shut against the explosive jolt that was pulsing through his head, blasting fragments from his skull.

It couldn't be . . . I couldn't have been that stupid . . .

Gentry hit the button on the tape machine, impatiently waiting for the tape to rewind. He pressed his palms to the sides of his head. The inchoate realization of what he had done shot through him like the flame from a blowtorch, setting his brain on fire.

"Mr. Gentry," the voice on the tape said, then hesitated. "You don't know me, but I'm Susan's roommate." The voice hesitated again, and Gentry found himself stupidly trying to will the voice to continue.

"I don't know if this is anything to be concerned about," the roommate continued, "but Susan went out yesterday morning and never came back. I'm sure there's a logical explanation for all this. You probably know where she is . . . I just thought, since she didn't mention anything to me, and her suitcase and clothes are still here, that I'd give you a call. Anyway, you've got the number. Call me if you want. 'Bye."

Max tried the number again, after getting the recording.

Again, the recording: *This number has been disconnected. There is no new number. Please check the directory for further information.*

He thought the phone company must have screwed up, maybe there was something wrong with the service in her area. He got into his car and drove to her house, thinking about what he would say.

He hadn't talked with Samantha since that day at the Embarcadero. Between working with Draper on the Fourcade investigation and preparing the Billy Darling trial, he'd had little time to himself. Keeping busy had been a mixed blessing. Facing the issues that Sam presented was something he knew he had to do, but didn't want to.

He'd finally decided to sit down and talk it through with her. His plan was that they'd both explain what they wanted from the rest of their lives and from each other. Get everything out on the table, no secrets, no hidden agendas.

If they felt that they could still see each other after that, then great. No guarantees or promises, except that each of them would be honest, neither posturing for the other.

In his head, he knew there was a chance that they could make a go of it, but only a chance.

He was screwed up over Rosalie and Ryan, and there was no way that he or Sam could just snap their fingers and have that emotional baggage disappear. He would tell her that. He would tell Sam that if she could deal with his problems, his guilt, the whole emotional mess, he would work with her, try to put the demons behind him. That he thought he loved her, though at this point in his life, he wasn't at all sure what love was anymore.

As he walked up the steps to her apartment, his thoughts began to seem much more confusing than they had earlier. He knocked on the door with the uncomfortable feeling that it wasn't going to work out.

He knocked again, receiving no answer, then looked at his watch. It was six o'clock, Mitchell's normal dinnertime. The drapes on the front window had been pulled. He walked around in back and noticed that her parking space was empty.

Phone disconnected, car gone . . . Where could they be?

He returned to his car and headed for the Embarcadero, trying to come up with ideas about where they might have gone, pushing aside what he knew was the very real possibility. Sam had decided to call it quits. She and Mitchell were gone for good.

The Embarcadero was almost empty, the tourists having returned to their hotels for whatever it was they had planned for the evening.

A light breeze was blowing in off the ocean, rustling the paper napkins, soft-drink cups, and tourist maps that skirted along the pavement.

At the edge of the world, slowly falling from sight, a fiery orange sun cast its remaining illumination on the buildings and water before sinking into the darkness of the sea.

The carousel was empty. An old man was busy quickly running a cleaning cloth over the wooden animals, talking to them, or perhaps to himself, as he worked.

Max thrust his hands in his coat pockets, suddenly feeling cold.

He'd waited too long.
The story of his life.
Now they were gone.

He was torn between racing up to Santa Barbara to look for his daughter and calling the cops up north.

It had been only a week since he'd dropped Susan off at the campus. She had called every day since then, but when she'd missed a day, Gentry had figured she was just busy. He'd never expected her to keep up the daily routine.

Now this.

He'd finally gotten back to the roommate, who wasn't able to say much more than she had in her message. She still hadn't heard anything from Susan, or from anyone who'd seen her. Susan had missed two days of classes, at least, the classes that they had in common. She told Gentry that Susan could use her notes when she returned.

Gentry had thanked the young girl, making sure that she knew to call him if she heard anything. He now sat on the couch, his right hand resting on the telephone.

If he called the police, he thought, they'd ask him how long Susan had been missing, take down the statistical information, and probably place the matter at the end of a long list of what they considered more important police work.

He thought about calling Max. But what could he do other than tell him what he already knew?

There was nobody in Santa Barbara to contact, nobody he could ask to check around and make phone calls for him. Hell, he'd never been to the campus prior to dropping Susan off. He was totally unfamiliar with the places a kid who skipped classes might hang out.

Not that that would have helped. Susan wouldn't have missed her classes, not unless she'd been forced to . . . not unless something had happened. And even then, she'd have called.

Unless . . .

The more he conjured up scenarios, the more upset he became.

He decided to drive up the coast right away, not

taking the time to pack a bag or even notify his office. He was at the door on his way out when the phone rang.

He recognized Susan's voice immediately. It quivered, and he knew she'd been crying.

She said, "Daddy?"

Then she repeated it again, as if terrified: *"Daddy!"*

Then another voice came on the line, cool and calm—and terrifying.

"Gentry," the voice said, "I think you know who this is."

And David Gentry nodded to himself, realizing that his worst fears had come true.

20

She awoke to the feeling of falling backwards. Her eyes focused on a window, a nearby table, a dark wood dresser, the bed on which she lay. She closed her eyes, allowing herself to fall dizzily head first through space. When she focused again, it was on the pair of feet that protruded from the end of the bed, long toes coming right out of the mattress, no body.

"You were out for a long time."

She turned toward the sound, first with her head, then the rest of her, but her arms wouldn't move.

"Just be still," the voice said.

She was trying to place the voice. It wasn't at all familiar. She could hear movement in the room, but was unable to see who was there.

"It'll wear off in a little while," he said.

Susan Gentry again tried to move her arms, only to feel a stinging burn on her wrists as she twisted first to one side, then the other.

"Like I said," the voice had moved closer, "just be still. You can't get away."

She could see the face now. She blinked, still thinking that this was some bad dream, and that if she tried hard enough she could shake herself awake. She started to feel cold, then realized that she was wearing no clothes, that the toes that stuck out at the end of the bed were hers.

"You're a sweet thing," he said softly, but not in a way that made her feel relaxed.

She watched as his eyes moved slowly down her body, stopping in the middle. He had a half-smile that made his mouth go up on one side. His eyes didn't move, but just kept staring at the same spot.

"Very nice," he said.

She noticed tiny bubbles of spittle in his moustache and at the corners of his mouth.

She remembered now: he had approached her, saying he was one of her dad's clients, that he had a message from him for her. He drove a van.

And she remembered opening her eyes and seeing the inside of the van, then drifting off to sleep.

"Do you know who I am?"

The voice was within inches of her cheek. She could smell something sweet on his breath, like sugary cough syrup.

She didn't know what to say. A name was floating in the back of her head, an easy name, one she had heard many times.

She didn't answer.

"You do, don't you?"

Again, the half-smile. There was something odd about his smile, and about the way his tongue seemed to move to make the words come out.

She nodded her head slowly.

"I thought so."

He seemed pleased, even proud. He stood close to the side of the bed so that she had to look at the bulge between his legs. He began to massage himself. She turned away.

"Look at me," he said, softly at first; and then, when

she refused, he got close to her face and yelled in her ear. She jumped as his voice reverberated through her head. She turned back toward him.

"That's better," he said.

He walked over to the window and removed something from a small table. When he returned, she could see he had something held tightly in his hand.

"I'm going to save you for dessert," he whispered.

The object in his hand was a curved piece of metal. With a snap of his wrist, a shiny blade clicked into place. He held the curved blade up to the light of the window, turning it slowly in his hand, inspecting it. The notch at the end of the crescent-shaped blade framed the light against the window like a tiny sun.

"Your father is an evil man," he said, still mesmerized by the glint of the blade. "And evil must be punished."

He looked away from the knife into her face, then moved closer, placing the knife on her lower lip, hooking the notched edge over her lip so that she could taste the cold metal tip inside her mouth.

"He took my father from me," he said, letting the tip of the knife trace a faint line over her lip and down her chin. He kept the knife moving, circling her breasts, then flicking at her nipples with the notched edge. She winced, letting out a constricted squeal, sucking the moisture from her teeth; it was like the sound balloons make when the air is let out.

"I suppose he never told you about that? No, he wouldn't. That wouldn't go along with his image: Mr. Lawyer, the DA of Death . . ."

Her mind was almost clear now. She'd hit on the name: Fourcade, Harris Fourcade, the one charged as the Ripper. Her dad's client.

The one he had gotten off.

She could see that she was tied to the bed, her ankles and wrists wrapped with electrical cord. Outside she heard the sound of birds. The chirping didn't seem to fit. She thought of what she'd read about his other victims, and that made the happy chirping of the birds sound as if they were mocking her.

She was with him, alone, tied hand and foot to the bed. Yet outside everything was as it should be, as if none of this had happened. Nobody knew; nobody would save her. She was going to be his next victim.

"What do you want?" she said, barely able to get the words out.

He looked back at her from where he stood, the knife poised between her legs. He let the tip move slowly downward, running it along the lips of her sex, then back up.

"Relax," he said, still probing at her with the knife.

She felt her legs, like steel girders, stiff and extended, motionless, afraid to move for fear that the sharp edge of the blade would slice her as it had the others.

"Relax," he repeated. "This is just a warmup. I wouldn't hurt you, at least not now."

He turned, taking in her eyes with his. He said, "You still don't understand, do you? You're not the one I want." He paused, then added, "When *he's* here, watching . . . when he's been through all that he put me through, when he's suffered like I've suffered—then it will be your time. You're just an added bonus, you might say, but by no means the main course."

"It will all happen right here," he said, his eyes glazing over. "Everything comes full circle. It must. It's my fate."

He smiled, and it struck her as odd that even now she felt the slightest twinge of pity because of his deformity.

"You're the bait," he said. "You're going to make a

307

phone call to your daddy, and you're going to tell him that for now, you're all right. Then we're going to arrange to have your daddy come and visit you. Just the three of us. Won't that be nice?"

Again, the smile.

"You see, it's your daddy that I really want, Susan."

His eyes drifted to the window for several seconds. Then he walked over to the table and a few moments later returned carrying two large notebooks.

"You must understand," he said, sitting beside her on the bed, holding one of the notebooks open in the palm of his hand like a priest reading Scripture, "I've kept track of your daddy." He looked down at the notebook, fingering the corner of the page before turning it.

"Your mother was an attractive woman," he said, as if to himself. "Too bad she had to die the way she did."

He was still looking at the notebook, not at her. Susan had given up trying to free herself from the electrical cord. Her only hope, she thought, was to yell, and trust that somebody outside might hear her. She screamed as loudly as her voice would allow, hearing the sound come out incredibly small and weak. No one would hear her.

He just looked at her, smiled, and moved closer. Still grinning, he shook his head, drew back his arm, and shot his fist into the center of her face.

She saw nothing for a split-second, then darkness. She heard a popping noise and felt the hard shaft of something sharp tearing through tissue, ripping into the space between her eyes. She wanted to bring her hand to her face, but couldn't. When she breathed through her nose, her nostrils exploded in pain, the ache like shards of glass stabbing into her cheeks and eyes. She opened her mouth finally, grabbing a breath of air, tasting the blood that was running down the back of her throat.

"You must promise me," he said, "that you won't ever do that again."

He was a blur now, though the voice was the same. She could no longer breathe through her nose, and when she closed one eye, she saw that part of her face, purple and broken.

She wanted to shut her eyes, go to sleep, then wake up to find that she was back in her own house with her dad.

"Promise!" he again yelled in her ear, and it sounded like cannons exploding. She felt moisture on her cheeks and it tickled her. She wasn't sure if it was tears or blood, or both. She nodded.

"Good," he said, getting up off the bed. "I have to prepare," he said, walking away from her to the window.

"He'll be here soon. We must both be ready for him."

There were really no decisions to make. Fourcade had said no cops. Fourcade had Susan. If he saw cops, if he even smelled cops, he'd kill Susan. He said he didn't care if he died or not. He'd kill Susan first, before the cops could even get near.

David Gentry believed him.

That stuff about the SWAT team swooping in like Israeli commandos and removing the victim from harm's way while neutralizing the bad guy was just so much TV bullshit. Sure, they got lucky every once in a while, but he'd seen too many "covert" situations turned into OK Corral shootouts. He couldn't afford to let that happen, not while Fourcade still had his daughter.

Gentry headed north on Rosecrans Boulevard, impatient with the five o'clock commuter jam-up. All he could think about was Susan, and how stupid he'd been. Max had seen it; Max had tried to warn him without making it seem like he was giving advice. There was no incredible coincidence. This had all been carefully planned, expertly laid out, replayed again and again until Fourcade had it down perfectly.

It was payback time, Gentry thought. He couldn't believe his own naïveté. As if someone like Harris Fourcade would actually know nothing about his father!

The thought now seemed impossible to believe, but he had offered it to Max as believable. He, the great David Gentry, the DA of Death, had committed the cardinal sin, he'd been sucked in by his client. He'd let his ego get in the way—his ego, and his guilt.

At Washington, Gentry turned east, heading toward the Hillcrest area and University Avenue.

Once on University, Gentry pulled to the curb and looked back, wondering if he had missed the turnoff. His heart was racing, and he cursed himself for wasting precious time. He swung the car back onto the main road, turning it around, almost colliding with oncoming traffic.

Heading back, he spotted the turnoff and maneuvered the car into the left-turn lane. After what seemed like an eternity, the traffic cleared and he was able to turn. He followed the street going south until it dead-ended in a remote corner just west of Florida Canyon.

Gentry found the spot, just a narrow mouth of blacktop that became gravel fifty yards from the main road. He was heading back into the hillside that abutted the canyon. After the first fifty yards, the houses became more scarce, and he felt as if he was in the middle of nowhere.

He followed the switchbacks as the road climbed deeper into the hillside, finally leveling out on a stretch of gravel parkway from which he could see the highway below.

He made a sharp right, cutting back into the mountain. The trail narrowed as it cascaded down a gulley and through some wild, low-growing brush. As he eased the car up the other side, Gentry looked to his left and saw the two-story house, like a sentinel, resting on an elevated plateau and set against a gray granite backdrop of jagged cliff.

Susan was there. The van was parked under a low-hanging eucalyptus partially covered with feathery tendrils of lush green growth. Both rear doors of the van were open, and Susan sat inside, her legs dangling out the back.

Gentry pulled within twenty yards of the van. Susan didn't move.

He looked around quickly, then got out of the car. Susan smiled, but the smile quickly disappeared. She was telling him something with her eyes, the way she held her head. He looked around again, seeing no one. Susan was silent, and Gentry wondered if perhaps Fourcade was inside the van, waiting for him.

Still, thought Gentry, even if Fourcade was lying in wait, there was nothing he could do; there was no choice. He had come for his daughter, and to his great relief, she was still alive. Fourcade hadn't hurt her. He had made it in time.

"Are you okay?" he said, putting his arms around her, then grabbing her hands in his. He saw that her nose was crooked, pushed in and bent. On both sides the skin had turned a dark mottled purple, as had the area right below each eye. Gentry looked into those eyes, seeing his own reflection, as the knives of guilt tore into his chest, laying him open.

"Daddy," Susan said, but that was all he heard. He saw something move inside the murky reflection of his

311

daughter's eyes.

Too quick.

The back of his head suddenly went numb with pain. He heard a ringing, the amplified sound of his own blood pulsing in his ears, a throbbing, deathly rhythm. He thought of Jackie, and then of Susan—and of how he had failed them both.

Then he felt himself falling, and everything turned to black.

21

David Gentry had called Max from the DA's office downtown, telling him what he'd discovered about Harris Fourcade's father. They'd made arrangements to meet at Gentry's home to go over the Jake Harrison material.

Max found the connection between the elder Fourcade and his son intriguing. Yet he still wasn't sure how it related to the rapes and the murder. And the Gentry-Fourcade connection was still a question mark for both men.

Max decided to take Cardozo along, since he'd missed his run the previous day, and the dog always liked to sniff around in strange territory. It was about as adventurous as his life got. Besides, Max needed someone to talk to about Sam, and what his next step should be, and Cardozo was a great listener.

Sam had left without a trace, not even a forwarding address. She wanted to start a brand new life, Max assumed. The last thing she'd want would be to perpetuate old relationships. He knew he had to think of something, that he couldn't just let things end like that. Maybe talking to Cardozo would help him decide.

Max was surprised, as he pulled into Gentry's driveway, to see the garage open but no car parked inside.

"It doesn't look like anyone's here, boy. Let's take a look inside anyway," he said.

Max stepped from the car and headed toward the front door, Cardozo a few steps behind him.

He bounded up the front porch steps and rang the bell.

No response.

He tried again, this time knocking forcefully. Cardozo barked for added emphasis.

Still no response.

"This looks funny, boy."

Max placed his hand on the doorknob and pushed the door open. He looked back at Cardozo, flashing an expression of surprise, and confirmation.

"Left without locking the front door," said Max. "Also not his style."

They entered the house slowly.

Max yelled, "David? You home?"

There was no answer. In the living room, the television was blaring. Max walked over and placed his hand on the back of the case.

"It's hot," he said. "This set's been on for at least a few hours, probably longer."

He moved toward the kitchen. Strewn haphazardly on the table were several manila file folders and a pile of loose paperwork. Max glanced down at the paperwork, casually poking at it with his finger.

He recognized the documents as Gentry's records on Jake Harrison. He found Gentry's personal notes on the Harrison case and began to read them.

When he'd finished, he walked over to the telephone, intending to call Gentry's office to see if perhaps he'd been called in on an emergency.

On a small notepad by the telephone something caught his eye. Someone had written the name "Fourcade," along with what appeared to be directions in a sort of shorthand scribble. Written just above Fourcade's name was Susan's name, along with a telephone number prefaced by a nonlocal area code.

An idea was beginning to present itself. An image formed behind his eyes, still vague and indistinct, but terrifying all the same.

Max dialed the number.

"Hello," said the young female voice on the other end.

"Is Susan Gentry there?" said Max.

There was no answer for a moment.

"Is this her father?"

"No," said Max. He explained who he was and why he was calling.

"I'm Susan's roommate," the voice said. "I talked with her dad twice already. First I called about Susan being missing, then . . ."

"Missing?"

"Yeah, didn't he tell you? She's been gone for a couple of days. I told her dad about it."

The image behind his eyes became clearer. In it, Harris Fourcade was smiling, standing at the counsel table at the preliminary hearing, just after his case had been dismissed. In the image, Fourcade was winking at Max, as he had in real life.

"You said you talked to David Gentry twice?"

"That's right. He called me again shortly after the first time. Sounded pretty upset. Wanted to know if I'd heard anything more."

Max stared down at Fourcade's name on the notepad. He was only half paying attention to the roommate, who was telling him about how strange it was for Susan to skip her classes. Max focused on the

315

handwritten directions, at least, what he thought were directions. He recognized the words University and Florida. Both were mere blocks from where he lived.

Max said goodbye to the roommate, thanking her for the information. He pressed the button on the phone, then punched in Phil Draper's phone number. Draper picked up on the fourth ring and sounded out of breath. Max related his conversation with Susan's roommate, and what he had discovered at Gentry's home.

"You don't think . . ."

"I don't know what to think," said Max.

It struck him that there was a loose thread to all of this. A strap that had once held everything together had now come loose and was flapping inside his head.

It was not like David Gentry to stay out all night, and it was not like him to charge out of the house leaving the television blasting and the front door unlocked. David had obviously been concerned over Susan's disappearance, which, Max thought, meant that he didn't know where his daughter was. The most likely explanation was that David Gentry was out there somewhere trying to find her.

Max suspected that Harris Fourcade was not an innocent bystander to all of this. Fourcade and his father were like Preface and Epilogue, their importance understood only after one has read the story in between.

Jake Harrison, a phantom from the deeply buried past, lay in pieces, like a puzzle, atop David Gentry's kitchen table. Harris Fourcade, a piece of that puzzle, had weaseled his way into Gentry's life, under false pretenses.

Max wanted to know why.

"That home," said Max, still talking to Draper, "where Fourcade was placed . . . the foster home."

316

"Burris Foster Home," said Draper.

"Yeah. You don't happen to remember where that was located, do you?"

"Sure," she said. "In the Hillcrest area, near Balboa Park."

Max stared down at the piece of notepaper.

"Why do you ask?"

Max didn't answer right away. He looked at Cardozo, who lay on the floor next to him.

"I think he's there," Max finally said.

"Fourcade?"

"All of them," Max responded.

22

There was an object opposite him, positioned between himself and the sun, backlighted in black. Its outline kept shifting, blurred, like a trout at the bottom of a shallow pond. A throbbing ache at the back of his head reached behind his eyes, tiny fingers pulling at his nerves, playing with his pain.

When Gentry tried to focus on the thing in front of him, it would click into blackness for a moment, then turn watery, indistinct.

He sensed that he was inside, but his eyes were telling him that he wasn't. He felt the shaded protection of walls and a roof. Yet the sunlight behind the figure streamed through a too-large window, and he could feel and hear the wind spinning around him, rustling at his feet.

Gentry closed his eyes, trying to remember the last image he had seen, trying to determine where he was.

Waves of recollection washed over him, dizzying him, filling his mind with incoherent bits and pieces of faces and events. Susan's face, battered and bruised, flashed clearly before him. He grasped it, concentrating on what had happened: her phone call; Fourcade;

driving into the canyon.

Things slowly began to fall into place.

When he opened his eyes again, he was still dizzy, but he could see him.

Only he was different.

Gentry thought he was still dreaming, so he let his eyes close again. He told himself that the thing he had just seen was part of a dream, not real. Like one of those hideous creatures, gargoyles, carved into the side of an old church or atop a stone column. He was afraid to look again.

What if the thing was still there?

"Well, how do you like the new me?"

Gentry thought: the thing is talking now. Either that, or I'm dreaming that the creature has a voice and is addressing me.

His eyes focused on the human shape seated in a folding canvas chair just a few feet away. The throbbing was still there, constant, like someone sawing metal inside his head. But his vision was clearing. He recognized the person, the monstrous creature of his dreams.

It was Harris Fourcade, except he'd changed. Someone had done something to him, or he'd done it to himself. Something raw, primordial. His face was swollen around the mouth and nose. He'd transformed himself. Gentry blinked hard, trying to focus.

"Bet you've never seen anything like this."

Fourcade was smiling, laughing. The barely noticeable cleft that had been hidden under his moustache was now clearly visible. Fourcade had shaved off his moustache, revealing a raw, purplish-red inflammation, like a tiny finger that had been stripped of skin, protruding from one nostril. The finger seemed to wrap around Fourcade's upper lip, hooking it, pulling it

319

back and away from the other side.

Gentry had, in fact, never seen anything like it before, and for a moment he thought it was just one of those frightful Halloween masks that kids wore. He had the strange sense that he was looking through the lens of a camera, trying to get the face into focus, unable to bring the right and left sides of Fourcade's mouth onto the same plane.

Fourcade said, "You haven't even asked about your darling daughter."

Gentry followed Fourcade's eyes as they shifted to his right. He saw Susan lying on her back, just a couple feet away. Her clothes had been removed. She looked to be asleep, or . . .

"Don't worry," said Fourcade. "She's just resting. I gave her a little something to help her sleep. She should be awake soon."

Fourcade smiled, a wild grin, holding his mouth open and taking short quick breaths. Snorts. Gentry thought of a rabid animal.

"I want both of you to be awake when we have our little party."

"Why are you doing this?" said Gentry. Thoughts of Jake Harrison flashed through his mind.

"Come on, now, counselor, you must have figured that one out by now."

"Your father."

"Very good. At first I was worried that you might put it together too soon. But then I realized that that wouldn't happen. And do you know why? Because a person like you, one who has taken it upon himself to play God, wouldn't remember some trivial life-and-death decision he'd made over twenty years ago.

"And, sure enough, when I came to you, flashing my money, you didn't have the slightest idea who I was. It

320

never struck you that you were looking at the orphaned son of the man you had wrongly sentenced to death."

"But he died in prison," said Gentry. "He wasn't executed. My decision had nothing to do with your father's death."

"Wrong again," snapped Fourcade. He squirmed impatiently in his chair, crossing and then uncrossing his legs.

Gentry was now aware that he and Susan were inside a van of some sort, and that the rear doors of the van were open, letting in the sunlight. He remembered seeing Susan seated inside the van just before everything had gone dark.

When he tried to lift his hand to touch the back of his head, he felt his wrists tied together behind him.

"You sentenced him to *death!*" yelled Fourcade.

He got off the chair, angrily slapping it aside with his hand. It rattled off the walls of the van, then tumbled out the back. Fourcade jumped from the van, then stood outside, looking in. Gentry could see that he was still enraged by the turn the discussion had taken.

"It was you, Mr. Gentry, you, the great DA of Death, who killed my father."

Fourcade had one foot on the rear bumper and was pointing inside as he spoke. Gentry heard Susan stir at his side.

"I've kept all the records," said Fourcade. He reached into the corner of the van, just inside the door, and lifted two large notebooks.

"Here, in these. I've got it all. All those years, when you were sitting up there in your nice, insulated office, deciding who would live and who would die. It's all here."

Fourcade had a notebook in each hand and was

holding them over his head, punching at the sky.

"So don't tell me that you had nothing to do with my father's death. Because I know better."

Fourcade placed the notebooks back inside the van. He turned his back for a moment, and Gentry could see his shoulders heave with heavy breathing.

"Take it out on me," said Gentry. "Do what you want to me, but leave her alone."

Fourcade turned around, the smile twisted to a snarl, his eyes flashed bright with satisfaction.

"It's not that easy," he said.

"You want to get even with me. Okay, I understand that. But leave Susan out of it. She has nothing to do with the decisions I've made."

"You're absolutely right," said Fourcade. "Nobody understands that better than me. But in this world, Mr. Gentry, the innocent must suffer. It's sad, but very true. You taught me that. You made a decision to take my father's life. Because of that, you took away *my* life, and my mother's.

"I've learned my lessons well. As I said, the innocent are destined to suffer, Mr. Gentry. Your precious daughter is going to suffer because of what you did. Because of what you *are.*"

"This is crazy," said Gentry. "You'll never get away with this. You can't kill us both and expect to get away."

"You just don't understand, do you?"

"You raped those women."

"Ahh, the great trial lawyer finally gets something right. It's poetic justice, don't you think, that the great prosecutor turns out to be the one who helped the Ripper beat the rap?"

Fourcade let out a belly laugh that echoed inside the van.

322

He added, "And you don't know the half of it, Mr. Gentry."

Gentry was trying to follow Fourcade's thoughts, while at the same time hoping he'd remember something about Fourcade or what he'd read in Jake Harrison's file that he could use to throw him off balance, buy some time.

"But I intend to explain all of that to you, counselor."

Fourcade lifted himself back inside the van. He removed a curved knife from his pocket and flicked open the blade.

"First," said Fourcade. "I'm going to have some fun with your daughter. And you're going to watch."

Fourcade knelt at Susan's side and dangled the knife between her legs, looking back over his shoulder to make sure his every movement was being observed.

Gentry tried to throw himself at Fourcade, but the ropes around his wrists and ankles were tied together by a longer stretch of rope, which had been fastened to a metal hook welded to the wall of the van. Each time he lunged, his hands and ankles were pulled further behind him, hog-tying him, preventing him from moving.

"She's still a little groggy," said Fourcade, getting on his knees, holding the knife at his side. "I want her to be awake for this. I want both of you to know exactly what I'm doing."

Fourcade turned and moved toward Gentry. He hovered over him, the knife pressed against his throat. "I want, Mr. David Gentry, for you to watch as I do to your precious Susan what I did to the others. I want you to suffer slowly, just as I have."

Gentry noticed tiny balls of spittle at the corners of Fourcade's mouth. He was close enough so that as

323

Fourcade spoke, he covered Gentry's face in a fine spray. Gentry sensed that Fourcade was aware that he was doing this. He'd been able to control his speech earlier, but now seemed to take some demonic pleasure in exhibiting his deformity—something else for which David Gentry was to blame.

Fourcade pulled the knife away. He moved toward the notebooks, picking one up.

"I want to explain this to you," he said, suddenly calm.

Gentry figured this was part of his plan, and was grateful for the delay, though he had no idea what to do next. Even if he hadn't been tied down, it wouldn't be much of a contest. Fourcade was young and in good physical shape, and was also filled with a rage and hatred that had grown stronger over twenty years. A fifty-five-year-old out-of-shape lawyer would be no match for him.

Still, he would have traded anything for the opportunity. At least then he might have had some chance of saving Susan's life.

"You see, Mr. Gentry, I've followed your career, your life, over the last twenty years. I even have articles from when you started in the DA's office. Old newspapers, back issues."

Fourcade smiled, looking down at the notebook.

"I've been very careful about my collection. There's a section for you, and for your family. Your wife's death. Even Susan."

He looked up, and an almost peaceful expression crossed his face. Gentry realized it was merely a mask for the hatred that burned inside. Fourcade continued to flip through the pages of his notebook.

"And then there are the men who were wrongly convicted," he said. "I must have over a hundred of

324

them here. Men, like my father, who were sentenced to death, sent to prison by people like you, Mr. Gentry, only for it later to be determined that they were innocent. Men whose lives were taken away from them, from their families, because people like you made a *mistake!*"

Gentry could see the anger boiling to the surface again. Fourcade was talking himself into a rage. His words became more slurred, carelessly strung together, mispronounced. But Fourcade didn't seem to care anymore. He seemed determined to teach his father's killer a lesson, to make him suffer.

Fourcade suddenly jerked his head from the notebook.

"Ya know, I almost forgot to show you."

He turned, and lifted a length of garden hose from the floor behind him. At one end of the hose a clear plastic mask had been attached.

"Let me show you how this works," he said. He placed the mask over his face, looping the strap over his head. When he spoke, the mask gave his words an eerie nasal quality.

"You see, this strap holds the mask firmly over the mouth and nose. I take the other end of this hose and fit it over the tail pipe of the van. The rest is simple. Just start the engine."

Fourcade threw up his hands like a magician after a magic trick.

Gentry felt his stomach twist into a knot.

"It's particularly appropriate, don't you think, considering what you had planned for my father." Fourcade removed the mask and carefully placed it at his side.

"At first I was going to build my own little gas chamber. But then I realized that that wouldn't be

325

necessary. This is much more simple, and just as effective."

Fourcade chuckled to himself, then suddenly stopped, raising a hand, demanding silence. He glanced accusingly at Gentry, then cocked his head, as if he had heard something and was making sure.

"I thought I said no cops."

"I didn't . . ."

Fourcade again held up his hand, then jumped outside. Gentry lost sight of him, then heard footsteps on top of the van. A moment later, Fourcade was back at the opened rear doors, breathing heavily.

"We have visitors," he said, working quickly and efficiently to pull Susan's body out the back. He propped her against the eucalyptus, then returned.

"Looks like your friend Mr. Becker. Too bad . . . this changes things."

Fourcade began looking around inside the van as he spoke.

"There was so much more that I wanted to tell you."

Fourcade lifted the coil of hose, then suddenly grew still, his brow furrowed in thought.

"But maybe," he said, "I'll tell your friend, Mr. Becker, instead."

His eyes grew wide as if a great idea had struck him for the first time.

"Yes," he said, laughing, "your friend, Mr. Becker, of all people, will appreciate my little story."

Fourcade climbed into the van and attached the mask to Gentry's face. After checking to be certain that it was on securely, he took the other end of the hose and disappeared under the back of the van for several seconds.

"You're going to love this," he said, sliding into the driver's seat behind the wheel.

Gentry felt the van rumble as the engine cranked. He heard the driver's door slam, then saw Fourcade through the open back of the van. He had hoisted Susan's body over his shoulder,

Before he left, he said, "It's a lot quicker than the way you killed my father. So long, Mr. Gentry."

Gentry heard Fourcade's labored footsteps becoming fainter. He tried not to breathe, holding his breath until his chest was on fire and he could stand it no longer.

The first thick smoky breath didn't put him out, and neither did the next. A few seconds later, though, he knew he was falling back into his dream, one from which he thought he would never return.

23

He'd met Draper at his place. Max had dropped off
Cardozo, and the two of them had driven in his car
following the directions on David Gentry's notepad.

Phil Draper was wearing a pair of skin-tight Levis,
one of her outdoorswoman Pendleton shirts, and high-
top leather work boots with thick corrugated rubber
soles. Hidden underneath her light nylon windbreaker,
attached to a thick leather belt, Draper carried a
Beretta Model 92F compact 9mm handgun in a tooled
leather holster.

"There's a gun in the glovebox," said Max, gesturing
toward the dash.

They'd just turned off the main road and were
heading toward the canyon. Phil Draper punched the
button, and the glove box door flopped open.

"Jesus, Becker, helluva place to keep a weapon."

She removed the Smith and Wesson Model 36 Chief's
Special that Eddie Deets had given Max a few months
back.

"I don't have much use for it," said Max. "Most
judges frown on lawyers carrying guns in court."

"That's too bad," said Draper, deftly letting the
cylinder swing out for inspection. "It would save a lotta

time to just shoot the bastards in court instead of waiting until they're paroled." She handed the gun to Max.

"You know how to use that thing?" she said. She removed her own weapon, inspected the slide, then placed it on her lap.

"I've been to the range," said Max.

He set the gun on the center console. He had been about to shove the gun inside his waistband, as he'd seen scores of detectives do in court and on TV, but then thought better of it.

"That's the old style five-shot swing-out cylinder," said Draper. "It's lighter than mine, but not by much. The problem is you've got only five shots to hit your target, then you gotta reload. I bet you don't even carry speedy-loaders."

Max shook his head.

"I didn't think so. See, with only five shots, even if you've got speedy-loaders, you're at a disadvantage."

Draper lifted the 9mm in the palm of her hand, as if weighing it.

"With this," she said, "you've got a semiautomatic. Fifteen rounds to hit your target, not counting the round in the chamber. Unless you're in a fire fight with multiple suspects, if you can't take care of business with fifteen shots, you shouldn't be out there."

She reached into her pants pocket and removed a rectangular black metal clip.

"But just in case you run out," she added, "all you do is slam this baby home and you've got another fifteen rounds."

"I'll keep that in mind," said Max. He felt something stick in his throat as he considered the possibility of a shootout with Harris Fourcade.

The road had turned from blacktop to loose gravel. It was wide enough for only one car to pass. Behind

329

them, on the other side of the hill they were circling, the sun had already dipped into the canyon, throwing the gravel road and adjacent hillside into twilight. As they rounded a rocky incline, the fiery orange sun reappeared, and both of them shaded their eyes, squinting to follow the road through the glare.

"That must be it," said Draper. She snugged the 9mm back into its holster.

A ramshackle wooden house rested atop a small plateau at the end of the road. The house was in a state of severe disrepair, with parts of the roof missing. The roof rafters, weathered gray by exposure, were visible in places where the shingles had been ripped off by the wind.

A long porch, like a gallery, stretched across the front of the house and wrapped around the side. Wooden planks from the floor and railing of the porch were broken, and bits of splintered wood were strewn about the front yard. Two rows of windows, most of which were shattered or missing, rose symetrically on each side of the front door.

The second floor of the dilapidated structure was an exact duplicate of the first, except for the porch.

A single-level structure, also wood, was attached to the house at one side. It was covered in brown fiberglass shingles and had no windows facing the front. It looked as if it had been added some time after the original.

Only two of the windows of the main house still sported the heavy wood-slatted shutters. Parts of shutters had fallen from the house and littered the yard and adjacent hillside, along with rusted automobile parts, a crushed and dented metal trash can, an old refrigerator, beer bottles, tumbleweeds, and animal droppings.

A van was parked about thirty yards away, at the far

side of the house, under a giant eucalyptus.

"That's Fourcade's van," said Draper.

Max eased the car to the end of the gravel drive and turned off the engine. He looked at Draper.

"You keep an eye on the front of the house," she said, drawing her gun. "I'll check out the van."

Max got out of the car, crouching by the front wheel. He could feel the sweat in his palm making the plastic grips of the gun feel slippery. He kept an eye on the front door, while watching Draper approach the van.

Draper suddenly jumped inside the back of the van. Moments later she stuck her head out, motioning for him.

When Max got to the van, Draper was in the process of giving David Gentry mouth-to-mouth resuscitation. There was a smoky-sour stench inside.

"Turn off the fucking engine," Draper said, between breaths.

Max jumped behind the wheel, but found that there were no keys in the ignition. He searched under the dash for a few seconds and found the hood release, then raced around to the front and started pulling wires until he finally managed to kill the engine.

When he returned to the back of the van, he noticed the length of rubber hose leading from underneath the rear bumper. He crouched down, spotting where the hose was attached to the exhaust pipe.

"He'll be okay," said Draper. She had David Gentry propped up against the side wall of the van. Gentry was coughing and still seemed groggy, but he was breathing on his own.

"Susan," he moaned, coughing and barely able to get the words out. Gentry jerked his head in the direction of the house. Draper was busy removing the ropes from his hands and feet.

"He's got Susan inside," said Gentry. "Fourcade.

He's crazy, Max. He's going to kill her."

Max started for the house.

"Where you think you're going?" said Draper, jumping out the rear of the van.

"Stay with him," said Max. "Make sure he's okay. I'm going inside."

"The hell you are."

She stood chest-to-chest with Max, glaring at him, daring him to pull rank.

Max's mind shifted to Susan: the evening of the women's meeting with Draper and Esther Morse; the day she had first called him her Uncle Max. He thought of Jackie, how much he missed her, and how much he loved them both.

And he thought of that last night with Jackie, and the guilt he'd carried with him over so many years, the lie that had eaten away at him, little by little, every time he saw David Gentry.

"Call for backup," he said, turning away from Draper. She paused, and Max wondered for a moment if she'd follow his orders. Reluctantly, several seconds later, she headed for the car. Max started toward the house.

He paused a moment just inside the front door. The place was silent, except for the rustling of leaves on the floor, and the sound of wind as it whipped in from the open roof. The breeze and shade from the overhanging trees cooled the house. There was the damp smell of rotting wood and something more pungent that wafted in on the edge of the wind, barely hinting at its meaning.

A wooden stairway led to the second floor. Max was trying to decide where to start when he heard the voice.

"I'm up here," Fourcade said. "No use sneaking around like some stupid detective, Mr. Becker. Just take the stairs."

This wasn't happening as Max had expected. The problem, he realized, starting up the stairs, listening to the boards squeak under his weight, was that he didn't *know* what to expect. Fourcade was right, the closest he'd come to anything like this was watching Dirty Harry on the big screen. Halfway up the staircase, Max doubted he'd have any use for Eastwood's clever repartee.

"That's it," yelled Fourcade.

The voice was coming from somewhere at the end of the second-floor hallway.

"When you get to the top, take a right. Follow the hallway until the end."

Max did as he was told. What other choice did he have?

He proceeded slowly down the hall. The .38 felt like it weighed about ten pounds. He could feel his finger sliding around the trigger. He wondered if he would have the guts to pull it.

"Why hello, Mr. Becker."

Max stood in the doorway of a back bedroom. He heard Fourcade's voice, but couldn't see him. Then he looked to the right. Fourcade stood in the corner. He had Susan in front of him and was holding her by the neck with a knife at her throat. Susan's eyes were half-closed. On seeing Max, she blinked, then opened her eyes wider, the paralyzing fear etched on her face.

"Don't do anything stupid," said Fourcade. "Put the gun very gently on the floor, then kick it over here."

Max hesitated, trying to think of an alternative. He was still reeling from the shock of seeing Fourcade that way, the exposed, raw tissue of his upper lip curled back against itself, his mouth hideously contorted, like the creature in the movies, a scientific experiment gone terribly wrong.

And that smile, as if he had finally tired of hiding his

deformity and now intended to balance the scales, to horrify—to get his revenge.

Fourcade tightened his grip around Susan's neck, causing her to let out a stifled scream. Max placed the gun on the ground and gently kicked it away.

"Good," said Fourcade, easing his grip on Susan. "Very good."

The window on the far wall was open. Max figured, mentally retracing his steps since entering the house, that the window looked out on the front yard. He wondered what Phil Draper was doing.

"Now," said Fourcade. "I want you to go to the window and tell that woman to stay put."

Fourcade dragged Susan toward the gun, bent down, and lifted it in his hand. "Tell her that if she comes inside, both you and the girl are dead."

Max went to the window. He felt Fourcade behind him, pointing the gun at his back. He wondered if this was where it would all end: a slug in the back of his head from his own gun.

Max saw the van at the side of the house. The squad car was parked where he'd left it, the doors still open. Phil Draper was nowhere in sight and Max wondered if she was inside the van with Gentry. A tiny voice inside him prayed that she'd decided to come after him.

"Don't come inside," Max yelled. "Stay there. He's got the girl. He'll kill us both if you come inside."

Max turned, blocking most of the window. He stayed there, hoping that Fourcade would not come to the window and see that Draper was no longer outside.

"You follow directions well, Mr. Becker. Just keep it up, and we'll all get along fine."

"Listen," said Max. "I know about your father. I know you think David Gentry had something to do with his death. But killing us isn't going to bring him back."

"That's true," Fourcade replied in a monotone. His mind seemed to be elsewhere.

"Let the girl go," said Max. "She doesn't know anything about this. Let her walk down those stairs. Then you and I can talk."

"Talk about what? What kind of fool do you take me for?"

Fourcade tightened his grip around Susan's neck. Max noticed the tears streaming down her face.

"And you, of all people, Mr. Becker, should talk. I wonder whether you ever told anybody that it was *you* who last saw her mother alive."

Max felt his heart jump into his throat. It stayed there, choking him. He wanted to talk, to do something to explain. He swallowed hard, trying to catch a breath. Susan's expression hadn't changed. Max wondered if in her terror she was capable of understanding what Fourcade had just said.

"That was a long time ago," said Max, trying not to sound surprised. The memory of that night began to come into focus. He saw himself clearly. He and Jackie Gentry, inside his living room.

Max said, "How did you find out?"

Fourcade smiled. "I know everything, Mr. Becker."

"But how?"

"Simple. I was there."

The scenes played out one after the other in Max's mind. He saw himself talking with Jackie Gentry, then saying goodbye to her at the door, and watching as the headlights of her car receded down the driveway.

Fourcade said, "I followed her to your place. I thought that was interesting, just the two of you, all alone. A little fun-and-games with your best friend's wife, eh?"

"Nothing happened."

"I'll bet."

Fourcade looked down at Susan, taking pleasure in the confusion he was causing.

"It was you," said Max, finally putting it together.

Fourcade smiled without opening his mouth.

"It was easy," he said. "So easy. Just a little tap on the coast highway, and off she went."

Fourcade made a diving motion with his hand.

"She probably didn't even see it coming, thinking about her Maxie instead of watching the road."

"You forced her off the road, making it look like a hit-and-run."

"And nobody was the wiser," said Fourcade. "I meant to tell your buddy out there all about it. I wanted to see him squirm. I wanted to tell him about you and his wife. I wanted him to know that the same guy he helped beat the rap on those rapes was the one that killed his wife. Ironic, don't you think?"

Fourcade laughed loudly, filling the room with his howling.

"It's perfect," he said, catching his breath. "Just perfect. He gets me off, and I come back and make him pay for killing my father."

"You'll never get away with it."

"Oh, but that's where you're wrong. You see, the three of us are going to take a little walk. We're going to get into your car, and we're going to go for a little ride. A rather short ride, where you and the girl are concerned."

The sound of Fourcade's crazed ramblings rang in his ears, the syllables melting together, overlapping in a barely coherent madman's slur. Max strained to hear any noise from outside. His eyes shifted quickly, wondering if Gentry or Draper was still there.

"And don't think your partner's going to save you," said Fourcade. "One move from her, and you and the girl are history. Believe me, Mr. Becker, I'd rather live, but if it comes to dying, I'll take both of you out with me. Now, start down the stairs. I'll be right behind you, so take it nice and easy."

Max walked out the door and started down the hallway. He heard Fourcade, shuffling behind him, hissing with every breath. Fourcade had the .38 trained on his back, the knife still held loosely at Susan's neck.

"That's it," he heard Fourcade mutter from behind. They had gone down the first flight of stairs and were at the landing in the middle of the staircase. Max glanced around, trying to locate Phil Draper.

"Nice and slow, now. Just like that."

Max started down the stairs, wondering if Draper was still outside. By this time, he thought, if she'd called for backup, the place should be crawling with uniforms.

He was at the front door when he slowly turned around. Fourcade was less than three feet from him, with Susan still securely in his grasp.

Max couldn't believe his eyes. In a split-second his mind told him to look away, to act as if he'd seen nothing unusual.

Behind Fourcade, wedged between the wall and the stair rail, pressed up against the ceiling, Phil Draper seemed to hang, like a human bat, the barrel of her 9mm semiautomatic focused on Harris Fourcade's back.

In that microsecond, Max realized that this was the right moment, the only moment. Draper would have to get off one helluva head shot to take out Fourcade, and any shot fired at Fourcade's back could go through him and hit Susan.

He also realized if he allowed Fourcade to read his thoughts, it would be over for all of them.

Max focused on his own reflection in the glint of the chrome gun barrel. He saw himself moving, as if in

337

slow motion, his arms outstretched, his fingers splayed out, reaching for the tip. His eyes traveled down the inside of the short dark cylinder, knowing what was about to happen.

He fell forward, twisting the gun away.

Then the flash, lighting up the hole, setting his hands on fire, sending the hot lead searing through his chest.

Someone was screaming, and a clap of thunder shook the walls of the house.

Max saw himself tumbling through space, the gun still exploding in his hands.

Epilogue

Two months after Phil Draper had emptied all fifteen rounds of her service revolver into the body of Harris Fourcade, and Susan Gentry had resumed her studies at Santa Barbarba, David Gentry found himself back walking the corridors of the downtown courthouse.

A group of jurors stood outside in the hallway, drinking coffee and talking with each other. Gentry walked with his head down, averting their eyes, aware that some of them stopped their conversations as he passed.

The inside of the courtroom was quiet. The clerk was at his desk, but the judge, bailiff, and lawyers were missing. The only other people in the courtroom were an attractive woman seated near the door, and a young Mexican male who looked to be sleeping in the front row.

Gentry took a seat in the back, where it was dark and where he could be alone with his thoughts. The clerk looked up from his desk, registered who had entered, and hesitated, as if he were about to say something, then went back to work.

Gentry rested the back of his head against the

cushioned edge of the chair. The rectangular fluorescent fixtures overhead were gray around the ends, and flickered on and off. On the other side of the wall, he could hear the rumble of the motors that operated the heavy lockup bars as they whirred open, stopped, then a few seconds later started up again. Then there was the final clunk of the bars slamming shut.

Gentry closed his eyes, letting his mind take him back. He knew it was no use fighting it. He'd tried that, during the weeks afterward, only to find that he could not rid himself of the images. So now, in the dark cool of the last row of the courtroom, he let himself go.

He opened his mind to the scene of Harris Fourcade inside the van. In his dreams, Fourcade's demonic appearance had become overshadowed by the monstrous cruelty of his deeds. Gentry saw himself looking down the end of the hose, certain that his next breath would be his last. He saw Fourcade, scarred and disfigured by fate, hovering over Susan, ready to slice her open as he had the others.

And all because of something he'd done, a decision he'd made over twenty years ago.

Jake Harrison, as it turned out, had probably been innocent. At least, Gentry had arrived at that conclusion after sifting through Fourcade's notebooks and doing further investigation into his own case file. He would never know for sure. The witnesses were dead or missing, the evidence cold. But it all seemed to fit, at least on paper.

Fourcade had statements from witnesses who admitted to lying at Harrison's trial. Fourcade had found a church worker who helped operate one of the local soup kitchens. The worker told Fourcade that some time after the trial, he had spoken to the transient who had been the prosecution's star witness, and the transient had admitted to being unsure of his identification. Two other men, both in prison, had confessed to committing the robbery/murder, and to reading about Harrison's arrest and trial in the newspaper. Fourcade had procured signed statements from both of them.

Gentry was aware that the discovery of such evidence, accumulated so long after the fact, was not that unusual. Witnesses could be pressured into changing their stories. Men serving long prison terms on other cases had little to lose by tacking on another confession to a crime too old to be prosecuted, especially if they saw it as a way to better their plight in custody. A few packs of cigarettes, some magazines, maybe an increase in privileges was worth a lot if you were looking at spending the next twenty years of your life getting cornholed by your cellmate.

But in the end, Gentry realized that Jake Harrison would have been convicted regardless of whether he had faced the death penalty. Nobody had created the evidence against the man, it had just happened. No one individual could be blamed if the system had, in fact, resulted in the conviction of an innocent man. Gentry understood that even if he'd had nothing to do with Jake Harrison, Harrison still would have been convicted and sentenced to prison, where he might have been killed all the same. The system—not David Gentry—had failed Jake Harrison.

Harris Fourcade was insane. Obsessed with the sorrowful plight that life had dealt him, Fourcade had fiendishly struck out at anyone he could find. Had it not been David Gentry, it would have been someone else, like the completely innocent women whose lives had been ruined by his anger and viciousness.

Gentry had remained at the Burris Home the evening of the shooting, after the ambulances had left and the coroner's wagon had pulled away. In the darkness, using flashlights, he had been there, behind the old house, when the smokehouse doors were pulled open. He had peered inside into the darkness and had stood in shock as the beam of light from Phil Draper's flashlight played over the rotting corpse. He'd had no idea who it was.

Draper knew, though. She took one look at the putrifying flesh and told them it was Leonard Burris. He had been bludgeoned to death some weeks earlier, then hung on one of the hooks inside the smokehouse.

They would later find the genitals of the four rape victims stuffed in the old man's mouth.

Susan and Max eventually told him about Jackie. The police had found the newspaper articles that Fourcade had saved, dealing with her death.

Hardly a day had passed since Jackie's death that Gentry hadn't blamed himself. Jackie had rushed from the house that night in anger; he couldn't even remember what they'd argued about. He'd always felt responsible for losing her. If only he'd tried harder. If only he'd run out after her, calmed her, talked it through.

Now he knew he was not to blame. He would never be able to lift the burden of a failed marriage from his shoulders, but the weight had become lighter. Jackie's death had not been his fault.

Gentry was awakened from his reverie by the sound of voices. When he looked up, Max Becker and Nathan Zellner were emerging from the judge's chambers. Max walked up to the young Mexican and said something, at which the Mexican nodded, then slumped back down in his seat. Max then came around the divider and took a seat next to Gentry in the audience.

"Jury's got a question," said Max. "Judge's let them take a break while we discussed how to answer it. He's

342

going to tell them to just follow the instructions."

"Yeah, I saw them outside."

"How'd they look?"

Gentry twitched the corner of his mouth, and put his palms up.

"Yeah," said Max. "I know. 'Who knows?' Right?"

"I'm sure you did your best, Max."

They were still seated, talking, when the court clerk walked past them and escorted the jurors back into the courtroom. Zellner had taken a seat at the edge of the jury box. He flashed a smile at each of the jurors as they walked past him on their way to the deliberation room.

"Has Nate been behaving himself?"

"What do you think?"

Gentry shook his head, then said, "That's the one good thing about Zellner. You can always be sure that he'll act like a complete asshole. It's comforting, you have to admit, to know that some things in this life will never change."

Gentry continued, "How's your client taking it?"

"Billy? Okay, I guess. We scored some points with the hotel maid. I guess she felt a little guilty about stealing the money. In the end, she admitted to taking the twenties."

"But Darling already confessed to hitting the guy."

"Yeah, except with the theft issue out of the picture, Billy's story about having to defend himself should carry a little more weight. I got some very interesting looks from the jurors when we showed the pictures of Kravitz lying on the floor in his birthday suit. Zellner never managed to explain that one. He just kind of sloughed over it, ya know. He would have been better off admitting that Kravitz was a kinky bastard, but that he didn't deserve to die because of it. Zellner talked himself into a corner in his opening statement. He thought the jury would swallow that 'pillar of the community' garbage. I'm not so sure they did."

"How did Billy come across?"

"Scared. Real scared. But that's good. He didn't sound like he was lying."

"Who's the Mexican kid?"

"A friend of Billy's."

"Looks familiar."

"You probably prosecuted him. Miguelito Gervas. He was at the hotel the day Kravitz bought it."

Gentry turned his head only slightly, and raised his eyebrows in a token gesture of surprise.

"I couldn't call him," said Max, in explanation.

"Don't blame you," said Gentry. "Trial strategy. Kid looks like a lying sack of 'greasy shit, right?'"

Max nodded. "Besides, he would've made something up. Mickie sees a witness stand and the bullshit starts pouring out of his eyeballs. Zellner would've killed him."

Both men remained silent for a few moments. The events of the last few months had shaken their faith in the effectiveness of the system. Harris Fourcade had been set free by the courts to wreak havoc on the community, adding an additional victim to his list, and almost taking the lives of three more.

And all the time, Billy Darling had remained behind bars, held without bail, unable to gather evidence in his own defense.

At that moment in time, neither man was without doubt as to the excellence of the American justice system, and their respective roles in it. Both understood that you had to have some of the gambler in your blood to throw your fate into the judicial ring. You hired a lawyer who would duke it out with the opposition according to rules originally set down by men from another continent wearing powdered wigs.

In the end, all you could reasonably hope for is that

you got a fair shake, and didn't get sucker-punched in the first round.

Max still wondered if Susan had told her dad the whole story. After it was over, Max had awakened in the hospital with a separated shoulder, powder burns on his hands, and a through-and-through gunshot wound that had come within inches of hitting his heart.

Susan had come to him then. To thank him. Max hadn't been sure how much of Fourcade's wild ranting had sunk in that deadly evening. Whether Susan had understood about her mother and her Uncle Max.

"I'm sorry about your mom," he had said to her from his hospital bed. She had just nodded, touching the back of her hand to his cheek.

"It's okay," she said. "It's okay. I don't feel any more of a loss, knowing how it happened."

They spent the next few minutes together silently, just being with each other. Susan said nothing of his meeting with her mother the night she was killed. Either because she hadn't remembered or because she didn't consider it worth discussing, the issue was never brought up.

Now Max felt it hanging there between David Gentry and himself. He wondered if Susan and her father had discussed it, and if Gentry had been the one to suggest that it be permanently put to rest.

Max screwed up his courage. He was tired of living the lie. Nothing had happened that night between Jackie Gentry and himself. Jackie had come to him filled with anger over her failed marriage. They had all gotten to know each other well and had often consoled one another in times of need. It was only natural for her to seek out the advice and solace of a friend.

Except Rosalie hadn't been home that evening. So the giving of advice had fallen onto his shoulders. And that was all he'd given her. Despite Harris Fourcade's lurid insinuations, the truth was that they'd shared a cup of instant coffee together, and they'd held hands and exchanged words of understanding and compassion. And that was all.

So why, Max asked himself, was he hesitant to admit as much to David? Why had he kept hidden over so many years the fact that he was the last person to see Jackie Gentry alive? Had there been something between them that night? Was there something in Jackie's expression, in the way she had held his hand and looked into his eyes, that had signaled more than mere friendship?

Max had attempted to respond to those questions, and dozens more, over the years since Jackie's death. It was the uncertainty of his answers that still troubled him.

"David," he said, "I don't know what Susan told you about that evening at Fourcade's."

Gentry furrowed his brow, giving Max a confused look. Max was tempted to let it end right there.

He went on, "I mean about Jackie, and the night she died."

Max focused on Gentry, watching for some sign of recognition, a glint in the eye, a knowing smile or grimace. There was nothing. Max was about to continue when he heard the clerk's voice.

"They've got a verdict," he said, the words echoing in the empty courtroom. Max felt his heart jump.

Max looked at Gentry, who smiled, patted him on the knee, and said, "Showtime."

Max stood, and started for the counsel table. It was then that he saw her out of the corner of his eye.

Samantha. *Sam.*

Seated in the shadows, watching him.

She's come back.

His heart was pounding now, racing ahead of his

346

thoughts. His head spun with confusion. He wanted to go to her, to explain everything, to tell her what a fool he'd been, and how much he loved her. All the things he hadn't had the chance to do that evening, standing in the cold near the Flying Horses Carousel.

The bailiff brought Billy Darling back inside the courtroom, and stood behind him as Billy seated himself at the counsel table.

Max smiled at Sam and made a stupid wait-a-minute gesture with his hand—as if she was really about to go anywhere! He quickly touched his hand to his chest, feeling his heart about to burst through.

She's come back . . .

He sat down next to Billy at the counsel table.

The jurors were then ushered into the courtroom, each taking their designated seat in the jury box. The judge had already taken the bench, and was directing his attention at the jurors, waiting for all of them to be seated.

"Ladies and gentlemen of the jury," he said, "do you have a verdict?"

A short man in the front row, the foreman, stood and said, "We do, Your Honor."

The judge watched as the clerk walked around to the other side of the courtroom and approached the jury foreman.

"The foreman will please hand the verdict form to the clerk," said the judge.

Without looking at it, the clerk took the piece of paper from the foreman and gave it to the judge. The judge reviewed the form for a moment, then handed it back to the clerk, saying, "The clerk will please read the verdict."

Max and Billy stood. Max looked at his client, putting his arm around the young man's shoulders. Billy looked scared. He was withdrawing inside

347

himself, like a dog that's been beaten, cowering even under a friendly hand.

Max glanced back at Miguelito, who was hunched over, balanced on the edge of his seat, his chin bouncing nervously on the wooden divider.

Behind Miguelito, David Gentry sat calmly, a tight smile on his face. Gentry gave Max a "thumbs-up" sign.

Sam had moved forward in her seat, her forearms draped over the seat in front of her. Max wondered what she was thinking at that moment.

In those few short seconds, with the clerk about to read from the verdict form, Max said to himself: "I've done the best I could. It wasn't perfect. I made mistakes. But it was as good as I can do." And as his thoughts turned to David and Jackie Gentry, to Susan, to Harris Fourcade—and to Sam, Max felt that the words had a special meaning now.

"We the jury," the clerk read in a clear, deep voice that seemed to echo in Max's ears and deep within his soul, "in the above-titled action, find the defendant, William Darling . . .

   . . . *Not guilty!*"

FOLLOW THE SEVENTH CARRIER

TRIAL OF THE SEVENTH CARRIER   (3213, $3.95)
The enemies of freedom are on the verge of dominating the world
with oil blackmail and the threat of poison gas attack. *Yonaga*'s
officers lay desperate plans to strike back. Leading a ragtag fleet
of revamped destroyers and a single antique WWII submarine,
the great carrier must charge into a sea of blood and death in
what becomes the greatest trial of the Seventh Carrier.

REVENGE OF THE SEVENTH CARRIER   (3631, $3.99)
With the help of an American carrier, *Yonaga* sails vast distances
to launch a desperate surprise attack on the enemy's poison gas
works. But a spy is at work. The enemy seems to know too much
and a bloody battle is fought. Filled with murderous rage, *Yonaga*'s officers exact a terrible revenge.

ORDEAL OF THE SEVENTH CARRIER   (3932, $3.99)
Even as the Libyan madman calls for peaceful negotiations, an
Arab battle group steams toward the shores of Japan. With good
men from all over the world flocking to her colors, *Yonaga* prepares to give battle. The two forces clash off the island of Iwo
Jima where it is carrier against carrier in a duel to the death — and
Yonaga, sustaining severe damage, endures its bloodiest ordeal in
the fight for freedom's cause.

*

Other Zebra Books by Peter Albano

THE YOUNG DRAGONS   (3904, $4.99)
It is June 25, 1944. American forces attack the island of Saipan.
Two young fighting men on opposite sides, Michael Carpelli and
Takeo Nakamura, meet in the flaming hell of battle that will inevitably bring them face-to-face in a final fight to the death. Here is
the epic battle that decided the war against Japan as told by a
man who was there.

THE SURVIVALIST SERIES
by Jerry Ahern

THE WINGMAN SERIES